GENERATION DEAD

ISBN: 978-1-7399188-0-4

Edited by E. Rachael Hardcastle
Formatted by E. Rachael Hardcastle
Written by K. J. McGuinness
Cover artwork by K. J. McGuinness

Published by Curious Cat Books, United Kingdom
For further information contact www.curiouscatbooks.co.uk

Also available as an e-book.

First Edition

GENERATION DEAD

by K. J. McGuinness

"I am eternally grateful you have taken the time to read my hard work. Please consider leaving a review wherever you have purchased this book. Tell your friends.

Thank you for supporting my dream and taking a chance on me.

For Mum, Joe, Emma, and friends.

And to my ex, who said I'd never do anything with it... how about now?"

WARNING

This novel is intended for mature audiences. It is a dark book with disturbing, triggering and distressing scenes, mature language, suicide, disorders and sexual content.

"You have been warned.
If I offend you, I have succeeded."

VOLUME ONE

PRELUDE

January 3rd, 2012

"THREE!... TWO!... ONE!..." KABOOM!

The superstore is suddenly engulfed in a giant fireball; a tangled fist of orange and crimson punches through the main entrance, sending shopping baskets and carts flying. Windows shatter, smoke and shrapnel erupt, cascading into abandoned cars in the parking lot, triggering a piercing choir of alarms. Thousands of pieces of glass, brick and steel batter the undead. Those alarms—now deafening—smother the crackling flames.

It's hard to believe a small DIY bomb can do so much damage, but it does. The explosion is seen for miles.

Despite the chaos, it conveniently blasts half of the attacking bloodthirsty creatures to smithereens, though the survivors—once strangers forced together—have created half-decent memories in that store. Now, however, those memories are consumed in flames. Everything from their film projector to the beds and the den is gone; their sense of home lost, their blanket of security quickly disintegrating

The blast wave ripples for miles, almost forcing their getaway truck into a lamppost. Will spins the steering wheel to avoid a collision at the last second. It would've been game over—his new friends turned into lunch meat for the nearby battalion of undead man-eaters.

Damon watches the supermarket explode and dives on his sister, Claire—praying he doesn't crush her tiny frame—to shield her. To their left, it throws Amy and Beth to the back of the truck.

Suddenly, Claire bursts to life from a bout of

unconsciousness, still weak and in need of help. Damon cradles his trembling sister; he strokes her face, elated to see she's unharmed. Claire passes out again in a hot sweat, equally bewildered to see him.

Now collapsed in Damon's arms, Beth glances back at the store—once their makeshift home. It is now a huge bonfire. Then she buries her face in Damon's sweater, emotionally drained.

But at least they're safe... for now.

***

Kieran appears amidst the burning wreckage of the superstore, flames so high the Great Fire of London would have cowered in fear.

He steps through the blaze like a machine, unphased by the bedlam, hell-bent on claiming a well-deserved prize after a long hunt on the scent of the fleeing teens in the delivery truck—a prize that will include his ex-boyfriend and the accompanying band of dishevelled teens.

He screeches through the thick smog, foaming at the mouth. The remaining infected follow him as he charges for the truck.

Kieran soon slows to a disgruntled stop, staring at the truck's arse end. Amy smugly offers him her middle finger as they speed off, disappearing over the horizon.

She knows he'll be back, and nothing can prepare them for what is yet to come.

CHAPTER 1:

THE END IS NYE

December 31st, 2011
Beth and Darcy's Bedroom
Leeds: Population 2,000,000
15 Hours, 10 Minutes Until New Year...

"Blood, Fire and Death..."

Beth sets her newspaper down and uncrosses her legs, reaching for her morning chai latte that has gone cold from neglect. That seems to be the Saturday morning tradition these days, taken from her father, her actual father that is. Every Saturday morning for as long as she can remember, Beth's father would mop up the night before with some carb fixture while reading the Saturday paper. He was always crossed-legged while her mum loitered, often getting lost in her own mind, procrastinating. Sometimes, she was ironing his work shirts or writing a new recipe from a cooking show. Her dad particularly liked the paper because he always said they 'reserved it for the best shite in town— shite you couldn't write'. She would sit eagle eyed and giggly with her cereal and colouring, expecting to be taken to the park. She adored her father, and he adored her. That was, until his seat became empty. It's amazing the subconscious traits the human mind picks up while thriving like a sponge in its infant years.

"Witch piss." She grimaces after taking a sip of the latte.

"Could you please just concentrate?" groans Darcy.

"HOW?" Beth replies. "Every page seems to just be blood and fire." She flicks more aggressively, disgusted at the state of decay in the world. "Look here, Nicholas Westship named as the 'Gingerbread Killer', a big lead as police home in… nine… no TEN victims… five of them children." If Beth had pearls, she'd be clutching them. "More homeless are missing, connected with a government scheme. Grime Flu fears grow from epidemic to pandemic as a lab burns down. And oh, look at this, two dead in Christmas meteor shower!" She throws her arms up, done with it. "No news is good news, eh? NEWS?" she says mockingly. "What even is NEWS?"

"Notable Event's Weather and Sports… NEWS," Irks Darcy.

The penny drops for Beth and her face droops to an annoyed expression.

"How did you not know that? Your IQ is like 140, it's like 20 behind mine!" reiterates Darcy.

Beth stares at her blankly before taking a breath, thinking of a smart comeback. "You know this whole sharing a room thing… don't think it's gonna work, DD." Beth turns for her make-up stand.

"She says after two years," Darcy mocks under her breath.

The girls share a room because the little Hyde Park manor on the corner has only three in total. There may be four of them, but as the other two are boys, the girls rightly protested when they moved in. Their room, though, is a wonderland for comic-driven recluses. They share similar interests, so it is hard to differentiate between whose side is whose. The walls are a red and cream which pulses in the light, sprinkled with various posters (mostly of New York, where the girls often delude themselves they can one day abscond together after university).

They met on a school trip—a week across Europe. Anyone who chose history as a subject got this opportunity. They had, sort of, purchased the same ticket. Beth was 2B

10

and Darcy was 4D and somehow, they wound up with the same coach seat. Neither was going to give it up, both being headstrong and selfish, so they took turns until the teacher found a better solution (by the time they were on the M25!). At first, they didn't speak. Beth was a thinker and let little out. But, by the time they arrived in France in the afternoon of that same day, they were chatting like old ladies. The rest is history.

"Rose or Peach?"

Beth hold ups two identical looking bottles of nail varnish under Darcy's nose. Darcy recoils in horror as if her best friend just presented her dead mice like a cat would for its master. Darcy is knee deep in paperwork and university exam books.

"B, the revision." She frowns, monotone.

"Come on…" moans Beth playfully.

"They're the same." Darcy's tone doesn't change.

Beth gasps, stumbling for her words. "That is an outrageous accusation!" She turns her attention to Rose and Peach. "Don't listen girls, she's just menstruating." She turns back to Darcy, jokingly. "There is a world of difference between these two bottles of dripping sex!"

Darcy sighs like it's the Nth time Beth has done something like this, but humours her nonetheless.

"Rose here… is a woman who is confident… sexy but sophisticated that gets that promotion, dares to be bold but also doesn't fail to be one of the boys."

Darcy's eyes roll.

"PEACH, however, tells the story of…" Beth thinks about it for a moment effervescently. "Hmm", she says, "I'm not a whore but I'm not a virgin, either."

"It is astounding you can tell the difference. More so the fact you studied psychology over fashion…"

"I enjoy understanding people."

"Look, if I just pick, will you help me with this work?"

11

"Of course."

"Peach, she reflects my inner feminist…" Darcy's eyes shoot back down to the paper, picking up her pen.

"We're bad feminists," chuckles Beth, swivelling around to her mirror.

The sublime difference between the pair is their attention to detail. Beth is messy—not dirty or unclean, just disorganised. Her duvet is on her bed, though she hasn't made it, resulting in lumps of various sizes and shapes of the covers that were once weighed down by her laptop. Her desk sits in one corner, littered with wads of paper, pens and stationery. Wooden shelves are fixed to the wall, filled with dusty books varying from high fantasy novels to 'Psychology: Thinking Fast and Talking Slow.'

Some books lay discarded across the floor.

She sits, letting her eyes roam the graffiti left by the last bunch of losers who rented the place. She goes back to the mirror, analysing herself; carefully, she applies a portrait to her face for the day as routine dictates.

Beth is graciously lip-syncing to her idol, Amy Winehouse, in the background, while Darcy tries to scramble together the last of her dissertation research aka the 'bane of her existence'. Her half of the room is beautifully organised, colour-coordinated and clutter-free, probably rooted in some suppressed undiagnosed Obsessive-Compulsive Disorder.

A smile flashes across Beth's face from beneath reams of liquid sunshine hair. It creates dimples and creases that move her freckles. She dips her head—never someone to be too loud or extroverted, casting her face to the side for the right light and contour. Each of her shoulders curls towards her chest, flexing her firm bosoms. She's a statue now, but her emotions are not so easily masked on her innocent face. Pain is clear in the crease of her brow and the down-curve of her full lips. Her perfect blue eyes show her soul. If someone were to look closely enough into them, they might fall under her spell. Beth remembers reading that very line on a bathroom stall about herself. Her eyes are also a deep pool of restless crystal—an ocean of hopeless grief. They have seen war in the ethereal sense, and if someone could look into them, they'd see the beauty of the universe.

Unlike her roommate, Beth's mission in life is not to let the world break her. She has always felt as though she has a point to prove. One goal: change the world. If that fails, she'll simply conquer it. If she is arrogant about anything, though, it's her hair, which adapts with the sun in summer and lightens a shade above 'goddess of the sun'. But, in winter, her snow-white hair returns to its buttermilk gold, draped and softly curling along the ends. Every time she appears, the day never ends, smiles never fade, leading everyone to instant happiness.

Plastered on the wall beside the mirror is a page torn from the 'Trek-America' brochure with a flawless red felt tip ring around an alluring camper van, concealing the cliché: 'Live, Laugh, Love,' burned into the wall for eternity by the previous tenants. Someone has tried to pick it off and replace the words in black marker: 'Drink, Smoke, Party,' instead. Probably, it's a droll attempt at 'Neo-Dadaism' humour—a representation of the epitome of teenage angst.

"Can you believe New Year's Eve finally falls on a Saturday?" Beth brings up, finally finishing her last toe of one foot.

"I know, it's the perfect recovery time, not like it's going to happen again for another five years."

"2016." Beth switches to the other foot. "What do you think we will be doing in 2016, still friends?"

Darcy scoffs, "Out of the question. All I see is graduation, men, success—"

"More men."

"Is that applause I hear? What's that?" Darcy turns to her

own table mirror, acting. "You want to give me the Nobel Peace Prize for Human Rights and Feminism? What? You mean you want me to hold the title from now until the end of time? Isn't there a law against that?" Darcy says, imitating, accepting her award with a hairbrush as Beth giggles. "But you changed the laws of humanity, time and space for me? You shouldn't have."

At 19, Beth stands as the matriarch of her household clique. Though not the oldest, she seems to have fallen into a mother goose role of her clan.

Darcy taps her pen on the paper rapidly and purses her lips. Her black ink hair flows down her back and her eyes are foxy with an icy, greyish-green hue, like the first sprouts of plants in snow.

"None of this makes sense!" she says, looking at the mountains of paper on her desk. She's been at it so long she's hallucinating, and her eye is twitching. "And, these soul-sucking vampires want 10,000 words by the third?" She licks her teeth, unimpressed.

Beth divulges how they are made for better things, and that somewhere out there her 'sugar daddy' is waiting, smothered in an American 'hot-shot' deep-fried pizza.

"2016 right? Think of that American-deep-fried-man-meat."

Darcy laughs. "Beth, you're disgusting."

BOOM!

An explosion outside their window shakes the room— books and bottles fall from their places. Car alarms wail and the lights flicker. Passers-by cry out, cussing and yelling at each other.

"MAN ALIVE!" Beth yelps as she smudges her toe.

Darcy leaps off her bed in a startled shuffle, almost pushing Beth out of the way for a better view through the window.

"Watch it, Toothpick!" Beth snarls.

Darcy's hand presses Beth's shoulder as she parts the blinds.

"That was right outside our house. These disturbances are literally happening on our doorstep now."

Beth spits out Darcy's hair from her mouth, flapping her hands and trying to get a view.

"Now that's NEWS!" chuckles Beth.

"DID YOU HEAR THAT? He just called that lady the c-word!" Darcy woos like a child watching their friend get in trouble at school. "It's getting dangerous out there. I don't think this party is such a good idea." Darcy returns to her bed. "I reckon it's the Grime Flu."

Beth snorts. "Pff. One whiff of the sniffles and the entire world loses its mind. Everybody will raid the supermarkets soon for toilet roll, pasta and hand sanitiser. What have I told you, DD? It's the media scaremongering the sheep. It will be dickheads getting a little too excited for tonight. It is New Year's Eve, after all. On a Saturday!" She Squeals.

"So you keep saying…"

"THE END IS NYE."

Beth shakes her hands to be spooky. She picks up her pen, acknowledging Darcy's's response, and returns to her dissertation.

"This is all nonsense. Jargon! How am I supposed to create a perspective on ten RFL's from an angle? WHAT DOES RFL EVEN MEAN?" She sighs.

"I don't know. Really Fucking Lost?" Beth sarcastically remarks, now wiping the nail polish off with acetone having forgotten the events outside like they were an enigma. She picks up the eyeliner. "What were we talking about?"

"Why couldn't these university tutors teach us something useful for real life? Like taxes, or how to get a mortgage without having an anxiety attack?" Darcy asks.

"Nah, they won't buy that; didn't you know everybody has anxiety attacks these days? It's a fashion trend," Beth remarks having perfected the perfect Egyptian eye wing.

Darcy ignores her comment amid her rant. "But no, they insist on teaching trigonometry and algebra in schools because that's definitely higher on the menu." Her tone suddenly lowers to a dull, mocking one. "Hi, yeah, I don't know where to find my tax code, but I can tell you the size of this TV and its dimensions. When-the-fuck would anybody use trigonometry?"

Beth tries not to break from her contouring but adds, "Well, it's used in oceanography, calculating the height of tides. The sine and cosine functions are fundamental to the theory of periodic functions, those that describe sound and light waves—" she babbles, curling her hair.

Darcy pauses and looks at her blankly. "Therefore, you're going to die a virgin." She laughs.

"Eat me, Danby," Beth chuckles, finishing her lipstick. "Oh, wait that's right, little miss skips meals."

"HEY!" It strikes a nerve.

"Forgive me." Beth tilts her head regretfully. "The worst part is that on top of all our studying and exams, we have a shit party to plan to save Chris's arse!"

"Well, after last night, I'm half-tempted to tell Kieran to go fuck himself!" Darcy says.

"And he probably would just to spite you." Beth tilts her face to the left, then right. Perfectly symmetrical. She air kisses her reflection in approval. "What do you want for breakfast... that *is* if you will eat—"

Beth brushes her fringe out her face, condescendingly gazing at Darcy.

Darcy finishes after a long pause, "Bacon."

"Do they serve much bacon in the castles in Sweden?"

"Uh, I guess, yeah, we call it sigfläsk… which is cooked ham… Skinka is basically our version of ham. But then again Skinka is also a name for a pig's butthole. So, it depends on its context. Asking for Skinka and eggs is different to saying my ex Jordan is a Skinka."

Beth yelps a solid 'ha!' and turns to the mirror once more. "Butthole and eggs, can I please have butthole and eggs." She murmurs to herself over and over, joyfully amused by her immaturity.

Princess Darcy Agnes Danby is the third descendant of some royal family in Sweden. If you don't already know her, you probably never will. Mostly, she finds anyone she doesn't know scarier than a horror movie, and she finds that so scary she won't even watch the whole thing. She's a freak by society's standard, but an angel in Beth's eyes. She'll easily read someone like a book in 30 seconds and they'll hate it. It's why she's taking psychology. Darcy is probably the smartest girl in the country (or has the potential to be), getting As in every school subject. But someone as hyperintelligent and hyper sensitive as Darcy is a daily civil war with herself.

She's had her family's royal blood and power to use, plus connections to get her to where she is now, but she is always humble. The only reason she bothered doing university was to avoid boredom, even though it is mundane. She likes to keep occupied.

Beth isn't the only one hiding darkness and demons.

People will decide they don't like her or just make an excuse to avoid her in the future. She is 'weird' after all. To Darcy, the world is weird; she claims normality is relative, like hot and cold, high and low. She isn't as tough as Beth, but the embodiment of love, wrapped up too thinly to stop it from spilling out at the edges. If she can let someone in, she'll light them up like she does Beth. Like all lights, she's blinding at first.

18-years-old and the youngest of the four, she is a self-entitled, opinionated, outspoken, vegan feminist, minus the shaved hair and loud colours, but she would still probably ask for the manager, anyway. Whenever Beth isn't vocal enough, Darcy is... much to Beth's reluctance, constantly.

Two opposites... somehow connected forever.

Will
Will's Bedroom
13 Hours, 47 Minutes Until New Year...

BOOM! The sultry room rattles. Down falls console games and statues as if they were all the king's horses and all the king's men. First the Buddha, then the stag, followed by the elephant. Up shoots a shell of a corpse underneath the black silk sheets from the super king bed. The sheet slowly falls off naturally to reveal a mousy blonde, athletic frame with grown out black roots, obviously from a bottle. Will's eyes scan the room like it's alien to him. A tatty half-smoked roll-up joint dangles out of his mouth.

"What the fuck was that?"

He can see barley anything because of the blacked-out windows, with blackout curtains and black everything. Why black? Because in the words of Will, 'black is the first thing that was and is the last thing that will be'. The only thing saving him from complete optical elimination is his games console home screen staring at him. He must have fallen asleep in a haze of THC. The TV is paused on that new show he was interested in.

"Oh yeah…" he mutters, with the joint still dangling in his lips.

Will has a secret soft spot for cartoons, a secret he means to keep from the others. The only other one who shares this 'grave keeper' as he calls his secrets, is Kieran. He thinks about him briefly.

"Fuck that."

He shakes his head to be sure he has got rid of the mental intrusion. If only there was a cure or therapy to erase someone from your mind. Will takes out the joint but nearly rips the skin off his lips from the dryness. He swings his legs over and runs over to the window to grab a peak of the commotion. It's muffled, but he's intrigued, regardless. He always been the type to nosey in on things, cars passing, people walking.

Who are they? What do they want? Are they trying to steal my grow? Or, harvest my organs?

You know, the serious question in life.

Will scratches the part of his boxer-shorts stuffed in his crack and adjusts before grabbing his dressing gown.

"Drama?" He peeks open the curtain. "Ooo-la-la, local drama!" he says gleefully.

The type of guy at the party who sees you have a pet and pretty much just sticks to it all night, ignoring any human interaction… he's Will. Will is the oldest of the bunch, always changing his age to suit his needs. The guys hazard a guess, putting him somewhere between 18 and 23. He almost forgets himself, not because he's lying or being deceiving, he just doesn't trust anyone anymore. The less they know the better. 'Fake names, wrong ages and birth places keep you safe', he would say. That's only reserved for strangers. If anyone's lucky enough to break him into submission, he'll do anything for them.

"How anti-climatic."

He fakes going back to the bed, scanning what he can make out. The room isn't quite a shit tip, but it isn't next to godliness either. If he takes out the eight pint glasses filled with different variations of water and maybe the snack wrappers, it will be a half decent batch pad. Will often cleans his room during what he calls a 'productive hour', sometimes on a day off when he's stoned, hungover, on a 'comedown' or even a combination of all three coursing through his veins. It is usually from a heavy rave or even just a few beers with the lads at the pub. Other than a glass of water he constantly has beside his bed for his cotton mouth and wrappers from the munchies or his 'junk draw', his room is mature for his age. The curtains are always drawn. Sultry, silk paisley, grey and black bedding spread over the super king. A feature wall of striped velvet, blacks, greys and whites. Will loves grey and all its shades, so naturally he has a draw labelled 'for the darkness within'. He won't tell anyone what's inside, but it works for an incredible sex drive.

It doesn't matter if you're a girl or a boy, Will is a kinky free spirit and the way he sees it, he'll simply 'loves everybody'. They discuss Will's sexual identity at parties, but he doesn't fall in love with genders—he falls in love with a spirit. It doesn't matter what you have between your legs; everyone has an equal chance at capturing his heart.

He sees a lighter on the mattress, probably there since before he was.

"Ooo, gimme."

He dives for it now, trying to spark the half-dead spliff. "Oh, suck a bag of dicks."

He tosses it aside after the 20th attempt. He pats his hands around. *Controller? Nope. Titty-bong? Nope.*

"OO! Rectangular small device that resembles lighter, bingo."

He clicks it and suddenly it starts his vinyl music player from behind. His favourite, Fleetwood Mac, plays and he momentarily forgets himself.

"AH! YES!" Will successfully pulls out a windproof lighter, the same one he uses when he gets creative with his 'medical' designs, i.e., another way to smoke as much weed as he can until the image of his ex isn't clear anymore. His last two inventions were a metre long blunt and four-way crucifix bong.

BOMMMFFF! The flame ignition nearly takes off his entire fringe and startles him so much he dives off the bed— definitely enough to take his nose hairs off.

"That's one way to wax," he says, blowing his nose as he creeps back onto the silk sheets.

Will leans back to the sound, hands behind the head, and takes a large toke from his 'medicine.' *Life. Is. Good.*

He looks to the nightstand on his left, a picture of himself and Beth reminding him of better times. Beth and Will are the oldest of friends within the group, albeit not always the closest. They do, however, know the most about each other and see each other through a lot. Their friendship, therefore, is one for history books. They attended all the same schools and were inseparable before high school, but once there, they never hung around the same groups. Will was a social butterfly, getting into trouble for smoking something he shouldn't be and fighting between singing practice. And boy, can he belt out a song! Anything from the incredible Jennifer Huston to Les Misérables. Beth, however, was too busy annihilating her adversaries on various debate teams between taking over the school, metaphorically. The peach painting pretty princess could wipe the floor with anyone in almost any subject.

It wasn't until they found themselves in the same performing arts club they bonded. They offered Will a part on London's West End but he turned it down to look after his mentally ill mother—one of his biggest (but most necessary) regrets. His mother is his rock... anyone even blinked at her the wrong way, he'd go from Gizmo to gremlin in a blink to put it politely. His poker-straight spiky hair (which he used to dye black, and these days lets grow to his natural thick and lustrous ash hue) is usually neat with a clean-cut and fade, short back and sides. It's been that way since he met his girlfriend, Ricca. She likes it that way, and that's usually the way it is.

His eyes are a mesmerising deep ice blue—flecks of silvery light perform ballet throughout. His face is strong and defined, his features moulded from granite. Puberty wasn't polite to him—blemishes and craters—but he came out glowing even if scars and said craters decorate his skin from his teenage acne.

Will's default expression makes him look serious. You will often find him in his room in a glaze of his favourite pastime, smoking blindly into a coma, when he isn't managing the alternative medicines section at his local health and nutrition shop. Being a self-proclaimed nutritionist, he will probably throw his certificates at you while trying to sell you weed, naming all the strains and their benefits. He practically camps near the cannabis-based products; you would think his area managers don't yell at him hourly to get out of there and delegate his staff. Saying that, he's been there that long he mostly only comes in to hold the induction course for the new starters.

Basically, Will's mind is an encyclopaedia of pills, biotin, minerals and tea. He sits pondering his never ending plan to open his own business.

"Candles, maybe? Oils? Ooo, no. Cookies, edibles. And face creams. I'll call it cookies and cream... GENIUS."

He reaches for his note pad locked away in a nightstand draw, above the sex one. Anything you talk about, Will can associate it with a vitamin, or a movie, or an article he read in the newspaper.

The room shudders from another ruckus outside. It takes a moment to register something has occurred. He can hear the droning, repeating car alarms and commotion of passers-by before he sits up, groggy.

He goes to his satin black curtains to see. The sunlight pierces his eyes. He falls back, cursing.

10:00 hours
Kieran & Chris
14 Hours Until New Year...

The late morning sun streams through the blinds. Something triggered the alarm, and it plays a familiar song. Kieran snorts to life, clearing his throat, coughing, and (as usual) everything hits him at once. He is more aware of his cracking headache than the layer of dehydrated saliva coating his cracked lips.

He angrily throws the alarm against the wall, not bothered that it breaks into several pieces.

"QUIET, SHE DEVIL."

21-year-old Kieran-James McKenzie pretty much towers over everyone. Though not the oldest, he is the tallest. He goes by K-Jay, or he will allow Kier if you know him on a more personal level since he despises it (on account of being branded 'Kier the Queer' through his tortuous years of school). Will eventually refused to call him K-Jay, seeing it as a facade or caricature that wasn't really him. No one feature makes Kieran so handsome, though his eyes come close. When he is resembling a gutter-witch of stale booze, they are an intense blue with hints of white and crimson fire —the only person known to have orange eyes, Will's second favourite colour.

From them comes an intensity—an honesty, a gentleness. But he's also broken and lost. The only flaw? His intense drug and alcohol problem. But it doesn't stop the flow of his flame-coloured, wavy hair like a Santorini sunset.

There is a face staring at him now, though. He's about to freak out when he realises it's Chris.

"What the fuck is he doing in my room?" he says so quietly it may have been in his head. He's so close to Chris's tanned face he can see it bears acne pockmarks. "Never noticed that before."

23

Kieran assumes it's natural. He always thought Chris had beautiful brown tousled hair and a Greek look about him. He lifts the covers to see they are both wearing boxers before sighing with relief.

"Oh, thank fuck." Kieran tries to get up without disturbing him. "Please, I can't sleep with any more straight men."

Not that Kieran doesn't like Chris, but the Friday, Saturday and Sunday night football chants at the pub with the lads is a dealer breaker for him.

"How did I get here in the first place?"

Once on his feet the room sways, almost causing him to lose balance. He reaches out for the wall. Everything is a blur, and he only remembers leaving after the argument with everybody the night before. His hand slips along the high sheen paint and he sprawls onto the carpet with a crash. The room swirls again before he uses the bedstead to pull himself to a stance. Meanwhile, Chris snores.

"How is this fucker still asleep?"

Kieran scratches his head, chest, then arse, burping and adjusting his orange designer briefs. He catches an aroma of his burp and gags.

"Wow, that was a lot of booze."

Kieran glimpses the seven foot broken mirror he hasn't replaced nor remembers how he broke it. However, his dried, bloody knuckles seem to hint at the answer. Despite the cliché, his skin is ice white (and it truly is). He looks more like a Viking as each year passes; the lines deepen on his face and he is more handsome still as his soul illuminates from beneath. He figures the lines and aging look of a Nordic woodsman could be down to all the abuse.

"But I don't care," he blurts out loud.

This feeling assures him he had some fun the night before. He doesn't remember getting home, as usual. But maybe something in the room can piece it together? He can smell vomit on himself, but looks confused, holding up his arm that's dry as a prune, with crusty concrete left over like when a dirty dish gets left out overnight.

"Fucking delightful." He murmurs, "That's not my sick, I'm never sick." He looks down at Chris. "And it's not you. So, who do you belong to?"

As he speaks to the dried vomit on his arm, he notices the green slime-like texture; it doesn't match anything he's come across before. Kieran looks down, distracted from his 'sick stick' arm, and sees he tried to cook—there are trails of crumbs, slime and dirty pots. His stomach turns.

"Hungry already, buddy?"

Everything slowly comes flooding back—the argument with the others last night leading to his rampage in town. After that, nothing. Trepidation hits and he dares not check his bank balance. He thinks the transactions might solve the blank part of the film reel that was last night! He walks through empty cigarette packets, dirty clothes and discarded beer bottles on his wooden floor as if a corpse just rose from its grave. A fry-up is probably the last thing he needs given his shitty IBS, but he'll have one, anyway. Perhaps if he can grovel, Beth will cook it for him. She's an excellent chef. But first, he has the hallway and the stairs to negotiate.

He digs his phone out of his jeans to text Beth, but there are a surprising number of social media posts to scroll through. He cringes, throwing the phone to the other side of the room. Accidentally, it hits the wall and plonks on Chris's head, who still doesn't wake.

He scoffs. "Not even the end of the world could wake you, eh."

There is little to be said for Chris other than him being an acquaintance of the group, studying on the same course. He doesn't live with them, but he has been staying as their guest for a few days because of some trouble with a drug dealer. He's very much into football, football and football...

oh, and drum and bass... and raves... and pills. A self-anointed hedonist with other layers to his personality.

He will smoke/screw/rob/snort anything, and will say yes to any suggestion if the money is right. He is keen on going to his psychology lessons as he is 'in love' with Darcy—the girl he describes as 'out of this world'. Then again, he pops that many pills, taking a shit in a porta-cabin is an out of this world experience for him.

Despite not being the sharpest tool in the shed, what Christopher lacks in academia he makes up for in enthusiasm. As he would put it, 'I'm just vibing off life, mate.'

Suddenly, a loud crash followed by car alarms and shrieks from the passers-by startles Kieran.

"What in Satan's name was that?"

He runs to his window, which looks like it hasn't had a woman's touch (or anyone's touch) since he moved in. Kieran watches two pedestrians argue violently after stepping out of their collided cars. Unbeknownst to him, Will is on the opposite side of the wall doing the same. He frowns, enthralled when he sees the driver has his head resting against the steering wheel—he's unconscious but not injured, and there appears to be green sick all over the windscreen and down the poor man's pale shirt.

Kieran looks at the fluid on his arm and back at the commotion outside. The colour and texture matches. He overhears one of the other drivers use the c-word before scoffing and coming away from the window.

Slowly, the door creaks as he peers into the hallway.

"Minimal damage, always good."

He darts to his bathroom on the opposite side and washes off the sick. He brushes his teeth too, trying to wake up with a few splashes of water. Unfortunately, he has to share a bathroom with Will and since the breakup neither of them knows what belongs to who anymore. It's a big ol' mess.

"Fuck it."

Kieran washes his face with energy wash before squirting himself with Will's aftershave. He knows full well this time.

Ugh, the beer fear is back!

He wraps up in his purple dragon onesie and feels for a pair of sunglasses in his pocket. *Perfect!* Kieran slithers out like the naughty child he is contemplating the stairs. As Fleetwood Mac echoes from another room, he can barley stand the noise drilling into him.

"OI PRICK!" He swings Will's door open. "Turn that shite down now."

10:07 hours
Hallway

It would be a lie if Kieran said he didn't have a guilty pleasure for the smell of weed seeping from Will's lair, and the sound of vibrato bringing back fond memories. Even now, opening the door, he remembers losing hours with Will in the fog. The feeling is intoxicating. But that quickly turns full on toxic. One could assume that's just what happens when you spend two-and-a-half years with someone in love. All the fond memories turn into shards of glass that attack the brain. A turbulent relationship, but, despite the difficulties, they were sickeningly in love. Kieran sat on an engagement ring for two weeks, trying to swallow his pride and propose. But, one day, Will eventually fell out of love.

"The fuck are you doing in my room? Piss off. You're not welcome in here anymore," Will yells, now out of his euphoric bubble but still too stoned to hit anger.

Kieran pretends like he isn't dying inside. "Jesus Christ, Bates. We have an inspection in two weeks, let some light in here. CLEAN. UP!"

"Speak for yourself, try looking in the mirror once in a

while, maybe use those tears everyone can hear you crying on a night to mop up that cesspool you call a room."

It's hard to read Kieran's emotions from behind a horned hood and sunglasses.

"Your statues fell."

"Oh no, Moose!" Will shrieks, picking up the stag statue.

"That's a stag."

"His name is Moose, you racist ginger clown."

The frustration from Will is still abundant even if it lives below the scratch of the surface, quietly on simmer. He imagines it like magma that spits every so often, mad for what Kieran has done in their relationship. It annihilated Kieran; breaking his heart (or as he will tell you, 'ripping it out and pissing on it') was the hardest thing he'd ever done.

Will grins at Kieran who tries not to grin back. Will's smile slopes downwards, and his usually playful smile is drawn in a hard line, dulling his dimples. But he has perfect pink lips, ripe for kissing, and his powerful hands are rough from past school quarrels. It's all Kieran can think about.

"Why does my body still react like I want to kiss that bastard?" Kieran mutters. "I'm so over everybody loving the way Will's voice quickens when he sparkles with a new idea or is enjoying a song he can lose himself in, forgetting the mask he wears for others."

William Bates goes by 'Gizmo' to his dearest and he is a self-proclaimed herbalist. He is the textbook definition of hyper independent with a cute, cheeky boy-like charm like a mogwai. His ash blonde-brown whiskers and puppy dog blue eyes resemble something small and fluffy, but with a bite! You shouldn't mistake his cuteness for weakness, though. His trauma makes him a weapon. You might think he's prescribing you the correct medication for your ailment, but what he'll actually give you is a concoction to poison your blood for a slow, untraceable and painful death —only if you're on his hit list, of course.

Will always says he isn't much for astrology but says it takes a lot to piss off a Taurus. Standing at five feet ten inches, Will is dark, handsome, and open-minded, with an interesting view of life. The lad can talk the hind legs off a donkey given the chance. He's the most introverted extrovert you'll meet; a nervous wreck to begin with, but after a taste of alcohol, he is the life of any party and also the reason the police will probably show up. He's handsome from the depth of his eyes to the gentle variations in his voice. From his generous opinions to the touch of his hand, he is sweet and kind.

Will swiftly met a nice girl, Ricca and dated her for a while, which pained Kieran even more. Will split up with Ricca and took Kieran back a few times, but he kept going back to the girl, unable to decide until he finally settled. Kieran got the short straw. This added so much more drama to their already unfolding 'Greek tragedy,' as branded by the others. More recently, Will and Ricca split again, leaving Will to enjoy time to himself. But of course, Kieran didn't take the breakup well and still has trouble being around Will. Their lives are intertwined; it forced them to live under the same roof. What makes Kieran more resentful is they act like distant strangers or estranged family members when they see each other.

"You say we're going to be friends. We are going to try but every single time, God! You treat me with utter disdain and hatred."

Kieran flounces out, leaving Will in his darkness, both in his mind and in his room. Why would either want to stay under the same roof with all that tension? When you sign the contract that binds you to live together for four years and you think you're going to be in love forever, you have no choice but to 'crack on'. Plus, neither can afford to move out, despite praying for a miracle, or wants to go first because they share the same social group. In Layman's terms, they are the divorced parents, and their friends are the children. Neither spends that much time in the house or the same room when the other appears, anyway.

As he walks down the corridor, almost forgetting about the impending bollocking that awaits him downstairs, Kieran thinks about how he lives with a glimmer of hope William will come back to him one day—his darkest secret, but that's the good thing about keeping it to himself; nobody can ever know and take it away from him. He can be as deluded as he wishes, be it five months or five years, so he takes out pent-up sorrow and anger on Will every so often. Kieran will deny it, but everyone knows. He's no angel; he played a part in breaking down their love, too.

Back in the day, Kieran and Will were quite the handsome power couple, and everybody wanted their relationship. They met in a nightclub where Will already worked on weekends for 'fun' as a release from his mundane lifestyle prescribing Bette and Dot their cod liver oil. Kieran had just started as the club's photographer—a passion of his. Part of their relationship's demise was Kieran being seduced by the shiny lights and nightclub lifestyle. It worsened his immaturity.

Will wanted Kieran to himself... marriage and the quiet life. Kieran wanted attention and the fun of being at what he thought was the greatest club in Yorkshire with Will at his side throughout. Kieran wanted his king, but he wanted the kingdom too. He couldn't have both. It simply wouldn't do.

As he broaches the stairs, the ill feeling of nausea, headache and irregular heartbeat stops for a second as the even more sorrowful feeling of Kieran's regret. He would despise the club in time (being the demise of his relationship), and would have gladly burned the place to the ground and watched the ghouls echo in the embers if it meant holding Will for just one last time before he set him free to Ricca, or whoever possessed his heart next.

Add in mistakes and traumas, and you have a recipe for a beautiful disaster.

That is one of Kieran's biggest regrets. All he had to do was grow up. When he finally did, it was too late, and it was soul-destroying.

"Should have, would have, could have."

The words spin like a cheap screen saver so harsh he might get dizzy and fall down the rest of the steps. And boy would he if he wouldn't get charged for the damage. That's the rule in the house, their rooms are their own domains. 'Live, destroy, defecate or flood your room,' as Beth would often declare, but the rest of the house was neutral ground or as Darcy likes to say, 'Sweden in all the wars.'

Their relationship wasn't all doom and gloom. It was also passion and fire. They did everything together. For a time, they were happy. Nothing else mattered. Most of their relationship was pillow talk and bonding. Will swore he couldn't fall in love with anyone since his first, Bryan, but Kieran was the exception.

As Will broods in his room trying to fix the antler that has fallen off Moose, he still cannot grasp why he loved Kieran so much. Maybe he'll always have a weakness for him. The more he tries to fix Moose, the more he fails. He sniggers for a moment, thinking it's almost like a reflection of his relationship with Kieran.

Will always thought Kieran to have so much potential. These days, Kieran is along for the ride until he figures out his calling, job after failed job after failed relationship. Despite several attempts to move on from Will, he can't quite find the right person. In his defence, everyone he meets all has a screw loose—more so than he, anyway. It's like every person he tried to befriend after had a disorder Kieran would try to fix and end up more damaged than the person he would try to help.

He tells the odd white lie here and there to cover his arse, which also contributed to the end of their relationship. Kieran was so scared to keep somebody as beautiful as Will, he would often lie to impress him. He even lied about his age to seem older to Will because he said he only usually went for older people. After he found out at an awkward revelation at Kieran's birthday, that was the first seed of doubt. How would you feel if you bought someone something that said 21 on every gift but they were actually 20, and in front of most his family and friends?

As that awkward and harrowing regret replays in Kieran's head, he sits on the stairs for a moment, trying to decide if it's for reflection or to not pass out. He thinks about how he's done a lot of growing up in the last three years, but struggles with regret like most people. The difference between society and Kieran is no one told him how to deal with it; he would often abuse himself in subtle ways so no one would pick up on it. Hence the smashed mirrors and injuries. Failed suicide attempts aside, he's accepted he must suffer through life until he gets hit by a bus or wins the lottery.

Because of the heartache, he turned to the bottle; he was angry for a long time, and still can't get over the break-up nearly four years later. He's a drunkard, plain and simple. His breakfast is vodka masked by orange juice to throw the others off, but they know. He slurs his words by lunchtime and passes out in the afternoon.

What little food he eats is as take-outs or pickles from a jar. He is a phenomenal cook; talented, making this even more depressing. He can match Beth in most subjects: fashion, food, film, acting, singing, sports. The world is his out-of-reach oyster.

His efforts to win back Will became futile, so Kieran no longer leaves the house for anything that isn't party-related or to attend lectures. He even pays the others to buy things for him, so he doesn't have to. Empty beer cans and spirit bottles lay discarded about the house. Wherever a can or bottle lands when empty is where it lives... until the others get annoyed and yell.

Before Will left him, Kieran did everything around their home. He cleaned the most, cooked the most, paid the most. Eventually, he gave up. The way he saw it, the only thing he had going for him walked out the door (though not officially), as Will now occupies the next room, and his proximity reminds Kieran of the ghost of his past, the former man he used to be.

Only a visit from his mum can prompt a quick tidy of the empties.

Kieran has known the group the shortest, but when he and Will became serious, he introduced him to the others and burrowed his way in, cementing their friendships, much to Will's resentment.

For now, Kieran plans to improve his hiding skills for his nasty habit. He drinks a little less to avoid slurring his words and hopes the rosiness of his cheeks doesn't give him away. He can stay anaesthetised through the day while planning exactly how he'll become paralytic by evening. This he does every day, often waking in a cold pile of vomit, either in bed or on the floor.

Essentially, he's just waiting to die.

Kieran
Hallway
13 Hours, 50 Minutes Until New Year...

Suddenly, the smell of bacon infects Kieran's nose; he can't quite make his mind up if it's nauseating or pleasing to his sinuses. The trepidation has taken control of his body like his legs are being hijacked by a puppeteer—he is but the stringed minion.

Before he knows it, he's off the step moping and in the

kitchen.

Ah, the good old kitchen! Somebody cleaned up since their last party. It's not too shabby. Yet, when you're a student, nothing erases the tea-stained, chipped mugs, coffee-stained counters, odd assortment of dirty dishes, curling linoleum, or the ancient stove with grime inside the cooker door from the last lot of losers to rent it. Oh, and not to mention crooked cupboards, last year's calendar askew on a rusty nail, and a wobbly three-legged table every tenant has threatened to get fixed.

Darcy and Beth are already up and dressed around that table. The back door is open, letting in a cold winter draft—cold that reaches in and strangles your soul—but with the heat coming from the cooker, it's balanced. Darcy is smoking a cigarette in front of her laptop. Beth is swilling around the bacon, which crackles in time with the hum from the run-down refrigerator. Both the smoke from the cigarette and frying pan conjoin in harmony, coiling in the air like a Van Gogh painting.

The silence is ironically deafening; you could fit an array of planets between them like a swelling balloon. The temptation for Kieran not to pop it becomes too great. He knows he's in the doghouse for last night.

"Parley?" he jokes, cringing.

If he had a tail, it would be between his legs.

Beth turns around. Darcy looks down her glasses, which she didn't have on before, probably to stop her eyes twitching from glaring at the same exam words over and over. She flicks ash into a tray and purses her lips, then returns to the tap of her fake nails on the keyboard. Kieran thinks it sounds like relaxing raindrops. Beth looks over at him, barely standing in his Spyro onesie, and he takes off the shades. She places Darcy's coffee next to her before returning to the cooker. The now galaxy-sized silence lays thicker and there's tension in the atmosphere.

Darcy crosses her legs and taps her pen on the table, which disturbs her coffee. Her hair is even neater than usual, dragged back in one long efficient ponytail, so thin if she swung it could whip Kieran into shape.

Beth places both their meals on the table and pulls out a chair. Darcy looks up from her screen, smiling in the tense, fake way she often does. One swift sip of her latte, and Beth is smiling the same way. Kieran imagines them holding a presentation for the student council, it's so awkward. 'Tits and teeth' Beth would often recite before going on stage.

"Did you hear about R'Poppy?" Beth opens in a broader than normal accent; her attempt to keep things light, already ignoring Kieran's existence.

"Oh, no. What about R'Poppy?" Darcy takes another sip, trying not to lose all her lipstick on the rim.

Kieran realises they are doing it on purpose until he says something.

"She got her midterm piece scouted by some fancy pants for London Fashion Week last week. She called me, all excited."

"London Fashion Week? Lucky, mad bitch." Darcy licks her lips.

"Makes a change from trying to order a taxi in a takeaway—"

"Okay I'll bite. Why is Christopher in my room?" Kieran suddenly interjects, breaking off their pointless morning matters.

The girls smile at each other. "We put him in there after your little tantrum last night. Didn't think you would come back for a few days."

"That's usually how it goes with you, isn't it?" Darcy doesn't bother looking at him.

"Well, we have a party to plan and a friend to help," he briskly says, avoiding the elephant in the room.

Darcy's tone becomes borderline demonic. She pauses,

then closes the laptop. "After the shit you said to us last night?"

Beth says nothing but offers a simple head tilt, inclined to agree with Darcy.

He sits quickly to suck up to Beth. "Can we at least talk about it?"

"We had to drop everything for this when we have university coursework to do, due in three days. You landed us in this mess," Beth explains. She grips her knife and fork, waiting to eat her breakfast like an orphaned child.

"I provided you with a solution. I tried to help. You were the ones who were going to walk away from Chris and—"

Beth cuts him off. "We were going to come up with something!"

"You orchestrated and manipulated a whole situation to work out in your favour, just so you could have your wild New Year's Eve party with total disregard for the ones who love you," Darcy adds.

"And even on the off chance you didn't plot this whole fiasco, you've landed us all in the biggest pile of shit since Will's mum tried to burn down the neighbour's house, all because he asked us the turn down the music," Beth says.

William's mother, Natalia is a genuine hero with a lion's heart, but she is insane. Constantly in an out of the psyche ward, she's a loose cannon; one minute she'll be making bubble and squeak, and the next she'll tell you she's put razor blades in it. Natalia loves her children and is a splendid mother, but you can wind her up and watch her go —where she'll stop, nobody knows. Will could never understand the connection Kieran always had with her. During one of her neurotic benders, he is one of the only people who can calm her down (other than Will). Many who've known her a lot longer have tried but failed. She won't listen to anyone else, like a speeding train without breaks. But, Kieran has become this blockade of fluffy marshmallows.

Maybe it's because Kieran's brain works the same way, like a psychotic whisperer? He speaks perfectly crazy without making others feel like they are. Will's mother didn't take their breakup well, either. On one hand, she had a heartbroken son and on the other, a 'son-in-law' (as she would say) who she worshipped.

"How was I supposed to know Chris was going to get drugs from the biggest dealer in West Yorkshire? I told him, 'just get some shitty skunk and pot from down the road'. Not only that, but he gets the drugs on loan and doesn't even sell any. That was his fault?"

"You know Chris is a moron who thinks with his willy!"

Beth realises her volume and looks over her shoulder to make sure he isn't there. She growls, exhausted with herself, knowing it's pointless saying anything to Kieran.

She continues, "You said some crappy things last night, and you were sober, which for you makes it worse!"

"Look, I'm sorry. I know to say sorry is like covering a bullet hole with a plaster."

"Yeah, breaking us yet again, then expecting everything to be fixed. All for history to repeat itself. You know what happens when you break something and try to put it back together, you can see the cracks!" Darcy can't help but blurt, "These days, the word sorry is so meaningless and overused. Saying sorry doesn't fix the heartbreak you have caused, the added fear and worry. Sorry is just a word. Sorry doesn't take back you told a total stranger and one of my closest friends my darkest secret. That's nobody's fucking business."

"I'm sorry, DD. Please."

His shoulders slump, his eyes cast down in a mournful gaze. His mouth sets in a semi-pout as he reaches out to take her hand. She too looks back despairingly.

"When I saw you the other day in Midnight Garden's

Mental Unit, running into the both of you, it was the first time I felt I wasn't hiding a dark secret. I was so shocked to see you in a place like that. But I knew within the first few moments of starting it would be okay. After the 'oh shit' feeling, I wasn't alone. This weight had lifted. I know you see me as the unpredictable neurotic fool, but you accept me. Maybe I am. But I am getting help. I love you guys so, so much." Kieran trembles and tries to hold back tears. "You don't get it, it's like a void," he continues. "A dark void. Never-ending, and it consumes everything, so you're left feeling nothing. Empty with a hollow soul away from any other human life. Because the emptiness is so consuming, it cannot bear to pretend everything is okay. Nothing is okay! People walk around this planet each day and pretend everything is fine and it always will be. Why can't we all just admit we are plastic dolls with a painted smiling face revealing no guilt, sadness, emptiness or emotion? That's depression. People think it's a rain cloud over your head but it's so much more—it is the unseen, unheard, silent killer; a pain too strong to cope with and an organic beast who constantly has a hand around your throat, suffocating you. It is something you can't escape, no matter how hard you try. It always swallows you again."

Kieran leans back, and the girls look curious for a change. He knows he has them.

He continues, "It constantly follows you around, like black smoke choking you from the inside out. Like a... a... demon clawing at your heart and mind, eating pieces of you until there is nothing left. It's why I lash out. It's why I said what I said to you both last night... and Will. I was horrible. It pushed me to the edge; all these thoughts and feelings of trying to hurt you guys back when all you were doing was telling the truth. There are times my brain just explodes. It's no excuse, I know; I own my behaviour, try to help, try to be good, and then a trigger flicks. I strike out at someone who loves me. In these moments, I am least proud of who I am, to show the worst parts of me like a damaged child. I know these are things for me to work on, not for others to mitigate. I am an adult, after all."

"Barely," Darcy mutters, still sore from his words the night before.

The girls look at each other, unsure but slightly moved by his performance; it helps he is still intoxicated—heightened emotions and all. He wipes the tears rolling down his beer-flushed cheeks.

A tear trickles down Beth's cheek, memories flood her mind. "I suppose we all wish we could go back, rectify our mistakes. But that's life. It is impossible. We have to live with it. You can't let guilt gnaw on you like a maggot at the core of an apple."

"If you guys still want me to move out after New Year, I will. I thought about what you said."

Beth hesitates. "No, it's okay. We can speak about it another time. You can stay for now."

"We spoke last night. I thought about what you said and it's true about admitting your demons; not wearing them as a badge of honour but addressing them. I was just angry," he says.

"No, we all think you're right. I can't keep pretending my secret is normal and I can just live my life ignoring an eating disorder. I need to go back to Midnight Garden and have been lying to myself that I'm any better," Darcy suddenly admits. "I feel like a new me and this year is going to be the first day of the rest of my life. Thank you, K-Jay." Darcy goes over to hug him and the embrace lingers. "I'm going to ring Dr Smith; I don't know when, but soon. Right now, we have a friend in need."

"What's for breakfast?" Chris enters the kitchen, stretching; he yawns, trying to come to life.

"Speak of the Devil."

Beth smiles at Kieran, wiping his cheek. She winks as Darcy returns to her seat. Chris pours himself a coffee, wrapped in a pink kimono.

"Have you guys made up? That was a pretty heated argument last night. Is that my dressing gown?" Beth double-takes.

"Yeah," he chuckles. Chris starts 'windmilling'. His hips and the outline of his manhood presses against the silk. "I'll wash and give it back!"

She grimaces. "Keep it. Then burn it." She gets up to make Chris a plate. "We're calling this one a truce, right Kieran?"

"Oh, thank God. I'm starving—I could eat another person!" Kieran is about to build himself a plate but turns to Chris. "Yeah, C-Dog, I'm sorry you had to witness last night. It wasn't cool of me. The things I said weren't true and we'll look out for you. We will not let any dealers come after you."

"Oh please, that was nothing compared to what goes on in my house. Usually, the police and SWAT teams roll up." Chris laughs it off.

"A bit like Will's 18th," Beth mutters.

"What happened on Will's 18th?"

"Natalia happened." She scoffs.

"Were going to have a grand party tonight and charge people for entry, sell Cloud 9 and pay off Aiden Wolfe with interest," Kieran reassures.

Chris sits focused on breakfast.

"We have to be honest, it doesn't look great," says Darcy.

"What?"

Kieran slides bacon on his plate and licks his fingers where bean juice has dribbled.

"Despite your..." Beth clicks her fingers, unable to find a suitable word.

Darcy interrupts, "...*cuntish* outburst."

Beth nods. "We still were trying to organise the party. But, we've hit a few problems," Beth explains.

The last one to enter the kitchen is Will, who has finally drawn out of his vegetative state in the cloud of THC in his room. He is wearing nothing but his black boxers and navy-blue dressing gown with the letters RDB sewn into the pockets, barley covering his five-foot ten frame and blonde spikey hair which is a bedhead picture like a toddler who just woke up from a nap. He has a look of childlike glee; he doesn't say anything to the others as he shuffles and squeezes past for the melamine bowls sitting mismatched in the creaky cupboard.

"You smell like what I imagine a drug dealer's car would smell like." Beth wafts the air.

"You weren't complaining when you used to smoke it with me," he laughs with a croak.

"That shit will mess with your brain," she claps back, "which is why I stopped."

He shrugs, shrouded in the cleverness of his intoxication. "It's different for everyone. Weed makes you see profoundness in the mundane. It can be positive or negative. If you have a predisposition, you're more likely to get unusual effects."

"Ah, yes and you're the perfect poster boy of flawlessness and no neurotic mental conditions," mutters Kieran.

Kieran suddenly becomes anxious and uncomfortable and crosses with Will, who smiles at him sporadically but awkwardly—somebody gave birth to another elephant in the room. Their unsettled eyes glance unceremoniously around and try to avoid catching each other's. Will pours himself a bowl of chocolate pops cereal doused in milk, making pleasurable groans and growls before leaving the room as Kieran sits in a standoff-ish manner.

"Oi, I made breakfast!" Beth barks, confused by his

ignorance.

"And I made cereal! Merry Christmas."

"Christmas was a week ago."

"It's still the holidays."

Will shuffles out, dragging his cute man slippers across the floor. He parks himself in the living room, switching on the 60-inch TV courtesy of Ricca at Christmas, which sits below a Katana mounted on the wall—a birthday gift from the same person. Will lifts his feet on the coffee table, high as a kite, and flicks through the channels. Their living room is the biggest shared space, large enough for a decent party. The girls make it attractive during their holidays. Beth takes pride in making sure her decorations are the best. If her front room was a showroom at your local emporium, hers would be the showstopper. A fireplace sits in the centre with a huge mirror above and some quirky artwork on either side. The walls are hung with shades of grey, black, and white fabric to make for a sultry atmosphere. It has a large silver-grey, smooth carpet, and dark purple silk covers the furniture. There are two sofas—an L-shape and a three-seater—which surrounds an enormous coffee table. The room is also home to each tenant's personal touch, such as photos of them hung up, posters, and more.

The only thing that doesn't quite fit in is their attempt at quirky Christmas decorations. Entering the front door, the staircase is immediately on the right. The stairs go halfway, before taking the hard-left, where the door opens right into the living room.

"It's like he just has a psychological need for the last word," grunts Beth as the gremlin shuffles out.

"OCD," suggests Kieran.

"Eh?"

"Two and a half years under him, remember."

"Fair point." Beth tries to clean up.

"And now I'm suddenly off my bacon at the intrusive

42

thoughts of him banging Ricca." Kieran drops his plate on the table.

"Aww, I'm sorry, sweetie." Darcy reaches over to take his hand for a moment compassionately before almost completely switching moods and going back to her laptop.

"Therapy still not easing it?" asks Beth stood by the bin, scraping what's left of her breakfast into it.

"As much as I beg for some kind of hypno-therapy treatment, I can't seem to get it… And Fanackapan in there seems to just forget reality all together," Kieran responds.

Beth, Chris, Darcy and Kieran lean over to the kitchen doorway and watch Will mind his own business from the kitchen, bewildered for a moment before returning to their conversation.

"Do you think you two will patch things up?" Beth bravely asks.

"I don't know. Last night was the worst we've said about each other." He sighs, looking into space as the rest of them gather around the table. "We can't avoid it forever."

"I sent out the invite to everybody on social media and then in the student union, who are going to forward it onto the council who will literally throw flyers out of car windows if I tell them to," Beth says.

Darcy's phone rings. "Hello… yeah… yeah… oh… okay, I understand." She slams the phone down, vexed.

"What?" Kieran chews with his mouth full, halfway through mopping up his hangover and washing it down with that special 'orange juice'.

"People are dropping like flies, everybody either has plans or they're sick. Like really sick. The sickness phone calls seem to outweigh the 'I have plans' phone calls!" Darcy throws her head in her hands.

"How is everybody so sick?" he asks.

"Where have you been? The news for the past 72-hours has been covering that new 'Grime Flu' outbreak, epidemic, whatever it is!"

"I don't watch the news; no news is good news!" he confidently says, shaking salt onto his eggs.

"AH! What did I say?" Beth shoots a stern expression at Darcy.

"The paper said everyone seems to have come down with it. Haven't you noticed people calling in sick at work on the online chat group? Or the students complaining via our inbox?" Beth asks.

"Oh, people check that?" retorts Kieran, confused.

Chris appears, anxiously shaking his leg. Kieran stops him. He takes Chris's hand romantically.

"We can still do this. We have people coming, right?"

"For now," Darcy says without confidence.

Chris takes Kieran's hand and kisses it gentleman-like, smirking a little. A part of Chris's face says it's okay, but it's his eyes that give him away. They're doubtful. Something about them that Kieran can just feel is wrong. So he takes a deep breath.

"I will let nothing happen to you, my little hooligan. You know the only thing worse and more dangerous than a woman's gay best friend?"

"No…" Chris smiles, finishing his breakfast.

"A straight man's gay best friend."

Chris chuckles with a gob full as Kieran kisses his forehead and gives a reassuring ruffle of his hair.

"So, let's do this!" He stands brusquely. "Up! We have shit to do, things to decorate, things to buy." He summons the rest of them, who look at him unenthusiastically. "Chris and I will get the speakers. I know a guy! In fact, he can DJ! I'll get the decorations, party poppers, those silly hats, some cliché 2012 glasses and it'll be the party of the fucking millennium. When people see it tomorrow, they're going to wish they dragged their sorry plague-infected fannies to this party. THIS. IS. THE. PLACE. TO. BE!" Kieran tries to get everyone motivated. "But first, I need a nap. I need to sleep this off. You know what? Chris can do it. Thanks, Chris!" He grins. "Also, you'll need to pick up some more alcohol," Kieran slips in at the last second.

"Why?" asks Beth.

"Somebody drank it all."

"Who?"

Kieran awkwardly grins.

Beth growls. "When?"

"Uh, let's see, the 24th, the 25th, the 26th, the 27th—"

Beth makes inaudible straining noises. "You really are a cheeky bastard! Alright, alright. If it gets me out of this last assignment! If I see one more RFL I'm killing someone."

Beth will accept doing anything else. Finding it mundane and bleak, she finally warms to the idea of the soiree.

Beth
10 Hours, 30 Minutes Until New Year...

Beth goes to collect her winter coat from the bedroom. She quickly hussies herself up in the mirror, displeased with what she sees, when something steals her attention.

She hears clattering and commotion in the streets, so hobbles to the window, tripping over the office chair, trying to ogle a peek. She splits the blinds with her fingers and watches like a nosy neighbour; there's weird activity as people are fighting over belongings. Then those fights spread throughout the neighbourhood. Police are desperate to contain the matter. She also witnesses a mugging and fears for her safety, even in her home. Despite being uneasy about heading out with the increasing violence and crime randomly breaking out in areas of Hyde Park, Beth vigilantly ventures into the unknown. The streets she knows like the back of her hand are alien to her, bleak and void of life.

K. J. McGuinness

14:55 hours
Leeds City Centre

Ah! The city in winter—there is nothing quite like it;
something about the stillness of snow that blankets it anew.
For a while, it will cover everything dark and cruel.

Beth is grateful to be out during the day, which makes a
change from waking up in darkness to going to sleep in it,
and barley having time to see daylight because of her part-
time job. She rustles her fur coat having walked from the
house, which is only a short 15-minute walk. The icy winds
come to breathe freshness upon the world as the snow
transforms the city into a dreamy blank canvas.

Depending on where you go, Leeds streets and back
alleys are capriciously cruel and things have got worse with
the increase of sickness and fear. Fear causes anger, anger
causes chaos. Most people probably don't even know why
they're fighting or stealing but to join the bandwagon.

Beth thinks those people are idiots.

Streets belong to the night walkers, the party animals, the
pimps and the drug dealers. The beauty of it is, they just
look like everyone else, hiding in plain sight. Even the
police stay away unless there is a complaint from a taxpayer
and even then, they arrive slowly. So, it is under the sallow
lamp-light most money changes hands from stolen goods
turning to smuggled narcotics. Right now, Beth is by a sea
of people heading in different directions.

The upper-class who have cash to flash strut down the
high street carrying their designer handbags and wearing
their Armani winter furs. The lower-class people shop in the
markets for hidden gems and the 'bargain of the century.'
Anyone below that sits on the littered floor, begging for
spare change. They have no fancy handbag to keep their
belongings in, never mind a thick coat to see them through
this harsh season. On every corner are buskers; some sing

46

with marvellous talent, others sound like a cat caught in a washing machine. One thing is certain... there are always a lot of stalls selling fast-food galore to make the homeless people's mouths water. It is enough to make anyone beg, cheat, lie, and steal.

The sun is about to say goodbye, and Beth is still struggling to find enough liquor for the party. After giving up on her travels, she accidentality comes across a corner shop she has never noticed before. She continues to see strange activity and yearns to leave the high street before the night crawlers claim their victims.

"Perfect!"

It puts a spring in her step and she cautiously walks in to find a few people minding their own business and a full aisle of alcohol with her name on it.

"Jackpot!"

She replays memories in her head, waiting in line. Anyone from the outside looking at her would know she was in her own world. An odd headline on the papers stacked on the till confuses her, so she picks one up and reads an article about missing homeless people vanishing from the streets, somehow linked to Grime Flu; it just reminds her of her earlier sentiment: blood, death and fire on a vinyl loop.

The sudden realisation that people like herself are so oblivious to the unfolding reality around them hits her.

"Miss?" the male cashier asks.

He distracts her, prompting Beth to forget about the article and put the paper down.

"Sorry. I wasn't being one of those people. I'll pay for it if you like?"

She blushes, and her eyes move to his name tag. There is something happy-ish about him—tall, at least six feet, but slim. He has the kind of face that stops you in your tracks framed by mid-length black hair, tousled, with dark stubble which can be mistaken for auburn in the light. He looks like the guy who must be used to it—the sudden pause in a person's natural expression when they glance his way, followed by an overcompensation, a nonchalant gaze and a weak smile. He fills out his clothes nicely. Beth likes what she sees.

"No, it's cool." Damon smirks.

"I was just miles away…" she explains, trying to get to her purse. "It's a shame about all these people getting sick."

"Yeah, it's probably just like Swine Flu and Ebola," he adds.

"Meh, hakuna matata." Beth smiles, flicking her wrist.

"Eh?" Damon looks blankly at her.

"Hakuna matata."

"Drinking problem?" he awkwardly asks.

"Excuse me?" She double takes, aghast.

"Sorry… a joke, it's a lot to drink, so I'm guessing you must have a New Year's party and you were rambling so..."

"Oh," she chuckles, unattractively looking down at the 16 bottles of mixed spirits. Thank God for Darcy's Swiss bank account. "Yeah, my housemates' idea." She tries to pack the bottles in a box. "It's Swahili; it means 'no problems' or 'don't worry about it'. I speak a few languages."

She's flirting. It's obvious.

"Do you want to hear it in another—"

"I've heard it before... somewhere."

"Yeah, I think it was in a movie."

"I had to grow up pretty quick, not many movie nights in my life I'm afraid."

"Well, your New Year's resolution is to watch more."

"Yes, Ma'am." Damon tries not to grin. "Happy New Year."

Later, the party begins with a spark now there's more alcohol, and hopes of ending in a bang.

Generation Dead

Will is kicking back in the lounge and smoking, concentrating on the TV. He is so high he has to turn the volume down to taste his macaroni and cheese. Once empty, he licks the rim unapologetically—he lets some sauce rest on his chin because he's too far gone to care. Will adds that bowl to the already three empty ones stacked on the coffee table.

"Breakfast, second breakfast, elevenses and lunch!" he announces, pleased, drawing the rope on his dressing gown. He looks for the remote before realising it's in his lap and laughs. "Oh, it's the little things."

"Something about the Leeds and Bradford first international terminal... skip." The channel changes. "Something about a billionaire Alexander Henderson franchising his new Tokyo headquarters for his 'Devil's Food' brand, part of the 'Devil's Food Corp'. NEXT!" He clicks. "Alexander Henderson Fundraiser Charity Ball, snoreeeeee! Jesus, is this guy everywhere?" The channel changes. "Gingerbread man hunt lead... mmmm I do like my serial killers but..." He gets bored.

Click! Click! Click!

Then he comes to the news.

Will leans forward and turns the volume up several times. It takes a moment for his ears to focus and adjust when he sees a couple of people dressed in boiler suits and hazmat protection gear. The dry cogs in his brain lubricate and pay attention.

"We have confirmed reports that the infirmary, specifically the newly built Mercy Heart wing, has been sealed from the public for two days now. They are treating patients reporting cases of Grime Flu only! We believe the virus is spread through bodily fluids, now up to 95% of

49

cases reported so far being fatal. Two Americans working in the city centre have been infected… one of them is Dr Karl Brandon, seen here on the left. The World Health Organisation and the Centre for Disease Control have told the BBC numbers will continue to rise if we do not put measurements in place. If you see suspicious behaviour, please ring this helpline. If you fear you have been exposed to the Grime Flu, we beg you to report to the Mercy Heart wing immediately. Treatment which is still being trialled. Do not contact anyone else, and wear a mask and gloves. Three people have died since the first reporting only last night. The World Health Organisation is calling it the 'deadliest outbreak on record since the black plague' right here in the heart of the United Kingdom. Shipment and travel by air, sea and land has been suspended. Emma Thomas reports."

His eyes widen. He puts on his black-framed glasses and clears his throat while trying to find a drink to cure his cotton mouth.

"Many violent outbreaks in the streets are being reported to be linked to Grime Flu, and earlier this year we saw the brutal violent acts in the London Riots. It appears history is repeating itself in Yorkshire. There are reports of looting, mugging and fighting. I repeat, many outbreaks are being treated at the Leeds General Infirmary which recently opened its brand-new wing. First of its kind: the Mercy Heart LGI wing is now the tallest structure that shapes the city's skyline. But sadly, the unveiling celebrations are on hold as the patient numbers have skyrocketed. If you or someone you know and/or love is displaying any of these symptoms, we urge you to call this number."

Will thinks the people coming down with Grime Flu are linked with the random violence in the streets of Leeds. The epidemic broadcast is followed by a contradictory 'no need for concern at this moment' announcement by some secretary official. Will takes too big a puff of his spliff, and his eyes widen—the nutritionist inside of him is screaming.

Darcy walks past wearing a pair of soaking wet rubber gloves and goes to pick up his bowls.

"Gizmo! What have I told you about smoking weed in the living room? It stinks up the curtains! If the landlord calls in on us, we're fucked! Smoke in the kitchen with the door open or in your room!" She snarls, wafts the smoke, and disappears back into the kitchen.

At least a good three minutes passes before Will puts down the spliff and asks her what she said, pushing his glasses up.

"I swear Darcy was just here," he mutters with glazed eyes.

He stands up, nearly falling back on the couch and trying to gain some balance, then proceeds to the kitchen where he finds Darcy. He pauses. She is minding her own business; her headphones are in, concealing her from the outside world. She has her hands planted in the sink, happily washing up as she belts out a tone-deaf verse of a Britney song about dancing until the world ends, when she glimpses Will from the corner of her eye.

"Fuck!"

Soap suds fly everywhere. She takes off her marigolds and yanks out her headphones with a look of disdain.

"What?" Darcy wonders. "You scared the shit out of me."

"I just came in to tell you something. I can't remember what."

"Jesus, Bates, how high are you?"

"I'm fine, thank you."

"No not, 'Hi, how are you?' I said... oh sod it."

Darcy throws her hands up and growls without bothering to finish explaining herself. She goes to dry her hands and picks up a load of laundry, clean and folded and sitting on the table waiting to be rescued.

Kieran comes in still wearing his onesie, having woken from his nap. Will bursts to life, suddenly remembering what it was he wanted to share.

He talks like a sloth. "This thing…"

Kieran and Darcy exchange confused expressions.

"Last night we were talking about all the people who couldn't come to this party tonight because—" He pauses, losing his train of thought.

Darcy helps him out. "Because they are busy or sick."

"YES!" He clicks his fingers. "Right before we got into the argument—"

Will stops and looks at Kieran, remembering their incredibly scornful insults from the night before. Kieran doesn't know where to put himself.

"OH, JUST SPIT IT OUT!" snaps Darcy.

"It's Grime Flu."

Both Kieran and Darcy groan with discontent. "We know, we spoke about it this morning."

She hesitates and picks up the laundry basket, heading into the living room.

"That's not what I'm saying. I just saw the news today, and it's getting worse. It's bad." He follows her, so Kieran does too.

"So? Pandemics and epidemics happen all the time. Swine Flu, N1H1, Ginger-ism... what's so special about this one?" argues Kieran, shoving his hands in his pockets.

Will licks his lips to lubricate his mouth. "Those all happened in other countries with cures, but this is happening in our town, down the street, literally."

"Again, SO?"

"I don't think it's a good idea to have this party."

"Oh, no! No! No! No! No! NO!" Kieran snaps. "You're not doing this all because of some fucking weed-induced paranoia!"

"No, seriously, you didn't hear what I heard. These

people are sick and it's bad. If we throw this party, we risk getting sick ourselves. We risk getting more people sick. People are dying."

"It's the media scaremongering, Will. You used to tell me that all the time when we were together."

"No K-Jay! Don't bring that up. Not after the poisonous words exchanged; I'm not talking about that."

Kieran chokes, shrugging, and shaking his head. Darcy growls before leaving upstairs, frustrated with the both of them bickering once again.

"I'm not being paranoid," Will states calmly, "but I know this party is a bad idea. I can feel it. We can find another way to help Chris pay back the drug dealer for Cloud 9. Listen to me!"

"NO! YOU LISTEN TO ME!" Kieran roars. "The girls and I have put too much into this now. Beth and Chris are due back at any moment with all the supplies. We have people RSVPing, and numbers are building. There is no going back. I will not let some jumped up little 'halfling' ruin this party because of his THC-induced delusion that everybody is going to infect each other and die."

"What's up with you two?" Darcy asks, changing the topic and returning with an empty laundry basket.

Kieran becomes erratic. "Will is trying to get us to cancel the party, saying everybody is going to get the plague and basically die!"

"That's not what I said."

Will pinches his thumb and finger on the bridge of his nose, shutting his eyes to stay calm.

"Next you'll try to tell me people are eating each other in the streets!"

Kieran waves his arms frantically and cavorts back into the kitchen. Darcy surveys the two of them, trying to figure it out.

"Gimzo, sweetie, what makes you think people are going

to die at the party?"

"That's not what I said; it warned people on the news... it was bad. I'm merely saying we can stop this from getting worse and also us getting sick if we cancel." He over-pronounces to get his point across.

"DELUSION!" Kieran's high-pitched squeal travels to the living room. "SMOKES TOO MUCH POT!" he continues, taking another jab at Will. "You're not stopping my party; this could be the event of the year."

"You throw this party, and this party WILL be your last!" Will retorts.

"WELL, I'M GOING OUT WITH A BANG! BOTH META. PHOR. ICALLY. AND. PHYS. ICALLY." Kieran gestures, sexually thrusting to the air.

"Charming."

"Stop pacing," Darcy tells him. "You're like a stressed tiger in a cage."

"Are we really going to listen to the same person who thinks we live in black holes upon black holes?" Kieran says, storming back in, having consequently run himself a glass of ice-cold water—mouth drying from the dehydration of the hangover.

"That theory was not disproven."

"Stoner!" Kieran grunts.

"Alcoholic!"

"Fuck! You!" Kieran snarls.

"Not anymore." Will smirks.

Kieran is about to swing for Will when Darcy tells them both to knock it off.

"Will, babe, you know I think you are one of the cleverest men in my life, who always has something to say, who I always listen to."

Will scoffs, "I know where this is going."

"Wait, all I'm saying is nine times out of ten I would agree with you but..." She pauses, almost reluctant to speak. "Kieran is right. We have invested too much into this already and it's too late in the day. Would you honestly listen to every single thing they told you on TV?" She caresses his cheek.

"THANK YOU!" Kieran smugly dances.

"That doesn't mean I'm on your side, ginge. Will isn't paranoid. I don't think we need to worry... yet! I'm sure it's something the government will deal with in the new year."

Darcy heaves a sigh of relief when she hears the door go. It opens from the living room, letting in a gust of cold winter air. The sun is already fading, and shadows are cast over the city. Beth and Chris step through with mountains of bags.

"Help us!" They nearly fall forward. "We have plenty more where that came from and we have guests arriving in two hours... we might pull this off."

The bottle bags clink, and the odour of processed food consumes the air. A strange man helps himself into the living room.

"Beth, what have I told you about trying to bring homeless men home?" asks Kieran, obviously poking fun.

"You know that's our DJ!" she growls.

"Close the door, it's freezing!" jokes Kieran.

Will stands beside him and they exchange a bland look, almost as cold as the air.

The late day is illuminated with that special chill and pale light only winter's sun can produce. Rain from last night makes everything glow with an icy kiss. It decorates the street as a birthday cake with frosting everywhere.

"Careful, your tears might freeze," snarks Kieran.

"Careful, your soul might freeze. Oh, wait..." Will retorts.

Kieran dances around in his bare feet like a maniac in the street. "FUCK IT'S COLD!"

"Quick, he's over here, come and get him Midnight Garden Clinic!" Will bellows out to anybody listening.

"Oh, ha-ha, report me to the insane asylum like always. Isn't that reserved for your family?"

Kieran laughs and playfully pushes Will. They share a tender moment. They stare at each other, standing so close yet worlds apart—they can feel the heat of each other's breath. It's a little awkward; the silence has gone on too long.

"Oh my god, I found it!" Kieran breaks the ice—so to speak.

"What?"

"Your frozen heart, of course."

Kieran reveals a snowball and launches it at Will. He cackles again and they play fight, distracted from the car full of bags. Beth and Darcy tenderly watch for a moment from the window before Beth bangs on the glass.

"OI, HURRY!"

17:16 hours
Beth & Kieran

It's as if only a few minutes pass before nightfall. Less than an hour ago, the sky was painted with hues of red, orange and pink, but all colour has now faded, leaving a matte black, starless canvas.

"Looks like it's a clear night tonight," Beth says, taking a drag on her cigarette and craning her neck.

"Yeah, they're starting early."

Kieran takes a drag too, referring to the echoing sound of popping and exploding in the distance, which soothes him.

"It always reminds me of what I think an apocalypse would sound like, all the explosions and bangs like gunfire —the sky is alive."

She grins. "You're strange."

He ponders, then says, "Aye."

"I'll tell you what *is* strange," she begins, "that you can hear the fireworks, but you can't see them."

"Strange things." Kieran flicks his cigarette onto the street and rubs himself warm.

"I think we might pull this off. We have a DJ, a few people have already turned up, we have a buffet and an endless supply of booze. However, that's half our rent and insurance gone!" Beth reveals, cringing.

"We almost didn't pull it off."

"What do you mean?"

"Vitamin dickhead in there tried to stop the party, he thought everybody was going to get sick by being here... including us. He seriously tried to suggest we think of something else and abandon ship because of what he saw on TV." He tuts.

"Oh, no! No! No! Albeit, I was against this at first, but I've warmed up. He's my best friend and your ex, so you know what he is like."

"Yeah I know, but I admit this has scared him, Beth." They look at each other, concerned. "In the back of my mind, I worry because I've never seen him react like that before."

They both look through the window at Will as he helps set up by hanging disco lights as the music pumps.

"I must admit as well..." she trails off.

"Go on..."

Beth feels chills rush through her. "Earlier, when I was getting the supplies for the party, I saw some freaky stuff. It was like the London riots all over again. People were going nuts; some people were walking around like they had no purpose, others were sick. I know my city. I live and breathe the streets, but this was different, like something had... *died*."

"We can't let this dampen our evening; we can deal with it tomorrow," affirms Kieran.

"Why do I listen to you? I can't believe I'm going to be

distributing narcotics at my party. I'm the student president! God, I'm going to hate myself tomorrow."

Beth flicks her tab end before shuffling inside, safe from the breeze.

This is going to be a night I'll never forget, she thinks.

20:20 hours
Darcy
3 Hours, 40 Minutes Until New Year...

Darcy looks down at her mobile phone and over her shoulder to see if anyone is there. She sneaks out the kitchen door, picks up a garbage bag, and hustles some trash in as an excuse to leave. It leads to a balcony outside with four or five steps descending to the bins and a tall, tan fence where there is no gate; it feeds straight to the alley for all the other student houses.

The guys truly don't know the perfect view they have; anywhere else on the street and you're blind to the horizon, shared by a glimpse of the outer city. Beyond that, lights illuminate the shimmering haze of pollution. Dots of green and red from the cranes and warning lights look like random stars in the sky. In the far distance, the silhouette of the skyline pierces through the warm glow like a jagged mountain ridge. Millions of lights cause the dense mass of skyscrapers beyond the endless row of suburban terraces to glitter. Terraces lead to buildings that rise higher and higher each year. People are needle points and cars are blood cells from here, flowing through the veins of the city.

The only vehicles on the road are taxis. No matter the weather, time of day or year, the urban decay never ceases. The hustle and bustle of the locals never halts. Neighbours are always out talking, kids playing, dealers dealing and students doing their thing. But this time, this one time, the streets are quiet... *too quiet*, like the Angel of Death has wandered through and snatched souls.

But Darcy has too many other things on her mind to notice the peculiar silence. She lights up a cigarette to add to the hazy cloud, lingering, spiralling in stagnant air, while making a call and waiting anxiously as it rings.

"Hi, is that Doctor Kim Smith? It's Darcy, Darcy Danby… yes." She chuckles nervously. "I'm sorry to disturb you, I know it's New Year's Eve and you have plans, but just with you telling me I can call whenever, no matter the time…"

"That's alright, Darcy. I'm at a boring charity function. Something to do with the Alexander Henderson Foundation. As long as I don't miss the countdown."

"Yeah, I think I need to see you again."

"Oh, why is that?"

"Some things have happened. I've been doing a lot of thinking and had a wake-up call. I lied to you, but mostly to myself. I'm no better and my New Year's resolution resolves that. I want a new year and new me, something stronger. Somebody said to me, 'once the soul is so thin the body follows, instead of a growing a sense of self-love and self-worth, there isn't the strength to climb to health.' And so, it is so very hard to eat more, even when it is a simple bite at a time, hard to listen to the part of the self that wants to stay alive, to be loved. It's time I claimed back the person I once was."

"I'm proud of you, Darcy. I'll call you in the new year and set something up. You are a strong girl, and this is going to be your year. Take care of yourself."

"Thanks, Doctor Smith. I have a good feeling."

Darcy ends the call and looks philosophically into the night sky, smoking her cigarette.

Will
2 Hours, 54 Minutes Until New Year...

It isn't quite a t-shirt; it isn't quite a shirt. Will has spent far longer than he wanted fidgeting with his bow tie, adding to his impatience and frustration. The collar plays about his neck as the warm heater blows air on his dresser, the only source for Will's room—he never liked the heating on much. The fabric is close enough to show the shape of his chest.

The door creaks and Will casts his eyes briefly in the mirror to the shadow in the doorway.

He knows who it is; Kieran's watching, if only for a moment, knowing that shirt would have been pretty in any colour and something Kieran wants to touch, hug, lose himself in, if only for that moment.

Then he catches his eye. "Enjoying the view?"

"I'm sorry, I honestly was just walking past, and I saw you struggling with the bow tie and thought you might need a hand."

Will hesitates for a moment but nods slightly, allowing Kieran into his world. Sighing, he is trying to offer an olive branch for the previous evening.

Kieran has a ramekin half full of pitted green olives. He silently holds one out, expecting to be praised like a cat.

"Olive?" Will looks at him funny. "It's the closest thing I could find to a branch…" He inverts his lips inwards, doing that half smile most British people do when passing in the streets.

Nothing but the sound of laughing, chattering, and base music pumping below fills the room. Cars are pulling up and guests are greeting one another.

"It seems to be going well."

Kieran comes up behind, almost caressing his body, resisting the temptation not to press into his perfect

60

curvature. He can smell argon oil, aftershave and the slight haze of THC—it's ironically intoxicating.

Kieran bites the inside of his mouth to keep a straight face, just like Will would.

"Yeah well, doesn't matter what I think anymore," Will can't help but throw in.

Kieran says nothing, which takes every shred of his being. He towers above Will by a whole foot. Will was always the small and nimble, athletic one in their relationship, and Kieran was always larger and higher. Will would never admit he used to love being held in bed with Kieran's arms and body wrapped around him like a bear, since they considered him the dominant party in the relationship. But while they are masculine, Kieran loves to be held as well.

The silence becomes awkward; it hangs in the air, suspended, like the moment before glass shatters.

"I've never been good at these; you were always the one who could do it for me," Will admits while Kieran fiddles, putting the olives down.

"That's kind of why I stopped, I wasn't sure whether to offer."

"There are many things I've had to learn to do without you and many things I've had to learn to live without. Suppose that's breaking the habit, isn't it?"

"Like a drug," Kieran agrees.

The silence continues, tearing them both apart. Will becomes anxious and takes a spliff from his side.

"About last night. What I said—" he begins.

Kieran cuts him off. "You think I don't remember but I do."

"You weren't drunk?"

"I'm not talking about that," confesses Kieran.

He finishes the bow tie perfectly and brushes Will's shoulders, then gives the bow tie a little jiggle. It's blue, one of his favourite colours.

"I was with you two years, Will. I know when I wake up with the smell of your aftershave on me. It's not all there, but I know something happened between us… I can still taste you."

"Oh, that…" Will's eyes dart around. He appears gloomy as he turns to face him properly. "Surprising to say, you drank so much. I'm shocked you have any taste buds left."

"Likewise, with the amount you put up your nose."

They stare at each other in the mirror, longingly, before Kieran turns away and Will moves after him.

"We don't have to talk about that. It will just fuck with my head even more. I want to say I'm sorry about the argument before, but you said some evil things." Kieran looks into his eyes, tears already forming; the pain comes from a dark place. "They already knew but thought maybe they had forgotten, and you just had to air our dirty laundry again."

"You hurt me with what you were saying!" snaps Will.

"So, your idea was to hurt me back but harder?" Kieran quickly responds.

There is something in that shout. Will watches Kieran's eyes. Then he knows the anger is nothing but a shield for pain, like a cornered soldier randomly throwing out grenades, scared for his life, lonely and desperate.

"We have to do it for our friends. We are like the divorced parents and Darcy and Beth and everybody else are our children. This needs to stop. Jesus Christ! This is just it! We can't even get through one conversation without it turning into a battle," Will erupts. He breathes in. "This is stupid, it's been nearly three years… we should have moved on. I moved on and got with Ricca and I built a future—she made me laugh. Then you started a job at the company I work at for God's sake."

Kieran sighs. "That had nothing to do with you. I was

desperate, and it was all that was out there. It's been two years since the bank of America collapsed, dooming the world into recession. You know what, I was good at it."

"*When* you showed up!"

"I had a lot going on, not that you would know. You destroyed my life, and I had to pick up the pieces by myself. All you had to do was to stay."

"UGH!" Will gets wound up.

"You know what adds insult? You just left, went AWOL, and that made me look stupid. I said nice things about you. I defended you in the group chats when they asked if you were a psycho."

"That's surprising."

"It was my job and my reputation on the line. I had been there for eight years. And you couldn't stop talking about us to people I wouldn't trust as far as I could throw. I was not ready for that," Will says.

Kieran grunts. "I wasn't myself—I was sick; you wouldn't get it. Trust me, I'm already fucking embarrassed about it enough. I have to replay those memories in my head when I'm alone in the dark. You wonder why I don't stop enough to slow down. That's what will wait for me in here." He taps his head, agitated.

Will strikes him with a look of fury. "Really, I wouldn't get it? With a family like mine? All that SHIT you know I endured growing up. A mentally ill mother, a baby sister to raise at ten—I was a baby myself. The street gangs! The drug wars! My first boyfriend—not to mention hiding the fact I was bisexual from everyone while in this secret relationship to maintain my respect and reputation at school and in the streets?" Will looks him up and down.

"You know, when I saw you outside the club that time with all your employees and Ricca having the time of your lives, I genuinely would have been so worried about what they thought about me for going AWOL. But now they

mean fucking nothing to me! They don't know my story—
our story."

"THERE. IS. NO. OUR. STORY!"

"Then stop fucking with my head, Will!" Kieran shuts
him down.

Will walks to his suit jacket and picks up his braces.

"You know I got sectioned because my aunt died, then
my brother killed himself. I had no choice but to leave. I
wish I didn't leave the way I did. You know me better. She
died suddenly, clear as day—head smashed against and wall
and PFFTT! GONE! I saw the blood dried in her ears from
where her brain leaked. And then a week later I walk into
my bathroom to see my brother swinging from the light
fixture 45 minutes gone. What else do you expect when you
take a mentally fragile boy who lost the only thing he ever
loved and then take away family members too?"

"Funny way of showing it." Will sighs.

"You even said despite all your friends hating me, you
knew me better."

"I don't know what I know anymore. We're different
people, we're not even the boys who fell in love with each
other. It's been that long and we have separate lives despite
living under the same roof. You had your shit, and I settled
down with Ricca. Which is now over thanks to yet another
one of your little stunts."

"I heard what happened. I'm sorry about that." Kieran
looks down. "You told me to kill myself."

"You called me a drug addict and came for my mother.
Those are lows blows..." Will wanders to his bedroom
aimlessly. "For anyone. There's a rule on the street, Kieran,
you know that! Say what you want but don't go after
somebody's mother. After all I taught you about my family,
the streets. After they accepted you and loved you. Why do
you think I text you to apologise last night?"

"At three in the morning?" Kieran scoffs.

"You know I've never been good with my words or feelings." Will groans in frustration again. "I'm not going around in circles."

There goes the deafening ironic silence again. Neither one knows what to say.

"I love you, but I don't think I am in love with you like you are with me. Something is there, but I can't give you what you want. I don't know—you seem to the be one that stands out. Not even Byran or Ricca or any other person I've gone through has had the same effect you did."

"You never even tried, Will. You came back for two weeks and then left me again for Ricca. Just because she ended up in the hospital. Do you have any idea what that did to me? She was sick, yeah..."

"She had cancer, Kieran!"

"You promised me on the phone that evening she went in, you would be back. You would be back even though I knew from the minute I dropped you at home after work—that was the kiss of death. Then I wake up and on social media she's bought that fucking Katana for your birthday that stares me in the face every time I walk through the door. And you didn't even have the guts to dump me, you didn't even care I saw it. I had to find out from my sister who showed me on her phone, on social media, NOT TEN MINUTES AFTER I SAID I GOT BACK WITH YOU! I WAS SO ENDEBTED YOU HAD GIVEN ME A SECOND CHANCE!" Kieran roars. "Didn't she fucking cheat on you, sending her body to every Tom, Dick, and Harry on social media while she was in that place? Didn't you say she was sending messages to her cousin about how she wasn't happy with you and the only fucking reason you found out was because they left it on a tablet?"

"That's none of your business. We had more communication in our relationship than you could even fathom. You know nothing about us." Will counters, "Love is hard, not a walk in the park; you fuck up, you forgive, you work at it. THAT's the POINT!"

Kieran scoffs harshly, "Wow. The fact you could say that about her and not us when that's all I ever wanted to hear from you."

"She's kind, and she makes me laugh and she's SORRY! Just like she knows nothing about our life together other than the poison you drip-fed her."

Kieran looks at him pleadingly; it's something he didn't want to hear.

Will glances away, hesitating. "Don't look at me like that."

"Like what?"

"You love me," Will says, trembling.

"You're under my skin, man. The fuck can I do?" Kieran presses his tongue against the roof of his mouth.

"I guess we're just destined to be fucked then." Will throws his hands on his head, grabbing his dark blonde spiky hair and taking a few steps back. "Life isn't fair. And it isn't a story. Those perfect endings comprise people whose lives suck to make themselves feel better about their regret! This isn't a story where the hero gets the guy or girl after screwing up with some grand romantic gesture. Sometimes you don't get to make up. Sometimes you don't get the closure you want or need." He puts his hands on Kieran's shoulders and looks into his eyes. "These feelings I have for you won't end until my body ceases to function, and it releases my soul for whatever comes after. I could deny it as much as I want, but I know when I'm alone you are there. I have to hope somehow that our love will endure.

"In a parallel world, we are together, married and happy like we were supposed to be here. And I don't know, maybe in five or ten years, we can go for a drink. Even on my dark days, you'll be in here somewhere, keeping my mind from sinking into that schizophrenic bubble that claimed me in the past. I know however deep I fear I've fallen, you will be there like the solid ground to steady me, giving me time to climb back into positivity. But for now, it is not our time." Will rests his forehead against Kieran's as he whimpers. "Always remember that."

"It's a bittersweet symphony," Kieran whispers back.

The moment quickly passes. Will wipes his eyes and looks up to Kieran, who does the same.

"Enough!" He sniffles. "It's New Year's Eve. I'm probably going to die of the plague but here we are at the end of the world." Will picks up his jacket. "New year, new beginnings; we should try to be friends, even if we hate each other."

"What's your resolution?" Kieran asks, walking to the door.

Will pauses for a moment to think about it, not sure how to answer. "Smoke more weed... save the world..." He turns and offers a cheeky, charming grin. "You?"

"Live." Kieran holds an expression of accomplishment.

"Hey." Will gets Kieran's attention and looks at him kindly. "Shave... you look better when you're..." He tries to think of the words. "Tidy."

Will tosses him an off-purple/deep pink bow tie.

The two of them smirk before Kieran leaves. He strides along, feeling a little melancholy when Chris bounds up the stairs.

"Fuck K-Jay! Fuck K-Jay! Fuck K-Jay! Fuck! FUCK! FUUUUCK!"

He springs so fast his suit becomes untucked. His face is drip white.

"Chris, what the hell, man? What's wrong? You look like you saw a ghost. You didn't take any Cloud 9, did you? That's for the guests!"

"No, you need to come with me. NOW!"

Chris tugs him into Kieran's bedroom. Kieran kicks up a

fuss about being aggressively manhandled while Chris acts hysterically. He dances, moving about the room like there's a hurricane inside him. He's moving as if his brain is demanding the energetic expenditure of an athlete but won't tell his limbs what to do. His eyes are wild.

"Chris, talk to me!"

"CODE BLACK! CODE TEN! DEATH CON FIVE!"

"Mate, what-the-fuck are you saying?"

His words are crowded together and some are missing. Kieran's protests are bouncing off him like hard rain. Now he's right in front of him. His fingers are white-knuckled and holding Kieran's vest, asking if it will be okay.

Kieran strikes Chris out of nowhere. The slap is as loud as a clap of thunder.

"Chris, that is the second time in two days I've had to do that! Get a hold of yourself and explain!"

"What's code for 'the fucking drug dealer is here'?" Chris nearly pisses with distress.

"What?" Kieran repeats a few times, now joining the anxiety cavort. "Aiden's here? Aiden Wolfe?"

They rush over to his window, peeking through the blinds; they look at the many cars and taxis.

"Wait, I don't even know what he looks like," growls Kieran.

"Cream suit, burgundy shirt, looks like he might chop your dick off with a machete, or his teeth."

Kieran scans the road until he shrieks. "Oh ding, ding, ding."

He spots the rugged-looking man in his early thirties walking up to the stairs of the front door: ivy blazer and burgundy shirt with the sleeves rolled up (as well as the jacket sleeves)—normally one would look like an 80s reject, but somehow he pulls it off flawlessly.

He is greeted by Beth at the door, oblivious to his identity. His curls are midnight-coloured and his eyes a dark brown, framed by graceful yet bushy brows, although maintained. His skin is tanned. He has prominent cheekbones and a well-defined chin and nose. Muscles ripple across every part of his body. Tattoos peek out of his shirt on his forearms and neck.

"Fuck! He can bite my dick off if he likes." Kieran sweats.

"You're sick! HOW IS THIS SUPPOSED TO HELP? WE ARE DEAD MEN!" Chris screams, hyperventilating.

"You mean *you're* dead? He does not know what I look like; you're the moron who got the drugs on loan!"

Chris screams. Kieran puts his hand over his mouth. squeezing tight until Chris is calm and controlled. "We will fix this!"

"Yeah, he kind of knows what you look like now."

"What?" Kieran's voice lowers below demonic; his head may as well have done a 180.

"I kind of… might have… accidentality showed him a picture of us while we were talking."

Chris scrunches his face up. Kieran's drops to a ghastly proportion as he slaps Chris, who forms a shell like an armadillo and squeals.

"Pathetic! How you call yourself a straight man I'll never know!" Kieran stops.

"I'm a lover, not a fighter."

Kieran paces. "Oh shit. Oh shit. Oh shit. Okay… this is fine. This is good. This is all part of God's plan. We stick to plan A!"

"Which is?"

"Fuck! You are hopeless! It's the only thing we've been speaking about all day! We sell Cloud 9 as normal, but we just explain and he can take the money as we go."

"Will that work?"

"I don't know." They lean back over to the window, ogling him one last time.

"Do you think he can see us?"

Suddenly, Aiden Wolfe spontaneously looks up in their direction, and they scream, ducking down underneath the windowsill.

"Shit, we need to do this." Kieran uses his might to pick himself up and glances at his watch. "We have two-and-a-half hours until midnight. You need to go throw some water on your face and act like nothing happened if he comes to you. You tell him you have the money and if he sticks around, you will give it to him. That's enough time for us to make the 500 pounds." Kieran gags. "I still can't believe you borrowed that in DRUGS!" Kieran quickly races to get ready. "Beth and Darcy should sell a few tabs of Cloud 9 for ten pounds apiece. There are supposedly 80 people coming throughout the evening which means we only need 50 of them to buy it."

"And what if they don't?" Chris is sweating now too.

"Then I hope you can live without kidneys!"

An invisible hand clasps over Chris's mouth; he feels his ribs heaving as if bound by ropes, straining to inflate his lungs.

"Oh, I'm joking! Everybody will buy some; people will buy some for their children and their children's children." He flaps facetiously. "Now go!" Kieran tucks himself in. "I SAID GO!"

Darcy
1 Hour, 16 Minutes Until New Year

Casa de la K-Jay is BOOMING! The drinks are flowing; the base is heaving, and the people are gorgeous in the Hyde Park household. People are drifting from far and wide, drawn to the pretty lights and euphoric sound. Moths to a flame; everyone is acting as if it's their last night on Earth. But it's their minds avoiding the thought of the hangover to come. The music excites people. The strobe masks so many of their movements, but each flash captures them in a different pose.

Tomorrow there will be hell to pay. But tonight, the alcohol is flowing on an IV drip.

That stupid, filthy rug atop an even dirtier grey carpet is seeing more dancing shoes than a ballroom—everyone with everyone bumping, jumping, grinding, spinning. The music escapes from every open window and door.

Darcy is playing host, keeping watch over her domain and her minions, catering to everyone's needs. She occasionally slips the odd bag of Cloud 9 here and there in a pocket, clutch bag or a clenched fist while raking in the money.

"You have turned this place into something better than any nightclub in the city! Your club is electric, everyone feeding off smiles and dancing. I could go like this all night long, feet moving to the crazy beat," the DJ shouts over the music to Darcy.

She smiles. "Thanks, I like dolphins too." Not having heard a single word he said, while multitasking, pouring drinks and selling drugs. She wears a teal gown made of soft satin fabric—long and loose to hide her petite figure.

"I love your dress," a 'customer' says.

"Thank you!" she yells back. "Green for envy."

A semi-circular, high collar made of faux silk heads the ankle-length robe. Darcy walks light as an acrobat; it makes her jet black wavy hair sing. Hardly anyone can see the dance floor; it's wall-to-wall people moving to the house music and 90s remixes. There's no room for any more so people overflow into the front garden and onto the street.

"I wonder how the Police haven't turned up yet?"

"Probably too busy dealing with 20 other parties like this." She throws her hands up, gyrating.

"I heard the emergency services were engaged this

afternoon. All services are indisposed, and the hospitals are rammed."

"Well, us northerners are quite the handful," she replies, not taking what she said seriously. "Excuse me for a moment," she adds after spotting Chris.

"Darling, you look like a dear in headlights—what's wrong?" She puts on a flamboyant facade for her audience.

"Aiden Wolfe," he utters and looks over her shoulder.

She turns to match his direction of vision where she sees the man standing in the corner, acting with clout.

"I'll take care of this. Chris, I need you to go stand with the DJ. Keep handing out drinks and food and stay calm."

Chris seems too jittery, paranoid by the strobe lights that shoot rainbows even into the darkest corners.

"CHRIS!"

She grabs his cheeks and looks deep into his royal green eyes, like she's looking into his soul. Suddenly, he kisses Darcy, and the world falls away—the moment is right, slow and soft, comforting in ways words can never be.

Their hands sit below each other's ears. Chris's thumb caresses her cheek as their breath mingles. She runs her fingers down his shoulders, pulling him closer until there is no space between them; even with all the commotion and pounding music, she can feel the beating of his heart against her chest. This is a dream come true for Chris.

"I know you like me and I like you too! If you can do this, I'll be back for more," she assures him.

"I have this."

Suddenly, he becomes strong and confident, like he can conquer the world, finally getting to kiss the girl he's loved for so long.

Generation Dead

Beth
1 hour Until New Year...

Finally, the lady of the hour, the President of the Student Union, first of her name, graces her guests by walking down the stairs like the red carpet. Of course, she would leave it to the exact hour... a Cinderella-type story.

Beth is flawless, whether she wants to do the party or not. She always attempts to be the centrepiece in any room and pretends not to care. Right now, she can feature upon any billboard or magazine cover but is better than those two-dimensional photoshopped models.

Somehow her imperfections make her perfect. There is a shyness to her, hesitation in her movements and a softness in her voice. Nobody can work out if it's an act. People are talking behind their hands; she doesn't mind as long as she makes an impression from the stairs. Donning a white cocktail dress, her ice blonde locks are pinned up, which must have taken the longest. It would be tens across the board with judges present.

The creamy sheets of the silk short dress slip onto her shoulders, peppering her body with soft, sensual kisses. Like a lover, it seduces the senses and conveys with the utmost skill in the art of pleasing, just how she likes it.

"Let the chaos begin," she chuckles, and her guests—her studio audience—laugh.

She clops down the last step. Darcy picks up her gown so she doesn't trip over and takes Beth by the hand.

"Beth, I know you're soaking it up right now, but I need you on guest duty—five pounds on our door and—"

"And ten pounds for the powder, I know." She rolls her eyes. "Why?"

"I think the drug dealer is here. I don't know what he wants but I'm taking care of it."

"The one from Midnight Mount, your group therapy

73

session?"

Beth panics as Darcy walks off. She curses before painting on an overly fake smile, enough to worry a clown.

23:05 hours
Kieran

Kieran slowly braves the stairs, having got rid of his hangover. He looks out among the ocean of people, many characters far and wide. He's giddy when he hears a voice.

"Wow, you look like you're not drinking yourself into an early grave for once."

He looks down to see Will holding two drinks.

"Was that your way of saying I look good?"

"Tell anyone and I'll deny it." Will smiles.

Kieran takes one of his drinks though it wasn't offered, and they manoeuvre between their guests.

"Thanks for the bowtie, we almost match."

They turn to glance at their reflections in a cabinet. Will tidies his dinner jacket while Kieran puts his on; they are both wearing the same item in different colours—one blue, one purple—white shirts and black tailored jeans with matching braces.

"We look quite the pair, don't we?"

"Careful, people might think we're back together." Kieran rolls his eyes. "You don't mind, do you?" he can't help but ask.

Will looks at him awkwardly. "Would I have given you my other bowtie?"

He smirks, walking back to the DJ stand while Chris tries to confidently mingle with the guests. Kieran stands for a moment, more dumbfounded than ever given their earlier conversation. "Christ, you are a mind fuck lad." He mutters.

He follows. "How much have we made so far?"

"350 and still going strong; these people are smashed,"

replies Will.

He smiles. "Yeah, none of them look too sick either."

"Yes, because they're so smashed. I'm letting the record show I'm still totally against this," Will reiterates, "but I'm the right balance of high and drunk to live with it."

"That's why I like you," Kieran says loudly over the music, only half-joking.

Kieran already knows he doesn't love him back, and he gets a sensation like something is yanking on his heartstrings, trying to pull it out of place. And it hurts. But he can't resist. God, he can't fight against his naughty thoughts; even Will's smell is flooding his senses now.

"I'm off to... there's a... go... over... something."

Kieran babbles his words and Will tries to speak, but they both fail like toddlers learning their first words.

Kieran walks off and grabs a bottle from the table. He swigs it neat and grips it in his hands as he watches Will talking to other boys... and girls. He can't help but be consumed with jealousy. His words replay like a broken jack in the box that just... won't... pop.

Being drunk is Kieran's coping mechanism; a bad day at work or an argument, drinking until the sunrise is always the answer. He staggers through dark streets, one hand on the nearest wall. If he's singing, he falls asleep harmlessly on the couch. If not, it's never a good idea to get in his way. An internal voice says not to ruin the New Year, but the sadness turns to rage and the rage consumes him. Suddenly, Kieran feels painfully out of place. Pepperoni has accidentally made its way onto a vegetarian pizza, that kind of misplaced.

Space magically opens up on the floor, calling to him. He slides past the people in intransigent euphoric bliss until he is higher than high, bottle raised without a care in the world. It doesn't matter if he dies. Nothing matters as he's dancing on the northern lights beneath the dry-ice smoke swirls and an array of blues, acid greens, hot pinks and shimmering gold. The music fuses with his body.

23:18 hours
Darcy

This is her hunting ground… a dance. The drug dealer meets her gaze with the smile of one who knows the upper hand is his. Darcy purposefully lets her leg fall out of the gap in her dress a little more than usual, showing her designer shoes like they are her greatest weapon. Yet, her face stays aloof, disinterested. It's a film noir 'standoff' of sexual power.

"You're the girl from the group therapy sessions. You were there two days ago," he begins as she approaches.

"Small world."

"Interesting,"

"Do you want to grab a drink and come for a smoke, maybe we can watch the fireworks out back? The view is pretty good," Darcy flirts.

He smiles ever so slightly, almost sinister, as he agrees. She leads the way through to the kitchen.

"Quiet in here."

"I know, lucky us."

Darcy plays coy as she leads him to the back and opens the door. Piercing cold air greets them. It's different this time, freezing like winter is angry; cold that gets to your bones, trying to cheat you out of your soul.

"So, what brings you to this neck of the woods?" Darcy angles herself in the moonlight: the next scene in the noir film.

Aiden sparks his lighter a few times before creating fire for his joint. "Seeing an old friend, you?"

"Supporting an old friend," she cleverly infers.

"What's his name?" he asks.

She lies. "Martin."

"Does Martin live here?"

"I don't know whose place this is." She lies again, a little agitated.

Aiden's tone and demeanour suddenly change, as does the atmosphere. "Then how the fuck did you know the fireworks would be good back here?"

She shrugs and becomes uneasy, rubbing her arms. "Lucky guess."

Aiden cuts to the chase. "Enough bullshit. I don't know who you think you are trying to fool, but if you haven't heard of me (which I think you have from the meetings), you know who I am and what I'm capable of."

Darcy drops the act. "It's not my friend's fault. He didn't know what he was doing when he got the gear from you. He has a good heart and was only protecting his friend. That's why we're having our whole stupid party."

She panics, trying to not quake with fear; she's a clever girl, searching the archive of her brain cells to dig up a miracle.

"You don't want to mess with a guy likes me. I want my fucking money."

"We're getting you the money. Seriously, we're nearly there. If you just wait and enjoy yourself..." She seductively strokes his arm, trying to calm him, "...you'll get more than you dreamed."

Aiden shoves her and grabs her neck, but his humongous gorilla hand almost consumes her face. She drops her champagne glass and it shatters.

"I could snap you like a toothpick."

He reveals a concealed hunting knife from his jacket; her eyes widen as she chokes, her feet scraping the ground like a park swing. Darcy's face turns a shade darker than purple; the blood boiling in her lips causes them to turn blue, and the vessels in her eyes burst, sending them bloodshot. She struggles to form her words.

K. J. McGuinness

"And I… could… use your balls… as… paperweights."

Darcy kicks her knee as hard as she can against Aiden's groin. He recoils in agony and drops her. Her green velvet-draped frame falls against the railing. She makes a run for it and only gets as far as the pile of bin bags before Aiden tackles her. She screams for help but her efforts are futile. Darcy lies on her back as Aiden matches her body's form. His hands venture over her curved body, exploring.

They pull apart and open their eyes, staring deep into each other's eyes.

"What's happening here?" Darcy asks, less worried about her safety and now more confused.

Aiden, full of wonder and lust, says, "Pretty girl like you? I'm sure we can come to some kind of arrangement. I have a soft spot for green eyes and I've admired yours since our first group session."

Darcy can't help but be curious and passionate, and she realises she can play this to her advantage.

"Promise you'll leave my friend alone?"

She looks down. He follows her gaze. In a turn of events, Darcy has the knife pressed up against his crotch, having stolen it in the struggle.

"Sneaky." He grins. "If you get every single penny and interest… We can call it even and I get to take you out."

She gasps. "You're insane!"

Aiden laughs. He leans in and softly kisses up and down Darcy's neck. She lets out a little whimper of anticipation. Aiden works his way back to her tender lips. As they kiss, she knocks him down, rolls him over, and lies on top of his strong, muscular body. She runs her lips up to his neck and lands an intense kiss on his lips.

He lets out a freakish moan, slowly followed by another.

She pauses, a little weirded out.

"That's not me…" he tries to assure her.

It happens once more, coming from behind the bins in the

alley where the back garden connects to the rest of the street. Their icy breath dances in the air; the fireworks going off in the background consume their silence. Darcy notices the amber sky, helicopters flying overhead. But still no fireworks. The longing ghoulish groan lingers once more.

She lets go of Aiden and goes to investigate. Aiden takes his knife back.

"Hello?"

Darcy is hunched over; she scoops her locks behind her ear, investigating the darkness. Nothing seems to be there.

Aiden urges her to get behind him. "Hey, where are you going?"

It startles them when a man falls out from behind the bin bags. He has dirt and grit all over his clothes and a grimy body. His dark grey shirt used to be white and is tattered and shredded where his heart should be. His veins are black, all of them visible to the surface. He looks like he's going bald.

Darcy takes pity on the unfortunate wretch, much to Aiden's protests. He feels an unexplained loathing at first sight and a need to protect tonight's fling. Even from this far end of the street, he can see the man's cruel, detestable, disturbing smile in a permanently sinister snarl. Sunken, milky eyes glisten with a hint of red and silver, but they are the only things sparkling.

"Cat eyes," she whispers in awe.

"Step away," Aiden orders Darcy. "It's not safe."

"Don't be cruel, he's probably had too much to drink and needs to go home. He looks like he's had a rough night."

"People are sick, they're fighting in the streets. He could be one of them."

"Well, we need to do something, or we will miss the countdown—we can't just leave him here," Darcy barks, turning back to Aiden. She steadies herself, facing the man in need. "Excuse me, sir, do you need a taxi? Are you homeless, do you need help?"

She extends her hand, slowly approaching him, fingertips inches away from his shirt.

Suddenly, the man hunched over—who has been repeatedly dry-heaving on the stack of bin bags—snaps. The skeletal creature shuffles like a decrepit, decaying old man towards them. As Darcy gets close enough to see his face, she notices he has a dislocated jaw, showing a torn tongue and blood-stained, razor-sharp, savage teeth. A flame of anger ignites within him. He lets out a piercing screech and charges towards Darcy with ape-like fury.

Will
10 minutes Until New Year...

"Why so blue, Gizmo?" Beth comes up behind him, ignoring that he's trying not to be noticed. "Where's Ricca?"

"We broke up." He takes a sip of champagne but misses, inebriated.

"What? Because of the house party in Headingley a few days ago? I thought that was just a disagreement?"

"Yeah, a permanent one. I think it's for the best, though. Right now, I need to figure things out." He looks at Kieran, filled with melancholy. "I think being alone to figure things out is this year's plan."

"Why don't you go talk to him?"

Will rolls his eyes at her unimpressed expression. "I already did."

"Well whatever you said, doesn't look like it did any good."

They both stare at Kieran, eyes almost rolling in the back of his head, sweating, completely lost in the music.

"What, the truth?"

"Look, I'm not saying you two have to be best friends or lovers or whatever, but maybe for one night, you can put your shit aside? That's what tonight is about, isn't it? It only happens once a year. It's a time when the hopeless can be romantic and a resolution can become a revelation. One night can change everything. Maybe it's time to put this chapter to bed," Beth says, slurring her words. "Then again, I'm drunk, and I've never done drugs but I'm pretty sure somebody put Cloud 9 in my drink because all I can see is green, GREEEEEN." She smiles and lifts her hand to show an empty square packet. "Oh, it was me." She falls into hysterics.

Beth watches Kieran as he's watching Will, who is watching them both awkwardly. They catch each other's eyes and look away, like a game of who can notice the other person first.

23:55 hours
Will, Kieran & Beth

Will is mingling with the guests; his vision darts to Kieran who is trying not to be noticed gawking at Will. Both are heavily inebriated. Their vision locks for a split second and darts away. Beth is rolling her eyes so hard they almost disappear into the back of her head.

"Children." She grunts to Will.

Suddenly, she takes a fishbowl gulp of her champagne and holds Will's hand. She drags him over to the dance floor.

Beth approaches Kieran, who isn't paying attention, and begins gyrating with Will. He's uncomfortable... at first. She points out how he's being stubborn and this whole thing is petty.

"It's literally New," hiccup, "Bastard... Year in five minutes..." She hiccups again, trying to keep a burp inside. "The pair of you are relentlessly stubborn. Don't end this shitty year like this, Will."

Will nods; in his eyes, he wants the same. Beth suddenly

81

gives him a brusque nudge into Kieran, then toddles off. More bothered about pouring champagne into flute after flute, she hands them out like a crazed homemaker.

"Here, give these out," she instructs Chris.

Kieran turns, about to reign holy hell on whoever pushed him and spilt his precious whisky and cola, but is caught off guard when he sees Will gazing at him. At first he pulls a grimace. Kieran awkwardly looks around before Will asks if they can talk, barley capable of stringing together a sentence.

"Why would you want to talk to me? You made your intentions and feelings clear; leave me alone to enter the year how I want."

Will leans in. "But it's not how I want."

"You only ever manage to talk about your issues when you're drunk; the sadness comes out with the vodka—it has always been your biggest flaw. Leading me on for months, only calling me up when your intoxicated! If we didn't live under the same roof, I'd assume you'd thought I was dead!" Kieran discards him.

Will growls and takes him by the arm, dragging him through the crowd to the kitchen without caring about who he knocks out the way.

"What's your problem? Are you going to ruin another year?" Kieran can barely open his eyes.

"Don't be like that after what we said upstairs."

"It's always frustrated me you never spoke to me sober."

"Because I've never wanted to show weakness."

"That's what you call a coward. A real man expresses and fights for what he wants."

"You're the only person who has ever seen me cry, lose my temper, lose my mind. Truly, the only person to see me vulnerable."

"I'm sorry for what I said. I didn't mean to call you a coward." Kieran hiccups again.

Will hiccups back. "Me too."

"We could die tonight... so we should dance. Why not?" Kieran suggests.

"This isn't a good idea..."

Kieran looks him in the eye. "What if this was your last day on Earth, if you knew at the stroke of midnight you were going to die?"

55 Seconds Remaining...

"IT'S ON! IT'S ON!" Beth squeals giddily, jumping up and down like a child in a bouncy castle.

She switches the TV to the countdown and clicks the projector, which shines a giant version of the screen onto the wall above the fireplace. The DJ moves out of the way.

She swills her champagne glass.

Will and Kieran seem to have a silent conversation. They both hold vacant, inebriated expressions, but manage to see past the pain and sadness. Kieran finally turns away and blinks through the tears threatening to blur his vision, when Will's hand encircles his. It is soft and warm—reassuring almost, as if the owner has sensed his cry for help.

"You clearly want to talk about something. Whatever it is, just come out and say it."

"It's nothing. Just things were getting a little..." he pauses, silently staring into Kieran's eyes.

"You're such an arsehole." Kieran grins.

Everybody chants in unison as the suspense builds. "Ten... Nine..."

Will leans in and gently kisses Kieran's warms lips. They pull apart and take shaky, shallow breaths. Confused, yet unable to contain themselves anymore, Kieran holds Will's head in his hands and pulls him into a fiery, passionate kiss.

His hands work their way around Will's body, feeling each crevasse, each line along his perfect physique.

"Six… Five…"

Chris waits for Darcy, trying to peer through the people in the corner like a confused meerkat. He's more fragile than the glass ballerina on Beth's dresser. Beth is having too much fun on the microphone to notice him as she leads the countdown.

"Two… One…"

***

Darcy recoils in horror; the man lunges, tackling her to the ground. There is a moment of serenity as his eyes dive deep into her soul before he growls, drools, and screams. Aiden redeems himself by trying to stop the attack with fear and rage of his own. He grapples the guy's shirt, but the beast's force is too strong. With one push, he shoves Aiden against the wall.

"Oh, you're a dead man!"

Revealing his reclaimed hunter's knife, Aiden charges at the brute and, without thinking, tackles him to the ground. They are locked in a test of strengths until the man overwhelms him and sinks his teeth into Aiden's neck. He wails in agony.

Darcy screams, petrified. But her body tells her to move; she tries to help by tugging at the man, now making mincemeat of Aiden. He stops and turns his attention to her. In a split second, he has her in his claws, too.

Suddenly, she feels an intense, agonising pain in her neck. Her brain cannot process the sharpness fast enough before she realises his teeth are in her jugular. He presses until his teeth are touching, mixing Aiden's blood and hers with his diseased tongue. He pulls as hard as he can. Her skin and flesh rip like an elastic band as she gurgles, and her voice breaks. It sounds like a malfunctioning fax machine. The man rips out her throat in one smooth motion. Blood gushes everywhere.

Darcy falls into the wall, wrapping her fingers around her neck. She has no throat—panic sets in. She gasps for breath, a hooked fish flopping for air on the riverbank.

***

"HAPPY NEW YEAR!"

The celebration is a riot of colour, and the projection explodes with life as it shows the River Thames firework display on the back wall. Everyone is a little more hyped up than they should be. But, that's because of the cloud 9. They scream with joy as their feet disturb the ground. Bodies move together as they celebrate, rhythmically breaking into shapes and colours chanting the usual NYE song.

"They're going fucking wild out there…" the DJ says to Beth, looking out the window.

"That's northerners for you." She hugs him.

Beth turns to see Will and Kieran lost in each other and ecstatic, claps from the other end of the room.

A boy comes to her for a kiss.

"Touch me and die," Beth jokes, but then she lets him peck her on the cheek.

"You're not just doing this because you broke up with your girlfriend again, are you?" Kieran's eyes droop.

"No, there's always going to be something there for you. I can't help it. I wish I could turn it off, but I can't. But we have a lot to talk about; for now, let's just enjoy the moment, even if we go back to hatred tomorrow."

"Good to know you're not a total monster then." Kieran smiles again.

Will offers a half grin. "No promises."

"Will you still love me tomorrow?" Kieran sighs.

"Ask me in the morning," he says as he strokes Kieran's cheek.

"No really, you need to see this…" The DJ's face drops as his surprise turns to horror, trying to get Beth to look outside.

Suddenly, the electricity shuts down. Everything goes black and it leaves the guests in drunken disorientation with a few shrill shrieks. The only thing keeping them going is chattering. The only light is natural from the moon. It seems to have gone out for the entire street... yet the distance glows orange.

Kieran and Will stop kissing. Guests linger in the dark, gasping, confused and annoyed. Beth stands on the table and tells them all not to move. She can fix it.

"BOYS!" she yells at Chris, Kieran and Will.

"Why is the sky orange?" someone asks.

"I don't think that's the sky…" the DJ states.

Something is wrong.

"Go about your business, talk among yourselves, and we will have everything up and running soon," Beth drunkenly announces. She approaches the boys. "Keep everyone calm. Kieran and Chris, stay here to entertain everyone. Look after Chris because that dealer is around somewhere! Will, I need you to go downstairs and try to fix the lights."

Will does as he is told, which leads him to the cellar. Beth informs him she has it all under control.

"Where's Darcy?"

"I don't know." He shrugs.

Beth growls and darts upstairs, heading to her room to look for a torch. She opens the door to find some human-shaped shadows stumbling around in the darkness and makes a horrific discovery when she accidentally walks in on two guests who look like they're having sex.

"Oh, sorry, wrong room." She apologies and slams the door when she humorously realises it's her room. "Wait a minute." She giggles.

Then, a gut feeling drops, and her hairs stand on edge.

She reopens the door.

"Sorry to break this up, but this is my room. Please don't fornicate all over it."

They don't respond but continue to stagger and shuffle. She realises they aren't fucking but in fact fighting; a girl screams for help.

"Shit!"

Beth doesn't know what to do; it's too dark and she can't make out what's happening. She storms over, trying to form a wedge between the two of them. The scrap turns into a bloodied mess. In a plot twist, the two guests turn swiftly on Beth as if to attack. Beth's vision is dull but they pierce her sinuses with a bitter coppery smell. She's wet too, and she knows that stench... but why?

"Blood?"

She becomes trapped, playing a game of hide and seek, so pushes the guests away as they snarl and lunge for her to jump on and over the bed. Instantly, she is slammed into the wardrobe by the male guest, so she uses the cupboard door as a weapon by kicking it open, knocking the man aside. He growls. The girl falls inside the wardrobe, failing to pounce.

Beth, not wanting to harm the two individuals, races out and slams the door behind her. She slumps against the door, trying to hold them back, when an arm smashes through the wood to grab her.

She screams.

00:05 hours
Downstairs

The small talk wears off. Chris and Kieran run out of topics, and guests are debating leaving as the DJ frantically packs up.

"Nah man, I'm not staying. There's some freaky shit going on out there, I'm out."

Kieran tries again when suddenly Darcy appears in the

kitchen doorway. A guest spots her and lets out a blood-curdling cry.

Darcy slumps as blood gushes from her neck; there's a chunk ripped out of her oesophagus. Red ink spurts everywhere and drains until her skin takes on the pallor of a corpse. Her stomach is sick, and then one by one she loses control of her limbs until finally, her head lolls. She can still hear but cannot control her body.

As she gargles for Kieran's attention, which is fixed on the DJ, he spins. Kieran double takes and panics, then tries to help her, asking what happened. Darcy cannot talk, choking, wheezing and babbling through her blood as she falls into his arms.

Without warning, Aiden comes bellowing into the room before he barges past Darcy and Kieran like a battering ram; his ivy jacket is drenched red, too, and he has an ear missing. Both his lips are gone, all his teeth exposed. One of Aiden's hands is mangled, and his right bicep looks like someone has chewed it away, exposing white tendons beneath. This is only speculation to the guests watching frozen.

They laugh at first, assuming it's a twisted joke or entertainment, but then in confusion.

Kieran is trembling and crying as he holds Darcy's skinny corpse. Aiden stops and stares at the guests, picking his next victim—his eyes are dull, replaced instead with red and silver speckles in the dark. His golden Greek god skin has faded to a grimy pigmentation, and his veins are black and protruding. He lets out a barn owl screech when he spots Chris and charges at him with ape-like fury.

Beth is free from the clutches of her attackers and runs downstairs to announce the party is over. "Someone call the police!"

Her face pales when she witnesses Aiden drive Chris into the buffet table, then over the DJ's turn tables.

SMASH! The window behind shatters and somebody grabs

the DJ. The antagonist nearly rips his scalp off, the skin peeling away from the skull by his pony tail when he drags him backwards, plunging every nail into his eyes sockets. The attacker has the DJ like a bowling ball before he rips away his jaw as if he was tearing fabric.

"CHRIS!" Beth screams.

Uninvited guests burst through the door and arrive on scene. They present an alternate party gift: death and violence. Bloody and rabid, they attack innocent guests. A riot breaks out in the living room. Ultimately, all hell breaks loose. Everything happens so fast, creating a total shit storm.

Kieran cries out for Beth, who comes to his aid, pushing past the people who are being mauled or trying to flee. The last bit of blood spurts out of Darcy's throat, hitting Beth in the face. The three of them hug and tumble further to the ground. It doesn't take long for Darcy to bleed out, and despite begging for medical attention, panic consumes the guests, and they ignore Beth's plea.

No one has any idea what is going on; flapping around, they are scrambling as blood and guts are thrown up the walls. The blood flows as a river on steroids, thick like gravy across a slaughterhouse floor and soaks into the grey carpet.

After a few moments with her lifeless body, Beth is about to let her go, crying hysterically and begging her not to die. Her grip loosens, and she relaxes in her arms.

One demented guest dives into another and they collide, causing the TV to spark and BANG! Beth's ears ring—she's in shock.

She spots Chris's headless, lifeless body, while Aiden uses his spinal cord as a toothpick and vomits.

She specifically notices four guests with their hands and mouths inside the abdomen of an innocent party-goer. They're still alive, crying out for their mother, watching their intestines be pulled apart. A chunk flies out and smears across Beth's favourite picture.

"Beth, we need to run out the back door! Come on!"

Kieran tries to get her attention, but the unfolding massacre muffles his voice. Time freezes for a split second when Darcy's eyes flip open. She springs back to life and turns violent. Beth is lost for words; it's impossible, she was dead!

Kieran picks up Will's Katana from the floor and shoves Beth out of the way at the cost of being mauled by Darcy. This advantage gives Beth a few more seconds, prompting her to sprint. Kieran tosses her the Katana, wrestling with Darcy's superhuman strength, and Beth escapes to the basement to find Will fidgeting still with the lights.

"What's all that commotion?"

00:09 hours
Beth

Beth is sweaty, and her ears are still ringing. Her eyes are unfocused as she squints at Will.

"B, what-the-fuck is all that red? Did you face slam the punch bowl?" he jokes.

Beth doesn't respond, she just breathes heavily, staring off into oblivion.

"What are you doing with my Katana? Was Kieran messing with it again?"

She continues to ignore him, face drip white.

"B, you're scaring me. Did you take too much Cloud 9? You take too much? Do you need a tamp?"

Will waves, trying to lighten her up and takes the sword away. Unable to gain a response, he shakes her shoulders and screams the next question in her face. Beth jolts to life, having blacked out for a moment, or as she calls it 'brain-farted'. She stutters and struggles to explain.

"What do you mean they've 'turned violent?' Did a fight break out?"

"They're eating each other…" she sobs.

Generation Dead

Suddenly, a frightened couple of party-goers break through the basement door, chased by a madman. Will drags Beth into another room. She slams the door shut and hops down the stairs to find three more guests and Will pushing a man around as he lunges to attack each individual.

Unexpectedly, the man bites and rips the flesh of one guest, horrifying the others.

Beth darts around, panics, and takes a pickaxe hung up on the wall without even the slightest thought. Everything goes black as she drives the pickaxe through the man's head. And behold, a fountain of red goo squirts up and out. It is now apparent they are stuck in the cellar and must seek another form of escape. Will continues to repeat 'you killed him' over and over as she pants, glaring at the body.

Beth has just killed her first man; it's as though she has temporarily left the building and someone else has taken over. What she's done sets in, and she tries to wrap up the victim's wound.

Beth barks at Will that it was self-defence. "I just... I..." she babbles.

Above in the living room, a blood bath unravels. People are being eaten, ripped and torn. Blood and guts spray the furniture. Guests shriek and run into the dead of night, to be met by other panicking pedestrians and the bigger picture is revealed. It isn't just an attack on Beth's party... it's the whole damn city.

The orange glow is the city burning. Choppers whizz overhead. Chaos is on every corner. Cars swerve. People run riot.

Back in the living room, Kieran (or what's left of him) springs to life. He sits up. Eyes bloodshot pins and veins black, he coughs, drooling slime and bile. He sees a woman cowering in the corner and attacks her. He pounces like a wild animal and claws her skin, chomping down on her throat—a tasty, medium-rare steak. He thumps her chest, making ear-splitting shrieks, then bites out an eye and pulls off an arm. It's as easy as snapping a Christmas cracker, except the sludging and crunching to follow is disgusting.

What's left of Darcy and Aiden join him.

A New Year nightmare unfolds; the inner-city skyline that defines Leeds is in flames, lit up with explosions and backed by the soundtrack of car and house alarms, plus emergency service sirens.

This is one New Year's Eve Beth is sure has just changed the world forever.

CHAPTER 2:

THE NEXT GENERATION

January 1st, 2012
00:17 hours
Central Leeds

The bloodshed is as barbaric as it is brutal from the never-ending massacre in Beth's living room. Surviving guests flee the house. It's bloody murder on the dance-floor. The house that once graced Beth and her beloved friends is tarnished, now warped in the dark and disgusting macabre.

There are many who aren't so lucky; they lie haphazardly in pieces around the room like dolls torn limb from limb over the grass at a little girl's tea party. Their bodies are at awkward angles, heads held in such a way they cannot be playing dead. One head rolls away with the spinal cord and some ribs still attached. They have striped the bodies clean. Flesh, gristle and mush flood the room in pools of blood.

Glitter and confetti contaminate the juices of the cadavers, and the repositories of people as alive as Beth and the others cowering in the cellar are now abandoned shells left to rot in the open.

Who will send the bodies away with a love song and kiss the breeze that carries them heaven-bound? These are sons and daughters, brothers and sisters. Smooth skin becomes torn muscle and blood, as raw as any carcass at the butcher. It has transformed the rest of the home into a scene from a slasher film, and what remains is a tapestry or finger painting of human innards.

Aiden, Darcy and Kieran have lost their damn minds; they are feasting upon innocent guest remains in a bizarre horror show where they are the stars. They crunch their victims. Spurting, some still gasp for life, twitching and calling out for their mothers and fathers as the barbarians pull outs their guts and fight like a pack of wild dogs. Who gets the juiciest parts? They sit together over a body, growling, chewing on beef jerky intestines as the person attached calls out, crying like a baby, astounded the shock hasn't killed him.

Darcy's lips are torn. Her blood runs dark on her skin, a gaping hole left where her throat should be. Kieran's hair, where it was once kissed by fire just yesterday, is now ashen. The spark has died, extinguished without even a wisp of silvery smoke—their lives abruptly ended by whatever this is.

Beth bravely peeps out of the cellar door. She is trembling, snotty and trying not to sob to the horror she is witnessing. She spots her two friends and the notorious drug dealer after watching them die. They are eating human insides right before her. She blinks and Kieran already has his beady eyes on her in a flash—he glares, a nice piece of pancreas dangling from his mouth. The strange humanoid shell that remains of Aiden stomps around the room. Beth steals a glance at his face. The sight could turn her to stone. His snake-like eyes have emerald green and silver with sparkles of red, which dart around with emotionless unkempt. His rotting lips are already half-destroyed. She hears Kieran's bones crack as his neck turns sharply, letting out a moan.

Death is staring at her, only for a moment. But he bounds toward the door with demonic rage. Beth slams it shut. Kieran hits the other side, repeatedly bashing louder and more violently with every strike. She screams.

Will scares her from behind and she cries out, confused

and petrified.

"Get away from that door!"

He takes her by the hand, putting his arm around her shoulder and they cautiously head down the stairs into the first room of the basement. Will's hands are clammy and sweaty, like the condensation in the January air. He practically drags her across into the next room, where the other three wait; two are pacing anxiously while one cowers in a corner. She has urinated out of sheer panic.

Will closes the door and Beth leans against the wall in a state of deep shock.

The sirens wail in the background, behind the sound of mass panic in the streets. Yelling, crashing and thudding—the noise that makes you sick to your stomach. She might as well be on a plane crash landing to her death.

Beth's face suddenly convulses; she turns drip white and runs over to throw up blue alcohol all over her shoes—simply shameful.

Nobody is making any sound; they all stare off into their own space. Will covers the body of the man Beth drove a pickaxe through with a dust sheet. They forced her to execute him, trying ever so hard not to have a cliché panic attack. But she can't breathe, as if someone is choking her. Her heart is racing, and all she wants to do is curl up in a ball and wait for someone to save her.

It quickly sinks in no one's coming or helping, since the others are right there with her going through the same motions. A choked cry for help forces up her throat, and she feels a drop on her cheek. It appears this is the end of the road for her.

The only thing she can focus on is telling her body not to piss itself like the other girl. But she's already thrown up in front of strangers, so what's the point of trying to be dignified now?

Will is drunk and high, trying to focus. He can't believe

K. J. McGuinness

his eyes and doesn't want to. He's never seen something like this, even in his worst nightmares. But that is only because his brain always wakes him up before such a horrific image covers his mind. And now he's seeing something his eyes won't ever be able to erase. He squeezes them shut and reopens them, and again, and again. It isn't going away.

Adrenaline flows through his veins, tricking his mind into sobering up, but he can't move a single muscle, not even to scream. The absolute horror completely paralyses him, and the more he thinks about running away, or simply moving a bit, the more he is discouraged and utterly terrified.

"I told you this party was a bad idea," he says, catching his breath as he leans against the cold cobwebbed wall of the cellar. "I can't move."

He doesn't remember being so scared, not even when he was held at gunpoint in a crack den when one of Kieran's deals went south. And that was just the beginning. That idea only makes it worse... if it's even possible. Beth has also had a substantial amount to drink—the other three guests quake in the corner. Her throat burns from the acid she just threw up.

"I'm too drunk for this bullshit. What the fuck is going on?"

Beth panics as she listens to Kieran and Aiden trying to tear their way into the basement.

"Here's the interesting thing about alcohol: alcohol is a depressant; it inhibits the adrenal gland, which produces cortisol, epinephrine, and norepinephrine. These are the hormones that all regulate your natural stress response," Will explains as his mouth works too fast for his brain. He speaks so fast the others barley understand him.

"Will, you're doing that thing again!" Beth puts her hands on her knees.

"What thing?"

"When you get stressed or nervous you over explain

everything and talk too much!" Beth tries to speak between each gasp. "It's like an impulse."

"But it's true that drinking lowers your inhibitions—it stifles the gland responsible for things like your heart rate shooting up when you talk to a beautiful woman or your anxious fidgeting, and so on. Stimulants have the opposite effect on the adrenal gland." He blurts everything out silver-tonged.

"Stop!"

"Think about meth-heads, caffeine junkies, poppers. When you experience an emergency, your kidneys pump out adrenaline, which is a natural stimulant. As a result, alcohol's effect on your adrenal gland counteracts and you go from having fewer stress hormones in your system than normal, to more than normal. It all happens so quickly, and it makes you feel you've sobered up." Will speaks way too fast and erratic. "That's what's happening."

Beth stands up straight and heads over to Will in a flash. She slaps him to get him to calm down, startling the quivering guests trapped in the cellar with them. Will holds his cheek.

"Tell your adrenaline to shut up, okay, Gizmo?" she says, looking into his eyes reassuringly.

"You slapped me," he utters.

"I need you to focus, you're the useless encyclopedia of this group, and I need you to search that beautiful messed up mind of yours to help us. What would your mother do?"

Will stands holding his cheek as his eyes dart from left to right like an intense ping pong tournament.

"Probably take off her heels and try to stab anyone that came near her."

He takes a deep breath and forgets about the slap.

"We need to get out of here," Beth says in a moment of clarity.

She wipes her mouth. Now they must look for a solution,

which Will tries to quickly conjure.

"Wait, where's Kieran?" he suddenly asks, looking dishevelled. Will asks Beth what happened to Darcy, Chris and Kieran, deep down genuinely concerned for his ex. "Did they run out of the house?" Will looks pleadingly. "Where did they go, B?" She says nothing. "Where is our family?"

He tries to hold back the water works and continues to avoid answering him. She stares off into space, aggravating Will to repeat himself.

He strains his voice. "BETH! WHERE IS KIERAN? WHERE ARE OUR FRIENDS?"

Beth's brain has shut down. She is clammy. There is the glisten of a cold sweat. Her eyes are wide, as if someone is coming at her to deliver a fatal blow. Yet, what she sees, no-one else can see. Trapped in her own psychosis, a living nightmare for one tailor-made by her brain to play on her deepest fears. The horrors of people being ripped apart in front of her eyes strike her like a bolt of lightening. Will approaches, biting his lip as tears form.

"No!" He puts his hands on his head, the realisation sinking in. "WHERE ARE THEY?"

He says it over and over, each version more aggressive than the last until he screams and kicks the wall, hurting himself. His former beloved and his best friends are no longer in this world.

"My best friend, your ex-boyfriend, my other best friend... died in my arms. And now they are trying to get in here to hurt us." Beth tries to fathom the words. "They were dead, Will. They died. And now they're not," Beth explains. "WE NEED TO GET OUT!"

She suddenly screams. Will stares into the abyss, having taken to the gravel floor, not caring about anything but the vicious sound of snarling and violence—the soundtrack to their unfolding soap opera.

The group is startled by a bash on the door outside the room. Aiden and Kieran have made it through the first and now are clawing at the second, so it won't be long before the locals or Darcy join them.

Tears stream down his face, and the other three strangers cry together. "We're going to die," one says.

The grief comes in waves and threatens to consume Will entirely. It's his master... for now. He's at the mercy of its whim and it bites with such ferocity he fears it will leave him an empty shell. Until something hits him like the flick of a switch. The answer to their prayers turns out to be the memory of an old hatch for beer barrels at the dark end of the room.

Will drags his lighter across his knee to light a fire and moves the flame toward that part of the room. It reveals a hatch with a chain and a ramp for barrels back in the day. Will remembers before their block of flats were renovated that the place used to be a public house.

"I got it, the old hatch. This place used to be a pub and we can get to the street from the tunnel for deliveries. I used to sneak down there to smoke weed before the guys knew about my habit."

"This means there is access to the street? A tunnel?" one bravely speaks.

"We're lucky we live in this house. Bless this basement!"

Will takes off his blue bowtie and undoes a couple of buttons on his white shirt. He takes off the braces from his shoulders and lets them dangle around his shorts.

"Beth, help me."

He climbs over some old furniture. He and Beth clear a way, taking down the clutter blocking the tunnel: paint cans, summer garden furniture, old DVDs.

"Locked!" He sighs, shaking the century old padlock and chain and blowing off the dust.

Beth and Will look at each other and then at the door,

giving way to the ongoing beating it is receiving from Aiden and the others. They look back at the dust sheet over the corpse in the middle of the room with the pickaxe still wedge in his head like a lever on a train track waiting to be pulled.

"I guess I'll do it," he says softly yet reluctantly.

Will walks over to the corpse. Looking disgusted, he hesitates at first before putting his left foot on the man's shoulder and placing both hands on the pickaxe. He tries to look away, jiggling it out. The crunch of bone makes everybody cringe.

Will strains and groans to pull it out as if he were pulling Excalibur from the stone. With a final yank, he takes it but rips half the poor man's skull too. Bits of red juice and brain-flavoured smoothie leak out and trickle down the drain: a slaughterhouse floor.

"Move!" he prompts.

Beth clears the way and Will takes a few efficient swings at the chain.

"Hurry, they're getting in."

The three guests talk over one another, trying to tell Will to hurry. He breaks out in an angry sweat, his muscles bulging as he takes every hit.

SNAP!

The chain breaks and they push the doors open. Dust flies.

00:32 hours

The three remaining guests are let out into the street, escorted by Beth and Will. With no time to lose, Will moves the debris blocking the tunnel to the stairs and helps the other guests, then he and Beth resurface. Once they come up, Will turns and closes the hatch doors, driving the pickaxe through the handles as a blockade. Beth and Will try to keep an undetectable path. But the three strangers have other plans and run in hysterics without even a thank you, never to be seen again.

Aiden and the party-goers have torn through the second basement door to an empty room. Kieran barges in, sniffing the air before screeching and exiting back the way they came.

Will and Beth join the mass hysteria and suddenly, the bigger picture becomes clearer. A neighbour of theirs witnesses them fleeing. Beth sees her older next-door neighbour.

"It's Mr Henderson!" she says; her feet are already walking—she isn't in control.

Will's eyes are darting around at the sounds, startling him every couple of seconds.

"We have to get out of here, B." He turns and sees nothing but a shadow of where she once stood, so he panics. "BETH?" He checks each direction before spotting her over by Mr Henderson's house.

"Do you know what happening?" she says with a vacant expression.

Will comes bouncing over. She's acting out of character from the dumbfounded shock; her brain stutters for a moment as her eyes take in the surroundings. She feels lighter than expected. Every part of her body is on pause while her thoughts catch up.

Her neighbour places one hand on Beth's shoulder. "It'll be okay, it will. I will fix this."

"What?" Her expression changes as he gallivants off inside, realising there are intruders in his home.

"Beth, we need to go."

Will takes hold of Beth, guiding her down the slippery porch steps, gently talking to her like an old senile dog who has wandered. A rude awakening to what is going on in the city now becomes clear. Not only was the power cut in

Beth's home, but the entire city. There is mayhem in the streets and nothing but the distant amber skies with the echo of explosions and gunfire.

They stand helpless, gormless in the middle of their street while people run rampant around them.

"Why are there guns? Guns aren't legal in the UK."

Will stutters, physically shaking, and his eyes widen. His breaths are ragged and harsh. His hands tremble at Beth's sides, and she jams her fist in her mouth to stifle the scream.

"Not if you're law enforcement…"

"Were probably not going to make it out alive, are we?"

Her legs are frozen in place. A shot fires and sounds like it was meant for them, so they squeal and crouch. Crawling, they drag themselves to a car parked outside their home, gasping and choking.

"They must have called the in big guns, literally."

"What-the-fuck is going on here? I thought only farmers and their mums were packing?"

Will tries to peer around the hubcap of the car. Police, S.W.A.T and civilians run wild among every high house and low suburb, each alley and side street, as Will watches human numbers deplete by the second. The sight clogs his brain as he tries to generate some smartass thesis.

"I got it. This has to be that Flu on the TV. I don't know how but I'm telling you, my gut feeling is telling me it's Grime Flu!"

Shaking her like a maraca, he can see she's not coping well. Beth's mind is failing, like an engine that turns over and over. She can't plan. Every action leads to more pain, and there is no way out of this chaos. No way out. She brings her hand to her throat. No blood. She glances at the floor. No trap door.

Will can see he is losing his best friend. He feels smothered by an invisible hand. "Look at me," he says, hands grasping tightly on her shoulders.

Her face pulls back, and her eyes are wide like an owl. Startled, she appears drugged.

"LOOK AT ME, BETH!" He grabs her, crushing her cheeks; her breathing becomes erratic, deep, then shallow. "Fight it. Fight the feeling."

Beth's body writhes to be free or shut down entirely. Not even the freezing bite of the air is affecting them anymore with so much adrenaline coursing through their veins.

"Each time this happens, part of you will get stronger, learn how to cope."

Will is handling the situation well, though he doesn't want to be brave. He wants to be like Beth, but it's up to him to get them off the open street. Beth has no choice but to agree she has seen enough to rationalise Will's theory, even if by nodding.

A horrible screeching from some nearby deranged people startles the pair of them. No, from their doorway. Will sees into the living room—the freak show left behind—and gags before spotting Aiden, Darcy and Kieran. Somehow, they have made it back up from the cellar. Kieran wanders into view. His heart almost breaks seeing someone he used to love in this condition. Smooth milky skin is now ripped and torn. Once mesmerising blue eyes are now silicone white and beady... bloodthirsty. Will swears and tries to approach them. Beth instantly grabs his arm, begging him not to go near, and he argues they are ill, they need help.

K-Jay and Darcy, growling and rampant, watch the pair of old friends arguing in the street from the living room. They are predators literally about to bolt and pounce any second.

Beth says, "I think they recognise us."

"Shit!" Will spits.

Aiden, Kieran and Darcy are fully under the infection's spell; they spot fleeing guests from the front door of their house and there is a moment of tranquillity in the chilly atmosphere as their eyes lock. Will's stomach churns with the dread of what's coming.

"RUN!"

Will springs to life, crushing Beth's hand as he holds on tight, sprinting from the car. The infected trio close in on their targets. They force Will and Beth to dart down the street. They join an endless horde of other people travelling in the same direction.

Will still has hold of Beth, struggling to keep up in her high heels.

"Don't let go," she begs.

"Hold on," he begs back.

In the blink of an eye somebody much bigger and faster knocks them apart. Beth falls over her heels, losing grip of Will's hand. She screams in inconsolable panic, then stands and keeps going, knees bloody. They lose sight of one another during a chase and wheel off in different directions.

"GZIMO! WILL! WHERE ARE YOU? WILL! ANSWER ME?" she cries.

"BETH, OH MY GOD, BETH! WHERE ARE YOU?"

It's just faces in the dark, loud noises and screaming. Will knows he can't stop because he can't tell who's infected and who isn't, who is a friend and who is a foe. He repeatedly curses, getting pushed left and right as people zoom and barge into him. He gets spotted by the ailed and they charge at lightning speed. Will nearly collapses—has no choice but to pick himself up, turn and run. He tries to keep his balance, not to tumble despite still being heavily intoxicated.

Beth takes a wrong turn to where she thinks Will might run; she heads down a road and looks back for her best friend. She can only see the back of Will in her memory. Has she lost him, maybe forever?

Aiden and Kieran are sprinting after Will, faster than humanly possible. Darcy breaks off from her 'pack' and targets Beth.

Beth freaks out, having lost her last friend. She cries, unable to get the images of her best friends dying, coming back to life, and then tearing other people apart from her mind. The flashes of blood, violence, and death send shivers down her spine. She can't slow down. Darcy is bellowing a blood-thirsty howl on her tail, but at the last second Beth climbs over a tall wall and dives over. She injures her foot, landing on it awkwardly. She falls and has no choice but to crawl against the wall. Fearing her life is at an end, she screws her eyes shut.

Darcy can't climb over the wall. Beth takes a mental note and allows for a moment to collect herself.

"Jesus, she's fast for a plastic bag."

After a few seconds, Darcy gives up trying to jump at the wall like a small puppy climbing onto the bed. She finds another innocent teenaged target and sprints into the shadows of the alley, pursuing them.

"How can this skinny draped frame of a girl hold such speed and strength?"

Hands through her blonde locks, leaning against the wall, Beth whimpers. Her watery eyes enlarge, and the hairs on the nape of her neck bristle. A gaggle of goose pimples laminate whatever naked skin is exposed. Beth glares at the dried blood on her arms and her satin white dress; the luscious red has dried to a deep maroon. She staggers down the alley in darkness, heels click-clacking on the tarmac, limping away from her fall. Starved for air, her heart races, her lungs shallowly rise and fall in time.

Satisfaction with security is nothing but a distant memory, and an invisible force crushes her from every direction. Her creative and vivid imagination makes her wonder whether it's her mind playing tricks from the drugs and alcohol or reality. She knows one thing... she is utterly alone, abandoned and lost.

00:38 hours
Will

Will is the most scared he's ever been, trying not to admit it. He knows it's dumb to be scared, but he can't help it. Will envisioned this scenario in his head many times, letting his daydreams run wild in the past from watching all those horror movies and survival shows, but nothing prepared him for the reality and the severity of what it's really like. That's just it; he knew it was a daydream then. That's what made it fun because something like this could never happen. So easy to get lost in books or video games. This isn't a nightmare; this is real people being slaughtered and attacking one another in the streets. He always thought he'd play the perfect psychopath, able to switch off his emotions and do what needed to be done. The problem was, he always over thought.

The way he sees it as he observes, he needs to do his best and whatever will be, will be. By the time he's imagined how this could end, he's surprised he's not in the foetal position in the corner.

Will uses his hand against the cobbled wall to guide him down an alley, keeping him upright as he wades through double vision. He takes a left. After losing sight of Beth, he tries not to panic at misplacing his last surviving friend. He's endured loneliness and isolation before, but not like this. This is foul.

He curses when he realises he shouldn't have spent ten years smoking all that pot. It's slowing him down despite having a nice smooth athletic build.

Out of the shadows, Kieran emerges, almost tackling Will. He pulls Will's shirt and swings him into a wall, lifting him off his feet. He has a new super strength! Kieran smashes Will into the wall like he's a pebble. He tries to bite him but Will struggles free, pushing him back.

Tearfully he says, "Back off, I don't want to hurt you. I don't know what's happened to you. You're sick. We just need to get you some help. Come on, we helped you before, we can do it again."

The tears roll fast; he jerks his knee back and forth in frustration. Kieran screeches at the top of his lungs, striking fear and discomfort into Will and he charges again, but Will doges at the last minute. He dives to the floor next to a blunt piece of wood and sees nails sticking out of it. Will takes it as his only means of defence because Kieran just won't quit. Will looks over his assailant's shoulder and sees other humans being pursued by similar monsters. The only thing stopping him from joining them is Kieran.

"I know you're in there, you don't want to do this, you love me!" he pleads one last time. Will gives him a final warning, which obviously Kieran ignores.

"I loved you!"

The tears stream down his face and he screws his eyes shut before Kieran lunges. Will takes the biggest swing of his life. His ex takes a hit to the floor, but he isn't dead. Either way, Will vanishes.

He leaves Kieran with a bloodied head and the scent of missed supper. He can smell Will's aftershave. Kieran roars. He forgets about Will and finds new victims to terrorise before vanishing into the darkness.

Will catches up with a few other humans heading in the same direction. He stumbles as they barge among others, seeking refuge wherever they can. People squabble over cars and belongings, buildings and safe spots on roof tops. He witnesses a man shoot another just to get in his house.

Will cowers in horror before spotting others climbing into the docking station of a warehouse behind some trucks, discreetly hidden. He gets called over as one of the other boys similar in age waves at him. Will seizes his chance, letting a few maniacs run by before he makes haste for it.

He avoids a car—the driver has lost control and is swerving up on pavements. He dives in at the last second and two boys pull down the shutters, letting random pursuers slam against the other side.

Will is on the floor, panting. Nobody utters a word. Everyone seems lost and confused, and people are literally pissing their pants.

"*What* is going on?" he says.

00:44 hours
Beth

Meanwhile, Beth looks out on the ghoulish park, slowly building courage from trepidation to limp across. The laughter of children in the park is dead along with the light of day, now replaced with the onslaught of murderous cries and shrieks as everybody runs rampant. Skeletons of trees sway, at first visible against a pale grey sky, then hidden by the blackest night. The park grows ever darker the further Beth staggers; it's as if they wait, mocking, as they guide stragglers to their doom. Soon the shadows will blend and the trees' silhouettes against the sky will be less pronounced.

As the view disappears, sounds emerge as if the volume is being steadily turned up. The breaking of twigs becomes the focus of Beth's attention as people slip and slight in the winter's sludge.

Beth glimpses the moon before a dark cloud erases its precious silver rays, shrouded in the amber glow. She hobbles over the giant skate park in Hyde Park where it famously gets its name. Distant screaming, popping and smashing causes her to look over her shoulder frantically every ten seconds. She no longer trusts her surroundings.

Falling from the wall earlier to escape Darcy made her twist her ankle. Movement is slow and painful. She tries talking to herself to calm down as she limps to some crossroads. The horrors at the other side convince her to take a fresh approach.

She moves in the same direction as other civilians toward the city centre, taking a moment to catch her breath as it drifts in the ice air. She remembers a nicer time when Kieran and Will were sat on the couch with her, watching their favourite horror movies.

Kieran and Will, mangled all over one another in a love-sick-spoon, basically formed one gross PDA blob. Beth, an obvious third wheel and slightly stoned, ate all the salted popcorn. The telly depicted innocent civilians being chased by monsters. Will, who was so baked he may as well have been a cake shop, smartly pointed out that in such situations, if you wanted to survive, "one would run completely in the opposite direction away from all the people," but Kieran pointed out that, "strength in numbers is what will win the war."

"What would you do, B?" they asked.

She took a moment to respond because of her sensory cognitive responses being slow. "I don't know. I'd stay in the basement and live off beans."

"Mmm beans," the three of them said in unison.

"And toast." Will drooled.

"If I turned into one of those monsters, you think you could off me?" Kieran asked while Will stroked his hair.

"Hard to say. I'd have the be in that situation. You think you can see yourself doing something until you're in the moment." Will had clarity. "I can't off the one person who can cook for me and give me the best head." He chuckled.

"Ew, TMI, get a room." Beth playfully threw a cushion.

Kieran laughed. "We are in one."

Back in reality, Beth realises she still stands at the crossroads and uses the memory to her advantage. Take the darkest route out of the light, the one people are avoiding because they're too frightened of what may lurk in the dead-of-the-night.

"If I die, I will kill you, Will."

Anything could be down here but it's a risk she's willing to take.

Beth is the only one of her friends to have been born and stayed to study in Leeds. Will hails from Baildon which is the rural side of Bradford, nearly the next town over. Darcy technically came from Sweden when she was five, and Kieran was born in the US but lived in Scotland until he moved down to study.

This advantage means Beth lives and breathes the city and has an entire map in her mind. She limps toward the centre, hoping to find help, hoping to find... anything... in this living hell.

00:44 hours
Will

The corrugate iron roof is domed some 25-feet above them like a shanty-town cathedral. Grain is piled high at the far end and for the farm rats, it's a free-for-all. At the other end are sacks of fabric and cardboard boxes ready for distribution. With the screaming and commotion outside, it's like all the percussionists in the world have gathered together to play on the roof and the walls.

Three other boys sitting in various parts of the room meet Will; one cowers behind somebody's work bench, hunched over and panting. The other two sit near the bay doors. Will is in the corner trying to process everything that unfolded—images play over and over of Kieran turning into a beast and going 'bat-shit' crazy, plus the massacre in his home.

The silence is too much for him. He needs to say something and keep busy.

"Will," he utters, looking at the guy near the workstation.

"Matthew, but you can call me Matt," he says like he's run a marathon and smoked a pack of 20 at the same time.

This medium-built boy, a little on the cushiony side with slicked back blonde hair, offers to shake Will's hand. They quickly become acquainted and familiar with one another when things quieten.

"You all know each other?" Will stands.

"No, we just ran in the same direction and got here a few seconds before you," Matt says.

Will suddenly recognises one boy. "Wait, I know you." He pants. It takes a moment before it clicks. "Yeah, you were at the library in our group the other day. You were at that party a few days ago in Headingley. Tilly-bops or whatever-the-fuck her name was! You know my ex... *knew*. Do you two know each other?" Will asks.

"Sort of, we're on the same course. Me and my friend here were at a club when people started dropping like flies around us. They invited us to a party but never made it," one says. "It's like it's the end of the fucking world!"

"Yeah, that will have been my party. Small world," replies Will. "I'm Will. I don't think I caught your name the other day during study?"

"Adam." He pauses. "We met twice!" *Is he insulted?* Will wonders. "I don't know if there's anyone else coming."

"It's too quiet," Matt says with his ear pressed up against the garage door. "What's your name?"

The third one looks the weakest, timid. "Joel," he utters anxiously. "What if somebody is in here already?"

"You mean like me?" A female voice from behind calls out, startling Will and the boys.

A female police officer who reveals herself from another section of the warehouse soon accompanies them. She calls herself Jules, clearly middle-aged, probably even in her 30s but by the look of her tan and obvious smoking, it has all taken its toll. Jules doesn't seem so welcoming or willing to share her hiding spot.

"Who's the leather bag?" Will asks Adam, still catching his breath.

"PC Stenson. You will call me Jules." She hisses, "You're in my hideout."

Jules claims she found the hideout first; she claims she went to look for food to prepare for a lengthy stay, knowing the apocalypse has arrived.

"You knew this was going to happen?" Matt asks.

"No, but it didn't take long to figure out it was coming. Locked me up a serial killer don't you know, I was ready." She frowns, explaining proudly.

Will notices her firearm. She isn't a PSCO or a beat cop, she's the full deal. No wedding ring, but a pale shade of skin where the ring used to be, which means she's recently divorced. With scraped back black hair, her tan is forced into view like over-cooked oven baked fries. Will is a clever boy—not exactly book smart, more the 'smokes and knows things' type. Observant, he instantly knows this officer will pose a problem.

"We don't want trouble, just want a place to hide."

The five strangers in the warehouse now have a pressing conflict. Will establishes himself as the most confident of the group, having gained back some momentum from his shock before he tries to negotiate with the officer reasonably, resulting in major consequences. PC Stenson wants them out while people are being torn limb from limb.

She draws her firearm, putting the others' lives at risk. Matt tries to defuse the situation, also establishing himself as a brave figure, but it's clear they are going to have to leave.

"Please don't," Will says with his hands up as if he's stopping traffic. He's suspiciously calm.

"We can all go when it dies down," Matt affirms, looking at Joel who is still terrified, having said barley anything since they arrived.

Adam doesn't take too kindly to having a gun pointed at him. While Jules and Will are deep in negotiation, he slyly picks up and conceals a tin can. It must have rolled away from Jules' collection. Jules states her authority, frantically whaling and throwing orders around. As a police officer, she implies her word is gospel and Adam smugly points out if it is indeed 'the apocalypse', her authority won't mean much anymore.

Adam takes his opportunity as soon as her attention is elsewhere. He launches the can at her head and it knocks her off balance. The gun fires straight past Matt into the control box to the shutters, which snap and raise like falling blinds. The noise attracts more violent people.

Will, Adam and Matt seize their moment before Jules can recover and choose to leap from the warehouse docking platform, running down the alley further to an abandoned car. They must act fast with so many infected people hot on their tails. Jules growls, recuperating, and fires wildly into the darkness.

Will is about to make a split from Adam and Matt when the two boys look pleadingly at him. He's obviously made some impromptu allies and shouldn't run. Will thinks back to when he, Kieran and Beth were watching a movie and Kieran made a 'strength in numbers' remark.

Maybe he was right?

"I swear to God," he mutters to himself, "that if you're wrong about this Kieran and you're not dead, I'll kill you myself."

He reluctantly stays with the two boys and walks down another street, void of life or havoc.

"No Creepers," Adam says

"That's good," Matt says.

He elbows the driver's window, opens the door and hot wires the car in the pitch black, which speaks volumes about his past and his character. Will and Adam exchange an awkward expression that subtly says, 'how could he know?', but it helps them not to ask.

The monsters screech as they close in, hard to see, harder to detect. The creatures are fast, vicious and strong, they ooze green bile and their skin almost changes to a grimy pigment. They are rotting decay on legs.

They force the boys to make an impromptu alliance and after swift interactions they all stumble inside, lock the doors, and attempt to drive. Matt, trying to steer, forgets to take the handbrake off. He panics until Adam corrects him, pushing the stick down from the back seat. They become trapped when the infected smash their way in.

Matt, having already broken one window, gets grabbed and dragged through first. The infected throw him aside. Will has half a mind to take the driver's seat and flee, but his moral conscience takes over and he gets out, punching and kicking his attackers.

Will drags Matt upright and they attempt to leave again. Matt finally puts it in gear, and they speed off into darkness.

00:52 hours
Joel

Jules turns around and tries to draw the shutters in the warehouse, but it sparks back.

"FUCK!"

She stands with her eyes fixed on the road, breathing faster. Joel sits in a ball, quaking. They have left him behind, but this is not a game of hide and seek. He is now a rigid statue, unable to help Jules through fear. Jules turns and is surprised to see him remaining; she ogles him for a moment then raises her gun. Jules takes another step, turns her head with eyes wilder than a deer caught in lights.

Joel hid during the little can-and-run incident, but now

he's stranded with Jules, the trigger-happy police officer. She has the gun pointed at him still as he ducks lower and behind merchandise before she sees a trickle of water forming on the crotch of his skinny jeans.

"Really?"

She lowers the gun, hesitating and dragging him out by the shirt. Jules is now on edge, knowing she has to carry 'dead weight'. Joel doesn't understand why she's calling him a piece of spaghetti, complaining he won't last five minutes outside.

Why would she be so cruel at a time like this? It's clear she is a bit of bully. She sarcastically points out she is going to have to protect him now—such an inconvenience!

Her warehouse becomes under threat again as the creatures try harder to break in.

CHAPTER 3:

HAPPY NEW YEAR

01:00 hours
City of Leeds

A fresh hell has plagued the city. Wide-set pandemonium is in full effect throughout the vast metropolis.

News reports pour through the cracks to address the uncontrollable and unsettling disturbances growing further afield. If not contained, this 'thing' could continue to spread throughout the country, they say, advising everyone to stay in their homes, and anyone in the surrounding area to leave.

The government attempts to act quickly by dispatching immediate military forces to the north to quarantine Leeds, hoping to stop the spread of anarchy.

The mayor attempts to keep civil law and order before being forced to leave with his council, heading for London. They take a special police escort down the M1 motorway as military convoys whiz in the opposite direction, heading to Yorkshire.

The city's emergency backup power bursts to life, guiding them like a beacon.

Beth

Dread owns Beth as she walks closer to the high street among the widespread pandemonium pushing against her like an invisible gale. It attempts to put her in reverse. Anxiety has her stomach locked up tight. Nothing getting in or out. Her face numbs from the cold, setting in like rigor mortis; with teeth locked, her jaw tightens.

Suddenly, the pitch-black silhouette of the city illuminates as the backup power paves the way. With the power on, the horror is foul and smeared on blood-stained streets. Beth jumps out of her skin as the streetlights flicker one by one. Looters in the streets, mayhem, violence, death and gunfire shroud the night as the sky turns to a charcoal amber and light ash dances romantically in the air. Beth imagines she is at a cheap family bonfire.

If anyone isn't sick from the virus spreading faster than idle gossip, they're rioting.

She trembles, cautiously trying to stay in the shadows and out of harm's way.

She stumbles and limps onto the inner-city high street. Hands against every building she touches, she drags her body along. Over dressed and overwhelmed—heels click clacking, she's forgotten all about them and takes the most familiar route she knows, trying to avoid being seen, in pursuit of finding help; soon, she finds the opposite.

A man zooms past on the back of a motorbike with a baseball bat, swinging it at anyone infected in a sick game. Another looter stabs a man repeatedly for possession of a TV, and not just once or twice but nine or ten times like a grudge. Beth can't help but think it's something in the air. Something has pricked the cortex of anger within everyone and everything making them want to rage and hurt. She finds it difficult to differentiate between friend and foe—can they tell she isn't infected?

And there are bodies in the streets, torn apart like a dog's chew toy; the life that dwelt within them has gone and they are safe from the perils of this unfriendly world now. Hearts that used to beat with love are still. Souls that felt so many wonderful human emotions are blank.

Traumatised and trying to fight the shock now consuming

her body, Beth tries to help any way she can by aiding fallen victims. It's hard to control all the people running wild and those frantically crying out for help. She spots a little girl calling for her mother and runs over to pick her up. The child puts up little resistance, and together they run for a few minutes until Beth spots a woman repeatedly calling out for her little girl. The woman seems more terrified than thankful when Beth hands her over, but nods before disappearing again into the darkness and leaving Beth bewildered.

She turns in every direction; anxiety overwhelms her. She mistakes a few infected citizens for normal people. Two suddenly overpower her and knock her to the floor. Luckily, brave and kind samaritans help free her from impending doom—the two street merchants tackle them, enabling her to break free. Beth helps all she can before she is pushed back as the merchants are overwhelmed and torn apart themselves. She decides to flee to the nearby liquor store where she shopped earlier that same evening.

She takes a moment to catch her breath before a bullet zooms past and takes down someone about to attack her. Beth spins around to see the madman inches away fall right at her feet, then hears a few more bullets fire. She screams and covers her head, then looks up and sees a boy on the balcony of a shop, aiming a rifle at her.

Beth pauses for a moment to see if he recognises she's still human before she sprints for the off licence below.

"PLEASE! OPEN UP! LET ME IN!" she begs. It isn't like Beth to beg or cry. Her whaling goes unaided for a few moments with more mad people stopping to notice her. "HELP!"

She exhausts her vocals and bruises her bloody hands from banging. When the door suddenly gives, she is let in as her assailants close on her. A man suddenly yanks her in forcefully. It's the cashier from earlier. She looks down at his name badge again: Damon.

"*You.*" She stands there, a sad, shivering, sniffling mess.

"Hakuna matata?" He stares at her and for a moment time freezes.

Damon clocks the rifle and aims at two crazies after Beth. FFFFT! SPLAT! He pierces one in the eye, causing the back of its head to open like a party popper. As they fall, the other leaps over going for the win. Quickly, Damon flips the rifle upside down and bats this one away. She falls back with a great whack into a bench as a group tries to pass. The assailant's attention is briefly broken from Damon as she sniffs and ogles her new prey. This gives Damon the few seconds needed to shut the shop door and lock it.

She bursts into tears and collapses into him as gunfire ripples out in the street. They duck down. Damon switches off the lights, so they can see only the amber glow and whizzing shadows outside.

The other two prisoners introduce themselves.

"Vern."

"Lia."

She collects herself, feeling calmer now there are other people around. "Beth."

Something about living bodies feels safer, though they all look desperate for an easy way out. There is a brief, tense moment as she locks eyes with them all; They clearly understand the subtext on each person's face.

What is going on?

Are they dangerous...?

Are they still... human?

Exhausted, she slumps and takes off her heels. She is still smothered in Darcy's blood and whimpers, admitting defeat as her emotions catch up to her.

The other people in the shop say nothing apart from Damon who awkwardly approaches and tries to comfort her. He puts a blanket around her shoulders.

"It's not much."

She says nothing but remembers Damon as the boy who served her before the party. She tells him he is the 'pretty boy' whilst sniffling. Damon nods and blushes.

"You're not so bad yourself, despite looking like shit. Hakuna matata girl, am I right?"

Damon sits Beth down. For a while they remain unnoticed by the general commotion outside, shielded by the grace of the shelter that is Damon's shop, which doesn't seem like much of a grave. Beth doesn't want to die here. Horror unfolding outside gives them mere minutes to talk, then the group remains in silence as they stare out the window from the back, tears streaming down their faces. No one has any clue what is happening. They watch the rush of people whiz back and forth—someone is blind because his eyes have been gouged. Another drags his feet—what was once a man is now snake-like with pink-grey intestines dragging in the dirt as it staggers toward them using only its ears and nose for guidance. They cover their mouths until it leaves and watch another woman running with her child, only for her to be snatched away and the woman pounced on. Her daughter watches as the mother's throat is ripped out, before she meets the same demise.

"What is this?" Lia whimpers.

"They've gone mad. All of them. Completely mad." Vern takes a peek.

"Judgement day, end of the world," Damon says as they watch. "We will be safe in here, let's wait for the police."

"I don't think there is any police," Beth stresses.

Damon and Beth seem to have an instant connection. The discussion reverts to panic, and their panic gets them spotted by the wrong people. Damon and Vern push a freezer against the door to stop the monsters getting any ideas.

"My friend seems to think it's the Grime Flu virus, an epidemic gone wrong," Beth says.

"Where is your friend?"

Damon watches her with what seems to be his default happy-ish complexion. It takes her aback for a moment, surprised by his sudden calmness.

"Somewhere out there." She gestures, too spooked to blush.

"I don't know what kind of Flu does this."

"My friends were torn apart, savages, monsters, people I knew. Eating each other alive." Lia cries hysterically.

Damon runs his hands through his hair, blending into the shadows. He exhales, frustrated, and walks to the back of his shop. He places his rifle down, perplexed. Something catches his eye atop the boxed goods beside the barricaded door to an alley.

"Claire, you sly dog," he mutters.

A handgun peeks out of a wrapped cloth. He scans it for a moment. Odd, it's the one he's always wanted. A note drops on the floor from underneath.

'To my big bro, don't say I don't listen to or do anything for you. Merry Christmas. Love CBear xo.'

"What were you doing on the roof before?" Beth startles him, meeting him in the back as the others cower on the shop floor.

He turns with the gun resting flat in his palm.

"Wow rifles, guns. Who are you?"

"Sorry, it's a hobby of mine, I like collectables… replicas. I live upstairs. This is my mum's store, but she left it to me and my sister. Which probably explains this." He spins the gun on the box. "Mum liked to collect them too and left them to my sister, Claire. Claire doesn't like them, she hates guns. Said she'd draw the line at my rifle. I thought we didn't have any others. I thought I got rid of them—all except my rifle..."

"Claire?"

"Sister... I'm not even that fond of them myself. She

thinks I am because I used to play with mum's."

"You know how to use one." Beth points to it.

"Ironic, isn't it?"

None of this is important right now, but to Beth him talking about anything just to create a calming atmosphere is enough.

"Where is your sister?" Beth places her heels on a box and rubs her feet.

"Somewhere out there," Damon explains, repeating what Beth said. "I sent her on a supply run because our usual won't deliver until—"

"I can't do this; I need to get out, this is too much and we're all going to die."

Lia is screaming from the shop floor, distracting Beth and Damon, who come bounding back into the room to hush her. Vern is trying to calm her as she paces frantically back and forth, hyperventilating.

"Please calm down, we are safe in here." Vern dabs her shoulder, only for her to pull away.

"I can't breathe, we have to get out of here." Lia's eyes scan her other contacts and the panic grows.

"Keep your voice down!" Damon hisses.

Beth looks ahead of him out the window and sees people being drawn toward the shop. Lia's panicking gets the infected to the barricaded door, including their blind friend and the one donning his intestines as a gilet. Lia snaps and removes the barricade to escape.

"STOP HER!" Damon yells, but before he can drag Lia back by her waist, she has already let the fridge collapse into the street.

Lia takes one step outside before she is pounced upon and torn to shreds. Infected civilians notice the others in the shop and before anyone has time to gasp, two monsters strike Vern down. Unfortunate for them but lucky for Beth, it buys her and Damon a few moments. Using their common sense, Damon gets Beth into the back room. He becomes a little heavy-handed as he shoves her, but she doesn't protest. Vern's organs get thrown around in a meaty food fight. Beth forgets her heels in the panic.

"We have to go *now*." He barricades access to his shop floor with a blunt wooden log and pulls her to the door leading to the alley. "Help me."

Damon removes the goods blockading the door to the alley. The monsters batter on the door to the shop, already giving way. Beth squeals, trying to not go into full hysterics. Damon giggles through his nerves, his keys trying each one.

Gold yale, no. Silver bic, no.

"Hurry!" she protests, looking back at the door, seeing chunks of wood splintering away.

Black yale... Twist.

"YES!" He does it too quick and the key snaps in half. "NO!" he turns pale.

Beth shrieks. Hands are now through the other door.

"Fuck this."

He reveals the Christmas Gift weapon from his sister and Beth covers her ears. With that he fires off the lock and performs a perfect round house kick, obliterating the flimsy door to the alley.

"How on earth did you learn that?"

"Rangers! Go on!" he says flippantly.

Damon stays behind to ensure there isn't any trouble following.

"You need to run now and fast, take this!" He pushes Beth into the alley, remaining in the door as he hands her the gun. Suddenly, the backroom door shakes to life as people force halfway in, putting pressure on the thin wooden log.

"Wait, you're not coming?"

"I'll hold off whoever is trying to get in, virus or no virus."

"Why would you help me then not come with me?"

"I have to find my sister because I sent her to the store. I can't leave her when she is *my* responsibility." Damon adjusts his rifle, ready to use it. "Find your friend. If this was under any other circumstance, I'd ask you out." He attempts a smile.

She thanks him for his efforts, but doesn't know why he is doing this for her.

"Looks like you're a girl worth saving. Take the gun and go. Use it if anything or anyone comes at you. Just use it!" he adds frantically.

"But I don't know how." She trembles, feeling about three feet tall.

"It's a revolver, it has a hammer. Pull it down and point. Learn! NOW GO!"

The door gives way.

"Thank you!" she tearfully says.

"I hope we meet again."

Beth takes the back alley that leads to an open car parked between her and the bus station. She does not know what her next move is or where to go. She reaches the station and quickly mobilises herself when civilians and infected are running rampant. She catches their attention from the other end of the bus terminal and they chase her down.

She cries. She points the gun. The first bullet shatters a window and another pinches the shoulder of one of her pursuers.

She slips through an automatic door, getting onto the carriageway. They charge after her, so she darts for her life despite limping in bare feet. She spots a double-decker bus with the doors still open. She dives aboard it.

Keeping herself low and quiet, Beth gets sniffed out by the infected who seem to have a keen sense of smell. She crawls into the driver's seat and closes the passenger doors as they bash the glass. Beth takes lots of deep breaths and makes a run for it from the driver's seat. The three villains easily crack and shatter the doors, climbing onboard. She runs up the stairs.

"NO! Stupid girl. Never run up the stairs in the movies."

Too late… only one way out the back. She bolts for emergency exit using the hammer to break it and drop, but she rips her formal white dress. Beth dangles for a moment eight feet from the floor, holding onto the ledge. Her attackers come onto the second-floor sniffing and shrieking. She does her best to remain silent, keeping it all in.

Don't scream, don't cry, don't even breathe.

One sees her pretty peach nails clawing over the edge when they screech and run for her. Beth screams and drops to the concrete, grazing her face, knees and arms. *Get up, get up, GET UP!* So much adrenaline.

"ARGHHH!" Beth attempts to run, but something in her ankle is wrong. *Is it a sprain? Is it twisted?* "Screw it!"

Now limping for another double decker in sight, she turns to watch the three stooges drop from the same hole she did and get up with no hesitation.

"What is this, a machine?"

With the infected on her tail, Beth hobbles and begins barging the doors to the bus until she reads the emergency open button. It hisses, and she's in. She dives into the driver's seat of that one and jams the entrance with someone's abandoned suitcase so the infected can't slide the door open and climb aboard. Instead, they bash at the windows.

Beth hyperventilates. The walls are closing in. She claustrophobic… it's so tiny. *Where are the keys?* They drop out from the visor above. Having only passed her driving test a few weeks prior, she slips, stalls and jumps the bus with no clue how to work it.

She slams it in gear.

Once moving, she puts it in a higher gear and speeds up. Beth outruns her pursuers, but hits a few more infected and looters as she's fleeing out of town. She does not know if they're alive or dead or even who is who, but she makes a clean escape with her life intact.

02:00 hours
Countryside, M621

The military reach the Yorkshire border and attempt an endearing struggle to contain this catastrophic outbreak.

The government instructs the unit to set up at every access point in and out of Leeds, and try to activate a city-wide quarantine, separating the city from the rest of the country. Every bridge, motorway, slip road, country road, station, airport and field are seized, now under the army's control.

The Mayor of London instructs them to set up a county-wide border to make sure nobody travels until they initialise a clean-up process. He addresses the Prime Minister.

"No one in.. and no one out."

CHAPTER 4:

SAINTS OF THE UNDEAD

January 1st, 2012
07:00 hours

The world is silent; the sun is still resolutely below the horizon, and the street is eerie, like a black and white movie.

Frost setting in on the fields is cementing the bodies that lay scattered. The silence forms the last wintry song, and icicles reflect the dancing sunshine in every direction. The Angel of Death has their work cut out tonight. It's a PR nightmare wherever he works. It's quiet now, sombre after a bloody battle. Birds sing their morning lullabies, blissfully unaware of the destruction. Most other animals and creatures have fled—they knew danger was coming.

With no place to turn, no place to hide, everyone is defeated and helpless. Anyone left alive aimlessly wonders the streets, walking dead bodies themselves. Refugees have already taken safer places, barricading off their personal territories. Lonely are the street-dwellers knocking on boarded shops and homes, desperate for help. Those fending for themselves ignore their cries. It's survival of the fittest.

The military has declared martial law following a state of emergency. They begin their county-wide quarantine and scramble all services with their technology, which means the media inside their zone has gone dark. They've demilitarised the networks and the internet. The government has ironically branded Yorkshire a dead zone for service. Only the army can communicate through landlines or the

STN.

The outside world has melted with the already brewing conspiracies and theories on what they've done to the internet beyond the prison walls but there has still been no comment from officials.

As the military seals off any exits, electronic devices go dark too. The government blocks every outsource: all phones, computers, smart televisions. They cannot have this getting out. Local networks are on standby via an emergency frequency.

Grid locked traffic jams every bridge, motorway exit and highway.

05:31 hours
Will, Matt & Adam
M621

The scarlet liquid is drying brown on Will's white shirt. *Imagine being covered in your loved one's blood.* He can't help but resonate. If Will had continued to hate Kieran, it might have been the perfect fantasy to relish in your ex's blood. But nothing had prepared him for this. The light leaves his eyes as the colour from his rosy cheeks vanishes. Alongside him, a woman's body lays limp; her soul has departed as Will stares from the car window.

They join the masses waiting in the traffic exodus. Will, Matt and Adam lose their patience and debate walking.

"I have a shit feeling about this. This is how it happens in the movies," Will, the least patient of the three, tells them.

They have more chance of dying, like sitting ducks.

"I've listened to my gut so far and I'm not dead so I think we should go."

He gives it five minutes before everyone runs like headless chickens back in the opposite direction. Something has gone wrong. They are about to set off on foot when commotion ahead distracts them. Chaos breaks out. Will rolls his eyes.

Matt gets out of the car to brave the cold. He climbs on its roof as the others look on in confusion to witness the infection penetrating the motorway between jammed cars, literally a few hundred yards ahead.

"Someone must have been sick." Matt abruptly announces they must get to higher ground immediately. "I think we should all listen to that gut of yours."

People attack one another again. They overrun the police on their noble steeds. Spooked, they toss off their owners and trample through the crowds as everybody is trying to get away at the same time. From far ahead, Matt sees rapid gunfire. He ducks and panics. This provokes the chaos to worsen and become more erratic—people are pushing and knocking each other down, trampling other one another in desperation and fear. Bones are crushed, heads kicked in.

"The old and frail," he says with a sadness in his eyes.

He hops down, and innocent civilians flee in the opposite direction towards the boys, bringing the monsters with them. They run wildly before they are ambushed.

"Get in." Matt throws his head round the back of his seat and reverses their ride, weaving between the cars and gormless civilians.

They must think of a place to go that doesn't involve lots of people.

"The closer we are to people, the more likely they are to turn, so the more likely are those things to attack," he mutters as the other two cling to the handles for dear life.

***

Meanwhile, the government finally calls a conference to address the rest of the United Kingdom on the situation unfolding in the heart of Yorkshire. A spokesperson, the

Health Secretary, stands in on behalf of the Prime Minister. He explains the situation in Leeds, trying to calm people down.

He is outside 10 Downing Street when the media begin rapidly firing questions at him. He barely steps up to the podium. The last thing they need is nationwide panic.

"Mr Health Secretary, is it a hoax?"

"Is it a terrorist attack?"

He softly raises his hand to hush the rabble. He tells the country and the media they can rule out any terrorist involvement and immediately lies and says they found a new strain of a disease and have already detained Patient Zero.

"It came from a crowded meat market where the food was contaminated."

He then informs the rest of the country to carry on and everything will go back to normal.

The rabble of press speak over one another in a frenzy.

"What about the families trapped who live elsewhere?"

"Why can't anybody reach their loved ones within the area?"

"Why can't the people of Lincolnshire and Manchester access the city?"

"Why is there an outsource block on web access?"

He handles himself well, clearing his throat. "The Prime Minister is currently preoccupied with finding answers to your questions and will release a statement. As for our loved ones, there have been hotels and stadiums temporarily set up as treatment wards and bedsits until we can let them go. We have to make sure we stay alert and control the spread of the outbreak. The last thing we need is this disease transferring to any other city. It is only a precaution. We have temporarily suspended access to phone lines, signal and web addresses so our best teams can focus, to stop fear mongering and rumours intended to scare the British public.

Yorkshire is in a state of strict lockdown."

The nation is told by the government that if anyone approaches the area, it will persecute them to the maximum.

"We have set a border up to monitor the access points of Yorkshire. Evacuation zones have been organised and people in nearby homes are being collected and taken to these wards until we can clear the city—it is merely a precaution. We have divided an inner perimeter in the West Riding area, further divided into five sections: Bradford, Wakefield, Leeds, Calderdale and Kirklees. The outer perimeter, in which the evacuation posts are being set up, comprises the boarders of North, East and South Yorkshire and their respective boroughs. The surrounding counties: Greater Manchester, Derbyshire, Lancaster, Cumbria, Durham and Lincolnshire, have had their access points temporarily suspended as we investigate. Any family or friends within that zone will be safe and will return to their homes shortly. I assure you everything is under control," he lies.

Much of the public are frightened and confused; many are asking about family and friends in Leeds. The Health Secretary says he can no longer answer any more questions. He's informed by the military that they are on red alert.

"Be patient—the infected will get to be reunited with family and friends soon once we arrange treatment," the Mayor lies when the Health Secretary disappears behind a police cordon.

The nation uses hash tags and posts questions on social media until it spirals out of control; people are complaining and moaning—what the British public does best. People are recording social media vlogs, making funny videos, filming conspiracy theories and acting like it's all a joke. Most who have taken to social media as an outlet are just trying to reach their families and friends. Others want to weigh in, misunderstanding the magnitude of the horror unfolding.

Flights are diverted and trains and coaches are cancelled until further notice.

Yorkshire is dead.

06:50 hours
Country Hillside

Will, Matt and Adam abandon the motorway. All the cars are at a standstill. They steal another car and try to drive along the border of the quarantine; the boys take a moment to drive to a hillside, pull up, and overlook the scene.

"Well, at least the news wasn't lying about this."

Will sighs as he ogles the giant quarantine wall from afar; military soldiers are fleas dotted around as the boys listen to the faint rabble of people.

"What news?" Adam says, scrolling his phone. "There's no news. I've had no signal for the last three hours."

"Me neither." Matt adds, "Google isn't even working. I can't ring my mum."

"How the hell are we going to get out through all that?" Adam says. He pulls out some binoculars from the glove compartment. *How lucky.* "I found these, probably owned by some birdwatchers…" He guesses by the contents of the car that elderly people must have previously owned it.

"Or people who enjoy dogging." Will tries to make light of that situation.

"This border-thing goes on for miles and miles, we have no chance!" Adam says, eyes glued to the binoculars.

Matt adds, "Everyone has the same idea."

"Trapped like rats in a cage," says Will. "Man, they built it fast, almost like they were ready."

"They can't do that though, can they?" Adam glances away.

Will protests. "Wouldn't you? 65 million people to look after and a virus breaks out in the middle of your country?"

Adam is sad for a moment, thinking about all the kids and old people involved in this mess.

"Oh shit!"

With his train of thought interrupted, he glances down and notices a fight breaking out in the crowd. He sees a section of people being eaten and chased by the infected as innocent bystanders flee their cars. Families are carrying luggage and scooping up younger loved ones.

"What?" the other two say simultaneously.

He gets back in the car, shaken but quiet. The other two try to get some sense out of him as he sits, staring blankly into space.

"Give me them!"

Will snatches the binoculars to see what Adam has. Matt awaits his response. The air is so brittle it could snap, and if it doesn't, they might. No one speaks, because what is there to say? Platitudes won't cut it right now. A day ago, they were all speculating too, ignorant to the surrounding signs... anything to ease the terrible burden of worry.

"Another breakout in the crowd," Will says faintly, heartbreak in his eyes. He tries not to cry and puts the binoculars down.

"Are there any creepers?" Adam asks nervously.

"Creepers?"

"Yeah. That's what I call them! Because they're creepy, and they creep… doing… creeper things?" Adam says this as if it's perfectly normal.

The boys are tired. Will is suffering with a terrible hangover from the party massacre, with a worse taste in his mouth.

Will learns Adam and Matt are also students staying and studying in the area. Adam is on Kieran's course and Matt attends the same university, only he studies engineering and quantum mechanics. They even hang out in the same bars and pubs but have never crossed paths.

"So, you're like a rocket scientist?" Will lights up with delight.

"Not quite. The quantum mechanics is just a unit, I say it to sound fancy. However, I cover mechanical engineering and electrical."

"What's that when it's at home?" adds Adam, suddenly intrigued.

"Circuits, power plants, planes, turbines."

"That's your dream? Turbines…" Will says ruder than intended.

They all try to solve what the hell is going on while they continue their mission to find a place to hold up for a few days. Adam and Will take turns with the binoculars as they deduce the military has built the wall around Yorkshire, and swiftly.

"Circumnavigating the city without entering it will prove challenging to find a safe place," Will says to his friends.

"How did this mess even happen?"

Matt tries to grasp the reality and severity of their 'predicament', as he calls it.

"Predicament?" scoffs Will. "I'd love to see what you consider a fucking catastrophe!"

Will, Adam and Matt have a wild discussion on their theories of this unexplained mess, tossing words and conspires back and forth including the Flu, riots, death, and what can only be explained as helpless victims coming back from the dead.

"I saw it myself; I can't explain it—I don't want to. But I saw people die in front of me and then just come back."

"And let me guess, start killing one another?" Matt finishes Will's sentence.

"I was going to say eating... but, yeah."

Matt and Adam laugh about it despite Will's disgust.

"Sorry, it's just, you know when something is so fucking messed up all you can do is laugh?"

Adam suggests people might have got sick of the state the world is in and are finally rebelling. Matt thinks it's the government. Adam then suggests the possibility of aliens, or a meteorite, and they laugh off the subject.

But Will brings it back up. "Have you idiots seen the news in the past three days? Non-stop talking about how dangerous this new 'Grime Flu' is. All the social distancing warnings, and look how quick they were to set up what I can only describe as a 'quarantine bubble'?"

"Dome?"

They stare at him, half insulted, half sad.

"It's not that implausible," he adds.

Will believes he has seen the signs. "People started getting sick and these symptoms are causing them to become violent, full of rage, with a total lack of humanity and a desire for tearing people apart and eating them... that's what I saw, my eyes do not deceive me."

"So, you're telling me that these things..."

"I'm not saying the z-word," stresses Will.

"Zombies? That is what you're implying!" Matt contradicts.

"I DON'T KNOW WHAT I'M SAYING!"

Will explains the victims may not be completely dead but infected with a disease that causes Rabies-like tendencies and violent outbursts. He's spent loads of time watching CDC documentaries and that it isn't technically impossible.

"The WHO and CDC said one day a disease may come along and cause the end of the world and this could be it. Just like that... just like this..." He looks back at the crowd below. "They said one day something new and unprecedented will wipe us out. It's nature; it will be our response to it that determines our survival."

"You call that survival?"

The boys look down at the massacre in the distance.

"What you are saying defies all logical science, all logical

EVERYTHING!" Matt looks out his window. "I feel sick." He opens his door to let some air in.

The boys agree people coming back from the dead and tearing one another's faces off are a little too far-fetched for their taste. Adam disagrees and asks Will to explain what he sees as he shoves the binoculars at him.

Will watches more people ripping into one another.

"This is just fucked up, they're like wild animals... one bites another or attacks another and then they start on the next person."

"So, like biting?" Matt asks.

"Each victim looks fatigued, their eyes glazed over almost blank, like nothing is inside. Their skin turning grimy like the neglected epitaph of an eerie graveyard."

"Are you writing a book?" Adam remarks.

"Okay then, genius, where do you think the biting and eating of the human flesh comes from?" Matt gets agitated.

"Maybe they aren't consuming the flesh, but it's a virus that causes the host to infect anyone who comes into contact? They revert to primal instincts. The basic human instincts are to fuck, feed and fight. But the thing that splits us from the rest is our advanced human instincts."

It confuses the other two, and they ask Will to elaborate. He explains humans are just animals, only developed. Any animal's basic instinct is to hunt, breed, and bite.

"The consensus is that the recognised instinct in man is stuff like: fear, anger, shyness, curiosity, affection, love, jealousy and envy, rivalry, sociability, sympathy, modesty. Shit that makes us less animalistic," he suggests.

"But animals have that? I have a cat who does all that shit." Adam pipes up, thinking he's clever. "Oh no, poor Mr Shadow."

"Yes, but we are the only ones capable of cognitive constructiveness, secretiveness and acquisitiveness. Whatever those things are, they have nothing. I don't even think they're people, just ghosts in shells of what we once were. The soul moves on."

They argue against him, but Will isn't saying they are real zombies, like on TV or in the movies. Close enough to have the same symptoms, maybe. Will's copious amount of weed smoking and watching all those universe and disease documentaries have paid off. He goes as far to say it's not technically impossible. The closest thing humans have seen is Rabies and Mad Cow.

"Rabies?"

"Mad Cow?" the boys repeat.

"There isn't a disease, be it mental or physiological, that makes people want to eat other people, at least none as currently recognised by medical science. Side note, cannibalism isn't considered a mental illness, but as a part of a larger web of psychoses."

They laugh him off until Will asks Adam how he so easily forgot what they'd witnessed through the binoculars. Adam observes the events unfolding, then suddenly, they aren't laughing anymore.

"You can't deny what's in front of you and neither can I, as much as I'm trying to rationalise this. For once I don't one hundred percent know. More like 80-20." Will smiles cheekily.

Matt's intrigue peaks. "Bit of a smartarse aren't you? How do you know so much?"

Will says he studied biology and criminology before his love of smoking pot took over.

"I was going to be an electrician like my father. Electrics led me to science that led me to biology and… people."

"And you come at me for being into energy saving?"

"People can change, you know."

Silence ensues.

"Drugs, then." Adam pipes up out of nowhere, and the other two look at him, confused. "Drugs!" he says again, expecting them to understand.

Adam flaps like he's playing charades, trying to find the right words. He explains it could be terrorists and drugs.

"Maybe they put something in the air... or the water supplies? Drugs can make people tear other people's faces off, because it's been in the news. That guy in Florida... didn't they shoot him like eight times?"

"America is the world's Florida."

Will stares at Adam like a moron.

"Do I have something on my face?" Adam subsequently asks.

"You mean that guy in Florida who took a dodgy batch of bath salts?"

"Dodgy batch of bath salts? You mean to tell me there's a GOOD kind?" Matt sarcastically asks.

Will pauses. "I had a rough break up and there may have been a bath salt or two in my bender."

Will dismisses Adam's theory as a bland attempt at contributing.

"If it was airborne or in the water, we would tear each other's face off too."

Adam keeps throwing words at him like 'witchcraft', 'alchemy', 'Ebola'.

"Ebola?" Will becomes irritated and confused.

Adam says he saw it on the news. When Ebola broke out in Africa, people came back from the dead. Will stares at Adam once again. Will sarcastically requests Matthew's permission to throw Adam out. Matt denies him.

"Illuminati." Adam says lastly.

"Shut up, Adam."

Matt starts the engine.

***

They decide to take a detour to where Adam says they can

re-supply and refuel for the road ahead. He knows a guy who knows a guy who owns a petrol station near his sister's, and from there they will decide on what to do later.

"Anybody else have family?" Adam curiously asks.

"I got a mum and sister but if I know them, they'll be out slicing and dicing. This hell will be their heaven. They'll have got out... I hope. I'm sure I'll find them soon."

Will sighs but doesn't look worried, which is concerning for the others.

Matt drives cautiously and chimes in. "My family is from Basildon in Essex. If this thing is contained, then they are safe. But I know they'll be worried about me."

"Do you, Adam?"

"Not really, I don't speak to my family…"

"I thought you said you had a sister round here?"

"I do, but that doesn't mean I have to speak to her."

Adam turns away. And as soon as he out of Will's eye line Will makes a face, mocking him.

They pull in to already ransacked petrol station. It's looks family owned. There are few family owned stations left in the 21st century. Everyone got bought out or intimidated into selling to the big companies. Matt turns off the engine, and it's quiet. Too quiet. Will can already see this business had seen better days, even before last night's attacks. Old, dirty and rundown on the side of the road.

"Just… keep your wits about you boys. I'm done with surprises."

Will creeks open his side and steps out. Something feels off, but then again, it has all night. He's dying for some water.

"Fuel," says Adam.

"FOOD!" groans will.

Adam tells the others he's going inside the tiny hut for supplies and petrol cannisters for later when Matt calls for him to stop.

"Take this."

And out he pulls a switchblade from the back of his waistband. And tosses it to him. It hits the tips of Adam's fingers, and he juggles the blade until he drops it.

"GOT IT!" he springs up.

"MATE! SHHH." Will shakes his head before turning back to Matt at the pump.

"You had that this whole time?"

"I don't do violence."

"Says the lad who can hot wire a car."

Will shouts, "And get me some crisps to mop up this hangover."

"Really? After you just told him to be quiet."

Inside, Adam sees the place is trashed. It's tiny, next to a garage with a boiler suit and overalls pinned up by the former grease monkeys who worked on the cars. There's one suspended in mid-job. They just upped and left—trails of cans and blood. He tries not to feel nauseous. Eerie comes to mind, this grotesque site. It feels like he misplaced something inside himself. Adam flicks the blade open; it's only about four inches but it's four inches that could save his life. He doesn't even know what to expect. Too many gloomy thoughts distract him from what he thinks he needs. There isn't much on the shelves or in the fridges left, anyway. It's all tourist-y, dirty sunshades and maps. If this were middle America or the outback, it would be an oasis in a desert. Adam packs a basket of treats and liquids before stuffing two five-litre cannisters to finish his collection.

Suddenly, something falls off the wall near the office door. Must have been a picture. It startles Adam straight, eyes ping ponging in apprehension.

"What's taking so long?" Will appears from nowhere, startling him again.

"Jesus." Adam has his hand to his heart.

Matt rolls his eyes from the pump. The car is ready. It just shows how the boys are still trying to get their heads around this nightmare. Matt convinces himself he's dreaming, and he's slipped into a coma.

"Just thought I heard something." Adam leans back, causing Will to do the same. The boys go about their business. Will takes what he wants while downing a bottle of water from the dusty fridge. Adam comes to the screen where they would normally pay at the kiosk... empty. *Figures*.

Adam ruffles his pockets for whatever money he has when Will scoffs.

"Seriously?"

"What?" Adam throws all his money down on the counter like it's perfectly normal. "We're not criminals... they have cameras," he whispers.

The boys leave as Will puts his arm around Adam, comforting him.

They hear a thud. They stop, turned away from the office door.

"Was that the noise you heard?" Will whispers anxiously.

"Yup..."

Will and Adam peer over their shoulders and Will asks for the blade, so Adam tries to free a hand from all the bags of goods. Trepidation puts Will in motion, trying to silence the sound of his boots walking toward the office door.

"No... pssst, Will!" Adam hisses.

His eyes meet the dimmed sunrise coming through the cracks of the door, blocked by something every couple of seconds, something moving... a shadow. Will takes a few more conservative steps, despite Adam's warnings. He leans toward the door, trying to listen, but doesn't hear much other than maybe what he thinks is the sound of glasses being crushed under something heavy. One thing is for certain: he can hear a telephone off the hook beeping.

"Hello?"

143

The shadow stops moving.

"I'm here with the police." Will gets the knife ready as if to attack. "We just want to talk."

His hand is already on the handle. Adam gulps with a cold sweat on his brow. Matt wonders what the hell they are doing as he looks around to make sure no one is nearby. Will loses his nerve if only for a moment before swinging the door open when he is met by a complete horror show. He shrieks in a near unbearable, high-pitched tone.

Before him is a man in a check shirt and overalls hunched over something. Will hears sloppy noises when the man turns.

"Oh, my god."

The man has half his face torn away; he glares at Will as if to say he's pissed for being intruded upon.

"I'm sorry," Will says, paralyzed by fear, looking exactly like a statue. He can barely squeak.

It's not what the man looks like that terrifies him, it's the corpse he has a hold off. In pieces. Will stares stunned for a split second at this poor person's innards smeared all over. The man has what looks like their intestines and kidney mashed into its claws. Ribcage cracked open, no face, no arms, no lungs.

Will turns to Adam. "RUN!" he commands, bolting for the exit.

The possessed man bellows, throwing aside his meal and is already on his feet in pursuit of the boys. Matt spots the commotion from afar.

"OH SHIT!"

Will smartly pulls a shelf down as he runs past, causing the bloke to tackle over it and smash straight through the shop window. Adam cries out, scared.

"Don't stop" Will shouts, tugging Adam as he drops treat after treat from the bag.

Matt is already in the driver's seat. He spins the car

around and the boys dive in as the man recuperates and chases the car. They whiz off.

"Oh my goodness, I feel…"

"Sick?"

"Alive." Will gulps, and they both look out the rear window. The man slowly loses momentum.

Matt watches through the mirror. "Let's not do that again, please."

***

When he is done with the melodramatics, Adam suggests looking around to help other survivors where they can. Will doesn't want to be an arsehole, but he hates that idea.

"Aren't we supposed to be looking for a subliminal exit to guarantee their safety out of the madness? We don't exactly want to be stuck running around like Mother Teresa, trying to cure the sick."

"Not sure that analogy works," Matt tells Will.

"You never know, we might become Saints of the Undead."

Adam smiles at Will. He's too perfect. His smile is soft, with a hint of femininity. His strong bone structure is all male, but he's small and skinny compared to the others. Adam lets his eyes linger for a fraction longer than is customary, his usual test. Sure enough, Will gazes back. Even if he is confused, he's unguarded and calm. He's so much younger than Will expects, with a grown-up choir boy appearance, except for the tattoos that swirl above the neckline of his light shirt. He's got the same floppy tousled hair as Matt, except not slicked back naturally—stylish, almost mockingly so to Will—but his eyes aren't brown… possibly green. Will tries not to stare long enough to find out.

"Adam?"

Adam's mouth is almost too dry to speak. He nods like an idiot and then croaks. "Yeah, Will?"

"Thanks… for the crisps…"

Now that Adam is next to him, it's far easier to observe him discreetly. Will gives Matt a break from the driving once they are safe again, so he hops in to take over. It's natural for him to look his way while they talk and for him to keep his eyes on the traffic. He's smaller than Will by a couple of inches. He must be too small for sports or a manual job. Adam toys whether to ask more but stops short.

After refueling with what little they could find, and being chased out by what looked like the former owner, they head back onto the empty road. Matt is surprised by how quiet and 'dead' the roads are. Will smartly suggests most people will hide; everyone else will try to 'get out of Dodge.'

"You have an answer to everything, don't you?" Matt glances at Will, both smiling.

Will responds that it's how he's programmed. "Ex used to hate it."

He thinks about Kieran again—flashes of him bloody and dead, hitting him over the head, wondering where he may be now.

Will snaps out of it. "Fuck! Road sign has been mowed down!"

They pull to a stop, causing a light creak of the breaks. The boys are about to decide which exit to take on the dual carriageway; their choices are returning to the city for survivors or taking the other road out to where the chaos hasn't spread.

"Does anybody Leeds?" Adam asks.

"I'm not from round here," Matt says.

"Is there an atlas or map in this car? If it belonged to old people, they wouldn't use Google Maps, right?"

Adam rummages around in the glove compartment for an old crumpled map. The one he finds is so big it consumes the front of the car. They mumble and argue whilst their view is blocked.

"How can something so big fit into something so small?"

Will and Matt try to contain their immaturity but end up bursting into full on belly laughter.

"What?" Adam says, dumbfounded.

"Ah, I needed that." Matt sighs.

"I think we all did."

The moment fades until they are left in silence again.

"Do you hear that?" Will asks.

"Hear what?"

Suddenly, their fun comes to an explosive end. Another vehicle smashes into the side of theirs, spinning the car around and flipping it over. It rolls twice before landing upside down. The car scrapes down the road a few feet before coming to a stop. The other vehicle capsizes and halts a few feet away.

The boys' fates remain unknown as the sun continues to rise on this cold New Year's Day morning.

CHAPTER 5:

NEW WORLD ORDER

January 1st, 2012
02:00 hours
Joel
Leeds City

Still stranded at the warehouse, Joel is convinced Jules, the insane police officer, has taken him hostage. In reality, Joel is too scared to admit he's petrified to leave her side; he likes the sense of security that law enforcement offers, even though she explains it's all useless now. She can't and won't protect him. So, Joel feels braver as a hostage, for now.

He continues to convince himself he will be okay if he follows Jules, though he knows she will inevitably get rid of him somehow. She seems insecure and won't hesitate to kill Joel if he changes into a lunatic. But having not grasped what is going on around him, Joel can't understand how it's every man for themselves in this dog eat dog world... literally.

Joel is a kindred spirit—quite sensitive, never speaking up or deciding for himself—always a 'go with the flow' kind of guy. Never take him on a date, because you will spend hours waiting for him to decide what he wants to eat (not that he would eat much, since he looks like wet spaghetti or a tiny flea).

A couple of hours pass when the noise dies down again. Jules leans against the wall, sharpening a combat knife and glaring at Joel. He can't help but wonder where she got it from. He's pretending not to notice as he peers off into space, waiting for something to happen.

Jules breaks the silence and decides to interrogate him.

"How old are you?"

"Me?" His voice croaks.

"No, the coffee machine."

"18." He whispers so she can barely hear him.

She sniggers. "And what is it you do, noodle? Let me guess, something in retail? NO! Better yet, sales, call centre?"

He says nothing. She laughs and tells him how the crazy people outside could probably use him as a toothpick. "You will not piss yourself again, will you, noodle?"

Joel says nothing. Every question she tries, he responds to with an awkward stare and only speaks with his puppy dog eyes. Jules sighs and grows tired of his silence; she has picked up he hasn't said over five or six words since he found her.

She startles him by throwing her knife at the wall beside his face. He cowers. She laughs.

"I'm a delivery boy, for Devil's Corp."

"Ugh, I hate that company!"

"Why do you keep calling me noodle?" He trembles.

Jules looks him up and down for a moment, almost pitying his sorry excuse for an existence.

"That's what you remind me of. A wet noodle. No backbone and bland without seasoning. Are you unseasoned? What's your name, kid?"

"Joel," he utters.

She tilts her head, not having heard him.

"JOEL!" he shouts uncomfortably.

"Joel… hmm… Jules and Joel. Sound's like a reality show, don't you think? If only you were manlier, we could rule the roost."

Jules tells Joel the shouting and noises have died down;

they should make a move. She twists the knife out of the wall and explains she's going to go back to her station and stock up, then find the 'cunts' who ruined her warehouse spot.

"It isn't safe anymore. They broke the control box to the shutters. A cable tie won't hold them down for more than a few hours. I'm going back to my station. I'm getting more ammo than Guantanamo, to hunt those kids down who did this. They won't have got far—if they're not already dead. Then I've got me a serial killer to find."

"Why?" Joel asks abruptly. His sudden surge of confidence stuns Jules. "I don't know who they were. They are probably long gone, so why does it matter? You're a police officer, you could do anything you want, so why worry about kids? Why not just go after your serial killer?" Joel continues, suddenly regretting opening his mouth halfway through. "Isn't your job to protect the law?" he speaks matter-of-factly.

Jules picks him up, making him appear lighter than a plastic bag. She has him by the scruff of his bloody shirt. She bangs him into a wall. Their eyes meet—she's inches from his face.

"I *am* the law! They made it personal! You're right, I am a police officer. They broke the law when they broke and entered my facility and assaulted me. Now, they have to pay." She growls.

"But, didn't you do that first?"

Joel realises he shouldn't have said anything as Jules's face turns a violet shade. She throws him aside and aims her sidearm at him.

"This place was mine, my haven and my hide out. I will not let three jumped up little shits ruin that. You're going to help me track them." She pushes him toward the door.

***

151

The two flee town as quickly as they can to a police station where Julie gears up. It is apparent this was her ward; a few hours of dodging, diving and ducking as they proceed to her station. The temptation for Jules not to bust up the crime unfolding before her causes a deep brood in her face, almost like a tiger's low growl before a pounce. But she is a woman on a mission and won't let anything deter her.

Ready to leave town after suiting and booting, she gives Joel the option of leaving but he continues to follow her; the more time spent with her, the more Jules appears to ease around him. She even offers him a firearm.

"You're going to need this."

It stuns Joel at her choice to give him a firearm, but it's probably because she knows he'll never use it on her—he's too frightened, and won't know what to do.

The old police station isn't technically old since the refurb which made it plastic and shiny, but it still feels dated. Nothing like the pale and frosty tones surrounded by plastic and metal to make anyone feel scared of the place. It's nothing like the steel and concrete monoliths around it. They built it back in God-knows-when with stones and replaced with thick marble, almost impenetrable, for a small-town station. Not like the fortresses around the city with the cells armed with convoys, like a true prison. This one only has classic green brick cells to hold the odd drunk and disorderly pleb from the local boozer or occasionally to hold someone who was due to be transferred to a bigger place for something much worse.

It has pleasant offices though, as if they've had a woman's touch. Probably some middle-aged secretary who took pride in their job, or the fact they deluded themself that they were an important part of the force's integrity. The walls are as thick as a medieval castle and the windows almost as mean with bars on. There's no flicker of light within, and the thick wooden doors are closed.

"They've gone…" she mutters, pushing open the wooden doors and seeing all the metal cells open. Papers everywhere, chairs overturned. "He's gone." Her tone becomes more frustrated.

"Who?"

"The person… why I gave you that gun, lad."

She has her firearm raised so Joel raises his, trying to mimic everything she does from behind. Click. Jules flicks her torch on and finally switches off her radio, which has been blaring for hours regarding the pandemonium everywhere.

"You ever hear of the Gingerbread Killer?"

"The one in all the papers, and on the news? The one who likes redheaded kids?"

"Yeah, the one that's been killing every winter…" She etches forward, scanning. "Two years he's been at large. Two years we've been on his case and tonight, we got him. *I* got him. They said that son-of-a-bitch was *twisted* with what he did to his victims… I would know, I've been to a few of his crime scenes and fuck me I've seen some dark shit, but that stuff kept me up at night."

Joel's surprised anything could spook a bitch like that.

"Would definitely put you in therapy for life. I was going to be a hero, maybe even get sergeant. But now that sick cunt's loose and the world has gone to shit. So you can tell I'm a little tetchy."

No shit, thinks Joel. He prays he didn't say it out loud.

"Stay here!" Jules lowers her gun.

"W-w-w-wait… Where are you… going?"

"Relax, noodle, I have to do a perimeter check. Make sure he still isn't here. Track him. Then check my team for survivors."

Before he knows it, she's gone, and he's left shivering in the dark.

Jules always thought the law should be strict. It took a

real mental capacity and special type of person to uphold it. Not the ancy-fancy-PC-snowflakes that walk around helping old ladies cross the street. But the real door-smashing, floor-storming, ball busters. Once upon a time she was 'all by the book'. But something changed.

There's nothing worse than being told there's a killer on the loose than a killer being on the loose in a vast sea of people that have lost their minds and want to kill the first thing they see. It's all Joel can think about. He comes up with a million different 'I'm screwed' scenarios and needs feedback on every single one. It's a feeling like the head of a medieval mace, loose in his guts. The more he stares into the abyss, every shadow he makes out he thinks, *is that a person? What was that? Was that a whisper?*

He whimpers and turns abruptly to his side, pointing the gun into the darkness. Tonight, he has to stay in reality, otherwise he could get his head bashed in by a cop who thinks there's a new world order. Joel tries not to depart into the fantasy life that demands his attention at all the worst moments. Why does the mind try to shape thing into your worst nightmares during times of panic? Being a 'watcher' is the perfect job for a daydreaming introvert like Joel but not like this.

"BOO!"

Joel screams and falls back over an office wastebin only to have Jules cackling over him.

"It's clear, idiot."

She offers a hand out to Joel and he stares at her gesture for a moment, trying to bury the fear and the annoyance.

They spend a few hours in the station eating rations and discussing their theories on the events unfolding outside. She seems to have a heavy bias and prejudice view on society. Joel gets to know her. He wonders how someone with such ignorance could become a defender of law and order. There must be a need for control and deeply rooted narcissism within her.

Jules scrapes the spoon around her can slowly.

"You don't talk much, do you, kiddo?" She glances at Joel, then back at her can. "Probably for the best."

05:33 hours
Police Station, Pudsey

Jules wakes to the sound of what she thinks is banging pipes and veracious screaming; war cries echo around the station, and she rises tense as steel. Joel sits upright moments after. She tells him to stay put and stay alive as she goes to investigate the breach in her fortress.

Not again! No, this time the station has been attacked by the 'crazies' throughout the night.

"Noodle, remember that gun I gave you? This is now what it's for. I knew this was coming. First, they raid the stores and drain every chemist, bargain booze store and supermarket from here to Dover. Not on my watch."

She springs to life, but Joel cowers at the thought of defending the building.

Jules looks back. "Gutless."

She heads out and down the street. Joel shivers and quakes, slowly catching up. He approaches the station entrance, cautiously hiding behind a wall. A bullet ricochets off the outside light and he recoils.

Trigger-happy Jules is now being dragged knee-deep in a shootout with other survivors on the suburban street. Clearly, she has taken the law into her own hands, killing anyone she thinks is unfit for the new society. She calls out for Joel as he watches her; her face is cold and motionless, there's a sinister look in her eyes, like her actions haven't registered yet. The penny drops for Joel that Jules is a psychopath.

Someone like Jules has been waiting for something like

this—the Yorkshire apocalypse is her playground, and he needs to get out… fast. He witnesses her strike down the shooters.

She is skilled with a firearm, so he isn't sure who fired first. Two shots to every heart, it's like poetry, double tap, bang-bang same spot. She runs over to check their pulses, then hurries Joel past them and takes their car, much to his judgment. He looks down at the bodies and discovers her victims aren't much older than he is.

"We can't take a squad car, that's asking for trouble, so we need to be incognito," she says, getting in the driver's seat.

Joel stares at the dead as blood trickles out from various holes. He's traumatised.

"IDIOT! Are you just going to stand there and piss your pants? GET MOVING!"

He snaps out of it, dragging his feet over to the passenger side and gets in, where he sees a picture on the dashboard of one boy Jules shot. He is cosy with a girl and a small baby.

"They could have been anyone. Kids just looking for protection."

"They shot first," she calmly states, eyes fixated on the road.

She turns on the engine and drives. Jules promptly discloses she intends to find the military and stick with them after she has found the assholes who jinxed her hideout. Joel just glares at her, trying to fathom how she can be this cool after gunning down six people like she was cracking eggs. Logically, her plan seems like a sensible option to Joel (aside from trying to find Adam, Matt and Will, who Joel never got to properly acquaint himself with). Maybe he should have gone with them and had more chance of surviving? He is truly stuck and can't get away. Maybe Jules was right? He wouldn't have lasted five minutes. For their sakes, he hopes they might already be dead; it's much better than what's in his imagination, wondering what Jules has in store for them. He shakes his head at the horror.

Jules interrupts Joel's thought process as she slams on the breaks. "Well, I'll be fucking dammed."

She spots Adam, Will and Matt parked on the dual carriageway. They look to be in the middle of a heated discussion, staring at a map. Joel feels the hairs on the back of his neck stand up—his skin comes to life as goosebumps ripple over his body. Not in the good way like when he listens to his favourite song or relives that epic scene of his favourite movie, but the type of goosebumps when he hits the drop of a rollercoaster, and his organs feel like they're going to vacate through the wrong orifice.

Jules has found the boys she was looking for; she jokes she thought it would be like finding a needle in a haystack.

"What did I tell you, noodle? Someone is looking down on us today!"

"More like looking up," he mutters.

She pushes Joel out of sight and conspires with him to take the boys out. Alarm bells ring in his mind... this isn't good. She attempts to seek revenge over how things were left at the warehouse, much to Joel's protests and pleads. He tries to convince her they should leave to find the military like she said, but there's no negotiating with a psychopath. He can see it in her face... she's lost her mind, not that it was all there to begin with.

Joel understands the traits of a sociopath and a psychopath may seem similar. He always thought sociopaths have a less severe lack of empathy and guilt. It is thought sociopaths may form some deep bonds such as, possibly, with family, or fall in love. A psychopath cannot. While a sociopath would feel no guilt about hurting a stranger, they may feel guilt and remorse over hurting someone with which they share a bond. Joel has contended with many sociopaths in his life, his boss at Devil's Corp for a start, and most of his love affairs.

Psychopaths have always appeared to have no concern of the consequences in Joel's life. His first school bully, who's probably in prison now and maybe even this serial killer Jules caught—while a sociopath may learn to avoid consequences over time by reducing antisocial behaviour, a psychopath is aware of their actions and feels nothing.

Jules feels nothing. Case and point. She grows tired of Joel's incessant pleading and cowering, so she strikes him and discreetly follows the boys to wherever they intend to go. She wants to kill them and will do so without batting an eyelid.

When she gets the chance, she notices the boys have pulled over to a petrol station near a huge superstore. Joel awakens, groggily, and sees they have moved closer to the group of lads. It is up to Joel to save their lives.

Suddenly, Jules is foiled when Joel finally mans up and attacks her at the wheel. He's gone from wet spaghetti to hard-boiled-badass.

"I am not a fucking noodle," he says, ragging the steering wheel as she yells profanities.

Maybe Joel just tapped into that psychopath cortex after being knocked unconscious? Either way, he feels there are no consequences now. They spin out of control into the middle of the dual carriageway reserve. Thankfully, the boys are just the right amount of distance away to not be disturbed by this turn of events.

Jules's head is bleeding. She is seething with rage and turns her gun on Joel. He draws breath, knowing he has sealed his fate as he looks down the bleak abyss of the barrel.

Unexpectedly, they hear a horn blare from Joel's side of the car. A double-decker bus is speeding toward them. Jules's eyes widen, and she tries to scramble out of the car. The bus collides with another vehicle a mere 15-feet from their car. It smashes into Joel's and Jules's car, causing their vehicle to doughnut in the opposite side of the carriageway and down a banking, where Jules recovers just in time to watch the bus smash into Adam, Matt and Will's car.

It flips and skids away. The bus loses control and capsizes, then skids to a halt.

It has rendered Joel unconscious again. Jules realises the momentum of what has just taken place and switches her attention to Joel. He's laying with his bleeding head slumped against the window, lifeless.

CHAPTER 6:

SLASHING PRICES

January 2nd, 2012
07:16 hours
Beth
Outskirts of Leeds City Centre

The problem with hallucinations, after being knocked unconscious, is their unpredictability. Beth is in a dream though she's awake; something has dislodged, and she wonders if this is what having brain damage feels like—up is down, left is right.

She can hear the slamming of lockers and children laughing only a few moments before she realises she is in her own mind. It's bleak and echoes. Last night's events spark in the cogs of her mind. Darcy, Kieran, the massacre in her living room... it floods back.

It's a new morning, and her head is leaning on the steering wheel. She is in worse condition than before; it's apparent she's crashed her bus, which she could barely drive to begin with. She is covered in blood. Not all of it hers. Her body is beaten—cuts and bruises scattered everywhere. She is dirty and tatty, with one cheek half-melted down the steering wheel, accompanied by a pool of drool.

After coming to, Beth tilts her head back, groaning. She eventually struggles out of the wreckage by first unclipping the belt, falling into the smashed window against the hard concrete. She uses all her womanly might to climb out the driver's door and pull herself up through the doors on the bus's side—now, it's the top.

She clambers out of the unusual frame and emerges from the bus doors like a jack in the box. She drapes a lock of her golden hair behind her ear, and tries to crack her slender shoulders, jiggling the glass out of her bra. Beth's white cocktail dress is now torn, grey from the dirt and stained red with blood. She can't help but feel exposed and cold.

"Oh, my god… did I… was that *me*?"

Joel & Julie
Five Minutes Earlier...

Jules seems to have forgotten Joel struck her over the head, causing them to crash moments ago. She ignores Joel's lifeless body and exits the car, rubbing her head, wiping the blood from her cranium. She cracks her neck. A few seconds later, Joel's eyes blink open. Thankfully, he remains in the land of the living. His head is heavy and pounding like a bus hit him.

Wait... what happened?

He gasps and turns to see a space where Jules should be. Joel is on edge, thinking about whether she remembers being hit and assumes she does, but is merely biding her time. He cracks open his side of the door, which hangs on by a single hinge. It looks like a one of those tin cans you get in the reduced aisle.

Jules crouches down and takes him by surprise. She tells Joel to stay in the car and out of sight, and hisses that there is a girl in the distance standing on the bus.

"The little bitch must have been driving it," Jules snarls.

Joel watches a beautiful girl standing on a capsized bus and is struck by her statuesque-like posture. Jules informs Joel the only reason she has not killed him after his random burst of bravery was because it was ballsy; she tells him such an attitude will come in handy for when they need to repopulate.

"Repopulate?" Joel nervously laughs.

Jules watches Beth from afar like a hawk, anticipating her next move.

"We have to follow her. Bitch stole my kills and nearly killed me too... she has to go."

07:25 hours
Beth

Spring grass glimmers. It has a gentle glow from within. The streets and the roads are still deserted. On a normal day, the traffic would already fill up for the morning commute. Apparently half-past seven was the sweet spot.

Beth cannot see who she has collided with, she just sees an array of messed up cars she bulldozed through. Luckily, the light has made everything clearer. She realises what she's done, and she limps away, hoping not to have harmed anyone in the cars she smashed off the road. Before she has time to investigate, a fire ignites near the engine of the bus and she panics and tries to limp to the edge, but shouts with anguish and grips her side.

Her body is in pain, but so much of her hurts it's hard to locate where it is coming from. Her shoulders ache. Her back screams. Her knees are raw. Beth lifts a tear in her dress where her appendix should be and finds a shard of glass sticking out.

"WHAT?"

She looks more shocked than in pain. All she can think is thank God she had appendicitis, which led to its removal in high school. Why can't she feel it?

The fire becomes violent.

"Come on, you can do this."

Her nails distract her; two peach-covered claws have come off at some point and she seems more concerned about that.

FOCUS!

After three or four sharp breaths, she tugs on the glass and seers in agony. She makes her mind up to go elsewhere and suddenly she's back in the kitchen with her dad at four-years-old, smiling at him while he reads the paper.

PULL!

"Gahhhhh."

Darcy's smile flashes to Kieran's loving stare. Her voice becomes a symphony of dial up tones as she pulls the glass out of her side with little thought of the consequences. She looks back at the fire. It's going to blow.

JUMP DAMN IT. Off the bus she jumps, hobbling to a safe distance. Little does she know, her last surviving best friend is unconscious in one car only yards away.

Fresh blood douses the grey of the dress where she pulled out the glass. She stops, crying in anguish, because it's deeper than expected. It distracts her from the fire travelling across the bus, only for a moment, but a moment too late. Suddenly, it explodes, sending her flying. Beth has truly taken a battering. Her skin grinds against the concrete. She smacks her head and the sound of laughing children, the classroom bell and whipping noises fill her mind again. Disorientated, she spits blood and turns over, clutching her side. Her head rests against the concrete as she peers toward to flames.

Then out comes Darcy. But not as the blood-soaked demon that possessed her. She's different, almost pristine and angelic; a bright glow appears around her, and she smells like fresh linen. She walks toward Beth, and when she arrives she crouches. Her voice is muffled and soft. Another hallucination, Beth concludes. Her vision goes out of focus, trying to concentrate on what Darcy is saying. It sounds like 'get up, get up', but her body is in too much distress. Beth screws her eyes shut and tries to stand. Once she brushes off the near-death explosion, she flees the scene, passing car after car.

"Forgive me, I hope no one was in there."

She looks up at the parted clouds, hoping someone is listening.

Bleeding, she staggers down the road, which slowly forks away from the dual carriageway down a hill. Without looking back, she steps onto the bank, up the grass into the trees. Beth stops abruptly in her tracks. Unknown figures, turned away from her, are traipsing through the trees. She covers her mouth as not make a single sound. She has no idea who or what they are but isn't going to take any chances. Taking the break, Beth moves her hand from the wound. It's bad. She needs to get to safety. She's weakening.

She takes a different path out of the trees, avoiding the lost 'people'. Then, she emerges from the jungle and comes across a supermarket with giant iridescent letters across the front reading 'SUPERSTORE 24HR'. She's familiar with this place and she didn't know it was the one near where her parents used to live—among all the panic and frantic hell breaking loose, she lost her bearings. To her amazement, it is clear of any raids or attacks, or any signs of life.

"Huge empty car park, a few cars scattered scarcely, overturned trollies and decaying groceries. Yeah, people left in a hurry."

Beth can't quite see the entrance from afar, especially concussed, so she heads for the doors with a limp.

"I would have thought the first place people would go is the supermarket. And now I'm talking to myself. I'm crazy. I'm not daydreaming."

It's blood loss, she knows it even if she wants to deny it.

She searches the cars remaining in the lot, some perfectly parked, others left as if people ditched their rides in a hurry. Her stomach rumbles and she's sobering up, which means the hangover is coming. That's why she crashed the bus.

Beth licks her lips, devoid of all moisture. "Not now, cotton mouth." She groans, holding her side. "How can you be hungry, you're bleeding? And now you're seeing dead people and talking to yourself. Get it together, girl!"

She searches the abandoned cars for food or water, but most of the fresh produce has either been squashed and ruined by an external force or gone bad.

"What was this, a food fight?"

She peers into each one, hoping to find something... anything. Her already chilly hands cup against the even colder windows, fogging up the glass with her breath. Beth trembles when she sees empty baby seats with a pair of bloody mittens in them. She gives up hope and heads toward the entrance instead.

"Of course, it's barricaded."

It's blocked sufficiently with heavy items from the store, from both inside and out—piles of trolleys to garnish, too. Beth tries rattling the blockade, but it's thoroughly jammed. The chains jingle and the doors creek.

"Someone did this."

People may be hiding inside. She risks finding a way in.

"Hello? Is anybody in there? I mean you no harm. I'm not like the crazy people. I'm hurt and I need some help! Please, anybody?" she cries before figuring out how to get inside.

She looks up at the security cameras. A red light is blinking, which means their power is still working.

"Fine, let's play the hard way." She scowls.

It's a mess in the store as she dusts a spot on the glass with her palm. Products are scattered everywhere—people were here, that's a fact, but no one can be seen. She knocks and calls out again.

Clutching her side for dear life, Beth's blue eyes dart around for an idea.

"Think, Beth, think!" Wasting all that time on those

survival documentaries must have taught her something. "A-ha!"

She notices a stairwell on the east wall of the building, slightly out of reach. The ladder is broken. Beth is too weak and injured to push a car beneath it, so she moves a couple of steel bins instead and attempts to jump, missing the metal bar by her fingertips. Each takes its toll on her body and the deepening wound.

Will

The boys are squabbling over which direction to take, torn between their choices for action. When the bus smashes into the side of their car, Adam, Matt and Will are thrown around more aggressively than the last mint in a plastic container.

The bus flips on two wheels, capsizes, and slides into the central barrier while their car spins out of control and rolls upside down. The three appear lifeless. Adam, having not worn his seat belt, rolled through the backdoor as the weight of his body swung it open. Miraculously, he is the first to move. His bones crack like a glow stick.

"Something is definitely broken," he grumbles. "Holy Fuck!"

He is astounded. How has he survived when his arms are sprawled like the Rio de Janeiro Christ statue? He scoffs as his eyes fall to his body. He cracks his neck—a dislocated shoulder, but he still pulls Will from the wreckage (before popping it back in himself), who has already undone his own belt with a few tugs. Together, they get free of the car. Adam drags Will out with one arm and they topple over one another. Will's face is messed up.

There is an awkward moment between them; they are so close, they can feel each other's breath—nose to nose. Will thanks him and picks himself up. Matt remains lifeless and there is no time to waste as Adam notices fuel gushing toward a naked flame by the bus, which Beth is trying to escape. Her best friend is less than 20-yards away, and neither knows it.

Adam notices a blonde girl fleeing the scene but is too delirious to know if it's all in his head.

"I see dead people."

He rubs his face before Will shouts at Matt, who is unresponsive, snapping Adam from his trance. Will bravely crawls back into the car despite the ocean of fuel running and sets off running towards the fire. Will pulls him out anyway. The three roll and limp, diving into the bushes as the two vehicles ignite and blow up.

A tyre hurtles their way, so Adam dives on Will. They duck and drop Matt's unconscious body.

The boys exhale with relief; they're alive... for now.

07:35 hours
Beth
Supermarket Entrance

"Mother... butler!" Beth seethes as she smells the wet gravel under her bloody knees. They press into the concrete —another failed jump. "That. Hurt."

She tries over and over. Bins, jump, fall, repeat. She's growing weaker and more impatient, then loses her temper and kicks one bin over, accidentally tearing her dress further; the noise causes a ripple in the air, a starting gun echoing around the abandoned car park. *Oh no, speaking of guns... I left it in the wreckage!*

A murder of crows flocks from one tree, startling her. She spins, eyes darting across the horizon, praying no one heard. She curses because she is still in the same bloody clothes. So hungry, tired, scared, feeling emotional again.

Beth clings to her imagination about what lurks inside the store. Maybe they have chicken nuggets inside? The only thing she craves when hungover. Beth is absolutely entering that stage.

Her hallucinations are becoming progressively less amusing—the weak sun presses into her eyes, blurring her vision. She is becoming a phantom of herself, though she can't explain it, and her brain cannot process it. She's watching herself from several feet away—an out-of-body experience.

Beth sways. "It has to be the blood loss..." She watches as juice pumps out of her wounded side. Her body temperature drops and if she doesn't get inside soon, she knows she will freeze to death in a matter of minutes.

Beth looks toward the window and pictures all the food and a change of clothes.

"Fuck this," she declares, snapping out of it.

She picks up a metal trash can and launches an assault on the window with all her womanly might. The trash bin bounces back and attacks her. She falls. On her back, she kicks the bin out of frustration and hurts her foot. Beth tries to control her temper but screams loudly in thin air, not caring about who is listening or watching.

"FUCK ALL OF YOU!"

Her voice echoes through the trees. She realises what she's said, having not sworn for months, and checks to see if anyone is around, then gathers herself. In a last attempt, Beth tries to run and jump onto the bin she moved earlier that's slightly out of reach. She takes one last leap of faith and grabs the last rung, swinging like an acrobat.

"FUCK!" Her bloody hand slips and it forces her to twist with the other. "No, no, no, no, no!" She fights, pulling herself up onto the stairwell.

Beth laughs triumphantly, taking a moment to regain her strength. The painted white rails have turned red. There's so much blood... she's still bleeding, still alive by some miracle, but it's showing.

She glimpses herself in a vent, white as a sheet. Her vision is now doubling and blurry, her eyes are growing heavy. She battles to pry her eyelids open. Her heart is failing. She grips her side harder.

Beth potters around the rooftop, finding nothing sinister so far as to alarm her, so she intensely scavenges for a way in. She stumbles upon a hatch and opens it up, which leads to a set of stairs held up by wires. Beneath her is an office which she stumbles into, then explores her surroundings.

She sees nothing, no life forms, crazy people... nothing. She cautiously hobbles, literally like a zombie, until she wanders into a security room where she can look at CCTV. Still she finds nothing hopeful.

"Hello?" she calls out. "Is anybody there?"

Beth tilts her head as far as her balance will allow and stares at eight screens. People have been here; she can see on the cameras the store is a mess, they have set bedsits, food has been opened and left. It looks like people have taken their fair share, but probably never thought of it as looting. They were waiting. The store has been a resource. Their stomachs were probably empty. Detective Beth takes over.

"Well, what would you do? If you had to put clothes on the backs of your children and healthy food in their bellies?" she mutters to herself before scanning the rest of the computer equipment.

It's pretty standard: two computers, desks with wadded up piles of paper and a safe.

"Chocolate bars and coffee?" Beth blurts out. She puts her finger in the half-filled cup. She knows it's coffee from the smell. "Still warm," she utters.

Suddenly, an unsettling dose of dread seeps into her veins. She isn't alone, after all.

She looks back at the cameras, clicking the mouse a few times, trying to figure out if what she's seeing is real or a hallucination. A dark figure appears in the doorway behind her, which she can't see because her back is turned. She is gawking at the CCTV. She deduces people must absolutely be in the store somewhere because there's a little campfire still smoking, sleeping bags, empty bottles and food all around.

Beth is perplexed... *could they have left or been rescued?*

"Blood?" she says, narrowing her eyes at one camera.

There's a red substance on the floor, trickling all the way down the aisle. Her eyes widen. Suddenly, her senses are tingling; she can feel someone behind her, but she daren't look back. Without warning, in the blink of an eye, she catches something in her peripheral vision.

Beth is taken by surprise. A butcher's knife comes slashing down. She darts out of the way. It slices the controls. They spark.

Before her is a man, practically foaming at the mouth. Her brain goes into overdrive. In that frozen second between the standoff and fighting, her eyes flick from this brute to the cleaver he holds. It's bloody. Their faces are unreadable: no fear, no invitational smirk. He's wearing a store uniform and his name tag reads: THOMAS. STORE MANAGER. He appears to have turned into a complete psychopath, and Beth can see it in his face. She is staring madness in the eye, probably because of his seclusion, she assumes. Though it's only been a day, she argues people have gone insane for less.

He yells something unintelligible and Beth screams. He charges. She dodges the attack and tries to leave the room, but he grabs her leg and slashes her ankle. Beth makes the worst noise.

She becomes a sniffling wreck and tries to crawl away from him, knowing she is going to die any second, maybe from heart failure at this point. It's a miracle she's made it this far. Those heavy eyelids take over and droop once more. He is about to kill her—raising his arm, grasping the butcher's knife. It shines like the north star. A girl interjects at the last split second, blocking his strike with a shovel. The sound of the two metals colliding is supersonic.

Beth welds her eyes shut, using her palms for protection until the girl renders her enemy motionless on the ground. She smashes Tom over the head with the shovel from the gardening department.

"Take my hand, it's okay," the girl whispers.

She blinks her eyes, allowing her lashes to flutter more majestically than that of the wings of a butterfly. Her eyes are spellbinding. Her left eye is a rapturous shade of cerulean blue, much more appealing than even Beth's, with a hazel-auburn rondure sphere orbiting in her right eye. Each one holds a coruscate gleam that enhances their beauty. Her ears are pierced with golden hoops concealed by dark blood orange-coloured waves, further enhanced by highlights of washed out pastel.

Yet, her attire is simple enough and smells fresh, as if brand new—there is not a speck on her, not a blemish on her skin. She's obviously not an employee.

Beth's saviour introduces herself as Claire while Beth is shaking uncontrollably.

"So many wounds, it's almost too much."

Claire tells her to stay put and promptly returns with lots of medical supplies. Beth can no longer take the force of being stood up, so she collapses into Claire, shivering. Beth should be dead, but Claire informs her the adrenaline is keeping her alive. Her ankle is bleeding too now, forming a pool of blood.

Claire apologises for what she's about to do, and she drags Beth out of the security office and tries to haul her up on a table.

"This may hurt some more, I'm so sorry."

Claire gives Beth the medical attention she needs and

injects her various times. She's too weak to ask what they are, losing control of her body and consciousness. Claire calmly tells Beth she is going into shock. She needs to be sedated.

Those words echo through her as the lights fade.

***

As Beth rouses from a heavy slumber, her eyes crack open, registering an emergency. She is first aware of the coolness of the air and its loamy fragrance unlike the air outside. There's a light breeze from a fan, plus the heat from computers and humming of the machines. The table is lumpy as if she's on a bed of soil. Her clothes are damp, too.

Beth is disorientated and has a nasty headache; suddenly, she feels violently ill and vomits yellow bile on the floor. She coughs and tries to make herself aware of her surroundings. *What a sour taste, ugh!* It's an office, and she's hooked up to a drip. It's painful to move because most of her body is bandaged. She's in her underwear.

"What the...? It's a miracle!"

Her ankle is fixed, her side and the rest of her injuries have been taken care of. There's a huge bandage around her torso and she can feel the stitches. Something has miraculously cleansed the dried blood and dirt from her skin.

"Oh, hello," Claire speaks chirpily, thrilled Beth is awake. She tells her new friend she had to give her a sedative, which explains her sickness. "I really thought I was going to lose you, and I hadn't even met you properly. You lost A LOT of blood. I'm actually surprised you're up so early. Most of my patients are out for a full day."

"You did this... how?" Beth says, thankful yet surprised.

"I used to be a part-time trainee for an ambulance service."

173

"*Used* to be?"

Claire giggles and says she isn't anymore. The world has ended, of course.

Beth stares blankly for a moment. "Did you say the world has ended?"

Claire pretends to ignore her response and places a pile of fresh clothing at the end of the makeshift bed. It smells fresh.

"And here's a bucket of hot water, among other personal items from the main shop floor." Claire winks. "You should stay here, even if just for the evening, until you're feeling better."

Beth thanks her for saving her life. It all seems a little much, but she just wants to know what happened. She struggles to sit up.

"Oh…" Claire sighs and tries to fathom the words to explain the past few days. She firstly apologises for the man who attacked her. "I've been hiding from that maniac store manager for a day or two—it feels like forever so I don't know. He lost his fucking marbles and took over the whole store as his kingdom. I was stuck in here with him playing cat and mouse, hide and seek. But it's over now."

Much to Beth's disapproval and horror, Claire tries to be upfront and honest about who she is.

"I'm not like that. What's going on out there?"

She realises the best way to tell her would be just to show her 'on one condition'. Claire asks Beth to rest until she can walk on her own again, then she will show her the CCTV footage until she's all caught up.

***

Beth wakes sometime later, with Claire still near her. She startles awake, because sleeping had become a dangerous act.

Her heart beats fast, and there is a buzzing in her ears. The exertions of the night were a marathon of erratic problem-solving, blood, gore and running. It feels like a bad dream, but it's more and more apparent this is her life now. Never has Beth longed so much for the sweet embrace of her crappy duvet.

An existential dread sets in that this is real. This day will pass as if she is hungover, but not from drink, not anymore.

She swings her legs off the table as Claire watches her with a little smirk. The first thing she asks is if there are others in the store. Claire looks away, disheartened. She says she and the manager were in a group hiding together, but Claire is the only one left alive.

"You should eat and drink," she finishes.

Claire hands her some orange energy soda, a bottle of water and a sandwich on a paper plate accompanied by some crisps. Beth can tell she's gone to the extra effort.

"Electrolytes and fuel." Claire ties up her ginger locks. "I guess you can see for yourself now. You won't need to worry about Tom. I put him in another room and tied him up, but it could be better. If you feel up to it later, you can give me a hand."

Beth nods, already indulging in her sandwich. She's trying not to devour the whole thing in less than a minute.

She waits a few hours before she can hobble to the security room on her own, and as promised she tells Beth to brace herself, because she will not like what she sees. She plays the surveillance from the past 48-hours.

175

CHAPTER 7:

FLASHBACK

December 31st, 2011
Claire
Supermarket
1 Hour, 2 Minutes Until New Year...

The automatic doors glide open, and Claire is graced with the presence of... no one. The store is empty! Throw in some food, bright lights, air-con, and wholesale goods and BAM! The supermarket exists.

Leeds is a society plagued by hunger, even if it was the end of the world, in the literal and abstract sense. Somebody is always yearning for something more; that's why supermarkets were invented. Humans are social animals feeling bound to social rules—they need to thrive around others. It's said in Leeds, one in five people lacked adequate nutrition, whether that's behavioural or environmental remains a mystery.

Claire can almost hear the howling wind from the entrance, drifting down the isles to the docking station below. The tap of her footsteps accompanies her, echoing loudly momentarily aesthetically pleasing, though a sound she isn't familiar with. Claire isn't used to her steps being the only thing she can hear. There's always hustle and bustle drowning them out.

She looks to her left. *No uniformed guard. Why would anyone want to be here, anyway?* she thinks. *It's an hour until New Year; security is probably off celebrating with his wife and kids, or maybe on the town blowing or drinking whatever he's earned.* She guesses that's why they call it pissing it up against the wall. He's had nothing to do but stand as a door greeter, anyway.

Claire has underwear more intimidating than most guards. She always thought it was because humans are docile and cooperative that the system has been in place for so long, and it's because of this that the system is redundant. She'll tell you food can easily be removed from the monetary system to enable the world to eat freely. *With better role modelling, the new societal expectations could be adopted, and we could follow those patterns instead.*

She breaks her train of thought. The depleted number of souls sends shivers down her spine as she moves inward toward the fruit and veg. The place is enormous, illuminated in florescent white, giving everything a gleaming television-ad filter.

"Not surprising that barely anyone is here, it's 11 o'clock. Everybody is fucked up in a gutter or spending it with their loved ones," she whispers to herself. "And yet my arsehole brother sends me on an errand here."

Claire looks to her right and sees a couple of customer assistants, one scanning items like they're about to end it all, and the other miserable fucker is filing her nails. Claire locks eyes with the boy at the checkout and thinks, *sad bastard.* The only thing that stands between her and everyone else in the aisles opposite are the travelators to the lower floor.

Anyone here on this day must have a story to tell. Who would do a food shop one hour before midnight on New Year's Eve? Those people either need medicating or don't have a lot going on.

It's as if they see pizza, ice-cream and staff as much the same. Products—things to gain and the means to gain them. It's a disconnect of sorts, a brain-blip. If these people met the cashier at a barbecue, they'd greet them, ask about their kids, enquire after their health and make jokes. But here there's a cold rudeness that comes from seeing them in the same way as an inanimate object.

'I pay for this food, so I pay for you. You are a living robot, a possession that serves me...'

Anyone who ever worked in retail would agree.

Claire is an exception to this rule, though; she talks to everyone as if she's met them at a family barbecue. She likes a real chat, the exchange that is kind and emotionally generous. It's why she loves Americans. She travels to New York or Florida whenever she can. Americans aren't afraid to start a full-blown conversation in the supermarket, ask someone what meal they're having at the restaurant or stop a stranger in the street to compliment them and ask them, 'where did you get that fabulous get up? Go you!'

But no, not British people, even as one herself she always thinks there is a certain coldness about them. They will barely make small talk unless it's complaining, shouting profanities at each other or getting drunk. Only then will they share their life story to never see the person again.

'Hello, I'm fucked up so I'm drinking! Would you like a shot?'

'Oh my God, yes, I'm fucked up too!'

'Let's be best friends, spend hours in the bathroom talking shit, take 20 selfies and never talk to each other again.'

That's usually how it goes. Claire might as well be an alien.

Look at them, she thinks, gawking at the girl cashier blowing an obnoxious bubble from her gum and scrolling on her phone. So involved with their advancing technology and noses in their phones, which people can only then find their online warrior persona to complain about the state of the economy, price of fish, or even disagree with someone's opinion for the sake of it. Despite Claire's irksome criticisms of people, it doesn't matter if they're black or white, old or young, or want to categorise themselves. This nature and love of community inspired her to become a paramedic, helping those who often cannot help themselves and discovering all walks of human life.

Claire's heart weeps for the staff as she knows the bane of working in retail (since she owns a shop). Still pissed off her brother is making her do a midnight stock run so close to the hour, she wonders why he can't get off his bony arse and do it.

Who even stays open on New Year's Eve?

Her brother simply told her they would make a killing, being one of the few shops open 24-hours, plus they need the money. Times are hard after the collapse of the American banks. If they remain the only place open so close to the student flats, they could sit on a motherlode of sales: kids running out of booze, party-goers needing cigarettes, grabbing that last piece of bunting for the living room. Claire can't stand it; she thinks it's an excuse for zombie-like 'piss heads' to 'fuck up' her store—a store left to them by their mother.

She heads down the vacant isles toward the alcohol, curious if it's been ransacked.

"Fucking panic buyers taking all the booze, the beans and the bog roll. We should limit idiots on this stuff, it's not like there's a pandemic!"

23:00 hours
Mitch

Mitch works as a Saturday boy for the supermarket and has done since he left school two years prior. Unlucky for him, too many have called in sick tonight to cover the graveyard shift. *Isolation, vomiting, another isolation, the list goes on.*

Nobody wanted it after the manager, Tom, received a memo from head office about their new policy, stating that the shop be open for 24-hours during this winter period. Ever since the scare-mongering of an impending pandemic, government legislation has stated they must remain open to supply the vulnerable. Mitch is regretting offering to cover.

But it's not like he has any friends, anyway. The reason he took this job was to stop himself from blowing his brains out. At least this way, he gets three minutes of exercise and scarce human interaction. Though, he would much rather be at home playing video games, deluding himself in his online gaming with people he's sure are his real pals.

Startled, a customer dumps their products at his till. Mitch glances over at the entrance and watches a beautiful redhead enter. He locks eyes with her. She looks miserable. Mitch thinks, *sad bitch.*

BEEP. BEEP. BEEP

It's the only sound drowning out his colleague on the till behind him. She's filing her nails, and Mitch wishes she would at least make herself useful and re-stock something. They haven't had hand sanitiser on display since Christmas eve!

She sighs and tells Mitch she's bored. She's going out for a 'ciggy'.

23:03 hours
Val

Valarie. The loudest girl in every room and the type of girl who will pretend to want to help you, but in reality, only wants the gossip. Every smile that lights up her features is wrong. She runs on cold malice and nicotine instead of genuine affection. Perhaps she was a baby left to cry, or has a personality disorder (though the doctors cannot fix or diagnose it)? Either way, she has as much empathy as a

181

medieval mace.

She is common as they come. If the streets of the worst parts of Leeds had a baby, she would be the afterbirth of said child. She speaks with a harsh Yorkshire accent—rough as a cat's tongue, and talks more shit than the newspapers.

Most definitely, she's the bitch that peaked in school. The one that is so popular with the girls and the boys that everyone thinks is going to do so well in life, but in reality, is actually one shag away from another baby, benefits and council pop. Her conversations are buoyant, intended to be heard. There is an unsatisfied thespian in her. When she realised life was as good as it was going to get for her, she panicked and enrolled in a course at the university, desperate to inspire a spark of something new now that her dreams of being a model and marrying a footballer have faded. She left school with a BTEC level two in hair care, but instead of using it, she wound up shagging some boy who now lives with his mother in Bradford, and giving birth to two of his offspring, selling pyramid schemes on social media to 'old friends'.

Everyone knows she got around back then. It was her most favourite badge by which to identify herself.

On every subject, Val is opinionated and if you don't agree, she's not angry but she does pity those who cannot understand the 'correct' way to think about things. She doesn't really have many friends either, mostly neighbours on the council estate who will happily trade her for a sausage roll. Yet, in her delusion, she considers them acquaintances while also twitching the curtains to report most of them to social services. In any crisis, she will happily sit and watch drama unfold, but act like she was the hero… anything for her 15 minutes—born with the ability to harbour a grudge.

Val slumps off her adjustable chair at her disorganised till and walks away from Mitch.

Val can't help but think Mitch is dull, and the only reason she agreed to cover the night shift is because she needs the money for her trip to Marbella in three days. Away from the kids. Away from it all. Government pay cheques only stretch so far. He is definitely one shift away from blowing his brain out.

"M'off for a ciggy."

Val convinces herself tonight isn't New Year's Eve but a pretend version. Hers begins the minute her cheaply polished toes step off the runway abroad. She walks past the redhead who just came in and tells her to sarcastically 'run while there's still time'. The woman, Claire, looks at her in confusion before smirking and carrying on.

Val lights a cigarette behind the entrance, out of sight from the CCTV camera, where her manager Tom will probably wank over her, anyway. Sicko. She walked in on him once in the office, touching himself over a bikini shot of her downloaded from her Facebook page. About 20% of her reaction was flattery—he thought she was 'wank material worthy'—even if he was a fat, balding slob in his late 20s. The other 80%, though disgusted, found this an opportunity to blackmail him into giving her the two weeks off for Marbella. She could have done anything, including asking for a rise or promotion, but she settled for Marbella.

Despite being one of this supermarket's longest and most loyal girls, Val wants nothing more than to fuck-this-place-off and pursue her dreams. To everyone around her, she acts as if she's given up.

She enjoys the puff on her cigarette, letting the cold air fill her nose. She can already hear the distant fireworks beginning, but the fun has only just begun.

23:03 hours
Claire

A cashier filing her nails passes Claire. "Run while there's still time."

Claire looks on in confusion, then smirks, appreciating the humour in the self-pity. She can't help but think she's crawled out of the gutters of the wrong end of town.

Claire heads toward the alcohol section and her suspicions are correct, they've been robbed.

"Fucking panic buyers taking all the booze, the beans and the bog roll. We should limit idiots on this stuff, it's not like it's a pandemic," she mutters.

All that's left are a few crates and two boys arguing over them. Claire wonders if 'nail file' girl will have any in the back. Maybe she can sweet talk her, one retail chick to another?

23:15 hours
Harry & Dylan

"Craft beer? What the fuck is craft beer? That's all that's left?" Dylan grimaces at the small, colourful can in his hand. It's almost as cold as the air itself.

"It's like any other beer, but more annoying. It's what happens when beer starts peacocking and says 'look at me, I'm different'," Harry says, half-interested while the glow from his phone screen lights up his face.

Click, scroll, click, click.

"Just put it in the trolley. We can't be picky. It's still alcohol, right?"

Dylan nods, unsure.

"Then put it in." Harry's voice lowers, imitating what he ignorantly thinks is a slow person.

"This is why Aunt Shelly doesn't love you!" Dylan bites

184

back.

"Aunt Shelly thinks it's VE day!"

The boys are hoping to get everything done on their list and get back before the countdown, which means time is of the essence, despite being disappointed there is hardly any booze left.

"We should have gone to the local like everybody else," Dylan mutters.

"No, that's where everyone will go. Besides, we are *this* close to a pandemic... avoid people." Harry gestures and tells him he heard it was dead here. "Like, everybody I know of is sick. I just found out this place was open tonight and thought we would hit the motherlode."

"Look around, dipshit! This place is a ghost town—they took everything with them!" Dylan points out, "Government just wants to scare people. People are sheep and our PM is the shepherd."

They scan the wide aisles and find the odd can, random bottles and crates left standing strong.

Harry sighs. "Is that a half-eaten sandwich from fresh-to-go?"

"Pigs!"

"We should just grab everything; everyone back at the party is waiting for us." Dylan tries to keep thing upbeat.

Harry loads the crates into the trolley when Dylan notices something out of the corner of his eye at the foot of the aisle. He looks up and finds the '10/10 bird' looking at them. Harry sarcastically tells Dylan not to help. He strains when Dylan smacks him to check out the chick at the bottom.

Harry nods in approval as she walks off. Dylan says it's Harry's ugly mug that scared her off, and the boys argue over her while trying to stockpile any beverages they can.

23:16 hours
Claire

Claire sees the boys ogling her from the top of the aisle, so she grimaces and tries to focus on the task at hand, find 'nail file' girl and get the booze from the back. She rummages in her bag to check if she has any extra cash. Maybe she can bribe the cashier? She looks like the girl who wouldn't say no to shiny things.

Claire isn't paying attention, scuffling between the mascara and glasses in her hand, when she collides with a middle-aged woman. Claire jumps and apologises profusely for her ignorance.

23:16 hours
Linda

Another lonely New Year's Eve brings Linda to her favourite pastime, wondering the isles in search of salvation. Divorced and alone, it's always a gloomy time of year for her—take an older fitness TV personality, shortened, and add a little weight, make her hair messy with visible roots, and add some freckles and crow's feet. Make the bone structure ill defined. Then you would have Linda. Linda doesn't care that much about her appearance anymore. She has accepted she's led a good life, married twice with beautiful kids grown up (now with their own kids travelling the world).

They say middle age is a fork, and people take either one path or the other. One takes the person onward to further maturity, an outward facing mentality geared to help others. The other is a path to narcissism, an inward facing mentality that puts the self first and others a distant second. The first path is a life that makes the most of the experiences, helping the next generation and the community. It is one that merges and builds on the loving relationships in life and allows the person to become a role model.

This is Linda. She was on the cusp of early retirement and had plans of taking up motorbike lessons and jumping from planes; she even thought about enrolling in an art course at university, now she would have all the time in the world after working so hard.

Ten years ago, Linda wouldn't have been able to fathom the idea of being alone on a night like tonight. But fuck it, a bottle of champagne and a midnight snack or microwaved misery will have to do.

Her friend is sick, and Linda thought it would be a delightful treat to surprise her despite it being so late. A minor part of Linda still can't handle the idea of being sat doing nothing, at home alone; it's a niggling feeling of taking the path of helping others instead of the one to suit yourself, but nobody wants to be sick on New Year's Eve.

She turns the corner of the next aisle and accidentally collides with a young girl.

"Heavens, what a silly mistake, pay attention, Linda!" she says, flustered as a gorgeous redhead apologises profusely.

Linda tries to laugh it off as they make small talk; she inspects the girl and is instantly reminded of herself 40 years ago.

"My, you are gorgeous, aren't you?" she says, throwing the girl off.

23:25 hours
Claire

"Oh, goodness, thank you. I don't know what to say! I don't feel that way!"

"You remind me of me a hundred years ago." They laugh. "Gorgeous red hair and milk bottle skin. What's a girl like you doing here; shouldn't you be with friends?"

"I'm just on a bottle run. I have something going on back at my shop… house… well, my shop is my house…" Claire awkwardly giggles.

Claire loses track of time chatting to the nice middle-aged lady who she nearly knocked over moments ago. She jokingly exclaims she didn't think anyone would be alive. The lady chuckles and agrees.

"Most youths will be dead in a ditch somewhere right about now."

Claire asks if there is anything she can do to help since she nearly bulldozed her.

"I won't take no for an answer." Claire playfully links the lady's arm and walks her down the main aisle. "What it is you desire?

Claire can tell the woman looks hesitant but then admits she's being a 'sad old cow' and wants a meal for one and a bottle of 'champz' to take the edge off. She tells her there is no shame in that but explains the booze aisles are completely empty, then reveals she is going to find the store assistant who is outside smoking and ask her for the pallets in the back (as she knows there will be a bottle with both their names on).

"How can you be sure?"

"I run a shop in the centre of town and my stupid brother made me 'stock-up' before the countdown. Knowing him, he's probably planning some cheesy surprise while I'm out."

She rolls her eyes and scoffs. Claire's new friend looks onward and sees two boys rolling their trolley with the last of the alcohol toward the tills. The boy cashier waits aimlessly.

23:31 hours
Val

"Shit."

Val looks at her phone. She's way over her five-minute break and prays Tom isn't scoping the CCTV. Then she thinks *fuck him, I'm the one covering this shitty shift, it's not like anyone needs me*.

Suddenly, she hears screaming and shouting in the darkness. She can't see beyond half the parking lot. Val squints and then checks her phone again.

"That's odd, there's still less than half an hour left? What's with all the screaming?"

She watches one other customer in the car park packing away their shopping. They're about six or seven cars from her, and scattered around the lot. One of those cars belong to the staff. Mitch is supposed to be giving Val a lift home when their shift finishes.

Val goes to check social media but has no signal.

"Fuck sake, every single year networks get so flooded and no one can get through to anyone."

She marches back inside. Nobody is to be seen apart from Mitch. *Ew, why is he staring?*

23:35 hours
Mitch

Mitch is gawking at Val at the entrance and wondering, *why-the-fuck is she staring? Dumb bitch.* He clicks his company radio and tells her to do something useful, so she flips him off and flounces off toward the kiosk where they stock cigarettes and magazines.

He swivels in his chair, ignoring the insult, sighing.

Then he clocks probably the only other two lads in the giant superstore, pushing their trolley filled with the last of

189

the booze toward him.

23:37 hours
Harry and Dylan

Harry grunts. They have ten minutes to get back to the house party where Dylan can unload all the supplies (since he broke his back putting it in the trolley).

They approach the cashier who is swivelling on his chair at the till, obviously in a world of his own. An awkward silence ensues as Dylan unloads the bottles one at a time. The cashier waits for them to finish. Harry tries to break the tension by joking bout how shit it must be to work New Year's Eve.

"I can see why they made him work," Harry whispers to Dylan.

23:35 hours
Val

Val's radio blows a raspberry as she picks up the static. She knows it's her colleague, Mitch. She rolls her eyes and answers.

"Go do something useful!" he jokes.

She flips him off; she'll likely just flick through a magazine before Tom comes from the manager's office and rips her a new tit.

Val is about to settle and read about her favourite celebrities when two females approach her for help.

23:37 hours
Claire

Claire has finally found 'nail file' girl after searching for her everywhere at the magazine kiosk, doing fuck all, of course. She aptly jumps at the opportunity to explain she and her new friend are looking for last-minute supplies.

"If you catch my drift," she adds.

Claire flashes a 20-pound note, raising her eyebrows.

'Nail file' girl says she doesn't have drugs on her and if her boss, Tom, sent Claire, he will have to do better than last time.

"Oh, no. I meant there is no booze left. I was wondering if they have any in the back? Me and Linda here need to get our freak on!"

Claire rubs the note in front of her and the two exchange a subtext. Val flicks a page of the magazine, legs crossed. She raises an eyebrow and blows a bubble on her gum, letting it pop. It echoes across the store.

23:40 hours
Val

Val dwells on the offer regarding emergency booze in the back and then shrugs. She tells them to wait over by her checkout where 'that dead-behind-the-eyes geek' is, and where two boys are standing.

Val passes the other counters, and the boys check out her arse. Playfully, she winks while walking toward the warehouse.

23:42 hours
Harry & Dylan

Harry gives up trying to make small talk with the gormless cashier as he slowly scans.

"What, man?" Dylan grunts, rubbing where Harry has jabbed him.

"Mate, you put your cock in that, it'll fall off. I know her type."

"Wait here," Val says as she shoves the money down her bra.

Dylan smiles at the youngest girl and says, "Hi."

Claire waves and smiles politely.

"Where are you lovely ladies headed tonight?" Dylan grins a little more than creepily.

23:45 hours
Val

A large empty warehouse. Scary, no lights—Val fucking hates it in here, plus it's freezing. If she wants to get to the pallets, she will have to walk through the chiller. She debates coming back to inform the ladies they are fresh out of booze and keep the £20. But something in Val's better nature calls to her when she sees a box of red wine gleaming. She bends down to pick it up and suddenly, fireworks outside startle her, causing her to drop the crate and smash one.

"Fuck!"

She watches it bleed through the white box, the same as a bullet hole spreading across a white shirt. She checks her phone, wondering if she missed the countdown, when a flickering light toward the back of the warehouse catches her attention and she sees a figure turned away. It's just standing there. They must have walked in from the delivery station.

"I'm not dealing with pissheads," she says to herself. Something isn't right, and she can feel it. Val isn't book smart, but she's street smart and knows when to smell a rat. "How-the-fuck did he get in here?"

Val calls out, telling the stranger he can't be back here in the warehouse, as it's for employees only. She cautiously walks to him, phone back in her pocket and a bottle at the ready. She tightens her grip and swallows the lump in her throat.

"Like fuck am I spending the countdown dealing with this arsehole!"

23:55 hours
Mitch, Claire, Linda, Harry & Dylan

Mitch has finally finished scanning (which took all of ten years!).

"How are you boys paying?" Mitch looks at them unenthused.

"Hazza!" Dylan prompts.

"Thank Christ, I thought we were going to have to camp here."

Harry, finally relieved he's finished, throws cash. He's pissed they are going to miss the countdown. Harry mutters, wondering if he could have gone any slower. Dylan tells him to ease up, and it doesn't matter if they miss it.

"We can crack open two cold ones of the pompous beer outside and watch the fireworks."

Dylan asks the ladies if they would like to join. Claire tries to not be disgusted by Dylan's flirtatious efforts and grins.

"Sorry, I must get back to my brother in the shop and my friend, Linda is joining me."

Linda double-takes in confusion and laughs. Claire winks at her. Harry snaps and tells Dylan how angry he is at the delay. This should have been done earlier.

"Cuz! If Mamma D ain't of gotten the Flu, we would have," Dylan passionately bites back

"That's why we are at Aunt Shelly's!"

"You leave my mother out of this, cuz." Harry points his finger, and the girls become uncomfortable.

Dylan goes a little too far and starts announcing a few

homes truths. He sucks his teeth, avoiding being shown up in the presence of the ladies.

"Since your girlfriend left you on New Year's Day four years ago, You've been fixated on making ever year some big fucking statement to get over her. Four years man, when's it gonna give?"

Now Harry is the one red in the face as the girls become uncomfortable.

"New Year's Eve, New Year's Day, Christmas, whatever! They're just a single day on a calendar, it means nothing, it's merely one day to the next like all the others."

"Orite, cousin," growls Harry.

"It's meaningless. Why do people have to wait until this day to decide they want to get off their arses and change the world or themselves? Any other day is as good as the rest."

Claire tries to not be impressed by Dylan's logic. She raises an eyebrow.

Mitch, Linda, and Claire stand awkwardly as everything falls silent. Dylan reels it in by apologising.

"One more time, how about that drink, ladies, out front, five mins?" Dylan tries effortlessly and despite being tempted, Claire is strong against his advances, even if he is cute. "Suit yourself, Red."

Dylan cracks open the coldest craft ale can and it fizzes over as the sound of the lid hitting the pressed floor echoes. Harry leaps back to avoid the spray.

"Cuz, do you mind? You nearly got that shit on my sports gear."

"You shop in markets," Dylan says matter-of-factly, while sipping up and winking at Claire. Claire playfully ignores Dylan's next comment and grabs Mitch's attention.

"Zombie Boy… Mitch," she says, reading his name badge. "Where's nail file girl? Like, what's taking so long?"

Mitch is about to radio for Val when a slam and crash on the window behind the group cause them to jump out of their skins. Dylan drops his bottle, and it rolls away.

"Aw what!" Dylan wipes himself down.

"What-the-fuck was that?" Claire stutters, hand on chest.

Suddenly, fireworks burst outside. Harry looks at his watch and scowls at Dylan. They only have five minutes left.

"A drunken man is banging on the window; it happens every year," Mitch says.

Linda slowly approaches and thinks the man is in destress. He is crying. It's getting louder, more urgent. Mitch apologises to his customers and says he will tell the man to move on.

"You should stay put for a few moments," he adds.

Harry grunts impatiently and tells Dylan to just leave with him as he wheels the trolley away. But, as Mitch moves from the till, unexpectedly, another person smashes into the window, this time blooded and crying, followed by another and another.

"Does *that* happen *every* year?" Claire questions.

The group freeze, dumbfounded. Linda takes Claire's hand. Shivers travel down her spine, attacking every nerve. Five minutes ago, they were all strangers who wouldn't look twice at each other in the busy street, none of them realising this could be the beginning of the end.

One has made it into the entrance. They look hurt, and slip on the beer spillage and cling to Mitch. She is begging him to lock the doors, announcing "the entire world has gone mad", but Mitch doesn't understand. He panics and radios his manager, Tom to come immediately. They have a... weird situation.

Civilians are continuing to bang on the window, unaware of the entrance further afield.

"Fuck sake." Harry mutters, now revealing a pouch of tobacco, "If we're gonna be stuck here, might as well roll."

A scream, coming from the warehouse, turns heads

toward the east side of the store, causing Harry to drop his filters. Val is calling out for Mitch's help; she has her back toward them and is reversing slowly. In front of her is a deranged man, creeping forward and forcing Val to inch nearer the others. Dylan sniggers and cracks open another beer bottle. This time, the other customer becomes more hysterical, and she bravely snatches the beer out of Dylan's hand. She smashes the bottle against the bagging area to create a weapon. She runs at Val's attacker and drives the bottle into his face.

23:52 hours
Val

Val is growing increasingly impatient with the customer who has wound his way into the warehouse. He isn't responding to any of her name calling. She goes from timid trepidation to irritated. She sighs and radios Tom to tell him there is a situation and he better come fix it. They don't pay her enough for this shit. She puts her arm on the man's shoulder to turn him around gently, but recoils in horror when she sees his cheek is missing.

"Oh my fucking God! Are you okay?" She can see through to his teeth—repulsive white flesh and muscle are exposed. "TOM, YOU NEED TO GET DOWN HERE NOW!"

The man lunges for her. Val screams and falls back, hitting her head. She gets up, but it's a struggle and tells the freak to back off. Every step toward her is a step back for Val, so she radios Tom again, aggressively. Val whimpers she doesn't want to hurt him anymore than he already is, and they should call 999.

She aims the bottle at him, but the monster knocks it out of her hand, much to her amazement. She squeals, working her way back toward the warehouse flaps to the shop floor.

196

The creature is drooling with a blood thirst in his eye.

She backs out onto the shop floor, calling out for Mitch. Out of nowhere, a frantic customer snatches a beer from Dylan and smashes it on the bagging area. She runs and nearly knocks Val out of the way; the girl drives the broken glass bottle through the monster's face, or what's left of it. Val gasps and covers her mouth as she watches the man fall.

Is he dead?

23:56 hours

The emotionally unstable customer snarls at Mitch to lock the front entrance and lower the shutters. Claire is too scared to move; they are all in shock. *Did this woman just kill a man in cold blood?*

"What-the-fuck is going on?"

Harry demands an explanation, looking at Dylan who has his beer-coated hand clasped over his mouth having forgotten about his soaked threads. In a moment of clarity, the woman says she can't explain it. She tries to, but doesn't, but does in some sense.

"People suddenly started fighting, looting and rioting in the streets. It's been all over the news for the last hour, and they're eating each other, tearing one another to shreds. It's those things out there." She points to them banging on the window. "They're dead, they're all dead, but then they're not."

"They don't look dead to me! Dead people don't make noise and bang on windows yo!" Dylan panics, backing up.

The water works begin the same as the morning sprinkler on a golf course. She can't explain it, but it's the truth.

"I want whatever she's smoking!" Harry scoffs.

"Mate, we have to get out of here right now! I told you this is some pandemic shit."

Dylan and Harry agree to make a run for it, but the

woman comes across their path and blocks them.

"If you go out there, you'll die."

Mitch walks toward the shutters when Tom finally appears after all this time.

"What the hell is going on here?" He swings his keys, snorting a load of phlegm.

Mitch pulls him closer. "Boss, ring the police."

He thinks the woman has injured some people outside and has just killed a man on the shop floor. Tom calls 9-9-9 while trying to negotiate with the woman and calm her down.

Claire notices Val is stood over the man's body, shaking. She lets go of Linda for a sec and takes Val over to where she's waiting. Her voice is unusually soothing for this situation.

"The police are engaged, everything is," Tom grunts.

Everybody else checks their phones. "No service!"

Claire looks vacantly along the floor. Everybody says the same thing—anybody who has service announces the emergency services are engaged. Harry says he's not taking orders from some crazy bitch and pushes past her, and Dylan tries to follow when they get into a fight over another beer bottle. The woman is trying to use it to strike Harry.

"You are not wasting another one of my beers, lady."

Dylan enters a tug of war with her. Her finely polished nails dig into his dark tanned skin. Tom tries to intervene; this situation is becoming increasingly exacerbated. Mitch goes over to the doors, where he sees people banging on the entrance. He feels for them, but he can't let anyone else inside. Of course, the woman thinks that's his plan, and sets off to beg him not to.

00:00 hours

It's too late. In a split-second, Mitch opens the doors—

198

savage people sprint in. In the flash of an eye, Mitch's face vanishes, practically torn clean off. Two attackers claw at him as he falls. They gouge out an eyeball, bite off his nose and tear off his forehead and lips. Claire's face drops, her face loses all colour in an instant—the sights have sucked the life out of her in a vacuum.

The mad woman screams as a monster dives on her and sinks its teeth into her shoulder—a medium rare steak.

Claire's eyes widen. The girls shriek. Harry and Dylan dodge out of harm's way and Val tells Tom to lower the shutters. Tom leaps over one crazy indulging on the body of the helpless woman as he slams the button, then tries to stop the increasing swarm of attackers from coming in. Several rabid people are on the shop floor now, though.

Tom signals the girls over while the monsters tuck into their human snacks. Linda and Val are frozen with fear, so Claire pushes them. Those left alive flee, following Tom. It's a bloodbath. Tom hurries the others up some stairs, across some offices, and into a security room. He bolts the door and tells them this is the safest room.

"Now what?" Claire demands.

The others catch their breath. Tom goes to the desk and enters a code on the system. He presses a button underneath the desk… a panic button. Tom explains the button is to be used if the store gets robbed and hostages are taken. The police have been notified and will be with them shortly. Dylan goes to the CCTV screens and watches the creatures on the shop floor scouring the aisles, on the hunt for something. He coughs, trying not to throw up, as he watches the others digging into Mitch. They fight over his insides, throwing bits of him about. Intestine and liver are smeared all over. Everyone is retching but Claire, which Harry notices. One monster cracks open his ribs and tears meat off his spinal cord like a rack of lamb.

"Nasty way to go," Dylan mutters.

"Don't look." Claire tugs him away.

He looks over his shoulder at the cameras, at the other people pulling the crazy lady apart who, now they think about it, probably wasn't that crazy after all. She is screaming while one has her arms and one has her legs and they are pulling apart until her all four of her limbs come away from her body and she flops down like a bug with ripped off wings. The blood gushes out the stumps.

CHAPTER 8:

SHOP TILL YOU DROP

January 1st, 2012
00:10 hours
Supermarket Security Office

The cries are soft now, only the whimpers of the group fill the room as they try to wrap their heads around the reality of the situation and the severity of the events that unfolded moments ago. Linda is pacing up and down the room, denying this is happening on today, of all days.

"Thomas! The manager, right?" Claire comes alive from biting her nails in a corner.

"The proprietor, yes!" he boldly announces.

"How long will the police take to respond to the silent alarm, panic call?"

He shrugs. "Never had to use it before, but in this zone that alarm is top priority, so maybe a few minutes. They're on a channel and can be here in under two if we have a shoplifter, but I've never pressed this button!" he reiterates rudely.

His demeanor and response rubs Claire up the wrong way; she already thinks he's a bit of a cock.

"You need to tell them to bring the whole SWAT team, helicopters, dogs, tanks! Call in the mother fucking army! Those people are running around the store looking for us, man! That ain't right!"

"Dyl. Chill," Harry says with a shake in his voice.

Claire tells the others, "It may help if we keep trying our

201

phones for the police or anybody."

"What if it's the entire city and all the services are indisposed?" Linda panics.

"No, they always have something even if they call from the surrounding boroughs. They always bring in something fast, terror threats, bombs, explosions… anything mass casualty." Claire tries to put her at ease. "Let's make you a cup of tea, look there's a machine there, that will calm the nerves."

"How do you know?" Harry asks.

Claire doesn't answer.

"Ey! You'll have to pay for that, love," barks Tom.

"Yeah cheers, mate," Claire huffs.

Val says she wants to call her mum, but the phones aren't working. She's a mess, her bun has frayed out and her heavy eyeliner and mascara has run down her face, not to mention the snot constantly leaking from her nose, causing her to sniffle every couple of seconds.

"Christ, will you shut up or find a tissue, silly girl?" snarls Tom, much to Claire's disgust.

They can hear people downstairs shuffling, banging, crashing and occasionally letting out murderous screams.

The bursting of countless fireworks ripple above them.

Dylan tries to brighten the situation. "Happy New Year." They all glare at him momentarily. He shrugs.

"I thought you hated New Year's Eve?" Claire asks, putting her mobile phone to her ear.

"No. I said it's the same as every other day of the year. I never said I hated it. Who are you calling?"

"My brother at the shop."

The pair approach the CCTV camera.

"Where's that cashier boy?" Dylan freaks out a little. "He was there like literally five minutes ago."

"I don't think there's anything of him left…"

What's left of Mitch is being consumed by his killers.

"My best employee, what a waste." Tom pipes up from across the room.

"Get fucked!" Val suddenly comes to life behind her wadded-up tissue and new dramatic goth look. "You didn't even like him!"

"Well, he did more than you did, cupcake." Tom shouts back. "If he wasn't somebody's chew toy right now, I'd sack you for being pure shite."

"You can't sack me, I quit," hisses Val.

"You are truly impertinent!" squawks Linda.

"Yeah, well, you ain't my fucking cup of tea either!" yells Tom.

"Prick!" mutters Dylan.

"ENOUGH!" Claire silences them. "Any more shouting and they will hear us."

Harry comes up next to Tom and ponders what has got into those people to make them kill and attack others like that. Everyone is now looking at a monitor, respectively. They stare at the monsters eating the flesh of the victims; they assume they aren't really people, not anymore.

"Few minutes and it'll all be over." Tom walks over to a cheap red leather sofa and puts his feet up nonchalantly as they come.

"What if it's the riots?" Val asks nervously. "You know, like the ones we had a few months ago. The London Riots!"

"I doubt ripping people apart and eating them constitutes a riot, love," Harry answers.

Minutes turn into hours and hours turn to the morning. Eventually, everybody passes out from exhaustion from waiting.

05:06 hours

Claire is the last to wake up. She knows it before she's opened her eyes because she can hear them all quietly scheming. Like most people who are awake before they open their eyes, she hopes they just roll over and go back to sleep. Maybe it's been a bad dream, a fever dream like that time she had Mono. Maybe she's back in her bed above the shop with her brother greeting her with a coffee and the smell of frying onions. But no, her eyes ping open and there is the shitty red leather pressed against her nose. Somehow, she made it to the sofa.

She turns to the CCTV screens staring at her; the humming of all the computer equipment is louder in this stuffy little room, hotter with their collective body heat. It all comes flooding back.

"How come the police still aren't here yet?" she asks, still half asleep. "What time is it?"

"Five I think… I've been trying all night." And still nothing.

He remembers what the 'crazy lady' said to them, how she came in just before midnight. 'People have suddenly started fighting, looting, and rioting in the streets... all over the news for the last hour. People are eating each other, tearing one another to shreds and it's those things out there…'

Dylan asks if that means it's outside, too. "Everywhere else?"

"The police are probably busy with all that then, as long as we're safe in here. The alarm has been sounded; we will wait!" Tom folds his arm. "I'm starving, anyway!"

"How on earth can you think of food at a time like this?" Linda speaks up, aghast.

He thunders over to a draw that only he has the key for on his zipline bouquet of keys. Tom jangles them until he's in and pulls out a protein bar. Without hesitation, he devours it. They watch him in disgust and slight hatred.

"Thanks for offering. Dickhead," Val grunts having cleaned up some of her face.

"I have pets!" Linda announces, "I need to get back."

"I need to see my mum, Aunty D." Dylan cries.

The group panics, worrying about their families, parents, kids, friends, spouses and pets. Tom shouts over them, spitting half a mouthful across the room, asserting his dominance since they are in his store.

Claire sits, taking a mental note of Tom's God complex. Harry comes and sits with her having poured a black tea from the machine.

"Sorry, I didn't know what you wanted, and they have no milk, anyway. I'm Harry by the way, you can call me Hazza, Haz, whatever. That's Dylan, Dyl or even dildo. Which is what he's acting like, I'm sorry for his behaviour."

"It's fine," she smirks, cupping the tea with both hands. "Claire… just Claire."

"You seem the calm one in this fucked up situation. Eerily calm."

"Oh uh…"

"It's not a bad thing, just an observation. Downstairs when that woman killed that guy, you didn't flinch. And up here with all the shouting and panic you just seem to chill."

"Long story," says Claire, trying to hide it all. "Are they still down there?"

"They haven't even stopped for a second, just skulking, screaming…"

"Nobody is going to come for us." Linda cuts them off from near the door.

Dylan says they surely will have the police and the army kicking arse outside, and somebody is going to come across their store eventually.

"It is one of the biggest stores in Leeds," Tom says, "the best, actually."

"And we shut all those people out, just like that?" Claire leans back.

"Actually, the two outside cameras haven't shown many

people trying to get in, one or two failures, but they keep getting chased off." Harry leans in next to her.

"That's insane, you'd have thought people would have come in hundreds for supplies."

"Think about it, they already did! All this pandemic talk about that thing…" Harry clicks his fingers to think of the buzzword.

Val speaks up, filing her nails on the sofa. "Grime Flu."

"Yeah, everyone shat themselves and probably already stocked up a week ago. Plus, Christmas supplies."

They both look back at the monitors, at the people outside running amok.

06:10 hours

More minutes into more hours; they seem to go around in circles. Dylan is pacing while his stomach rumbles and Val has taken it upon herself to take off her shoes, put her feet on the table and flick through a glossy mag on the red sofa, now more bored than scared. They are becoming irritated, tired, hungry and need to use the facilities. Tom barges into her feet, forcing her to move them.

"You are so fucking rude. How the fuck did you become a manager?"

"And you are a stain on society love, fuck off back to your council flat."

Linda shakes her head from her chair. Tom slumps next to her, practically in Val's lap, so she bashes him with the magazine moving toward the edge. He rags it out of her hand and throws it across the room, landing near Claire.

"Stop breathing, you'll use up all the air," Val directs at Tom.

"This room is air-conditioned, and the controls are in here, you fucking specimen. Do you know how air works?"

"I don't need this; I need to be on a plane to Marbella."

Generation Dead

"Do you have any idea what the fuck is going on right now? Or is your head just shapes, noises and fucking cigarettes."

Val's jaw drops, insulted.

"Mate, you can't talk to her like that," Harry points out.

"What you gonna do about it?"

"Harry don't," Claire softly urges.

Suddenly Tom lets out an earth-shattering belch, repulsing everyone. "Augh… Need a piss."

"We all need a piss, mate," Dylan adds.

Tom gets up and walks over to the small waste bin in the corner.

"No, you're not going in here!" Claire protests, and everyone complains. He pisses in a corner, much to everybody's disgust.

"Just turn your fucking backs." He lets rip a fart, too.

"That stinks!" Val moves.

"We have to get back to the shop floor!" Claire says, wafting to covering the stench. "At least for food and to use the bathrooms."

"Are you sure about this?" Harry pulls her to the side.

"It's that or we starve with him."

They glare at Tom, shaking off.

"Thomas. Tom. Or Boss whichever you prefer."

"I understand you're in charge because it's your store. We recognise your 'tough guy' act." She tries to level with him. "I need you to understand we can't wait in this tiny security office; people are weak and acting out."

Tom and Claire look over their shoulders at what looks like an appeal advert. Tom glares at the CCTV, looking at the dead bodies and the one or two creatures now stagnantly wondering the isles. He grunts like it's a massive chore.

"Really, you expect us to shit in bins?" Claire folds her arms.

Dylan and Harry can't help but overhear and ask if they

are seriously going to go out there with those psychos.

"We may not have a choice; we don't know what's going on outside, we can't stay in this room and it's three against six."

Harry proposes one of them should go into the store to gather weapons one-by-one and bring them back.

"Weapons?" Linda chokes.

"This store is huge, it's surely got utensils. Knives and garden tools, all sorts."

"I don't fucking think so!" Tom shouts.

"Mate, I get it's your shop, but we need to defend ourselves if those mad fuckers sniff us out, or we'll end up like slave boy on the till," asserts Harry.

Dylan asks why someone can't just bring back supplies to the room. Claire glares at him until he succumbs and tells her she's lucky she is pretty.

Tom silences them. "I don't take too kindly to you calling the shots and using the products in the shop."

Dylan, Harry and Claire exchange a look of uncertainty regarding Tom's odd comments and hostility toward them. Linda and Val are nervous wrecks, so whatever task is at hand, they are out of it and it's between Claire, Tom, Dylan and Harry. They all opt to go first so, to settle it, Tom picks out four pens from the stationary pot on his desk: one red and three blue. He turns them upside down. He exclaims whoever picks the red lid gets the honour of playing hide and seek with 'those munchers'.

One by one they draw a pen, covering the end and reveal what colour they drew.

Everybody looks at Claire. She gulps. "Bad day to like red I guess."

She holds the red pen in her sweaty palm, smiling awkwardly.

Dylan stubbornly but kindly volunteers to go in her place, but Claire refuses. The plan is simple: return with enough instruments or sharp objects so they can defend themselves. Do not get discovered, or it's game over. She feels like she must prove her worth to the boys, being the only strong female of the group, given Linda is of a certain age and Val couldn't give a fuck. Harry makes Claire promise if she feels like she is in danger or struggles, she must hold three fingers up toward whichever camera she can see first.

"Why three?"

"I don't know, it's symbolic."

"This isn't a game." Dylan snorts.

Harry hits Dylan. "Yeah, well, you're going to need a lot of aloe vera to sooth what I'm thinking of doing to your face," Harry snarls.

"You love me really!"

"BOYS!" Claire yells, clapping and drawing their banter to a premature close.

Tom gives Claire one of the employee's earpieces attached to a microphone. Claire gets hooked up and Tom quietly asks her if she can hear. She can.

Tom says, "Harry and I will be your eyes from the CCTV. We'll warn you wherever the dormant creatures wander."

11:05 hours
Claire
Shop Floor

The fear courses through Claire's veins but never makes it to her facial muscles or skin. Her complexion remains pale and matte, the makeup on her face subtle but now stale and crusting. Her eyes are steady and alert as if she's shopping for the pair of summer deal shoes. She lets out an understated, very shaky sigh and turns to leave, showing she isn't too rattled. She can feel her steady heart pace as her eyes narrow.

"The lion's den."

209

Two feet donning warn Converse trainers dangle from a vent and Claire silently drops, making a superhero landing. She's at the far end of the store. Claire looks up at the vent flapping freely.

Please don't break, please don't break.

It's well away from the entrance, but if there is any noise, it'll only be seconds before she's found. She is astonished by her acrobatic skills when her feet didn't make a whisper on landing.

Tom radios in her ear. "You can take tools or knives, anything sharp to fend off those fuckers." Anything may make useful weapons against the assailants. She can hear the odd screech and growl in the distance from far away aisles. Every tone is a heartbeat skipped. She does not know what she is up against. So, keeping low, she begins in the frozen produce, working her way through the alcohol aisle until she reaches the bakery.

Halfway there, no monsters yet. A voice asks how she is doing. Claire looks to the closest camera and puts her forefinger to her thumb, showing that she's okay. Her shoes squeak on the shiny floor. She pauses and screws her eyes shut.

Sqeaaaaak.

"WRAAAAAAAAGH!"

"Why did she stop?" Dylan panics, ogling the cameras.

Claire has her eyes tightly shut. She can feel a sweat coming on.

"I don't know, dude, step back!" Harry grumbles.

She's suspended in time, ever so slowly lowering to her laces. They watch Claire take her shoes off.

"What is she doing?" Linda asks, panicked.

Harry squints to work it out. Now barefoot, Claire proceeds, looking up at the cameras.

"Ah, clever girl," Dylan says through biting his nails.

"Silent footsteps," Harry confirms.

"She best get a move on, not got all fucking day!" Tom growls.

Harry nervously watches through his hands. He tries to radio in, but Tom shoves his hand away and tells Claire one monster has gone back to the corpses at the lobby and the other two are scouring the poultry, tearing into bits of meat.

"They can smell it," Harry whispers, taking mental note.

Claire is now petrified. Her cool as a cucumber demeanour has left the building. Her adrenaline spikes in her fingers; she can feel every heartbeat and breath like it's her last and worries she might evacuate her bowls to keep from having a panic attack. She spots the aisle with the kitchen essentials.

"Come on, girl, you've done great so far..." Harry mutters to himself.

Don't let them see you falter, keep it cool. Claire pauses for a moment, taking the biggest inhale of oxygen, calming the lines in her face. She's ready. She turns to an aisle thinking she can cut across to the travelators.

Upon turning, she accidentally bumps into a promotion stand with a tower of Devil's Corp pasta sauces. Her soul leaves her body as if she has fallen and awoken the second before death in her sleep, slow motion. The well-crafted tower collapses. Some bottles smash and others roll away.

Linda and Val gasp as they watch in suspense. Dylan puts his hands on his head.

"DUMB SLAG!" Tom screams.

"Mate, will you pack it in?" Harry claps back.

Claire tries not to move, screwing her eyes shut, listening to bottles roll away.

"WRRRAURGHHHHHFFF!"

The monsters from the other side of the store prick their ears and squall their lungs as they dart toward the source of the noise. Tom and the rest of the group watch the undead duo switch from camera to camera, bolting toward Claire.

K. J. McGuinness

Tom says nothing, and Harry tries to fight him for the earpiece. He presses down on the microphone.

"Run for your life!"

Tom pushes Harry away, and Dylan comes to his rescue, standing between them. Dylan headbutts Tom for the earpiece and Val tries to break up the situation, poorly. A fight breaks out among them. They all begin shouting over one another, pushing back and forth. They leave Claire in the lurch.

"What's going on?" she hisses to them.

She takes the advice and legs it down the aisle to the escalators to the lower floor. She meets with the monsters foaming at the mouth. They launch an assault. She lifts herself up through the travelator, sailing down its rail. One beast reaches out but the other accidentally tackles it, and they both slide away and smack into the balcony wall, cracking the glass.

They slip and slide upright, pursuing her down the travelator. Claire screams hysterically, trying to lose her attackers. Her instincts take over; she throws and pushes objects from the shelves as obstructions. She has a moment to choose her path; she runs straight into the clothes section and climbs into a rail of the 'Devil's Corp Fashion' winter range. The winter coats form a good camouflage to the other side.

Claire is crying but forces her mouth shut with her hands to breathe steadier. She can hear the psychos so close on the other side of her hiding spot, sniffing and drooling. They growl and bark. She shuts her eyes tight and after a few moments, something inside convinces her the coast is clear.

She briefly and cautiously pops her head out. She pokes one leg through the clothing rack.

BOOM! One attacker surprises her right next to her face. She screams and tries to make a run for it, but the animal takes hold of her leg. Claire thinks she's done but wriggles free and loses her headset. She uses the cord to wrap round its neck and pull until it turns purple. She tosses it aside.

Claire tries to slip and slide away. The brute recuperates and slowly, mockingly, creeps toward her as the cable falls. There is a gruesome look of death in its eyes as it raises its claws. Claire gasps. *This is it.*

WHACK! Harry appears out of nowhere and drives a fire axe straight through the monster's chin. Undead skull and brains splatter around. Claire uncovers her arms from her eyes and watches Harry panting. She glances at the corpse with the enormous axe gaping from its skull.

"Two to go!"

Harry is bleeding. Rather than being in shock about the murder, Claire is more concerned about him.

"I'm fine," he reassures, "a slight disagreement with management."

Harry helps Claire up and they exchange a moment, staring into each other's eyes when she feels a funny butterfly-like feeling in her gut. Claire places her palm on his cheek. It ruins the moment when they hear a villainous cry from the other beast. Harry takes the earpiece and tries to radio Dylan.

"Cuz."

"Haz."

Tom is nursing a soon-to-be black eye in a chair, and Dylan has the earpiece monitoring the screens. It's clear who won the fight.

"I'm sorry bruv, no good news. One of them is sniffing around the entrance back to the office," informs Dylan.

"Shit. Right… where's the other one?" groans Harry.

"One psycho is near the door! He's coming upstairs to the security office!" Dylan shouts.

Dylan groans and turns to scroll through the CCTV cameras and their various angles.

"THERE!" Linda comes to life, finger clicking and

pointing for him to go back.

"It's downstairs, mate, toiletries. Garden tools are five aisles over. Go now and be quick."

No time to lose. They run, ducked down, around each aisle. Before making it to the outdoor palace, they gain some garden tools and kitchen knives.

"Let's go!" Harry nods.

"WRAGHHHHH!"

Claire and Harry pop up like meerkats.

"That was close." Claire tells him. They both run off back to the travelator.

"Oh wait, wait, wait." Claire stops Harry at the top of the conveyor belt.

"What is it?"

Before he knows it, she's already back with a basket.

"Survival!" she boldly announces.

Rope, lighters and solvent cans. Harry tells her that once they subdue the psychos they can play around later while they wait to be rescued.

One psycho is missing, and the other is in the way of returning to safety upstairs. Harry peers his head over the first aisle they encounter returning to the upper floor, which gives him an excellent view of every aisle down below, but still no psycho. Claire shrieks before covering her mouth and stopping in her tracks, causing Harry to bump into her. What she sees horrifies her beyond all comprehension.

It's Mitch, what's left of him. It's very little, but judging by the torn rags of clothing and adult braces chewed and discarded, it wouldn't be a farfetched assumption. They scattered his innards across the lobby. There's no body anymore, just a head. But that's not what shakes Claire. More impossibly, it's what the head it is doing. His head is making noise, almost like it's alive. Mitch's severed head faces her. He gnashes and groans, jaw still moving. It haunts her to her very core.

"I've seen some nasty shit, but that's the stuff of nightmares."

His eyes are vacant and stale. A misty fog has rolled over and consumed him, almost like a spell.

"How can this be?" she struggles to utter.

"We don't have time for this, Claire. Keep your wits about you," urges Harry.

She then sees the monster in the doorway, procrastinating. It's waiting for them. Harry looks around impatiently and sees the magazine kiosk. A light bulb pings.

"I'll be one second."

"What, wait. No!" she hisses.

She nearly has an emotional breakdown about not wanting to be left on her own, staring at this head, staring back at her, with its menacing expression. It knows her and yearns for her. Claire wants to look away but the more she tries, the more she's invested in this freak show.

Harry returns in a jiffy with tape and a few mags.

"What the hell, I got tape?"

"Look, I saw this in a movie and it could help."

He wraps two magazines around both their arms and tells Claire they are going to have to give their friend the old slip and run. She's not following, but before she can even say the first syllable of his name, Harry pushes cans off the shelves and lets them roll away as he shuffles backwards.

Claire overreacts and tries to stay close to him; it's only a few seconds before they draw the blooded psycho to the noise. By this time, Claire and Harry have made it to the door.

"Next time warn me!" she scolds Harry.

"It was that or we use one of us a bait."

The deranged creature kicks Mitch's noisy severed head, and it spins away.

"And another thing—"

SMACK! Claire is shoved into a wall; the missing psycho

215

has found them. She falls and Harry tries to incapacitate the monster—they become gripped in a fight for his weapon, which he holds like a riot shield.

The monster has great strength, a firm grip and sharp teeth splitting the wood on the handle of Harry's axe as it bites down is if it were some rabid dog pissed off at the game.

Harry pushes it away but slips in some blood. The two hit the ground and the psycho climbs on top and tries to bite Harry, but he shoves his weapon between its teeth again, trying to force it away. The monster just keeps the pressure down on Harry's bulging arms.

Linda opens the office door and tries to help, slapping the creature repeatedly (yet poorly) on the back. Claire comes to. It was quite the impact. She's not the weakest of people but not the tallest. Without thinking, she rummages into her basket of tricks and finds a flick knife.

"MOVE!"

Linda stands back, nearly falling over herself. Claire stabs the psycho. Nothing.

Harder jab. Nothing.

Again and again, they are horrified because it won't budge.

"What the?"

Claire loses her edge now, just stabbing and stabbing more veraciously with every swing. It bleeds, yes. But it doesn't care.

Finally, after letting rip a war cry even King Arthur would cower at, she plunges her butcher's knife into its spinal cord right at the base of its neck. Suddenly the brute goes limp, just like that. The dead body collapses on Harry. Claire may as well have pulled the mains from a computer.

Harry whines and tosses the body aside. They regain their strength and Claire enters in shock.

"I just killed someone." She stares blankly at Harry,

queasy and ready to sit down. Harry looks at her holding the knife so blasé. She's got spots of red on her face and hands.

"You're okay, you're okay." He pulls her in, but she doesn't hug him back.

She is quickly snapped out of it when Linda cries out and points for them to, "LOOK OUT!".

Harry gasps. The last psycho comes darting around the corner. He pushes Claire out of the way so hard that she falls again and slides across the floor. The monster misses her colliding straight into Harry. This one bites Harry's chest. He yells out in anguish, pushes the beast back, and they stumble. Out of nowhere, a knife tip appears through the demon's eyes. Tom stands over it, much to the others' surprise, having drawn a blade through the back of its head. Linda helps Claire on her feet, and they stagger back upstairs.

Harry puts his hand on his chest, glaring at Tom, who is glaring back.

"Did you really think there was only one way to access the office above?" Tom dingles the keys, obnoxiously.

"You could have told us this ten minutes ago, you fucking muppet."

"Come on, I'll check you out." Claire puts her arm around Harry who is hunched over in obvious distress.

Despite this tension, the group can finally relish in their victory of taking back the entire supermarket. They decide to sit in the office, reflecting on recent events.

"We just took back our store!" Dylan catches his breath with a profound sense of achievement.

"*My* store!" Tom adds.

"Yeah, but we just killed a load of people," Val says.

Harry aches all over. "They were trying to kill us; besides, I don't think those were people anymore after being up close and personal with them."

"It's all on camera, there's no way anything will hold up

in court," Dylan adds.

Harry shoots him a sarcastic look. "You'd know."

Claire interrupts. "We need to clean everything up. Those bodies can't stay there, it's not sanitary. Help will be coming." They look at one another sporadically. No one wants to go first. "Fine, I'll do it since I seem to do everything." She tuts.

"Wait. I'll go with you," shouts Harry.

"No, you're hurt, stay here so I can get the medicines. Anyone else hurt should stay and I'll take care of it!"

"Who died and put you in charge?" snarls Tom, turning his icepack around.

"I'm a paramedic. Save a life and you're a hero, save a thousand and you work for the NHS."

Claire goes back to the store and literally cleans out the medicine corner. She takes the important stuff and leaves behind the secondary stuff she can come back to. Right now, it's about disinfection, gauzes and pain relief. The group becomes a little more acquainted while Claire tends to any injuries, focusing primarily on the nasty bite Harry received.

"Follow me, I need mirrors."

"Where we are going, you going to seduce me?" Harry smirks through the pain. Dylan shoots him dirty looks.

Claire & Harry
Staff Toilets

"I'm sorry, you're going to have to take your t-shirt off. I need to deal with it properly."

"So you are having your wicked way with me!"

Harry doesn't hesitate as he lifts his shirt, seething in pain. Claire tries not to gape openly as she observes his sharp jaw, chin, and cheekbones. On either side of his straight nose are two blazing hazel eyes. Warm brown with smooth green hints. His dark brows are graceful. Thick, warm chocolate curls that meet his overgrown stubble frame all of it. His muscled back is bare except for one upper tattoo; a canvas that looks like a work of art, clasped hands in prayer with wings holding rosery beads. She cannot see his chest for a moment. Part of her wishes she could. The other exceedingly small part of her says she should get a hold of herself. She lets out a shaky sigh.

He turns back around. His prominent jaw curves gracefully around and the strength of his neck shows in the twining cords of muscle that shape his entire body—thick arms, bold thighs and calves, a firm chest and abdomen. His skin is brown and smooth. Claire feels a flutter as she is trying to concentrate. She sees the nasty gash in cleaner light.

"So that's why you've been so calm and collected. A paramedic." Harry breaks the silence.

Claire replies inspecting the wounds, "I'm technically a student, but I have been in a hospital since I was like 15."

Ew, this one is nasty. It looks alive as blood runs down his chest.

"Do you want the truth or a beautiful lie?" She smiles.

"Give it to me."

"It's grim. But I can fix it, however this is going to scar."

She patches him up pretty well, and it will do until rescue arrives in the next few hours. She cleans the wound with tea tree oils and TCP, using butterfly stitches with needles and thread which she has soaked in rubbing alcohol. Harry barely makes a sound or flinches during her process.

"Interesting," she whispers.

"Huh?"

"Sorry, I didn't realise that was out loud. You don't flinch... doesn't happen often."

"Not my first time."

"Now that really is interesting."

"You can't tell because I tattooed over most of my scars."

"Don't take this the wrong way." Claire puts her thumb on the thread and yanks it off. "Are you religious?"

"Oh, the tats... sort of. I'm Puerto Rican. Most of my family are die hard Catholics. But I didn't exactly go down the path that was chosen for me. I have faith though."

Claire says nothing, and an awkward silence falls as she scans his body for more scars, fascinated by his physiology.

"What is TCP?" he breaks the silence.

She sews him up, dabbing blood away every so often. "Antiseptic liquid. It will stop any infection. It's deep, I think the bastard nipped an artery." Claire doesn't break eye contact with her work.

"Can't say someone has bitten me before."

"Nor have I dealt with a biting," Claire reveals.

"No, I know that, but I meant I wonder why they called it TCP."

"Well, it's better than its chemical name trichlorophenylmethyliodosalicyl."

He burst out laughing. "You just made that up."

"I swear, look it up. Not exactly the easiest thing to be bought off the shelf, is it?" she giggles, and he smiles.

Suddenly, Val interjects. "Tom wants a word."

Claire and Harry exchange a look of uncertainty before returning back to their uncouth host.

"Try to keep calm," Claire says, quietly packing.

Already Linda and Dylan wait frantically. "What do we do if rescue doesn't come? What happens if they do and see all the dead bodies?" they ask.

They've killed people.

"Calm down, we will think of something," Harry says.

"Ey! This is my shop, I'll do what I like. Don't be a dumb twat. Look at the 20 screens you geriatric. It's all there. They can't do shit since we acted in self-defence. It's not even my problem. You did the killings. I won't give a fuck to sell you out in a heartbeat. Think of all the money I could get from it. Wa-hey!"

"You mean you didn't do shit!" Dylan is leaned forward, pressing a knife lightly into the tip of his finger as he rotates it.

"Tom, could you please just stop with all the nasty name calling, we don't want to be here any more than you do. We all need to get along until rescue comes. It *is* coming. At least now we can use the rest of the supermarket, get clean and get water and food in the meantime."

"Not without my say!" Tom dangles his keys again.

Dylan sniggers. "I don't think so, boss man." He jingles a pair of keys much to Tom's surprise.

"Where the fuck did you get them?" Tom advances toward Dylan menacingly.

"Back the fuck off." Dylan has his blade pointed at Tom, the looks in his eyes states perfectly he intends to use it.

"Dylan!" Claire yaps.

"I am NOT going down there. It's safe in here. Downstairs has all the blood, dead bodies and guts everywhere." Val protests, defusing the situation.

"Then I'll move the bodies."

Dylan

Being brave means being afraid, or at least it does for Dylan. It's a conscious choice. The two go hand in hand. First is the fear, then the determination not to be ruled by it. Dylan grew up always choosing to face fear, to conquer it. At least that's what Harry, his older cousin, taught him. He may appear to be dim-witted, but he has a lion's courage. Harry acts like his older brother, though the two appeared more like best mates found on the side of the street. Dylan holds Harry's humanity in check, keeping him down to earth, whereas Harry makes sure Dylan doesn't wander into traffic. If only they'd have just stayed in to look after his mum, it's all he can think about. The idea of her being helpless right now makes his chest ache.

For how else are we to make genuine progress in life? I am a warrior at heart. Faced with adversity I have an ability for calm and rational thought—to me that is a blessing. I'm coming mumma. He thinks to himself, traipsing through discarded remains. *Look at this mess. Look at them.*

He's seen nothing like it. Dylan can't make out where one person starts.

"Cock it."

He throws his hands up and walks to the cleaning aisle, dragging almost every product they offer. Mops, cloths, all the liquids, and goes to pull all the corpses he can find to one side including Mitch's severed remains. It's not the easiest task taking on solo, but it helps that he can vacate his own mind. Dylan can go through entire movies, songs, or games in his head, putting his body on autopilot.

He comes to Mitch's snarling head and then the 'crazy lady'. He observes the milky tint in Mitch's eyes, glaring directly at him, as his jaw grinds and twists. A sense of grimace and disgust comes over Dylan. How can this severed head still be moving? He uses his knife to push it slowly through the ear, like cutting a cake. The flesh has become tender. Slowly, Mitch's snarling stops. A machine that's clogged and shut down in an instant.

"Fascinating and creepy AF," he whispers to himself, before Harry walks up to help.

"Why are you holding zombie boy's head?"

"You would not believe what just happened…"

They put sheets upon sheets from the home section over the bodies to improve conditions. They layer them until they can see no more stains of blood. Dylan even takes some air freshener and showers the corpses in lavender spritz.

"Cuz, man. What-the-fuck?" Harry sighs like it's the nth time Dylan has done some embarrassing shit.

"What?" he says spraying. Tsssssst! Tsssssssssssssst... tst! "Yo, these bodies are gonna start stinking up the place. It's like a sign of respect, innit." Harry stares at him. "Mate, if I was gonna be chewed up for somebody's lunch, I'd want the rest of me to be laid to rest in..." he looks at the label, "Lavender... Night's Kiss."

"We could just put them in the freezer on ice... slow the process." Harry wisely points out.

Dylan stares at him for a moment, "Next to the icecream I have my eye on?"

Fuck. After a thud and shove, they pile remains in a freezer, jamming it shut having cleared out some space.

"This feels wrong. Like cannibal wrong. They're going to arrest us. Throw away the key."

"Dylan."

"Innit tho. They're take one look at us, see we're a different colour and..." Dylan gestures slamming his fist into his other palm. "Jailbait."

"Dylan."

"I'm too pretty to be in jail. I'll get bummed. Nuffin against gays but I'm not a bottom."

"Jesus Christ, Dylan... ENOUGH!" Harry growls, walking away.

"They'll call us the cannibal cousins of Camden." Dylan follows, carrying on.

"I'm the one who got fucking bitten, lad. I'm the victim."

Val slithers through the office door when she knows the bodies are out of the picture.

"Aww boys, thank you so much for that. I can't believe you had to kill them." Val flounces off like she didn't even give a shit.

"Wow, she's as fake as press on nails, isn't she?" Claire comes up behind them.

"Still would." Dylan grunts.

"Mate, get tested."

"You are just a creature, aren't you?"

Dylan shrugs nonchalantly.

"Where are you going?" shouts Claire.

"Need some fake tan, ready for my holidays."

"Of course she does."

Linda is next to appear. "I needed to get out of there! It was hot, stuffy, claustrophobic. I'm so shaken."

"You know what? I don't think those peeps was alive to begin with."

The group look at one another, scared and unsure.

Linda is going to get water and find something to rest on. Tom is last to emerge and follows her, repeating his authority. His appearance wherever he goes is really setting the tone, sucking all the niceness from the energy of the room.

"Um, I think you'll find I will watch what you take, love."

"What a 'thunder cunt' Tom is." Claire shakes her head.

The boys look at each other and burst out laughing their arses off. Suddenly, Dylan becomes a green-eyed monster as he watches Harry and her bond. Dylan playfully asks if Claire wants to get that drink still after they get out of here. She smiles sweetly but doesn't answer.

22:00 hours

The supermarket squad, chosen by Dylan, spend their first night securing the complex, ignoring everything outside and wait for help. Things are looking bleak; it's nearly been 24-hours since they tried to call the police. Still no phones and no news.

"Seriously, it's nearly been a day! Something is wrong. They are not coming." Val scoffs, filing her nails, chewing her gum.

"Maybe they're just busy. That crazy lady said everyone lost their minds out there. It's probably a lot to clean up—they will come for us, I'm sure," Linda explains.

"Or maybe they're all dead?" Dylan says, leant against a wall, picking the crud from his nails with his knife.

"Keep it the fuck down. Don't fuck this up. We don't know who's out there!" Tom warns.

"No one by the sounds of it, it's nearly been a day and not one person as tried to knock."

"Knock? You think somebody's gonna knock like we just ordered a pizza?"

"We need to stretch out," Harry suggested.

"What we going to do, huh? Sit on bean bags with a guitar and sing campfire songs?" Tom roars. He suggests they camp out back in the store, under his watch, of course.

Linda wants to be in the open near the front.

"Oh, nobody's fucking talking to you, Linda. Stick a pack of fags in it."

Harry pulls Claire to one side. "This knob is nothing but aggression and control. He's dangerous, Claire. If help doesn't come by tomorrow, we need to get out. We need those keys." Tom's behaviour is becoming sourer the longer they wait.

"God, you really are insufferable." Linda abruptly stands to leave with her bag.

"Oh, knit me a sweater, you old crone."

They proceed down the stairs as Tom continues to argue with Linda. Claire is watching them suspiciously, heeding Harry's words, while she helps him down, having changed his dressings once more.

"I'm sorry the stitching isn't great. It might be a big scar, and it will need proper attention soon." Claire looks at him and notices how hot and sweaty he has become.

"You need bespoke antibiotics I don't think the pharmacy

downstairs has. It doesn't take a paramedic to see you need a hospital."

"It's just the shock of everything, I'm sure." It isn't.

Dylan rubs his hands. "It's always been a dream of mine to be in a supermarket where I can do whatever I please. I'm starving," he says, yawning and stretching.

"Why not have some of your friends, cannibal?" Val winks, walking off. Dylan smirks and checks her out again.

"You touch nothing without my say!" Tom bellows.

Val yells, "Are you really that much of an arsehole? We haven't eaten in nearly 20 hours, Tom!"

"Anything you touch you pay for!"

Tom is about to rip into her when suddenly, the power in the entire shop floor switches off and the supermarket is thrust into darkness, causing Linda to shriek, spooked. She says she can't do it. The trail of blood and the idea of being around death sends her into a weird dance type seizure. She holds her blouse and apologises; she is going back to the office.

Val, Tom and Dylan are squabbling again. Claire and Harry look at each other. Why must they break up the calm? Friction rises every five minutes.

"So, this is how democracy dies. In the dairy aisle." Claire folds her arms.

Harry barks at everybody, causing him to cough and tell everybody to knock it off. He kindly tries to compromise with Linda already near the office door.

"If I get rid of every trace of what's happened, will you stay?"

Linda considers it. Harry then turns his attention to Tom and angrily suggests he stops being a 'Nazi-walrus-bastard' and lets people eat. Tom walks off, following Dylan to the food. Claire comes up behind Harry.

"Nazi? Walrus? Bastard?" She smirks.

"Yeah, he looks like a fucking walrus, with teeth bigger

than my head," Harry says in his broad southern accent. "And fat."

"Now, now. No need for the playground insults."

"If the lights don't come back on, we have about two days before all the fresh produce goes off and we have a dangerous situation on our hands."

"My shop. I'll do what I like," Tom says from afar.

"You are the manager of a chain, middle management. This food doesn't belong to you, it belongs to the consumer or at the very least the farmers." Dylan rummages in his pockets then throws £20 in his direction. It floats to the ground.

"If it truly is the end of the world, money will be the last fucking thing to worry about."

"Places like this are the new currency, water and food."

Dylan gives Tom the middle finger and playfully summons Val and Linda. He's going to take them on a double date, anything they want.

"What about me?" Claire suggests.

"Ah, you had my heart Claire, but alas this voyage must remain on course for new islands." He smiles, putting his arms around both girls.

One can almost smell the rage brewing inside Tom who flounces off back to the office, probably to watch from his ivory tower.

"You don't have to do this, Haz." Claire pulls Harry aside again. If he is coughing and sweating, his wound could be infected.

Harry sighs, calms her. "I'd rather keep busy. I can keep an eye on Tom."

01:00 hours
Dylan, Linda & Val
Shop Floor

The hungry trio have made themselves at home. Right at the front, in the open just to spite Tom, having brought blankets, beanbags and pillows from the lower ground floor's home section. They are sitting around open bottles taken from the booze aisle, drunk and mellow, not much left and none of it was the good stuff but it will do. Dylan is eating jalapenos straight from the jar. Conversation is a little stale, so he reads the jar and explains how he's obsessed with them; he's always been a spice freak and for some strange reason, he just loves eating them from the jar.

The label reads: 'Some like it hot, made by The Devil's Corp Food.' Dylan points out. "Wow, I always see that company cropping up. They must own half the stuff in here."

"Well, they are the biggest company in the world," Linda explains.

They specialise in food, gaming, home furniture, clothing. She thinks their headquarters are based in Tokyo, that the company is owned by another that's owned by another... not that it matters. Dylan nods his head and continues to munch on his spicy snacks, then washes it down with a bottle of Châteauneuf-du-Pape.

"I think the owner of, like, all the corporations is called Alexander Henderson. He's bigger than the other richest businessmen in the world *combined*," Linda foretells.

"Never heard of the cunt." Dylan swigs the wine.

"You like conspiracies?"

Val is twisting a frying pan in her hands in her own world when Dylan throws a jalapeno at her and smiles.

"I tell you what's a conspiracy, all of this. If you would have seen what I saw earlier, holding that cash boy's head,

228

you'd want to be lobotomised."

"Oh, please stop!" Val objects.

"I'm serious. He was gone, but… not. He was still looking at me, mouth going, blinking. Just a head in my hands. Something said put your knife in him. It's like the nanosecond I got to his brain, silence fell."

The others look at him, aghast and uncomfortable.

"So… what were you two boys doing here in the first place?" Val tries to fill the void of silence.

He squints, trying to see through his double vision.

"Last night in the shop, why come to a supermarket an hour before the celebrations?"

Dylan and Linda awkwardly look around. They both dislike New Year for separate reasons. Hate is a strong word, because it's more neither of them gives a shit about it. But Dylan answers Val's question with another question.

"Let me put it this way, why did you decide to work on New Year's Eve?"

"Shouldn't the store be shut by law?" Linda backs him up, having come out of her shell, but that's most likely the wine talking.

"You haven't heard?" Val scoffs. "All the businesses are extending their hours by law because of the new epidemic."

"Well, I knew people were raiding shops and stockpiling, but I stay away from the news. No news is good news. I'd end up being the last person to find out. And I'm okay with that."

"It was Tom's doing."

"Your pig of a boss?"

"Ex-boss!"

"I was supposed to be getting off abroad and was going to celebrate there… just needed the money." Saddened by the realisation she will never go, Val tries to deflect the question back on Dylan. He never answers.

"Me and Hazza are cousins, more like mates, but we're

good friends with a 'lad' he worked with. He thinks his name is something like William, and William's ex-boyfriend was having a party. But my mum got sick; she's vulnerable to whatever is going on. I miss her a lot right now." In all honestly, Dylan professes he doesn't care for New Year's Eve, it makes no difference to him; it's just one day leading to the next. "Why do people have to wait until that night to make stupid changes?"

Val raises her eyebrows as she swigs the wine, intrigued. Then her attention is on Linda.

Linda jokingly admits, "I'm 62, twice divorced."

What else would she be doing? A few moments of silence and crunching go past when Val abruptly asks why Harry's friend would still live with his ex.

"Millennials," Dylan shrugs, trying to catch peanuts in his mouth.

01:17 hours
Harry
Meat and Cheese Aisle

Harry can see his distilled reflection in the still fresh blood on the floor. He slops the mop around, trying to remove any trace of violence and death to make the place feel less… bleak. He can feel the aching in his bones as his breathing grows heavier. Wheezing and coughing, Harry tries to push himself to remain focused on the task at hand, he's a runner on the treadmill determined to do that one last mile before he pukes. His eyelids are weighed, and he moves sluggishly. Worry becomes anxiety; he knows something isn't right in his body. Hospitals will be out at the same time as accountable law and order. He runs through supplies in his head. Ibuprofen. Paracetamol. He can feel the call of the void ringing in his ears as he struggles to focus. He imagines the sensation to be as if he were walking in the

Sahara.

He looks up at the light, trying to flicker. It's blinding and sensitive to his vision. Harry likens it all the symptoms of a hangover. The ringing and sweat dripping is a crescendo when suddenly Claire places a hand on his shoulder to check on him. He jumps and drops the mop. She informs him he looks 'a little green around the gills' and he should take a break to eat something.

"I am absolutely not hungry!" he insists.

"Well then, at least let me check your war wound. You saved my life. I owe you."

He compromises and takes a break. "You don't owe me anything, this is my path."

He looks over at Linda happily distracted, deep in conversation with the other two. There is no sign of Tom. Claire has placed battery powered torches and click lights all around the supermarket to light the way while they continue to wait. She takes him over to her makeshift den in the supermarket's corner. He hobbles to a sleeping bag.

"This is what you've been doing in the meantime?" grins Harry.

She sits him down and reveals his bandage. It's a grizzly sight of oozing puss and blood, nothing like she's seen before. But what surrounds the wound is interesting. She cleans it out while gargling the hand-held flashlight, and to her amazement, notices Harry's veins around the infected area have turned black. She leans in closer, almost sticking her nose in the little bite mark, and watches how the blackness is spreading ever so slightly like the ink inside a thermometer.

She takes his temperature, dresses the wound and gives him medication she thinks will help.

"Can I be honest?"

Harry nods.

"I don't think anyone is coming. In fact, I wonder if Tom

even called the authorities."

"He's probably the worst person I've ever met, but I saw Tom try to call for help or back up or whatever. It's funny you should mention such a thing because it's peculiar."

"What is?"

He recoils in pain momentarily when Claire accidentally pricks him with a needle. She apologises as he continues.

"Not one person has tried to get in here." He has heard no noise from the outside since they lowered the shutters.

"Maybe the outside saw the shutter and knew not to bother."

Harry likes Claire's optimism, but says, "Trust me, if people wanted something bad enough, they could get in. In this type of situation, no law enforcement and no rules means everybody can do what they want and run wild. Looting, rioting, robbing banks and shops. It's just like the London riots." He further explains, "The store, this shelter is a 'fucking goldmine' of medicine, water, canned food, weapons and supplies for the end of the world, put figuratively. This place should have been ransacked by now."

Harry tries not to cough up a lung.

She dabs him. "How do you know all this information, the magazine trick, what happened in the London riots, etcetera?"

Harry looks at Claire for a minute like she is an idiot, knowing her ignorance is bliss, but secretly she is just trying to read him.

"I have had my life experiences," he says ominously.

"What would you do if it was the end of the world?" Claire scowls.

"Apart from all the shit I've already done? I have always wanted to trash a supermarket, drive a Porsche at 200 miles per hour. Kill my ex's boyfriend."

Claire giggles, trying to concentrate on sticking Harry up.

"Trash a supermarket!" she repeats.

He carries on. "Yeah! I'd start here because like I said we are on a gold mine. Look, if there no societal rules and there would be no consequences, I'd love to go nuts in here!"

"What do you mean?"

"Think about it, do you never look at the stuff all prim and proper, every placed window display and perfect mannequin. All the symmetrical and organised things in the aisles and just think I'd love to just trash that shit?" He barley laughs as his voice croaks.

Claire can't help but grin. "I guess."

"It represents commercialism, conformity to the dull and mundane repetition of law and order, rules and regulations... how things must be."

"Ah, so you're a fan of breaking the rules."

"No, I'm a fan of breaking the illusion that we must abide and obey in a society that expects us to be sheep."

"It's not the fact you want to trash the things for chaos but because of..."

"What they represent, yes. When I've had my fun, when the economy falls, water and food become valuable and currency. I'd set up a perimeter, a community, and trade."

"Trade what?"

"I don't know yet. Weapons, protection maybe?"

"What's stopping anyone just taking it by force."

"There isn't. You would just need great charisma and the art of selling."

"Wow, you've really thought about this. What are you not telling me?"

Harry smirks and then answers Claire's question with another question. "How did you know to take your shoes off to make your footsteps totally silent?"

"Fair point." Claire smiles and looks away for a moment.

"Things don't last, Claire, whether it's a 1000-year dynasty or a civilisation that collapses one day, it'll all just crumble because of something so trivial. Take this supposed pandemic they're all raving about on the news. One organism that threatens our existence has the potential to collapse our society. To stop the spread, they will have to shut everything down. Which means no income or revenue. Places will gather dust and go under. Then, the stores will be robbed. Rome wasn't built in a day, but it collapsed in one."

"Six actually."

They lock eyes again—that strange feeling coming back to Claire's stomach. Then Harry explains the truth. His girlfriend dumped him on New Year's Eve 4 years ago, so he joined the army. Picked up a few tricks. He was also at the first wave of the London riots in Camden and watched the city burn. Harry confesses it would be the first thing he would do if he got the chance.

"What would?"

"Rob a bank or loot a phone shop."

Claire looks at him, judging his choice after his speech about conformity and commercialism.

He smiles and asks her, "Have you never once had an impure thought of stealing something or wanting to just set something on fire?"

Claire pauses for a moment, wanting to deny any evil urges or intrusive thoughts, but she giggles and moments later, she confesses she's always wanted to trash a supermarket too.

"Go down to the alcohol section and start throwing bottles down the aisle, eat a can of peaches on the spot or just pour a box of cereal out and make the cereal version of a snow angel. And I've always wanted to kick a toddler in the face. They just fuck me off when they scream, noise upon noise, and oh my gosh when they gawk and stare at you for no reason."

Harry pauses and jokingly tells her she is fucked up. They laugh and a moment of silent passes.

She quietly remarks, "It must liberate you to do something like that, not out of badness but just freedom; as long as it didn't hurt anyone."

"Kicking children in the face?"

"No!" she chuckles. "Just the freedom to do it without consequence. Some look at it as criminal damage, others see it as a means of release to not kill themselves. Which is probably why they have rage rooms."

Claire admits she is rambling and swiftly changes topic, asking Harry why, if he had the urge to join the London riots, didn't he? Harry explains it's because that's the difference between true psychopaths and rest of society.

"Even though I wanted to, for the same reason you want to trash a supermarket, we didn't."

He leans in and says it's because they're the true crazy people—the ones burying the thoughts down. Claire is unsure for a moment until they burst out laughing, and Harry coughs and chokes. Claire tries not to grimace.

"Is there anyone out there for you?" he asks kindly.

"Just my brother. I'm worried he'll come looking for me but he isn't here yet."

She pats his forehead with a wet towel and the two kids stare at each other for an awkwardly extended amount of time. Anything over four seconds is weird in Claire's rule book. Harry brushes her ginger hair behind her ear and Claire's heart skips a beat. She doesn't know where to look or put herself, but she knows what's coming. Harry slowly leans in and Claire does the same. Suddenly Harry's face abruptly misses her and projectile vomits down Claire's arm. She doesn't freak out, but sits there and pats his back awkwardly. Harry can't stop apologising.

"It's fine. You're not the first and you won't be the last."

However, it stinks, green and gooey, nothing like she's ever seen before. *Black veins, green bile... what-the-fuck is this infection?* She then insists they must go to a hospital.

"Fuck Tom's rules. Nobody is coming. We need those keys; we're trapped in this place until then. You need to save your strength. We're going to a hospital."

Harry looks like he is about to argue. Claire shows him what he looks like. She gives him a hand mirror, and his own reflection takes him back, aghast. He reluctantly agrees.

"I guess that settles it. We will need to take as many supplies from the supermarket as possible because we do not know what is out there."

The last thing they agree on is they mustn't tell Tom. Claire gives Harry a sedative to help him sleep and leaves the den.

01:55 hours
Dylan, Linda & Val

Swirling his drink, resulting in about three spillages, Dylan drunkenly and mockingly puts on a posh voice. He smells the glass, noting how one smells 'red' and picks up another, noting how that one smells 'white'.

The ladies have let down their guard as they surround themselves with bottles of wine, pickle jars, and bread. Val insists they must take a 'selfie' to commemorate the moment for when they are rescued and hopes they stay in touch; she hiccups as her sombrero falls. They've all found items of clothing to suit their procrastination. Linda looks like she's barley in the room with her Russian-style woolly hat slumped over her face. She's getting too old for this. Dylan has drawn on what appears to be a moustache with stationary from downstairs. He clings to a tall, half-eaten, French baguette and works his beret, pulling the cheesiest smile as they cosy up for their moment. Val captures it on her old phone.

Claire pops out from the corner, stumbling upon the tipsy

soiree. She's still rubbing her hands after sanitising them and putting Harry to sleep. She looks at the amateur United Nations party and rolls her eyes.

"Oh hello, m'lady. Have you come to join the comradery? Where is prince Harold of Camden?" Dylan keeps up the posh voice.

"It's nice you've let your guard down guys, but someone still needs to keep a level head. Harry is sick and he needs medical attention. I'm a just trainee which means I can only do so much, so I've given him a sedative. He may be strong enough to move." She crouches down to get them to listen in. "I think we need to get out of here."

The others aren't taking much notice, so she sighs and heads toward the bathroom to wipe Harry's vomit off her.

02:02 hours
Claire
Bathroom

Claire hasn't seen her reflection in almost two days. She stares at herself, trying not to lose faith—she will see her brother again, who is surely looking for her right now. She does not know what-the-fuck is going on outside in the real world, but she's going stir crazy. If Tom wasn't watching them like a hawk, she would have tried to get everybody out by now. She takes one glance at the blood-soaked vomit stained clothing and thinks about how fatigued she looks, having not slept in a full day.

Her stomach grumbles. What she would give for a pizza right now. She thinks about the last 24-hours again; the flashes of the people eating one another, the death and the killing. Macabre images scar her mind and suddenly she isn't hungry anymore.

"What if he's dead?" she asks.

Claire knows her brother is a badass. After all, he brought

237

her up after their mother died. If he could say anything to her now in this situation it would be, 'don't lose your nerve now Claire bear'.

After scouring herself red, in what seems like forever because of the tiny basin, she leaves the bathroom which is on the bottom floor in the corner of the clothes section. She can hear the others upstairs laughing away. While Harry is out, it will be up to her to plan. Claire picks out some easy clothing—nothing fancy. Spaghetti string T and skinny jeans, even a nice, chequered shirt to go with it. She'll need a coat, it's freezing out. She looks down.

Shit, my shoes are still upstairs. Fuck it.

She picks out some new shoes that are easy to run in… just in case. She takes off her blood-stained jeans and top, not realising the cameras are behind her.

02:23 hours
Tom
Office

After getting over his little sulk, the stubborn and obnoxious manager cowers in his throne room, so he can monitor his subjects. A part of Tom doesn't want anybody to come, at least not yet anyway. This is perfect for him. Soon as the shit hit the fan, Tom intuitively knew this was something that would stick around, and instantly thought of the 'killing' he could make.

As he eats his yogurt, watching the screens, he casually overhears Harry explaining about the looting and rioting and like Harry, Tom realises what a gold mine he is sitting on. When the people come looking, Tom will start cooking.

He is tucking into some beef jerky stashed away in his draw to fulfil his obese needs, when he double takes at one screen. He belches and leans in, then slowly smiles. A satin-draped Claire is undressing in the clothes section. He puts down the jerky to perform his own. Tom unzips his pants and licks his lips.

02:25 hours
Claire

It's not perfect, but it will do, and at least she feels more human. There's still a girl under there.

"Right, time to get into action."

Claire goes up to the escalators and walks to Dylan's spot. They're drunk. Trying to not be irritated, the others have become too comfortable now. Fearing nobody is coming, Claire tries to get them to concentrate.

She reiterates. "Guys we need move Harry, he needs a hospital. It's time to pack up." She isn't joking. If rescue won't come to them, then they will go to it.

"What about my dick drip boss?" Val asks.

"Ex-boss," Linda corrects her.

"Oh, yeah!" she laughs.

Claire pauses and looks around. The red light on the camera is blinking. She quivers.

Fuck, he probably saw me changing.

She sits down next to Dylan and puts the blanket over her lap to make it look like she's joined them. Nothing suspicious to see here. She tries to get serious with them.

"We will not inform the manager. We're just going to leave. But first we need to get his keys. So, I was thinking we either wait until he's asleep or we take them by force. I was really hoping to avoid the latter."

"I'm not afraid of that walrus. I battered him once I'll do it again. He's all mouth." Dylan goes from happy drunk to angry drunk in an instant.

"Well, he can't keep us here. We have rights. The only reason I've even pandered to staying so long is the hope of rescue! He's an awful man; they'll remove him!" Linda

239

shudders.

"Look, are any of you sober enough to pack? You know… grab rucksacks?"

"Did you say snacks?" Val stumbles over her words.

"Claire, my crimson Goddess, being drunk and packing is part of the fun." Dylan relaxes again.

"Okay, I want you to grab bags, pack a few cans and dry stuff for the journey, warm clothing. Water is key. Find a suitable weapon for each. But for the love of God, don't make it obvious. Tom is watching our every move. Make it subtle and meet me here in 15."

They all agree they are able. So, they get to work.

02:30 hours
Tom

The flushing of the toilet echoes down corrridor as Manager, Tom opens his personal toilet door, grunting before he spits and fastens his belt. He comes back to the screens.

"Shut-the-front-door," he says—they're gone from their spot.

Tom calmly flicks through the screens, channel to channel, and finds them individually packing products into bags. Tom growls and storms out.

Claire

Claire has returned to her makeshift den to check on Harry. The others agree to leave when he comes to, but something feels wrong. She sees his shaking, and the sweats have stopped, but also there's no coughing. He's calm now. Black veins and pastiness ever so slightly stop his new state from reaching full bliss.

She touches his forehead. "Ice cold?"

She can't tell if that's a good thing or a bad thing, because he's so precious… a male sleeping beauty.

Dylan calls her over to the main entrance with the shutters, which are locking them in. Claire strokes his hair back, kisses his forehead and pulls a blanket over him.

The entrance is the most open part of the store. There is a doorway to a fast food place to the left, aisles behind, tills to the right and entrance to the front.

"Look what I found." Dylan reveals keys on a lanyard, the ones he took earlier to spite Tom. "Forgot I had these."

"Dylan, as soon as we are safe, I'm taking you up on that drink!" Claire embraces him.

She can see they are ready, but Claire is having a sudden change of heart.

"I think somebody should stay with Harry and I'm worried about him—somebody should go out and get rescue, rather than move Harry there."

"Don't you think it wise to wait until the morning, a few more hours can't hurt? We can sleep off the alcohol. It may not be safe to move at night and Harry may have had a nap by then."

"Yeah, listen to them, Claire Bear."

Unexpectedly, they are all startled by Tom having cropped up behind them at the entrance. He's caught on.

"You should wait until morning for Claire's boyfriend."

He is arrogantly walking with his hands behind his back. Suddenly, everybody's hairs are on edge and Claire can feel her adrenaline spiking.

"It's over twat-head, we're out of here." Val gives him the middle finger.

Claire notices Tom holding a butcher's knife, and he's twisting it in his palm. Val tightens the grip on her frying pan. Dylan gathers the girls behind him aside from Claire, who stands alongside.

02:35 hours

"This doesn't have to be messy, bruv," Dylan says with a menacing stance, protecting his ladies.

Tom can feel the sharp butcher's knife almost chiming as he twists; he's pissed off—they are trying to leave. He told them they can't, so he is going to have to assert his authority.

"You didn't even invite me to dinner."

"You can't control what we do mate, it's a free country."

"Oh, fuck off. I'm in charge now."

Claire firmly explains, "Harry is sick, his wound is septic, and he needs medical attention, rescue is not coming…"

He cuts her off. "THIS IS MY STORE AND MY RULES. NO ONE GOES IN OR OUT UNTIL THEY COME!"

"I vote leave, all for one and all that!" Val raises her hand.

"Oh, you would, specimen."

They no longer feel safe in the presence of Tom. Claire and Dylan exchange a look of uncertainty. This may get messy. His frantic shouting becomes threatening.

"Great, fat boy's turned into a psycho."

"If anyone tries to leave, there will be consequences."

"Four against one, mate, you've lost. Pray on some other dumber group." Dylan jangles the keys like a carrot in front of him, enraging Tom.

The others complain they want to find their friends and family. Claire insists she has a brother who will look for her, Harry is sick, and so on. She must play it cool, because Tom reminds her of her stepfather (an abusive narcissist who drank too much and terrorised Claire and her brother, so much they had to run away). Despite this bringing up some old skeletons, she knows how to handle 'his type'. She tries to level with him halfway. She will stay if the others can leave, even if it's only one of them. Because they need help.

242

"Think about it, it'll help you. We can bring back more supplies, more people for you. That's what you want, isn't it?"

Tom knows Claire is trying to sweeten him up, and he isn't budging. "This place will become my kingdom, and when the economy falls, you'll all have to stay and set up a business because they *will* come," he says.

Val whispers to Linda that Tom has lost it. Linda holds her blouse, trembling. Val tries to comfort her. She butts in, telling Tom he is scaring the others, and, in all honesty, he can't control jack shit. He can't keep anyone from leaving.

"I'd like my P45! You fat monster."

"You don't even know how to work the sodding keys," he viciously snarls to Dylan.

"I do! Buh-bye!" Val picks up her rucksack and takes Linda's hand. She goes to the door and enters the code for the shutters.

"With or without anyone, I have worked too hard to not be going on a plane tomorrow. I don't care if England is rioting!" she curses.

If it's one thing Tom does not like, it's not getting his own way, not being in control.

"Dyl, go with girls, I got this." Claire doesn't break eye contact with the manager.

At first he reluctantly waits, staring at Claire. She shoos him and promises to catch up. Dylan picks up his rucksack, promising to come back with the army and a bouquet if he can escape.

Tom can feel his adrenaline spike. He screams out, watching the others ignore his commands.

"Right, I need you to breathe and calm down. Take a breath with me."

Claire remembers her training, how to calm a volatile person at a scene. That was one of the good things about Claire's classes, keeping her wits about her. It could calm a crying child, someone having a breakdown or even someone in shock. There were several factors.

Val comes up to the tiny alarm box sifting through keys next to the automatic doors and punches in the digits.

One drops from the bunch and bounces away. "Oh balls, damn alcohol."

"Don't worry, I got it." Dylan smiles and bends down to get it as Val turns the correct key to raise the shutters.

SPLAT!

Linda Screams horrifically. Val's arm drops from the keycode. Dylan looks up, recoils and pulls Linda away in horror. Claire looks on paralyzed with shock. Tom has thrown the butcher's knife perfectly at Val's head, and it sits as if in a slab of wood, sliced into her cranium. Blood trickles down her ear and lashes, and her eyes roll to the back of her head. The poor girl is motionless, twitching ever so slightly—eventually, she caves and falls.

"W-what... did... you... do?" Claire whimpers, moving her hands from her mouth.

"*I* hired her... can do what I like." He sniffs and wipes his nose. "Besides, it was meant for him. I told you there would be consequences."

11:02 hours

Beth Recoils in disgust from the CCTV screens, having just seen this mad, murderous manager taking down a girl in cold blood. Claire is sat on the table behind, and looks down. A tear rolls off her face. Beth wants to look away but can't.

Tom is eerily calm to say he just struck down his ex-employee.

244

02:27 hours

"You... you *killed* her." Linda breaks down.

The group has discovered truly what a monster he has become. Claire comes to life and screams at the others to run. She must rescue Harry. Dylan takes Linda's hand and runs off with her down to the checkouts. Claire narrowly escapes Tom's reach when he lunges.

Fuck me, it's not like I'm going anywhere. I'm a rat in the cage.

Tom walks up to Val's body, puts one foot on her back, and yanks out the knife. The satisfying crunch and flick of the blood as the life leaves her body is euphoria. He slowly walks after the others.

Claire has lost sight of Linda and Dylan but prays they are escaping through a different exit.

It's as if he has just ignored that Claire is there. She looks back at the keypad with the lanyard still swinging. *Shit, we need the keys to get out.* Claire rips them away and runs off after them.

02:59 hours
Dylan & Linda

Linda is whimpering and Dylan is trying to quieten her, so they won't be discovered. They come to the door that leads up the stairs to the office. Surely there must be another way out if Tom could make it outside? They are about to flee through the open door when out of nowhere, Harry emerges from an aisle. Dylan knows something isn't right. He slows down. Linda thanks God.

Dylan nervously tells her, "That isn't Harry."

Harry is gormlessly glaring at them with a vacant look of despair, drunken.

"Don't move!" He tells Linda to stay put for a few

seconds, but her whimpering turns to hysterical crying.

The infection has totally consumed Harry; his veins are black, spread all over his body. He's grey and green and pale… grimy. He wheezes and his eyes are bloodshot. Drool dripping from his mouth resembles a thirsty bloodhound.

Linda looks around for Tom, trembling, gripping her own kitchen knife for dear life.

"Harry, you okay?"

Dylan thinks his infected wound may have caused some kind of delirium. Harry comes to life and lunges for his best friend, startling Linda to drop her weapon. Dylan pushes Harry back with some force.

"HE'S ONE OF THEM!" Dylan screams, wrestling his cousin. Their new enemy lets out an ear-splitting roar. "Fuck off, bruv."

He forces Linda away as they both fly down the travelators. He then shoves her into a rail of clothes, climbs in, and covers Linda's trembling mouth. They can hear Harry's war cries in the distance.

"WRAUUUUGH!"

Linda can't take the sound, causing her to sob through Dylan's hand. He realises the CCTV still live in the office, which Tom can play back to find them.

Shit!

Dylan must get to that room and get the tape; they can use it to clear themselves. It's means having to leave Linda for a few moments. She is in no position to join him.

"Linda, I need you to stay put—"

"No, no, no, n-n-no."

"Sh, shhh, I need to do this, if were going to get out of here." He has to cover her mouth again. "Please shut the fuck up, I'm begging you, lady."

Linda loses it and begs him not to leave. The commotion causes her to sprawl out of the hiding spot between the rails. Dylan, who tries to crawl out after her, shrieks and calls for her to look out. Linda turns—in the blink of an eye, she feels a slash across her throat. Her eyes widen. Suddenly, her throat gapes like Niagara Falls.

Tom holds his butcher's knife high after slitting her from ear to ear and doesn't hesitate to attack Dylan. He must have already got to the cameras and tracked them down. Dylan shuffles out the other side and trips over a rail. The fall causes Tom to miss his swipe and, instead, he ends up slicing Dylan's right hand clean off.

Dylan stares in complete shock at his missing limb. It bleeds uncontrollably.

Tom laughs at his misfortune. Shock turns into searing pain; Dylan cries out and falls.

Linda squirms from the gallons of blood pouring out of her neck until she dies, unable to gasp for air, terrified, scared and alone in her last moments. The blood flows out thickly, as red as any flower in bloom.

Tom creeps toward Dylan who shoves his arm under his left pit.

"If you all want to leave, then I will make a statement to anyone who comes here. I'll hang your bodies from the entrance! This is my place. They will not fuck me. I'll use you as bait for your mate."

02:59 hours
Claire

Claire has crawled from aisle to aisle back to her den, trying to keep out of sight of Tom; she prays the others have got away through a different exit somehow without the spare set of keys. She shuffles away from the blankets and bottles of wine they were enjoying. Claire makes it back to Harry's den but finds an empty bed. She looks on in confusion. *How? Where?*

Suddenly, she remembers the cameras in the CCTV room.

247

She can see what happened and maybe she can spot Tom.

She moves toward the open office door leading from the shop floor to the stairs when a bellowing scream startles her.

What-the-fuck was that?

Tom emerges from the door in front of Claire, but his attention is drawn to the noise. If he glanced to his left, she'd be discovered... caught out in the open. Her soul leaves her body again. Then Tom walks off, missing her by the skin of her teeth.

No time to lose! She bolts to life and sprints up the stairs to find out what the hell happened to Harry. She finds the footage, and it's puzzling; he gets up lethargically. He staggers slowly away from the den. She checks another screen and clicks onto Dylan and Linda concealed between clothes rails. She sees Tom on a separate camera and gasps —she must help despite being scared shitless. But first she takes out the tapes and switches off the cameras. She stands on a table and puts the tapes in the ventilation shaft. This will buy her some time if Tom tries to find her and will be evidence to send this motherfucker down when they finally find some rescue.

11:15 hours
Beth & Claire

"Actual blood is nothing like movie blood, just as actual death is nothing like movie death. There is no amount of horror that can prepare a person for seeing the life leave another, the hopelessness, the tearing as the soul departs," Claire says as Beth's tears dampen her pale face.

The tape ejects, and Claire informs her that was the last tape she hid. Since she switched the cameras off, there was nothing else to record, but she figures it is enough to put Tom away. Beth is unsure. Should she tell her about the state of things on the outside?

"What happened next, where are your other friends?"

"Let's just say I'm glad the cameras stopped rolling, because let me tell you, you will not *believe* what he did."

03:03 hours

Claire jogs down the stairs, back onto the shop floor, hoping to rescue her allies. She stops and ducks, peering through the clear banister. She spots Tom walking up toward where she thinks the other two are.

Should she shout something? *No, it's too late!*

Linda emerges, not paying attention to what's behind her. Dylan tells her to look out and Claire screams, but Dylan's cry masks Claire's echo. Tom slices the butcher knife from one of Linda's ears to the other. She falls. Dylan trips and his hand is amputated.

Claire falls to her knees, covering her mouth as tears roll down her face.

Dylan says something she can't make out, then Tom repeatedly 'butchers' him until he is unrecognisable.

03:04 hours
Tom

Tom lunges for Dylan, but he misses his footing over a rail and stumbles back. Tom gets Dylan's hand. He chops it clean off and watches Dylan dwell in a state of shock, gawking at his missing limb. Tom laughs and tells him he didn't mean to do that, but it's even better.

"Just like twatting that council estate skid mark."

Dylan collapses, slowly drags a shirt from a rail and applies it to his bloodied stump. He then crawls backwards as Tom excitedly moves in.

"All you had to do was just sit tight. And now look at the fucking mess..."

K. J. McGuinness

He will negotiate and save Dylan's life if he complies. *Thank God Dylan is still drunk, his stump doesn't hurt half as bad and his blood is thin, maybe he can get out of this one.*

"Go fuck a corpse, mate!"

Dylan grins and uses his remaining hand to give Tom the middle finger. He knows he's a goner. It's like a twig snaps in Tom's tiny head.

Dylan can see the cogs turning like a machine processing data. Tom's brain has printed out a receipt that says, 'does not compute, kill, kill, kill'. Tom sees red and his neck cricks like an involuntary response. He has left the building. This monster in control strikes Dylan.

Swipe, there goes the middle finger. Dylan uses his arms to protect his face and chest. Tom goes for his gut, slashing at him twice. He cuts so deep a part of Dylan's intestines falls out; he goes silent, but he's still conscious. It'll be over soon.

SLASH! His face is mush. Tom feels the spray of the blood. He is alive. Who knew this was his calling? No rules, his own kingdom.

He grabs hold of Dylan's braided locks, who is now unresponsive with gashes all over his mug. Tom takes it upon himself to extend Dylan's neck and raises the cleaver over his own head. He brings it down with a great fury. CRUNCH. Up over the head and down into Dyl's neck. CRUNCH!

There's wheezing from Dylan's half torn windpipe as the blood banks spew open.

"Come on, it's not concrete," Tom strains.

SWING. CRUNCH. SWING. CRUNCH.

Tom cackles and wriggles Dylan's head, twisting, jiggling.

"NGHHHHH! UGH!"

Finally, he takes the last swing and whoosh! Dylan's head

comes free. Thomas brings up the head and looks at his sunken eyes, floppy tongue and missing nose.

"I think I'll take my keys back, pal." He laughs.

Tom remembers that ginger bitch Claire is still loose in his domain. He smears the blood already splattered across his face.

"Wow, got a bit of a sweat on. That's a whole new meaning to the phrase slashing prices."

He spins his head to the second floor. He spots Claire and smiles, holding poor Dylan's severed head. She witnessed the whole thing.

03:05 hours
Claire

FUCK!

Tom spots her. She ducks down, then BOOM! She's yanked backward by something. She turns to see Harry has got a hold of her shirt. But it's not Harry, not anymore…

Something has consumed him.

Claire tries to break free from his spitting and snarling. She frees herself by getting out of her shirt as he tugs, and makes a run for it with Harry hot on her tail. Tom appears around the corner, butcher knife at the ready.

"SHIT!"

Claire's instincts take over and everything happens so fast she power slides underneath Tom, between his legs. She punches as hard as she can.

"Right in the boys!"

Tom

No amount of pain could equal the deadly blow Claire delivers between Tom's legs. He drops to his knees and releases his knife. The pain is overwhelming, but as he

251

looks up, Harry is coming toward him. He reckons being lunch would be worse. Claire rolls away, gets up, and runs off.

Claire

Good, I've lost them for now.

Claire's brain is telling her to get the hell out or hide where they will never find her. She is going to have to play cat and mouse with her infected ex-friend and this crazed killer.

She does not know why Harry is acting the way he is. Eventually, she wraps her arms in some magazines like he taught her and comes face-to-face with them both at either end.

11:17 hours

"That girl, you said her name was Val. I knew her. She used to hang around in my group... she was..." Beth tries to not to think about seeing Kieran and Darcy's bloody corpses get back up and rip people to shreds. "... a friend of a friend. At the same university."

"She didn't look like the uni type, or act like it... or even sound like it."

"That's not the strangest thing to happen in the past two days."

"I'll say."

Beth asks, "How did *you* get here?"

"First, I need to show you something." Claire takes her hand. "Tom spent the time looking for me."

Beth's heart goes out for Claire. She says it must have been the scariest thing of her life.

"Both Haz and Tom sped at me from either end of the store. I was piggy in the middle. I crouched and barged into

Harry, he flipped over me, and then I span and put my arms in front of my face. Tom hit me that hard, he tore through the magazines on my arms."

"Damn, that's pretty cool!"

"I grew up with an overprotective bother, I had to learn how to put him on his arse a few times between play fights."

"How did you get away?" Beth ponders.

Claire relives it. "I just kept running."

She kicked Tom. Harry tried to stand, so she just 'legged it'. She watched Tom kill Harry by crushing in his skull and repeatedly kicking it. Tom hunted her like it was sport. Claire reveals she hid in the vents where she put the tapes. She watched Tom scour and search for hours through the cracks, hopefully convincing him she had left the building, but he kept circling.

It was almost poetic.

Claire cries. "Just when everything seemed lost, people tried to seek refuge by banging on the doors, but Tom left them to their fate. Help never came. Eventually, their screaming stopped."

She pauses in her stroll until she comes to the bathroom door and swings it open.

"Oh." Beth lets out.

There he is, tied up and gagged with duct tape all over. Tom. He glares at Beth, muttering and passing stifled screams at her.

"How?"

"Turns out it was easier than expected when he finally took a break. He came back to the office to find you and I just slid down from the vent." She holds an invisible bottle in her hand and pops her tongue. "Dragging him was the hard part. I'm not a killer either, I was hoping the police would come while I was fixing you up."

She does not know the state of the outside world and doesn't understand why no one has come. She had to listen

253

to him whine and call out for her, and it made her cry, but she said a silent prayer and mourned for the dead, because those images were now burned into her mind and all she could do was cower and hide.

"I just keep replaying what he did to them all. Single-handed." Claire tears up again.

Beth won't lie to herself that she feels a little more uncomfortable now than sympathetic. "It's alright!

"Is help out there, Beth? Is help coming?"

Beth flashes back to her own nightmare and looks away.

"What is it like out there?"

Beth doesn't know how to answer, so she looks away again.

"That bad?" she asks.

"I don't know how far this thing goes. I'm certain the army is coming, though all we can do is wait, make sure no one tries to hurt us, or take this place."

One thing Claire can't get her head around is why her friend turned on her. Beth flashes back to Kieran and Darcy; she watched them die and then she watched them reanimate and start hurting and eating people. It's clear now this isn't just an isolated incident, it's spreading.

"A friend of mine was convinced it was the Flu on TV, the virus was making them violent and evil. We got split up, and I lost him. I just hope he's okay. I think he was right all along!"

"I couldn't bring myself to go back down once you got here. I just think I needed someone to be here. Let's go back down. So we can move my friends out of the way and put them to rest," Claire begs.

Beth is reluctant. If her story is anything like what she has revealed, it will be grim. The girls go onto the shop floor. It's bright and quiet, the intercom radio is playing from the speakers.

"I thought you said the power went out?"

"It just came back on, randomly during the night... I turned the music on because it made me feel less alone."

Beth is struggling to trust her own shadow. It's clear now she wasn't lying. Everything is where it should be. It was on camera, but something made Beth doubt it. *Maybe it's just the absurdity?* They stroll past the freezer containing the first set of remains and then to the banister. Way yonder is a body with a skull crushed in and what looks like bits of white and pink chunks surrounding the corpse. Claire turns around, breaking down a seventh time.

"I'm sorry."

"It's okay."

Beth sees the bodies are scattered. Linda, Dylan's head, and she even spots Val's body turned away in a foetal position over the other side of the travelators near the food court.

"I don't have the heart to kill him, but that cunt needs to pay when the army gets here."

Beth takes a deep breath, exhaling in frustrion. She puts a hand on Claire's shoulder.

"I've seen some really, really... uh... God awful things in the last two days. I understand. I'm here now."

"Thank you." Claire randomly embraces her, much to her surprise. Beth is left stood with her arms spread, wide eyed and confused.

"Yup," she says sharply, pursing her lips inward. "I image you'll want to change, wash and eat when it is done."

Out of nowhere there is a tremendous crash... inside the store. Beth and Claire jerk their faces to the entrance as a lorry steamrolls straight through the shutters.

"Fuck me..." she mutters.

"Wow!" Beth goes slack jawed.

"That's not good, come on. DANGER!"

Claire runs back to the office to grab two weapons. Beth watches, horrified, a little stumped on what to do so she just stands there bewildered. It is a delivery truck with the supermarket's logo, smashed through the entrance, destroying the front doors and shutters.

Luckily, it has formed a cork, halfway lodged into the hole. Beth and Claire go to investigate.

Trouble is brewing.

CHAPTER 9:

THE BEAST FROM THE EAST

January 2nd, 2012
12:33 hours
Superstore

The violent clattering of metal falling is deafening. The cladding from the front of the entrance dances on the marble floor, echoing out a shock wave.

"Here!" Claire almost chucks a bat at her.

Beth and Claire slowly approach a lorry that has come steaming in and crashed straight through the front barricade of the automatic doors, lodging itself halfway in the entrance. The front of the truck has smoke seeping out of its front. Luckily, it's acting as a cork, stopping the door and half the entrance from collapsing on itself.

Beth and Claire notice the lorry belongs to the shop.

"This one's from the car park!" Claire exhales.

"Someone has done this on purpose. Ready yourself!" Beth shuffles Claire behind her.

This is no freak accident. Claire is on edge with the butcher's knife having taken ownership from Tom, cautiously ready for anyone who leaps out. An ice-cold gust of wind coming from the outside greets the girls. It's freezing. Beth shivers.

My head is already pounding!

"I'm going to batter whoever did this!" She looks back at Claire. "Do you know where these lorries were?" she whispers.

"Docking station downstairs, I think. We could never get to them because we didn't have time to figure out all the keys."

Suddenly, a boy pops out from the driver's side and jumps from the truck. He is vigilant and holds a blunt instrument as his only defence. Beth holds her arm out, pushing Claire up against the side of the lorry, out of sight. She can hear the boy talking to another muffled voice; it's a deep base tone, so she assumes it's another boy who follows his friend.

One comments how big the store is. The other nearly tears him a new arse screaming about how idiotic it was driving a truck through the front doors of a supermarket.

"Well, it was locked, and the shutters were down... you saw that. Besides, we don't know who's in here. Show them we mean business."

"That's the second time in a day we nearly died in a vehicle driven by you, no less!"

"You're alive, aren't you?"

The other, having ignoring his protests, tells his friend they should be quick as the crash would likely draw unwanted attention. The first one explains they are at a stalemate until their other friend wakes up.

"So, there's three of them."

Beth and Claire talk in signals. On the silent count of three, the girls jump out and let rip a war cry with their weapons drawn to scare them off.

The two boys jump out of their skin, screaming, and one drops his weapon out of fear. The one who crashed the lorry into the shutters turns, trying to not react. Beth's face drops. The person responsible for crashing into the entrance is none of other than her best friend, Will. He, too, is just as surprised.

"GIZMO?" she shrieks.

"Well, I'll be dammed."

Will and Beth are reunited. She can't believe her eyes; she runs to him as Adam cowers behind Will, revealed to be the other boy. Beth buries her face in his shoulder and squeezes him until he almost passes out, even though he is just as grateful for the loving embrace. Claire looks on in confusion, still poised in attack formation. Beth turns to Claire and gleefully tells her Will is her friend and they lived together. They were having a party when everything 'went to shit'.

Claire is a little hesitant. She scowls at Will, having lost her trust in people. Beth ignores her and turns back to Will. She confesses she thought he was dead, and she would never see him again.

"I thought I lost you back in that street alley. *What* are you doing here?" She pauses, frowns, and playfully slaps him hard.

He asks, "What that was for?"

She looks over his shoulder at the mess in the doorway, the smoking lorry. Sarcastically, she tilts her head.

"THAT was for driving a monstrosity through Claire's hideout."

Suddenly, Will is struck by an ethereal force when he sees Claire. It's like Will's reality has slowed by a tenth of a second. He thinks he's laid eyes on the most beautiful girl he's ever seen—a redhead, just like Kieran, and boy how he loves redheads. Her perfect crimson hair rests right above her shoulders. This is hair that could fold nations. *Those eyes!* he thinks; *swills of emerald green in the cosmos that is her iris.* Her perfect skin is so fragile yet so soft and the unerring number of freckles around her nose makes him melt. With cheeks the colour of pink roses and eyelashes longer than anyone's he's ever seen, her out-of-this-world body catches his attention. She has a small waist with a huge posterior hidden under a checked shirt, stopping at her curvy hips, and they fit so perfectly in her dark washed blue skinny jeans. This is the girl, the girl he knows will change the way he looks at life, because he hasn't felt this way about anyone since Kieran. He feels so wrong for being captivated by her while he still feels attached and betrothed to Kieran, but then he remembers what happened to him.

He's gone, William, a voice says. Will realises he's clinging to a memory, a perfect idea of someone who isn't even alive anymore. His chest hurts.

"W-w-who is your friend?" He grins, trying to swallow the heartache.

"Is he broken?" Claire says curtly.

He's not usually the guy Claire would fantasise about. For a start, he's ash blonde, and she's always liked black hair on men, and taller. But she thinks he has the nicest blue eyes. She prefers men with a handle on the world of business, a critical thinker, and she thinks he doesn't look like he's got two pennies to rub together. *He's not special-looking, or well-dressed,* she thinks, but to her he stands out from the other two, and she can't quite understand what it is yet. There's something about Will—a slight confidence and inflated ego perhaps, that has Claire briefly muddling her words and blushing uncontrollably. Will explains their intention was to completely drive the lorry through the barricade and pack the truck with supplies.

"I assumed this place was closed for the holidays." He defends himself. "When I saw the shutters still down, I didn't know if this place was untouched or if people were inside. We had to risk it. We need to eat."

"You could have just knocked!" states Claire, far from impressed.

"Listen, if you went through what I went through in the last 36 hours, I doubt you'd be in the mood for knocking," Will retorts, escalating the conversation.

"Oh, you wanna bet, mate?" Claire squares up to him.

"Whoa! Whoa! Whoa!" Beth comes between them. "This

is all a misunderstanding, I assure you."

"You mean to tell me you turn up here on death's door looking for help and a few hours later a truck smashes into my safe place and it is *your* friend. After what I've just done for you?"

"I know how it looks." Beth tries to calm things down.

"You we're scoping this place out. WEREN'T YOU?" Claire raises her voice.

"Whoa! Please, Claire! I can't explain it. I don't know how he's here, but it is a freak chance event. Truly. I'm a good person. We are good people. We've known each other since we were six!" Beth tries to keep her full attention as Claire becomes a cross between menacing and jittery.

She finally takes a breath. "I'm sorry. I just think I'm a little unhinged. Don't make me regret taking a chance."

"What happened here?" Will realises he's missing something obvious.

"It's a long story. But she needs our help and our love, Will."

"Look, if your truck acts as a second barricade, I can live with it... for now."

"Who's the skinny boy?" Beth asks, directing her attention to Adam, still slightly cowering in confusion. "Wait. I recognise you; you were with our group in the university library and then again at that house party in Headingley a few days back." Beth clicks her fingers as Adam tries to find his words. "Uh... ADAM! Kieran's classmate."

"Seriously, another one you know?" Claire's face turns mean.

"I just picked this guy up and he won't leave!"

"HEY!" Adam finds his voice.

Will realises he has brought company. "Okay! I picked Adam and Matt up a few minutes after fleeing our home the night before."

"Matt?" Beth wonders.

"Kid in there passed out. He got hurt in an accident when some nut job crashed a double-decker bus into our getaway car a few hours earlier. We were out for some time."

"We missed like an entire day."

Beth's eyes widen from the realisation he could be talking about her. She quickly ignores it and desperately tries to change the subject.

Will, Adam & Matt
34 Minutes Earlier...

Having passed out from exhaustion, Will comes to. He is nose to nose with Adam's snoring and the warm breath on Will's face feels peaceful for a moment. Suddenly, he properly awakens and realises Adam is still a stranger to him. Will convinces himself he must have been dreaming; he tries to remember what it was about.

It's like one of those vivid flashes of a dream that feels like an eternity ago; dreams so powerful and raw until ten minutes pass and then it feels like a different life—the type of dream that would mess him up for the rest of the day. Maybe it's because he still dreams about Kieran every so often, but he'd never admit it, especially not sleeping next to Ricca or the puppies. Will loved him, but they just weren't meant for one another even if the pair of them lived in hope they could try again in five years.

Too late now, his inner conscience speaks.

All that's left are the constant flashes of Kieran eating someone on the living room floor, tainting the wonderful memories from when they were together. He remembered them cuddled in bed until then, in the beach house on a cool April afternoon, followed by the long late night walks on the moors. But now all he can see is Kieran screaming violently into the night, poisoned by the epidemic.

If I can get the image of him fucking someone else out of my head eventually, I can do this too.

Will gives his head a shake and checks his phone. *Still no service—the battery is getting lower.* He breaks free from Adam's grip, who grunts and turns over to Matt. Matt is still unconscious from the accident, and Will doesn't like the look of things. He scrolls through his gallery and finds a picture of Kieran from when they were together, cuddled up. It's a stillness in time, and no heartbreak can poison that image—proof they were genuinely happy once. There are a million things Will regrets. He should have said something before he died.

Suddenly, he remembers where he is, gripped by the cold midmorning air. This is no dream. The reality of the situation is becoming more overwhelming. Will does not know what to do. He sees they are still on the grass bank where they toppled over from explosion earlier. Will notices the tyre and sharp debris that nearly took their lives neatly spread around them. A small burning fire has kept them shielded from the dangerous winter conditions so far, but is now just dying embers.

There is a pale sky, smoke in the distance coming from the direction of the city, and it's quiet now. He sees the wreckage of the bus still blissfully ablaze. *No one is there.* It puzzles Will how he can go from a blind panic and everyone running in every direction to a ghost town.

He checks his phone again—a repetitive tick he can't help. He sees the date and time and he goes slack-jawed.

"A complete day has passed, no way!"

Suddenly, rustling from way yonder in the bushes startles Will. He tries to pull some debris around his body to defend himself. Ready for whatever is coming, Will tries to swallow his fear and raises a blunt metal instrument. A beautiful golden retriever with the lead still attached emerges from the bushes. Will slowly lowers his blunt object, surprised by the canine. *Must have had an owner.*

Will sees a severed hand is still attached. The dog sits and pants, casually staring at Will. Their eyes lock for a moment. This pup is one of the lucky ones. It gets up and runs back into the trees. Will shouts for the dog to wait and jogs over, but the dog has already disappeared.

As he emerges through the bushes, there is another small bank that descends to a car park.

'Wow!"

Will gasps when he is presented with an enormous car park complimenting a massive supermarket with 'Superstore: 24 hours' written in green over the entrance about 100-feet away. There is still no sight of the pup, though.

He momentarily forgets about the dog and returns to the trees, back through and on to the end of the dual carriageway. This time he isn't alone. When he spots some figures in the distance wondering around, Will wakes Adam. It takes some doing. He becomes more frantic despite trying to remain out of sight and quiet.

Are they friends? Foes? Monsters? Will doesn't want to stay and find out. Adam comes to in a cold sweat, screaming, when Will dives on him and puts his hand over his mouth. He is shushing him desperately.

He leans down to Adam's ear. "There are people. In the distance, and we need to get up and go. I've found a big-arse supermarket."

If they leave now, they might see if there are any trucks, so they can stock up on supplies and get the hell out of town before the army comes. Adam doesn't have much choice other than to agree after seeing the surrounding devastation. They both try to carry Matt into the trees without being detected. Adam suddenly vanishes, leaving Will in the lurch. Will turns in every direction. They are stranded. Adam goes to the car they were in… he's up to something. He crawls into the charcoaled remains and opens the glove box, not noticing the strangers getting closer. Luckily, he finds what he came for and pulls out the binoculars.

"Uh-oh…"

Adam is about to crawl back out of the wreckage when he hears footsteps dragging toward him, then feet come into view. They stagger closer. Adam tries not to move and remains silent, quivering. He can't make a single sound, not even to breathe, otherwise whoever or whatever will find him.

Adam thinks the coast is clear, but to be sure, he waits a few more seconds. He makes a mistake that nearly costs him his life.

He lingers but in doing so, his foot scrapes some glass across the ground, giving away his position. Feet come wandering back, now spooked and enraged by the noise. Adam panics and rapidly shuffles out of the wreckage. He is grabbed and launched back by the creature. He yells out in pain as they toss him into another car.

He's risked everything for a stupid pair of binoculars. The foaming beast picks Adam up and drops him again. This isn't like one of the other ones—it has way more superior strength. It is not sluggish or hunched like the others, and walks like a person... fights like one too, like it's kept some of its default humanity.

Adam stands and tries to fight the menacing being with great posture and pulsating limbs. He throws a punch, but the attacker blocks it by catching his fist with its hand like a wall. Their eyes lock. Adam stares into its red and silver sparkling pupils. It screeches and bends Adam's hand backwards, causing him to lower further and further, crying out in pain.

Without warning, a clunk over the head causes Adam's oppressor to fall. Stood over him are Will and his trusty piece of mental.

"Thanks for leaving!"

"I was only trying to help." He hands Will the binoculars.

"What was that?"

"I don't know. But it was different!" Adam rubs his wrist, concerned. "It's like it knew me."

They return to the bushes where Will has laid Matt down and concealed him in some branches. The two boys then lay on their stomachs on the grass and investigate. Will can see one or two docile infected wandering the large car park, but he says there is nothing else—the coast is clear, and the shutters of the entire store are down.

"Either they never opened, or the people inside locked themselves in."

And just like Will suspected, he catches sight of four delivery trucks lined up outside the warehouse bay.

"Bingo."

13:00 hours
Shop Floor

"Your friend doesn't look too good there." Claire gestures to Matt. "I can look at him."

"Are you a doctor?" Adam strains as he and Will carry Matt out of the truck.

"Lucky for you, you just steam rolled into the hands of a first responder. I'll see what I can do."

"Looks like fate brought us together!"

Adam and Will carry Matt over to Claire and Will fetches a sack of potatoes close by from a promotion stand. He fits the sack under Matt's head; he is now conscious but heavily 'out of sorts'.

"Can you hear me, mate? Are you able to talk or make any noise?" Claire opens his eyes, shining her trusty mini torch in his eyes.

One pupil is slightly dilated. Sign of trauma to the

266

cranium. Bleeding from the ears. No other visible lacerations. She goes over the details in her mind.

"You know you can stop staring. I won't bite! Unlike everybody else out there," Claire says without looking at Will. He darts his vision elsewhere. "Sorry, just a rough night, hard to trust anyone." She sits Matt up. "Are you dizzy? Can you say something to me?" She tries to get him to look forward. She flicks his collar bones, knees. "He's hit his head really hard, but he has a reflex, which means he might still have motor neuron function. Do not let him fall asleep again."

"Water!" Matt can barley produce sound.

Adam runs to the 'ready to go' food and brings back a small bottle. Matt downs almost the entire bottle and a few seconds pass before he turns green.

"Matt?"

He suddenly spews everywhere, swaying slightly, holding his head.

"Oh my god, is he going to die?"

"Hold him. No. The vomiting is good. I need you to look in the vomit for blood anything that you think shouldn't be there."

"What am I gonna look for, pennies?" Will shrugs but does as she asks… reluctantly. "Just bile and water I guess."

"That's good. It's a sign that he might not have internal injuries or any organs bleeding. The vomit shows dizziness and nausea which leads me to believe he's concussed." Claire explains, holding Matt's arm for his pulse: 70/120 BPM.

"Okay!" Claire decrees.

Will is hypnotised, watching her. It's riveting.

"The only thing I don't like is that blood from the ears that means a bleed in or on the skull. We're going to need to get that seen to. All I can suggest is we watch him and keep his core temperature down."

267

K. J. McGuinness

She tells Matt she will give him some painkillers and an ice pack, despite the freezers thawing out. Matt looks at her like she has two heads, swaying, trying to concentrate. She looks over his shoulder at the boys and up to Beth, stood over them.

She reiterates herself. "The worse thing he could do right now is sleep. You could lose consciousness and slip into a coma or even die. He will need a little rest when he wakes. No sleeping."

"Alright! No sleeping!" Will looks over at Beth. "Is she always this colourful?"

"If you saw what I just saw over the last 24-hours, you'd be a little skittish, too." Beth folds her arms.

"I have a medic den, near the back of the store. We can set him there. Do you think you can carry him?"

"Aww what?" moans Will. "I could barely get his fat arse through the door."

"It wasn't exactly a question; more you need to do this."

Will thinks for a minute as the others wait for his response impatiently. "I GOT IT! Wait here."

Claire scoffs in confusion as he runs to the travelators and vanishes. She looks at Beth, who just shrugs. They can hear all sorts of commotion echoing out, pans falling, cups dropping and Will muttering to himself.

"COMING!"

Before long he's back carrying a heavy contraption. He dumps it in front of them. "Ta-da. Solved."

"A pram…" Claire's face droops "A fucking pram."

"What's wrong with a pram, we can squeeze him into it? Wheel him to your little drugs den!"

Claire stares at Will, wondering if he's serious, but they get him into it, regardless. She takes them to den while Adam wheels Matt in the buggy. Matt can be placed in there as long as someone remains with him until he can focus.

"Wow, she is pure fire isn't she?" Will refers to Claire and whispers to Beth as a term of endearment.

"NO! Don't you dare, William." She gives him a stern scolding. "This girl has been through things twice as vile as us in less time; she does not need you creeping around. Like some slithering snake."

"What? it's just a compliment. Besides, if she has PTSD I am the perfect medicine." He flexes.

13:20 hours

It's the middle of the afternoon and Beth is investigating the lorry wedged in the entrance. She has her arms folded, lips pursed to the side and hip relaxed. Deep in thought, she thinks the delivery truck will hold for now if they want to get out. Leaving through the customer entrance is no longer an option.

"Hi," Adam tries to say, quietly approaching from behind.

Beth jolts, scared out of her wits. "You know, I'm getting a little sick of jumping out my skin every five minutes."

"I just wanted to come and check on you. Claire told me what happened… what with your little glass injury and all. I'm Adam."

"We've met!" She rolls her eyes. "Kieran's friend, right?"

"Oh yeah, you're the smart blonde girl who was trying to get your friend out of the drug trouble they were in." A light bulb illuminates in Adam's mind. "How did they work out?"

"Just great. The drug dealer tore a chunk out of my friend, who tore a chunk out of my other friend, and all three turned on the friend with the drug problem and ate him alive. So, just fabulous."

They shake hands and she walks over to the others, leaving Adam staring into space, turning a shade lighter than white.

Will

Think of something stupid!

He tries to break the ice with Claire, who is fixed on taking Matt's blood pressure, trying to get him to talk.

"I'm so sorry for smashing your doors in." *What the fuck was that? Smashing your doors in, seriously?*

Claire turns her head, looking at him with a grimace.

"Wow." Even Matt cringes.

Will turns red as if he was having a reaction. *Please, just let the ground swallow me.*

"I MEAN! Not like that. I meant the front doors. The supermarket front. Entrance. Doors. Not your… Oh my God."

He covers his hands with his face after becoming a baffling baboon, slamming a typewriter repeatedly. He daren't look.

She smiles. "It's alright, at least you put a cork in it."

Beth catches up to them just in time; she can feel the awkwardness like she's just walked into someone's fart. She looks at Will.

"You said something stupid, didn't you?"

"Go away, witch!" he snaps playfully.

"I just wanted to ask how you got here. There's no sign of a break in before we trampled through—do you have a part-time job here or something?"

"I was in the wrong place at the wrong time." She applies steri-strips to Matt's superficial scratches. "It went downhill from there."

"So, how did you two meet?" Will asks another question.

"You like asking a lot of questions, don't you? Do you always interrogate everyone you meet this way?" She doesn't bother looking at him again while working on Matt's arm. "Small sips." She encourages him.

"I'm simply building a profile; she could be a psycho

here and killed everyone in the store," Will stresses.

Beth and Claire exchange an expression of sadness. Beth sees her opportunity to intervene to save the embarrassment. And she explains she was in the area looking for help, food and shelter when she found the supermarket, avoiding the fact she smashed a double-decker bus through a pile of cars and had to flee the scene.

"She is not a psycho. Trust me."

"I honestly still can't get over it—both of us at this side of town, at this supermarket. It's so weird." Will concludes, "Do you believe in fate, Claire?"

"I believe in everything happening for a reason. Slight moments that can alter the way things go." She smirks.

"Claire, do you want me to stay with this boy? You haven't slept yet, and I'd urge you to get some rest; you have looked after everyone." Beth offers to stay with Matt, and Claire makes sure she understands he cannot fall back into a deep sleep.

"He might not wake up. Don't let him sleep!"

"I know!" Beth walks up to her and rubs her shoulders for emphasis. "Go. To. Sleep!"

Claire nods, looking like she's about to burst into tears so she walks off.

"Wait!" Will tells her to wait up. "I have more questions for you!" Claire tries to conceal her dismay. "Why were you here when the place got overrun by people? What was that look you gave Beth?"

Claire puts it bluntly, finding his relentlessness irksome. "I was doing a midnight stock run, got trapped with others, the manager went crazy and killed them all. I'm the only one left, if you must know. So, no, I'm not a psycho who killed everyone. I'm the psycho who had to put the psycho down," she barks.

"Oh my god, that happened?"

"In a sentence or two!" She smiles sarcastically, irritated

by his child-like curiosity. Will wants to know where the manager is. She tells him she tied him up upstairs. "What is with all the questioning? Listen, if you want to know, go upstairs and watch the security tapes! See for yourself!"

Claire walks ahead and realises she is being flippant and dismissive of Will, who feels fascinated by Claire. He stops in his tracks as she rolls her eyes and continues on without him.

"Bitch," he yells.

Claire slows down slightly, looking over her shoulder and smirks before walking off. She goes to the bodies of her friends and the strangers she has covered up in a different part of the store, and grabs a pillow and a bean bag, placing it next to the covered corpses. She curls up and finally shuts her eyes.

15:00 hours
Matt

Beth is reading a magazine next to Matt, trying to get him to sip water every couple of minutes, so he doesn't completely fall into a deep slumber. He comes to. At first it's blurry. All he can make out is this yellow siren figure. The florescent light makes it hard for Matt to focus.

That girl with the blonde hair. He is star struck when he meets Beth.

"Are you an angel? Am I dead?"

A thousand shades of gold and white that make new mosaics each moment hit him like cold air. A chorus of hues. She's beautiful. One glance of those blue eyes tells of a lifetime of struggle that had never been put into words.

Beth smiles and calls for Claire.

"Where am I?" Matt doesn't know what is going on or where he is. "And who are you?"

She tries to explain the best she can of who she is, and all she knows. Adam comes racing over, panting.

"Get Claire!" orders Beth.

14:52 hours
Claire & Will
Security Office

An hour was all Claire could handle from her slumber. It's like her body won't let her rest, too many flashing images and trauma racing through her mind. Sleep was all she had and now she feels like a shell of a human, so instead Claire is stacking and packing things in the office as Will watches the footage from the night before. He can't believe his eyes. This time she hasn't bothered to watch them with him. She can't relive it again. He understands why she has become so icy and sceptical.

"How did you…?"

"The manager killed my friend who got bit. I hid until your friend came, which gave me a fighting chance to sneak up on him. I suppose I owe her for that one."

"And where is…?"

"He's in the staff bathroom."

"I will do nothing to hurt you. I'm a stranger, I know, but I'm here to protect you. I can be trusted."

"People who usually feel the need to say they can be trusted... can't." She finishes stacking, putting the fear of God into Will just by using her expression.

"In that case I guess you'll find out."

Adam slams into the doorway, trying to catch his breath, interrupting them. "It's Matt… *gasp* … Awake… *gasp* … needs you!"

"I guess I will." She heads out of the room.

"Do you need me to hurt him, Claire? I'll do whatever it takes," he says, following her down the stairs.

"Who?" Adam wonders.

273

He's trying to impress her, and though she doesn't believe in violence, she is flattered.

18:00 hours

For the first time, the group has come together to sit near the front of the store on a table Claire has arranged. She sets plates, pours drinks and calls everyone to dinner. Everybody is somewhere around the shop floor, exploring, procrastinating, anything to keep themselves distracted and busy in the meantime. People are a little lost, because nobody knows quite what to do or say, so they keep themselves to themselves—they are strangers to one another, they would have easily passed each other in the street without a second glance. They only talk when they must.

Beth comes up the stairs to a fully set table and a controlled fire bin burning away on the shop floor. She pauses for a moment to grasp what is in front of her, then shrugs it off. It isn't the weirdest thing she's witnessed recently. She sees Matt, the first sat at the table with an ice pack strapped to his head, as he smiles at her presence. Matt helped drag the fire bin upstairs and light it, so now they can cook without needing electricity.

There're sleeping bags and blankets around the fire to prepare for what looks like a lengthy stay. Beth doesn't quite know what to say as she sits awkwardly at the table.

"This is very above and beyond, Claire. Wow!"

"Well, my brother was always the bread winner growing up, we were in foster care! I was very much a homemaker, and while he was out, I'd learn how to do something new. So whatever money he brought in, I used it to go the extra mile, it's no biggy. Anything to keep distracted."

Will and Adam eventually join, blown away by Claire's hospitality. "You've obviously come prepared and formed a

274

mother goose like complex over the group—making sick bays, building tables and controlled fires to keep warm using resources from around the supermarket."

"I mean, the power switched off again an hour ago. So there's that! I have to make use of the fresh food which will go off any day now."

She explains she did not know what everybody liked or didn't like, so she just made everything. Suddenly, Claire puts down beautiful smelling masterpiece dishes from Chinese to Indian, Italian and Mexican.

"I just used the camping equipment to cook it."

Beth is lost for words and doesn't know what to say. She takes Claire's hand and thanks her for taking her in and healing her. Matt also thanks her despite saying his head feels like 80 hangovers at once.

Claire pauses and looks down; she breaks down and admits after what happened to her, she didn't know what she was going to do, or if she was going to make it out alive. If it wasn't for Beth distracting Tom when she did, she surely would have starved or died at his hands.

Beth looks at her new friends awkwardly. Claire weeps and she hugs her.

Will tries to break the ice. "So what do you think we should do if the food is going to run out?"

"We still have non-perishables," Matt says to a quiet ordinance.

"We need to get your head checked, mate," Claire points out.

Over dinner, the group then tell each other their stories of how they survived and were thrust into this bad luck, including how Adam and Matt came about meeting Will. Beth makes a revelation in Claire, discovering they have a bond which brings them closer over their ambitions in life and they begin to get on famously, promising to look after one another. It feels strange to Beth like she is betraying

Darcy, who is probably out there somewhere.

Everyone informs Claire of what they have seen, which makes her fear for her brother, who is probably looking for her, and may have perished. She explains if she ever got out, she was going to go to their shop/home to find him. Claire explains she can't fathom or understand what she saw, that they all saw, on the tapes.

"How can someone just be normal one minute then 'lose their shit' the next?"

An awkward silence ensues. Will casts an awkward glare between himself, Adam and Matt... a call back to their earlier conversation.

"What I'm about to say is going to defy any explanation, but it's like the people I encountered were dead," Claire says, "and then..."

"Not dead!" Will finishes her sentence and she slowly nods.

"Harry got bitten by one of the 'crazies' and it's like he died but then came back." Claire inhales deeply at the memory.

"Like a zombie?" Beth asks.

"It sounds stupid but..."

Will cuts her off again and reassures her it isn't stupid. "Crazy, yes, but not stupid... We can't deny we've all seen the same thing. We have all experienced the same thing and they can't deny what was on those tapes. We need to accept that this is the Grime Flu." He concludes once and for all this virus is turning people into flesh-eating maniacs who are full of rage and violence. "The dead don't actually die. They are coming back as the undead... dead but not." Will sees the confusion and denial in everybody's faces. He doesn't understand it fully, but it has something to do with the green Flu. "Are we on the same page?" He looks for reassurance.

"So, you get the infection, the infection kills you?" Claire asks.

"And then it does something to you to bring you back. The bottom line is… infection is a death sentence."

"I just realised something!" Claire has a revelation, not a good one. "I gave Harry tablets to help him sleep. He never woke up. I think *I* killed Harry."

"No, honey!" Beth strokes her hand.

"He was dead from the moment he was bitten," Will interjects

Nobody speaks, but they consider his notion.

Claire asks, "Is that what's turning all the people?"

"It depends."

Beth says she saw her two other best friends turn in seconds. Claire says her friend Harry turned within an hour after going to sleep. "He must have just gone in his slumber."

Will puts down his fork and sits perplexed, trying to work out an answer for everything.

"But not your other friends? Dylan, Val, Linda? They didn't turn."

"They were executed like animals." Claire stares off into space.

Matt finally calls out, "Everything doesn't always need an explanation; maybe we should go along with something that defies all over logic and science and accept it—because it's happening, this is real. The sooner we adapt and move on the better."

They beg the question of how big this thing actually goes, and whether it's just the city or the entire country or worse, the world? Claire trembles, trying not to be emotional. Matt goes back to his original point and says nature has found a new weapon.

"Before we came here, we tried to get out," Adam reveals.

"They put up a border around the county line. All hell

broke loose in this mass exodus; it must have reached the border. It was pure bedlam and insanity. People running, screaming, the police shooting and going nuts. So, I'm not sure if it got through the wall."

"I don't think it's the world yet. Even an epidemic takes at least a month to become a pandemic," Claire explains, using her medical background.

"Isn't that what they said about Grime Flu?" Beth asks.

"They were talking about a lockdown, maybe that's what they've done?"

"No, they would have told us, not cut us off."

"We were at the edge of the city. We were even at the edge of the Yorkshire border. The army had already set up a giant perimeter locking us in this hell hole." Will nods to back up Adam.

"We don't know if it got through the border," Matt explains.

"Maybe that's why nobody has come for us yet," Claire agrees. "It has spread across the country, and they have forgotten about us."

"It's the worst thing, no knowing, just hanging in limbo."

Silence falls, making everything uncomfortable.

"Delightful topic."

Will can't help but be turned on by Claire's intelligence. Even if he is about to disagree with her slightly.

"Actually, simulations have shown that the chance of spread in individuals travelling away from the centre of an outbreak drops off exponentially."

"Here we go." Beth plays with her food.

"The chance of spread vs distance travelled drops by half every ten miles. The disease spreads as a relatively slow wave." Nobody has a clue what Will just said. He sighs, frustrated. "Look! Let me put it this way, the chance of distant travel drops by half every time the distance is doubled. It would let the disease get out of control. Where long-range jumps are exceedingly rare, epidemics spread in a slow wave, typified by the Black Death. The invasive caseload also spread in a slow wave after being introduced to Australia in the 1930s. When long-range jumps are common, the disease spreads rapidly as with SARS which spread around the world by air travellers. We haven't considered the medium, mode and range of long distant travellers from Leeds to the rest of the world." Will goes off on one of his famous scientific rants as the other eyes glaze over. "What is wrong with you? If people have left and got out into the countryside, the spread will slow. If they stay, it'll move faster. A disease can't move if there's no people."

"OOOHHH!" the group says in unison.

"Why didn't you just say that?" Claire asks.

"I did!"

"But the army and government won't let this happen, they'll shut the airports down," Beth contributes to the conversation.

"Unless it's the government behind it," Adam adds.

"I think we've established this isn't the government," Will responds.

"Government experiment cover up... army experiment gone wrong," Matt chips in.

Will rolls his eyes as Claire leans over to Beth. "How come he knows so much?"

"A ton of weed, a nutritional job history and a lot of documentaries." Beth whispers, "He's my useless encyclopaedia." She grins. "Trust me, the only good thing about the phones being down is that little brainbox."

Claire smiles and bonds with Will over their knowledge of all things in medicine and health. Adam disagrees and says it could be anything, since anything is now possible. It could be God, having grown sick of his creation, and wiped them out.

Will raises a brow, unimpressed. "You really think

religion is behind this?"

"My theories are just as valid as yours. You can't prove yours just like I can't prove mine."

"I believe that's a shot to the back of the net," mutters Beth.

"Really, you think science is a theory, Adam?"

"Technically, a lot is theory!"

"With evidence. Show me evidence of your theory other than a magical book that says you can't have a wank, eat shellfish, leave your abusive husband and talks of a magical man in the sky."

"William!" Beth slams down her knife and fork.

"I take my religion seriously, the same way you do. It's called respect." Adam wipes his mouth. "The Bible gets things wrong just the way science does."

"One thing is for sure, the infection is spread through contact, blood and biting so far."

They can all agree those things aren't people anymore; they are not their friends, family or loved ones. They are gone, and only the monsters remain.

"Former ghosts of themselves in a dead shell."

"So why did my friend turn in an hour and yours in ten seconds?" Claire asks in a tone.

Will pauses. "That I don't know. That could be the person, metabolism, health, location of bite. Bigger the bite, faster the spread?"

"Oh, wow, you don't have an answer for this one... someone call the police. Oh, wait..." Matt sarcastically throws the comments his way.

"Fuck you, man! I never said I had an answer for everything. When I don't... I don't. And I'll be the first to admit it."

Beth gives him the side eye. "Reluctantly."

The group talk over one another, yelling their theories on terrorism, bio weaponry and aliens. Suddenly, a gust of strong wind screams outside the entrance. The whole building shakes and aches from a blizzard attacking the supermarket. It silences the group. Will assures everybody it will be the winter weather from the east coming in, as it is that time of year.

The supposed 'wind' flares up, sounding like a whining ghoul, a beast in the night. Beth watches the snowflakes get whipped around in the air. Above them are glass windows arched into a pyramid that looks out onto a clear night sky. Claire panics and wonders if it could be thugs, or worse...

Will is surprised nobody has tried to loot the store since he had the same idea. It is agreed some ground rules should be set. They should alternate watches and take turns cooking. The group decides they should get some rest and Claire tidies away the rubbish. Will and Adam stop her and insist they take care of it.

January 3rd, 2012
00:05 hours
Shop Floor

A gale force blizzard from the east tears through the county, blowing strong winds and snow, blanketing the car park.

Matt lies awake in the makeshift sick bay bed, staring at the ceiling. He's supposed to be on the first watch but he can't sleep because of his mind working in overdrive, the howling weather outside, every creek and moan... it feels like it's game over.

Every time there is a strong howl or shift of wind, the anxiety of impending doom fills the group with dread. Adam lays awake around the dying campfire, the only thing keeping the entire shop warm. The amber glow reaches the corners of the far away walls.

Will sits near the entrance keeping a lookout, wrapped in a heavy coat, shivering, responsible for the reason the wind is blowing in. He tries to stuff blankets and towels in the cracks, even a cement filler, but his attempts seem futile.

Claire and Beth lay awake, unbeknownst to the others. No one is sleeping.

The one thing they all have in common right now is all anyone can think about—there are poor souls taking refuge wherever they may be huddled together for warmth out there. All the helpless elderly neighbours, pets wandering the streets, babies who can't fend for themselves, not to mention the homeless who had it rough, anyway. Beth can't take it anymore; her brain won't turn off. She can't decide if it's the wind keeping her awake or being alone with her thoughts for the first time since the party went south. She tosses and turns. Will comes over.

"Well, this is shit."

"Bethany Brunerfield, did you just swear?" Will acts aghast. "That has to be the most horrifying thing yet." He chatters, tossing a roll up cigarette into the fire.

"I know. Must be the cold air, brain freeze."

"Yeah, sorry again about the whole lorry into the doorway thing."

"Speed 3: Supermarket Sweep," she sniggers.

"Fast and Furious: *How Diary Crash*."

"Wow, that was bad even for you."

The two share a tender moment listening to the cackling fire.

"You know, with all the events that have unfolded, I completely forgot we were due for the worst storm in decades."

"Could be worse, we could be in it." She sighs.

Hours are passing by until she whispers for Claire, who luckily is in the same boat. Beth gets her up and says she has an idea. Moments later, Beth returns with an electric charger and a projector to shine onto the white wall. She tells Claire to pick a DVD and spreads them out. Will,

Adam, and Matt all notice the glow from the projector and the faint sound of a movie starting. They too aren't sleeping away in their own little bubble, left with the imperfect thoughts and demons. It's quiet enough to not cause alarm, but loud enough to subdue the arduous, howling gales.

One by one they all slowly head towards the glow. They come to find Claire and Beth snuggled up in mountains of quilts on a sofa taken from downstairs. Will watches from some distance and feels a sort of warm and fuzzy for a moment, like the outside doesn't exist.

Claire has raided the confectionary aisle and the two are immersed in piles of sweets and dips. They aren't aware of the others watching from behind. Claire and Beth sit before a newly lit, even bigger fire.

Adam joins the pair, followed by Matt and Will, who grab another sofa. No one particularly says anything to one another other than a few genuine smiles. Adam cuddles up to Will as Will lights a spliff. The two don't really say anything about it, and Matt is happy to watch at the foot of the sofa. The crunching of food and drinking of booze replace the impure loneliness and the sound of the veracious howling wind.

For a moment, everything seems calm and peaceful again, like recent events were a bad dream. One by one, the group tires and eventually drift off on one another. They sleep through the night undisturbed for a rare and thankful change.

09:54 hours

It's morning, and Beth naturally wakes up on the sofa. She is holding Matt. Although strange, she is quite grateful for the company, and can't believe she fell asleep. In the vicinity is the smell of bacon and frying onions.

How? Dreaming again?

283

She wipes the drool from her face and sits up. Empty bottles and wrappers and a quietly cackling campfire surround Beth. Only a few embers remain.

"Nope, not dreaming?"

The smell of frying onions instantly takes her back to when she would wake up in her tent at Leeds Fest every morning, still 'bamboozled' out of her mind. She always put her tent near the burger van because she loved the smell, and it would be a natural alarm clock at the festivals. She very much enjoyed festivals and would always try to do at least two every year—they were her sweet release from normal society, and she could be as bohemian and free as she wanted... plus, as a singer-song writer in her spare time, it was wondrous to explore music. To Beth, music was once solace in a mundane world and her only sense of freedom.

She snaps out of her nostalgia to another blistering howl of the wind, but the blizzard seems to have calmed until a further roar changes that.

Spoke too soon.

The others aren't around. It rouses her from her daydream about the festivals. *Where is everyone?*

Suddenly, she is presented with a plate including two eggs, bacon and fried onions stuffed into what looks like a bagel. Adam is smiling, chewing his food. She clears her throat, thanking him as she tries to wake up properly. She's not hungry, though.

She goes over to the dinner table with her plate and sees Will and Claire are flirting. Instead of eating, she pours herself a cup of coffee. If her stomach is empty, it'll both refresh and fill it. Back when things were normal, she could fly through six cups and three quarters of the day before realising he hadn't eaten.

She sits quietly, watching Will worm his way in under Claire's skin.

"How'd you sleep?"

Suddenly the attention is on her mid-sip. "Umm, as good as can be, I suppose."

Will tells her the movie night projector was a good call, but they really should get down to business. The other survivors are wondering round the store playing with what they find, taking time for leisure.

"We were just saying this is something we could get used to."

"I suppose there's no harm in having a bit of fun, we have the projector."

"I found a generator, in the docking station. It could power electricals. Providing games maybe." Claire smiles.

Something is wrong with Beth; she herself doesn't quite know why she's off kilter, but it doesn't seem right, and Will knows she isn't acting like herself.

"We are all grateful to be alive right now." She nods.

"Morning!" Matt comes to the dinner table.

Beth suddenly lights up and sparks are flying, it's obvious. "Hey, how did you sleep? You look…" Beth tries to be kind. "So much better."

Matt doesn't have his ice pack anymore. "Better. I mean my head still feels a little heavy and I can't make sharp head movements, or I get sick."

"I'm going to check you out again later. We are quite limited in what we can do. Which brings me to my next point." Claire hates to break it to the others. "It's somewhere between day three and four now for waiting for somebody to come." She puts down her coffee. "I fear if somebody was to come, they would have been here by now, which is why my original group tried to leave before Tom massacred them."

Beth sips a coffee while trying to wait for her appetite to come to life. Will gets up in a dressing gown and slippers, smoking a spliff.

"You've made yourself at home, I see." Beth raises her

eyebrows… "What do you propose we do?"

"Well, there's the matter of Thomas, the manager. I took him some water in a bowl and took off his tape. He's been quiet but he'll wail every so often."

"Like a dog?" Adam sits.

Now the full group is present.

"Well, she can't exactly loosen him. The man decapitated a lad!" snaps Beth.

Claire is visibly uncomfortable.

"I say we leave him." Will is straight in there.

Tom, still restrained and bound in the staffroom office, continues to draw in unwanted attention from his occasional screaming. "He hasn't eaten in a day or two… I should probably feed him," Claire suggests.

"That's because obviously you're a good person!"

"Let him starve!" Matt sides with Will.

"No! That just shows we are as bad as him. We are not resorting to that three days into isolation."

"People have done it for less, B!" Will says.

"The man is already a mass murderer; he'll gut us like fish if he gets loose," protests Matt.

"Claire, this is your call. He did these things to you, and this is technically yours, first dibs and finder's keepers and all that."

Beth folds her arms as eyes turn to her. Claire looks down, having a serious moral crisis. *Take him something? But he'll have to eat it with his mouth. Paper plates?* Deep down she knows she's trying to buy more time to decide. Half of her wants to really fuck him up for killing those innocent people. It was somebody's son, mother and friend.

"Well, I'll go shut him up. If anyone else goes he won't be safe."

Matt stands to take his plate to the bin they dragged over, but he loses his balance and falls into Will, still sat.

"Shit, I'm so sorry, buddy!"

"Matthew, are you okay?" Will says, caressing him.

"I just lost my balance, lightheaded."

"Let's get you sat down, mate, back at the den!" Will looks back at Beth and Claire, who look at each other, now unsettled.

They stand to help guide him.

"Someone is going to have to get help! He needs a CT. I suspect brain bleeding." Claire says slyly to Beth, walking slightly behind.

"I think the army may have started with the bigger areas, such as the city or the outskirts, to prevent the disease from spreading. Adam, Matt and I watched from a hillside two days prior—the military was setting up a quarantine when people were in the middle of a mass exodus."

"That's a great idea. We should join and leave. Everybody else has the right idea. We get your friend the help he needs."

"Maybe that's why you've been left alone in the supermarket for so long?" shrugs Will, now sitting Matt back on his bed.

"There's just one problem." Will looks disheartened. "It didn't end so well for those people."

"I need to clean. Helps me think!" Claire abruptly walks off.

"But... Matt?" Beth calls out for her.

Adam

"Who knows, where the hmmm, hmmm. Where the hmmm hmmmmm. Only time."

Adam happily hums to himself... one of his vices in stressful situations. He stares at the hot bagel, tempted to spit on it, or worse. Adam's mind wanders at the various possibilities as he braves the office stairs. He isn't exactly

287

flat out petrified, but he isn't confident either. It's like facing his fears, which he would rather take right now. His throat runs dry, itching at every swallow. His palms are clammy. The air is so brittle it could snap, and if it doesn't, he might. He debates whether to knock. Adam leans his ear against the door. Not a peep, odd but expected.

"Okay, food!" Adam says plainly.

The door swings open and Adam gasps sharply. He is ashen. The stare is enough to set the room in ice. The plate falls and food scatters.

There's no one there.

Adam's eyes still locked on the tape left behind, his breath even yet deep.

"Fuck."

The Den

"Leave her, she's been through a lot," says Beth.

"But what about Matt?"

"I'm sure she will come back in a minute or two!"

"You remember what it was like when you split from Kieran, you didn't stop. Any decision someone ask you to make was overwhelming!"

"DON'T remind me."

"I'm literally fine. Just a minor defect left over. I mean, the bruising is out now, isn't that good?" Matt tilts his head to the side.

"Is that fresh blood from your ears, dude?" Will cringes.

Adam comes sprinting back, stopping the trio in their tracks. He tries to catch his breath.

"Tom…"

Before he can utter another syllable, Beth has already burst to life. Shock is the electric ramification of the brain stuttering. Beth's brain immediately begins working overtime.

"Adam. Get those spare keys from Claire! Go with Will now. Find every single possible door, back door, secret door, access in and out to the rest of the supermarket. Put every key in every lock and break it. Snap it off. Leave one door. The door to the office." They need an escape route or at least know where the exits are to catch Tom.

"How do we get out?"

"We will take your truck, rev it out. That's our door." Beth has never thought so fast on her feet. She astonishes even herself. "Stick together! Take what protect you can. Back-to-back. Wrap yourself in magazines like Claire did. GO!"

Beth takes Matt's arm. "Come on bugga-luggs. We need to get you safe."

"Seriously, I'm cool. I should help. I can make stuff, traps!"

BANG!

Adam and Will freeze, as do Beth and Matt.

"That sounded like a gunshot!" she exclaims.

Something that sounds like fireworks rings out, echoing throughout the entire supermarket.

10:22 hours
Claire

The breakdown from the hospital was so long ago now. Claire is one of the lucky ones. She recovered. She's a different person now, also the same person. That's what it is to mature and grow. After the stormy seas of what the doctor did to her, she was sailing in open waters under a friendly sky. But the two days have really tested the weather in her stratosphere. From this place of feeling safe and well, her shakes are back, the paranoia. All the questions and decisions of what to do with another man's life. Sure, he deserves a life in a box or even death but who is she to play judge, jury and executioner? Claire has only ever done that for the right reasons in the moment of saving an epileptic child or amputating in the field to save someone's life.

Cleaning up was Claire's reset button on the brain. Clarity and perfection, she can still remember her mum's goofy clean up song after all this time. For her it's about taking back control, stability. It's a skill she always thought practical in her everyday life, perfect for emotional clean ups, academic clean ups and so on.

She screws up a plastic cup so tight her hands turn purple, trying to take a deep breath. She knows she should go back, and she will, she just needs two minutes. Claire is in the middle of cleaning up leftover breakfast, putting things from the table into bin bags, trying to keep on top of their temporary living quarters. Every stroke of a cloth, every spray from a bottle is a wire reset from the OCD Pandora's box. All she wants is sleep. Her muscles sink to gravity like laundry hung out on a snowy day.

Inner peace, inner peace, inner peace. She's in her own business when she picks up the trash bags and walks around the corner from their den. She looks up with content, that quickly drops when she stumbles upon something that makes her gasp.

BANG!

She looks down, her eyes widen at a pool of blood on her left-hand side. Claire has been shot in the abdomen, fatally wounding her. It takes a moment to register what has just happened and all she can think about is *how*? For a split second it's painless, pure bliss of not having to feel what it's like to have a hole in her body. Then this sudden rush of the worst pain she has ever fathomed takes hold. Sirens ring in her head.

It takes seconds for Matt to come speeding around the corner. "That sounded like a gunshot!"

"Matt, don't run too fast!"

He makes it just in time to catch Claire, who collapses in his arms. The trash bags spread out. Matt can't believe his eyes. The others come flooding in.

"Claire, look at me! What do I do?" Matt panics, holding her cheek.

She can't speak, the pain is too much, her ears still ringing.

"Claire, was this Tom? WAS IT TOM?" Beth holds her head.

Will and Adam come to the rescue. Will's heart sinks.

"Tom is missing, loose in the store," Beth explains to her. "Stay awake!"

Matt shakes his head, insinuating it was not Tom who shot her.

"Please tell me what to do!"

Beth is in shambles—she may have lost a sister before they could leave.

"UNEXPECTED PSYCHO IN THE BAGGING AREA!" Tom roars.

Out of nowhere, Tom, in a vengeful rage, charges the group reunited with his butcher's knife.

January 2ⁿᵈ 2012
13:45 hours
Joel

Joel and his officer have been scoping out what the deal is with the giant supermarket, after watching what Jules refers to as the 'blonde bimbo' bamboozling her way through them in a double-decker bus. On the outside world, it's mostly Jules watching and plotting from their car while Joel quietly cowers and follows.

"We are getting in there and taking it. I will make them pay."

Jules snarls, almost like a ravenous blood hound, striking

the fear of God into Joel, who simultaneously is still amazed to be alive.

"Jules, please, we can just leave it. You have me, take me and let's go!"

"QUIET! I've got justice to uphold—teenagers can't just go around doing what they please and getting away with it."

She has a trick or two still up her sleeve. This entire time she has been watching and waiting. She watched some blonde-haired bitch pulverise through a sea of cars and stupidly capsize a bus. Then she watched the same girl run off in the superstore's direction and climb to the roof after many failed attempts to enter the building (much to Jules's amusement). Jules watched as Will, Matt, and Adam—the 'bastards' who sabotaged her hiding place—follow in the same direction.

Jules and Joel are heavily armed with riot gear and guns from the police station. Joel understands she could have shot them from any length. The penny finally drops; this is a game to her, not justice. *It's sport!*

"It really is a lot just for one little vendetta!" he bravely points out.

Joel thinks Jules may have lost it, but before he can summon another burst of bravery to take her out, Jules makes her move. Joel must get out of the car and keep his head low as he tries to keep up with her. The two enter the bushes and submerge into a carpark overlooking the supermarket.

Jules shoves Joel down who stands gawking in awe. She declares they will overthrow the store as their own and figure a way to get in. The sound of a clicking gun causes her to turn around. Joel is pointing a gun at her. To his shock, she bursts out laughing, creasing the crow's feet on her tan-abused skin. She knows he won't do anything, which sadly he doesn't. Instead, he hesitates before lowering the gun. She turns around and focuses her attention on the store, looking through her military-grade binoculars. She sees the shutters are down and that there is the rear end of a lorry sticking out.

She mumbles, "Those arseholes must be inside—the entrance is breached and there must be an alternative way in... like the roof."

She doesn't get a response from Joel, so she turns and sees he is still pointing the gun at her, shaking, but determined. She gulps and tries to remain unnerved.

"Well, are you going to do it, then?" She presses her head against the tip of the gun and smiles. "BOO." She cackles and disarms him, emptying his chamber, then throws the gun. "Now you have a real toy. The tough guy act in the car was surprising and fun for a hot minute, which is why I haven't scattered your brain matter over the tarmac. Now it's boring! I knew you wouldn't pull the trigger; you're a pussy and there is nothing you can do. I'd rather have been stuck with the one who threw the can at me. I already won, and it's pointless trying to fight it. Now focus because we have a job to do. You will come in useful."

Jules turns back to the supermarket and tells Joel the only reason he will not end up like his friend is because she needs someone to repopulate the earth with when they have settled into their new business investment. She wants to make him watch as she kills his friends.

"I don't know them, for the last... wait, *what*?"

Joel's face drops, and he says nothing, resorting back to the scared little mouse she said he was. He fears for whoever may be inside. Jules's wrath is coming for them— she is ruthless, cold-hearted.

She hurries Joel along and they dart across the abandoned car park. Jules aims her weapon and takes out a few of the wandering undead creatures, like a silent assassin. They don't even know what hit them, and they didn't stand a chance. Joel's gut instinct is that she has done this before, pitying the poor bastards who crossed her. Before he snaps out of it and realises Jules is making him climb up on the roof first, she points the gun; she isn't fucking around. He glares at her before conceding. They enter through the same vents Beth did, and they drop into the security office. There is no one to be seen, just spots of blood on the floor.

"It fucking stinks!" she declares.

"Of what?"

"Death."

She sees the security cameras are out, broken computer equipment, and an intercom to the store. Vigilant and silent, the slick assassin descends into the main room, watching her back at every corner. She walks past a movie projector, empty bottles and two sofas, like people were making themselves at home.

"There was a struggle, many struggles." Her gun is ready and her combat boots squeak along the floor.

"How can you tell?"

"Fuck, you're useless! Look… dried and fresh blood. Dried blood is darker, which means it's a day old. A mop soaked in blood. They trashed this place. Maybe we are dealing with pros! I underestimated my opponents." She moves in closer, near the fizzy drinks. "I can hear voices."

"Yeah, I bet you can," Joel mutters coarsely under his breath, wiping his nose.

Julie pauses for a moment. "Look at this place, it's better than I ever thought. We could build an empire here, trade products, and could run the country in mere months. Water and food will be the new currency! Change of plan, we stay here, we trade with the army!"

Joel thinks it's scary how much thought Jules has put into this plan; how she really thinks she has a chance against the army. It's only been a few hours, and it's like she has been preparing for the apocalypse all her life.

Jules marches on and turns a corner where she is startled

by a tall, ginger, angelic creature carrying two bin bags in her direction.

Claire is stunned. She only has a nanosecond to gasp.

Jules genuinely makes a mistake and fires a shot at Claire. The bullet hits her in the gut. Seconds later, Matt rushes to Claire's aid.

"Shit! That wasn't part of the plan. She is not on the shit-list! Who is she?"

She mistook Claire for a zombie, which may have attracted unwanted attention. Matt looks up at Jules and Joel cowering behind; he briefly remembers them both from their unfriendly encounter back at the warehouse, and he frowns.

"You!" He tries to get Claire to stay with him. "What did you do?"

"Move it!" Jules pushes Joel away as Beth comes around to Claire's aid.

"Did Tom do this, Claire?" It echoes down the aisle.

Tom, in a vengeful rage, charges the group reunited with his butcher's knife until he sees Jules with the gun and dodges her by dipping down an aisle. So begins a vast game of deadly cat and mouse.

Matt

"TELL ME WHAT TO DO!" Matt repeats.

"Pressure!" she gasps… barely. "Find…. towels and exit… wound."

The group struggles to band together to hatch a plan, bringing a mad man down when Joel and Julie enter too.

"Adam, I need towels and hot water. Matt, keep pressure and keep her conscious. Who did this?"

"That police officer bitch from the warehouse! And that scaredy cat kid was with her!" He talks to Will.

"That mad copper? She made it here? She must have

followed us!"

"What?" trembles Beth, not understanding.

"Long story! What a psycho! What is her problem?"

"I don't want this pretty girl to die on me. Stay here!" Will leaps up.

"She has a gun, Will! Don't!"

"We are sitting ducks."

"Oh, God! I sent Adam out there alone," shrieks Beth.

"STAY!" he bellows.

They do not know what's going on around them until they grasp a lunatic is on the loose.

"Get her off the main walkway. Take her to the den. I'll be back!"

"Will, no! I just got you back. It's suicide."

Will is already too far. "SHE WILL KILL US ALL!"

"Help me with her!" Matt commands.

"No!" Claire shivers. "You move me. It'll... damage... inside..."

Adam trips up the escalator with hot water spilling from a bucket and towels over his shoulder.

FFFFFFFT! PING!

A bullet zooms past Beth and explodes a cereal box behind her. The shot rings out.

"OH MY GOD!" Beth cowers.

FFFFFFFFFT! TWANG!

"Help me!" Matt yells at Adam as more shots fire. They are out in the open and bullets are whizzing past them, getting closer with each shot. It covers Beth in cereal and she can't see where they're coming from. Every blast rips through the air.

"MATT!" Adam calls from a stall and tries to wheel it toward them.

"BETH!" Matt signals for her to take over, holding pressure down on Claire.

The two boys drag over the metal card which acts as a

shield. Bullets ping off the cart.

Will

Will has gone downstairs, keeping a low profile. He's currently in the garden and outdoor section, worrying about the two psychopaths loose in the shop. The hunt is on, but the question is… who is hunting who? He's defenceless, and he knows it. But he's creative.

Idea.

Sometimes the only way to beat the monsters is to think like the monsters. Become the hunter of hunters.

Wire. Fireworks. Plyers. Propane tank. Hairspray.

It surprises will at all the things available at his disposal. Time for those science lessons to pay off.

"Monsters are in my castle." He mutters while he builds and moulds. He has to work quick; time is against him.

BANG!

Then another shot, and another. He can hear the ricocheting and the cries of his friends.

Faster, William. Faster!

Jules

There are two kinds of joy, one is mellow, warming and goes to the core. It forms links between the body and the soul, helps the person feel at home in their skin. It helps to love more strongly, to feel connected and do what is right. The other is a high, more akin to overeating sugar. It comes fast and brings on an impulsiveness, and an indifference to others... and this is how the killers are.

Jules is hollow inside and laughing even as they warp beyond recognition. Dipping in and out of the lower aisle, she taunts the group by firing from below every time she sees that blonde bitch dipping in and out of view.

"Shit!"

They moved a cart in front of themselves. She goes back to her low profile, between clothing racks until Jules spots Will and open fires. He vanishes. And she marches over to him but slows near the cosmetics, Joel slowly behind her unsure of what to do.

She moves as the shadows do. Jules is startled and turns 180-degrees in a blink at a small siren noise.

It's a toy... a small colourful robot with flashing lights moving towards her. Something about it gives Jules the urge to move toward it.

He's messing with me.

If her limbs are moving, the anxiety is gone, or at least she can ignore it for a few moments.

Then Joel sees it, only by accident. It shimmers in the light for a split second, but a light goes off inside him. A wire spreads right across the walkway, which Jules is about to cross just as the robot dies down. Joel's eyes follow the wire which goes up the aisle at either end. The wires are wrapped around two cans of hairspray and there he makes eye contact with Will, laid on his belly. Will puts his finger to his mouth.

Joel's heroism intervenes once more, this time putting his foot down once and for all. He pushes Jules, so she trips right into the wire which triggers the hair cans to spray all over her, temporarily blinding her. Jules cries out and falls, letting the gun go off, missing Will.

Will rolls off the top of the aisle, deflecting her shot, alarming Will. The gun goes flying.

"OI! PC PRICK," he yelps.

She pings open an eye, trying to stand, growling.

"Nobody likes bent coppers!"

Will uses his lighter to light a firework taped to the propane tank and lets go of it. It shoots out of his possession and cannon balls her in the chest. The fire reacts with the spray and she goes up like the fourth of July.

"DOWN!" Will covers Joel and drags him into the aisle.

"WAUGHARGHHHHHHHHHH!" Jules screeches.

Will daren't look but he can smell it, cooking meat and a fabulous sweet scent of hairspray, so he grins.

"LOOK OUT!" Joel pushes Will away from him as a butcher's knife slices down between them.

Tom.

"Run!"

Joel and Will begin sprinting down aisles to lose Tom, screaming profanities, almost drowned out by the echoing of Jules.

After a couple of minutes of almost running in circles, Will spots the gun a few feet away on the other side of the walkway. He peers round and sees Tom huffing, scanning, hunting him also a few feet away.

Will takes his opportunity and dives for the gun only to have camo boots kick the gun away and then strike him in the face.

"You think I can't handle a little heat?"

Jules

Will's eyes rise, working their way to her face from the floor, nose bleeding. The pain takes over a portion of his brain, as if dealing with it is energy expenditure enough, without the effort of new thoughts.

Nice and charcoaled.

Jules is practically sizzling. She has taken minor skin damage, but her protective equipment is singed and blackened, some of it melted to her. Jules pants slow but heavy over him.

That's gotta hurt!

She goes for the gun, giving Will a second or two to crawl backward. *Damn these slippery floors.*

And now she's pointing the gun at his face, hammer cocked.

THWACK!

Something hits Jules hard in the head. Will watches it slide away; it's a bottle of conditioner and when he looks over, it's Joel.

"REALLY? CONDITIONER?" she says, more surprised than enraged.

"Looked like you have a few burnt tips." Joel's suddenly found his balls.

Will pulls a mean face and kicks her as hard as he can in the shin, causing her leg to jerk back and fall. The three of them have eyes on the weapon. Will scrambles. They fight over the gun. They push, shove each other's faces. Joel steps into the fight to overpower her, but all he can think about is when she called him a noodle, and she is too strong. It's like PTSD.

On their knees, she punches Joel in the crotch, making him fall to the ground, and she practically throws Will into a wall.

"YOU'RE DEAD, NOODLE!"

She fires again but will grabs the first thing he can find, tossing it at her arm. This time she hits Joel in the thigh.

As Joel recoils in agony, Will quickly recuperates like nothing happened and nimbly pounces on Jules. The gun goes soaring through the air and slides under a clothing rack. Jules growls and heads for the gun, ignoring the searing burning prickling her skin. She momentarily forgets about Joel, who is already staggering away.

Beth

"Do you know first aid?" she says with a cold shake in her voice.

"No!"

300

"Shit, me neither!" Beth tries to keep pressure on the wound. "No exit wound... that's good, right?"

"I think so. Only for like the first few minutes. She just said look for an exit wound."

Matt says the bullet should act as a cork for the time being.

"Claire, what does that mean, is it good?" Beth tries to get her attention, but she's already fluttering.

They hear gunfire in the background coming from different parts of the store. A blood curling howl and a bigger explosion suddenly overtake the shot.

"Where did Tom get a gun?" Adam cowers.

"It's not Tom, it's that crazy copper from the warehouse when we met."

"NO WAY!

Beth wants to know who it is. While trying to keep pressure on Claire as Beth hysterically searches through pills and potions, Matt tries to remain calm and explain they had a heated run-in with some people when they tried to hide in a warehouse.

"A crazy bitch claimed it as her own and our position was discovered. I have not a clue why she is here! She has someone with her, but I didn't get a good luck, did you?"

She shakes her head.

"Great, two psychopaths loose in our new home. We've been here *one* night!"

Joel

Pain. It's all he can feel, it's affecting every nerve.

My god, not even breaking bones is anything close to this.

Drip. Drip. Drip. Drip.

Joel is hobbling down the walkway when Tom emerges from one aisle. He's spotted by an enraged Tom as he tries to hobble away. Tom is too fast.

"No, no. NO!"

Joel limps up the escalator and then looks behind. Tom has vanished. Joel thinks the coast is clear as he reaches the top of the triviality, only to be startled by Tom.

How?

Joel pauses, and suddenly the only present thing in his mind is that he can't breathe. Then his throat opens like the satisfying glide of scissors across paper. Blood pours out.

Tom slashes Joel's throat: he cannot flee because of his thigh wound. He bleeds out, flapping around like a fish out of water, and dies in seconds. His body falls back down the escalator, rolling to the bottom.

Jules regains her concentration and sees Joel's body. She calls him an idiot, picking up her gun. She fires at Will again, who after being hit tries to crawl away. Tom, who is finishing Joel off, spots will. He hacks away at Joel's lifeless body, butcher-meat-factory style, as if his right hand was a pendulum. He spots Will trying to silently crawl away and is about to march over until Jules reloads her gun and fires in Tom's direction.

"Get out of my store, bitch."

"Clean up on aisle you." She shoots.

Tom flinches and draws his attention away. Jules is reloading her gun again, taking her eyes off the prize for a split second, when a direct hit to the frontal lobe from Tom strikes her—her face twitches. Jules goes down hard. Will screams. Tom calls out for the others who are dotted around the store like headless chickens.

Will's life is in jeopardy, and he continues to crawl toward the home goods just as Tom pries the gun out of Jules's dead, stiff hands, including his precious cleaver.

I'm a dead man; don't worry Kieran, I'll be home soon. Will shut's his eyes calmly.

Beth and Matt come around the corner of the aisle, both

with a basket full of cans and cutlery. They throw viciously in Tom's general direction. He shoots the gun wildly, blasting the hair dyes. It creates a beautiful cascade of colour as the two of them seek cover.

In what Will would usually brand a plot twist, Tom charges toward him, defenceless and about to die. When Tom falls in front of him, slipping in a trail of Joel's blood, he flings forward and the cleaver cuts Will's calf.

"A perfect accident." Tom grins. "I don't know who the fuck you are but I'm gonna shove you through the mince grinder."

Will screams out in agony and Tom picks him up, shoving him into a makeup counter. He can feel the gun being wedged under his chin as tears form.

POP!

Will is sprayed with Tom's blood across his face.

What the fuck?

The manager tries to utter some words; the air leaves his lungs and he drops.

"Oh no, here I go." The pain is too much for Will and he collapses slowly down the counter, trying to ogle his rescuer.

Tom tries to crawl until two further shots are fired, striking his legs from out of nowhere. He cries, now paralysed—someone has crippled him, preventing him from making any movements other than rolling around in pain.

"Is it clear?" Beth asks with a jar of bolognese in her palm.

Matt takes a breath and peaks half an eye out. He gives a swift nod. Beth and Matt rush over and see the psychotic manager in a pool of his own blood, swearing.

"I don't understand." She looks ahead. She sees a figure she can't quite make out. "No way!"

It's Damon, the boy who owns the shop, who stayed behind for her, holding a smoking rifle from the entrance.

Beth and Matt are temporarily distracted, enabling an injured Tom to roll away from the group and slip into hiding. Damon reloads the rifle and repeatedly fires a shot at Tom, slithering away.

Another girl (a stranger to the group) who he must have picked up on the way, accompanies Damon. She has dark skin, is tall, mysterious, giving the others a sexy librarian vibe. She looks to be around their age. There is something about her afro so beautiful and bold, those tousled spikes pushed back by a red bandana. It's a sort of visual joy reaching upward to the heavens—confidence and strength, natural and pretty. Damon has a cold sweat across his forehead as Beth ogles the strange girl standing in a dressing gown.

13:35 hours

Beth slowly walks to Damon. He watches her draw closer and closer, confused.

"Hakuna matata!"

She embraces Damon, happy to see him alive and well, but also confused by his presence. He rests his chin on the top of her head, taking in a breath of her hair like freshly baked cookies.

"How are you here, of all places?" She parts from him.

First Will and now the boy who saved her in the shop? She tries to not read too much into another gift from the universe. Seeing him alive brings a smile to her face.

"I thought you had to find your sister?"

"Yes! This is where she is supposed to be!"

"What the hell is going on?"

"This is Amy."

He persuaded her to help him find his sister, who he believes is here. The afro-haired bandana girl gestures a quick salute. It inspires Beth to believe more people are coming; more people must be out there, and to her dismay, it means everyone can see them since they are sitting ducks. They should really work on securing the building.

"I have no idea what the hell just happened, but I really should have expected it. People with guns and now you…"

"I wouldn't count on being rescued, princess!" Damon interjects. "Everywhere is a ghost town, people either fled to quarantine zones or are hiding."

The noise they were making must have caused them to draw attention. Damon assures they are safe for now.

"The way I see it. That isn't a bad thing."

"How do you know all this?"

"We walked," Amy pipes up.

"From town? To here?" Beth's brows go as high as they will go. "That's like ten miles."

"Hence why it's taken me this long. But what was going on in town is going on everywhere."

"We know." Beth shakes Amy's hand. "Welcome. I guess. You caught us with our pants down."

"What the hell was all that about?"

"I have no idea."

Matt comes past with Will wrapped around his shoulder, half in and out of consciousness.

"I'm taking him to the den."

Where to go from here? They will have surly attracted attention from the commotion. They also have to figure out what to do with Tom.

"Who was the guy trying to kill the kid?" Damon nods to Tom, crawling off slowly.

"A real piece of work!"

Damon hands his rifle to Amy assertively. "Stay here!" And he walks toward him. With one swift yank, he picks Thomas up, who can only wriggle.

"You hurt my friends!"

13:45 hours

And just like that, Damon has bound him in chains to a pipe in the staff bathroom. He fittingly gags him tightly this time and chains his legs also to the radiator.

"I really appreciate that," Beth says from the doorway. "I need the new corpses gone, we're going to need to shift everything down to the docking station, it's cold enough to slow any decomposition."

"Wow, you're pretty good at this leader thing." Damon laughs as they walk out.

"We can take care of it. Thank you for taking us in," Amy affirms.

He asks about his sister in case she is in the building. She was supposed to be doing a midnight stock run for their shop. Damon admits the whole thing was a rouse so he could surprise her with a firework display when she returned to welcome in the New Year.

"My sister!" Damon suddenly says as they walk toward the den. "Have you seen her?"

He shows Beth his phone's background, it's a photo of the two of them. It makes her gasp.

"Oh no! I think you should follow me!" She groans. She suddenly flashes back to Claire, explaining she had a brother who would look for her. "Matt, I need you to get anything related to medicine that's left. It doesn't even have to be from the pharmacy. Look for uhhh, herbal stuff. Tea tree, towels, bandages, vitamins. Bring me basins, salts, whatever… I need alcohol, clear spirits if you can. Amy, this is Adam."

She instructs them to clean and dispose of the new bodies of the unwanted guests.

"What's wrong?" He can tell her brain is stumbling, overthinking as her eyes dart around.

"I need you to not freak out." She's stood in the way.

Damon discovers the girl who got shot is his sister, Claire. He's horrified, heartbroken and enraged at the same time. He runs over to see Will with pressure on her abdomen, also having sustained a leg injury from Tom.

"Who did this? She is barely clinging on for dear life."

"It makes perfect sense now. Claire was saying her brother would have been looking for her. You're her brother!" Beth explains, feeling accomplished, like she's come to the epic revelation of her favourite mystery novel.

Damon is stroking his sister's hair, trying to not get wound up.

"This is insane," she mutters.

"I should have never sent her for stock, thank you for keeping her safe this long."

"I'm so sorry!" Beth says.

It isn't long before Beth works out it is inadvertently her fault that the both of them are in this situation. Beth was the one who purchased all of Damon's liquor in the shop; if it wasn't for her, Claire would have never had been made to go out and get more. She walks off, mournful, trying to process her shocking revelation.

"I should have never agreed to throw a party."

"You need to see this!" shouts Adam, throwing her out of her trance.

Adam takes Beth to the office, walking past Tom who is gagged and bound in his manager's toilet. Adam points to the cameras and Beth watches people running up to the walls of the complex and smashing into them repeatedly. The numbers build.

"Creepers!" utters Adam. "Wasters!"

They have the place surrounded by the infected. They gather in numbers, and the barricade will only hold for so long. Tensions begin to rise.

18:00 hours
Damon

Damon refuses to leave his sister's side, trying to help her any way he can. The rest of the group can tell he is angry and frustrated and he demands she be made more comfortable.

"I have pillows, blankets, hot water bottles and anything else."

"She needs a hospital!"

"I'm sorry. We are surrounded right now; we have to wait until they disperse…" Beth says softly.

Most of the survivors see this place as a sanctuary and a haven. They don't want to leave, only wait for rescue. Claire was one of the few people who wanted to venture out to find her brother, and now she has her wish (though she does not know he's right beside her).

Will is sitting with his leg up, staring at his feverish sleeping beauty while Adam works on his leg. Matt is sitting playing with metal scrap, he looks like he's building something.

18:30 hours
Beth
Rooftop

Blackness comes with such completeness it obliterates the memory of the day. With the thick cloud above, no relief comes from either the moon or stars.

Dense cloud obscures utterly the usual friendly smattering of stars. Ordinarily, Beth would stay in the Hyde Park Pub on a night like this, despite the first bite of winter in the air. Beth would have to be slow, silent, unseen.

Will creeks open the door to the roof access, struggling

from his injury. Adam helps him and uses him as a crutch. They only accessed the roof for maintenance and window cleaning before, and maybe the odd patch job if ever there was a leak. Beth feels like she hasn't seen the outside in forever. She's been cooped up indoors for nearly three days, so when the fresh air hits her, she has to sit down. All she can make out are silhouettes of buildings in the distance, and shadows of things that once were. It takes ten minutes for her eyes to form the shapes of the buildings. Maybe the odd fire to light an amber sky becomes the backdrop; it's a shame there's so many clouds blanketing the night sky, because she bets the stars would be seen in the trillions right now.

She is greeted to the icy wall of the winter blizzard. Snow lightly dances in the air. The most haunting thing about it that makes her shiver is the near silence of the rest of the world—not a soul or a peep.

"So, this is where you're hiding. It's taken us forever to find you!" Will creeps up on her.

Beth and Adam are standing by the edge of the rooftop above the entrance. Beth rubs her arms to warm up as her breath evaporates. Will escorts her to where she looks upon maybe hundreds of undead.

"Oh, it wasn't like this earlier." She cringes.

In vulgar and squalor, they climb over one another, reach up, snarl, shout, scream in a violent rabble. They are hungry and thirsty, maybe a baker's dozen more than earlier. The undead have gathered in their forces and the only defence separating the living from the dead are the shutters acting as a barricade. The lorry acts as a secondary one but if the monsters figure out how to push the truck through, they'll all be dead.

Beth's soul leaves her body. "This is bad, like terrible," she concludes.

The boys agree and think they would show her because

she may know what to do.

"Why would you ask me?"

Will points out she has been doing a good job of running things as of late, and it just seemed to make sense. Beth gulps. *This is what true fear feels like.* She sits down on the edge and asks the boys if any of them have a cigarette. Will pulls out a pack he swiped from the kiosk downstairs.

"You don't smoke!" Will says, suddenly jerking his hand away.

"Yeah, and the dead aren't supposed to walk."

"This is more like the old Beth I remember." Will smirks.

He gawks at her before shrugging and pulling out two cigarettes for them.

"This is awful." She coughs.

"This is just maybe 100 zombies, and there are two million people in Leeds alone, so what if more come, then what are going to do?"

Will barks at Beth, but she remains silent and focused. You can almost hear the clogs turning.

"Don't call them zombies—they are people, this is not TV," Adam stresses.

"What? They are not people anymore. I thought we all agreed on that?" Will interjects.

Will and Adam begin a heated debate, and Beth's eyes glaze over. She has completely gone off in her own world as she twiddles her thumbs, flicking ash on the ground.

Matt's head peers around the door. "Do you know which aisle the electricals are kept on?"

"NO!" both Adam and Will say returning to their squabble.

Matt notices Beth thinking off into space. She looks chilly. This is his moment to swoop in, a knight in shining armour. He calmly crouches and takes her hands.

"What are you thinking, girl?"

Will and Adam continue their disagreement. The stress is

getting to the group, tearing them apart. It brings panic among poor survivors, so they'll have the place reinforced and abandon the main supermarket shop floor. Death has tainted it.

"Zombies is what they are..."

Adam cuts him off. "No, that's bullshit. Zombies go around with their arms out moaning braaaaaaains! Those things down there were you and me."

"Oh really? And zombies weren't people either? What? Are you living in a black and white 60s horror movie? What-the-fuck would you call them then?"

"PEOPLE! SICK PEOPLE! INFECTED!" Adam raises his voice. "THEY NEED HELP! HELP IS COMING!"

Matt stands and tells Adam to keep his voice down. They both need to knock it off.

"Adam, literally the definition of a zombie is a person who is or appears lifeless, apathetic, or completely unresponsive to their surroundings." Will tells him to look it up.

"Oh, I'd love to if I had a working phone!" Adam sarcastically remarks.

"There is a book aisle downstairs, and I'm sure it will be written somewhere." Will wittingly points out.

Will squares up to Adam's face, almost pressing against his nose. "Zombies are corpses said to be revived by witchcraft, especially in certain African and Caribbean religions. THE SAME SHIT YOU SEE IN A MOVIE! A person or reanimated corpse that has been turned into a creature capable of movement but not of rational thought, which feeds on human flesh."

Will repeats the word, slowly winding Adam up. Adam feels his adrenaline bubbling until he calms himself down and sarcastically tells Will he looks cute when he's angry.

"I have a feeling my fist would look cuter up your fucking arse BUT I HAVE A SNEEKY SUSPICION YOU

MIGHT LIKE THAT." Will pushes Adam back.

"Oh, yeah?"

"YEAH, why don't we get down to it while we drink ZOMBIE COCKTAILS? That's also another definition of ZOMBIE. You ever had a zombie, pretty boy? Y'know lots of rum, liqueur and a fuck load of fruit? Fruit the little fruit boy?"

Adam pauses for a minute and the little fruit remark drives something inside him to suddenly snap. Adam headbutts Will as hard as he can. Will grabs his face. Will loses it and dives on Adam. Matt tries desperately to break them up.

"You homophobic cunt!" Adam squeals.

"You don't know me at all!" Will says as they roll around.

"That's it…" Beth has an epiphany. As she looks up from her head between her arms, she wipes the cold sweat from her eye. "Cocktails…" she whispers. "COCKTAILS!" She screams at the boys; Matt is wedged between Adam and Will. "Don't you get it? Cocktails... that's how we can get rid of them. Will, you're an arsehole but a genius."

"Thanks," he says. "So, like what? We're going to get them drunk? You know those things can barely stand as it is, right?"

"Yeah, but they have the strength of 20 men. One literally threw me into a car," Adam adds.

"No! Molotov cocktails—we can burn them. It's the only thing I can think of that would get rid of them when we have no guns and no way out," Beth explains.

"We have a gun," corrects Will.

"It has two bullets in it," counters Adam.

"Perfect, one for you and also another one for you." Will smiles.

"You could risk burning down this building, not to mention the ball of fire could draw more of those things in or anyone living, which I feel is more dangerous than those things. Look around you. We may as well be the sun," Matt responds.

Will scowls. "How does that make us more dangerous?"

"You're alive, that already makes you more dangerous than them!"

"Yeah, you may as well turn this place into Blackpool illuminations with a sign that says 'all you can eat'!" Adam scoffs, still grappling with Will.

"Shut up, Fruit."

"What else do you cave dwellers suggest? You two are beating the sexual tension out of each other and Matt, what have you done since you got here? Apart from collapse every 20 minutes from brain damage?" Beth snaps.

"Blonde bimbo says what?" Will says too fast for her to understand.

It registers. "I will slap you!"

"Oooogh! Violence is against the Brunerfield code," mocks Will at his best friend.

The boys look at one another and let go. Matt's feelings are clearly hurt, and Beth realises what she has said. She tries to fix it, but he walks inside.

Damon passes him. "Did I interrupt something?"

Will and Adam stare at him, both bloodied and confused and deny anything happened.

"Self defence lessons!"

"I don't want to be rude, but I want to take my sister and get the hell out of here."

Will and Adam want to wait for rescue, though— something they can both agree on, and Will doesn't want Claire to leave, so he tries to make excuses.

"She is too sick."

Beth tries to defuse the rising tensions and disputes by trying to meet the group halfway. She gets Will to go back inside and clean up his nose.

"Adam go and..." She tries the think as Amy

313

approaches… "do something else." She keeps Adam away, knowing separating the two will calm them down.

Discarded like an old newspaper, yesterday's news; if he was a flower, he would wilt instantly. Amy see's this and tries to help.

"Hey… do you want to go… and… try on the shoes?" Amy sounds so serious it could be mistaken for sarcasm; he looks at her for a moment.

"Fuck yeah." He grins, walking away.

She sits Will down, looking over his shoulder at Matt who is facing away, sat on his claimed blow-up bed. She feels bad.

"Stop pissing people off!" She dabs Will's nose.

"Am I still beautiful?"

"It's not broken, if that's what you mean?"

"Wow, that little twink packs a punch."

"Then stop getting punched!"

"I will when people stop being stupid—OW!" Will recoils.

"HOLD still!" Beth gets him to focus like a child.

Will rummages in his jogger pockets to reveal a crumpled spliff. He lights it whimsically.

"PUT THAT OUT!" She knocks it out of his hand as he bursts out laughing.

"How you were planning to adopt with Ricca, I will never know. Look, I need a favour… I need you to assess the severity of infected surrounding the area. Collect as much paint as you can gather." They will create signs on the roof for helicopters. "I need paint and bed sheets, anything to make 'alive inside' signs, or SOS, or anything anyone from above may see."

"Not bad, but who the hell is gonna see it?"

"It's for the daytime moron!" Dab, dab, dab.

"B! It's the dead of winter, we get five hours of daylight, and every day looks like a day on Neptune. BLGHH!"

"Look, just do me a solid. This place is about to fall apart. Get Adam. I need to talk to him."

"WHY ME?"

"Because you're the bigger person, Gizmo, you know that."

Will groans, getting up and trailing his peachy bum to the fashion show that is Adam and Amy. He looks down at them from the upper floor, laughing and posing in the mirror. When he puts his fingers in his mouth to whistle. They look directly at him and the fun stops. Will jerks his head for Adam to come up.

20:18 hours

Adam and Beth are intensely working up a sweat, brushing white paint on the roof with rollers. The freezing cold doesn't help when Adam suggests they use battery powered torches or light many candles during the night. Beth thinks the idea is sweet, but it's wrong for two reasons.

"We do not want to draw unwanted attention to our safe house, and the weather would surely ruin our chances. We are doing this so it can be seen during the daytime; it's better we work through the night so no one can see us!"

He apologises, and she tells him not to be daft.

"I'm sorry. It's bugging me too much. Do you hate me?" he says out of the blue.

"What?" She loses her balance. Adam waits for an answer so she says, "Oh, my goodness. Honey, no! What makes you say that?"

"It's just everyone else gets some level of respect and I just get orders thrown at me…"

"Oh, my gosh! I am so sorry if I ever made you feel that way. That's the last thing I wanted." She sighs, trying to think. "There's just a lot of pressure to be a certain way and delegate when I do not know what I'm doing." She tears up.

315

"I forget myself, there is a reason I am the way I am, truly. Come here." Adam brings his paint brush with him and embraces her. "If you ever feel like that, you look me in the eye and you say: Bitch! Don't talk to me like that!" They both laugh, sigh and go back to work.

"So, is Will gay or...?" Adam tries to bravely change the topic.

"Why, you scared he's homophobic?" Beth chuckles.

"No, just curious."

"Trust me, if Will was homophobic and meant it, I would kick his arse faster than you could say apocalypse."

Adam smiles, and a brief silence ensues as the snow fades to one flake every minute. Things are calmer now, and only the drowning sorrows of the undead snarling below in a mismatch choir of demonic angels fill the void.

"No. Will is 99 percent sarcasm and one percent uh, filled with a mental thrill-ness. He's my best friend. Learn to take him with a pinch of salt or in his case, a bag." Beth continues, "I take it you like him?"

"What? Uh."

"Adam, it's okay if you do." She stretches back to paint. Adam feels awkward. "Everyone is a little gay these days. I wouldn't rule out lasses from time to time, but I like my men too much." Beth smiles and explains, "Will is... complicated, he's a free spirit, doesn't care if you're man, woman, demonic entity or the flying spaghetti monster." She pauses and tries to fathom the words. "What I'm trying to say is, you may have a chance—he's just stubborn. I've only ever known him to truly love one guy. My other friend, who I watched die."

Beth looks off into space with flashes of Kieran dying in her mind. Adam watches her silently. He goes back to painting. She lets the heartache pass.

"They were cringe-worthy in love, two psycho peas in a pod, perfect for each other! But man, it was messy toward the end, a case of who could out stubborn the other. It was always the two of them—they shared things with each other, no one else would understand. I used to get so jealous of what they had behind closed doors, but again they were my best friends, and I was always picking up the pieces when it went tits up. Kieran would drink, Will would smoke, until they met in the middle. Will always wanted more than Kieran was willing to offer until it was too late. One day, Will just threw in the towel for good. Then Kieran got his act together, finally did all the things Will wanted, to prove he could be the one he was going to marry and spend the rest of his life with. Kieran kind of did it for himself. He realised it was time to grow up. But, Will had met a girl by this point. It broke Kieran's world in two and sent him over the edge, threw everything away. He didn't see the point in going on." Tears form in Beth's eyes as they both stop painting. "That was the day the light went out in his eyes. I've never seen a truly broken shell of a person or soul until that happened. He lost the will to live." She sniggers slightly. "The irony of that phrase… and I had to pick up the pieces. He had to watch the only person he ever truly gave himself over to, someone who accepted him whole-heartedly, love another. Can't imagine that. Her name is Ricarda or *was*… fuck knows if she's alive. Some southern girl Will met. It convinced Kieran Will loved her and he kind of did, but it was all the love he had for Kieran. We all saw Will didn't love her fully. She was a distraction to numb the pain and loss. She stuck around even though we all knew he was still deep down in love with someone else."

Adam doesn't quite know where to put himself. Beth realises she's making Will sound like he is hung up on Kieran.

"I mean, he will always care about him, it's just fucked up, isn't it? Watching someone you were so in love with die in front of you! I think this is how he is dealing. Like I said, they were both my best friends, so it was complicated and messy. Will technically has been my longest friend, but I had a deep connection with Kieran. I love Will, but I'll always hold a little resentment for what he did and somewhere deep down I think he will resent himself too. But Will says Kieran did it to make himself feel better about breaking him. Will is no angel by far. The thing that used to make me angry so much was them screaming about who fucked the other person over more. They would see who could hurt the other, then feel bad about it. Rather than just taking a step back and being sorry and forgiving themselves as well as each other. They could have had a wonderful friendship if they let everything go. But, I suppose when you find your soulmate, apparently, that's love. Weird, man."

"You ever been in love?" Adam asks.

She thinks about it. "I don't know. Apparently it just hits you, so maybe not. I've had boyfriends, but my ambition and career were my love. What it did to Kieran put me off because it wasn't their time, like maybe if they had met ten years from now it would have been perfect, if the world didn't fall apart that is." She puts the paint brush down as Adam purses his lips. "But it doesn't matter because he's dead now and this is what we have to do, paint a 20-foot HELP sign on the roof of a supermarket because the dead have come back to life. A week ago, it was Christmas!" They both snigger. Beth gets serious again. "I don't say this to put you off, honestly, but I want you to know why he is the way he is; he has high walls, and it's going to take a lot to knock them down. So, make a difference."

Adam smiles and nods. Beth tells him she needs more paint in hope it will pass enough time for rescue to arrive and for Claire to recover. Amy tries to make herself useful by tying bedsheets together to make enormous signs and she weighs them down with large, loose chunks of snow left over from the blizzard.

Will calculates a couple hundred infected surrounding the complex and they are at high risk of breaching the shop floor. He has fixed his nose and comes to help paint, but he pulls Adam aside and apologises for their argument earlier. Adam says he gets it and leaves it at that. The two embrace.

00:09 hours
The Den

Claire's situation doesn't look to be changing soon and Beth may run out of options as Damon grows impatient.

"Is there a way out of here?"

"There was," utters Will, "until Barbarella over there made us break every one of them."

"There was a mass murderer on the loose, and I was trying to save everyone. A little gratitude would go a long way." Beth scoffs.

"By trapping us in a fishbowl and yet more psychos still got in!"

"We should stay, we will clear as many as we can out—"

"I know what's best for my sister... we leave."

Beth can already detect some over protection. Damon can smell the infatuation oozing from Will for his sister, and it is abundant the guys dislike one another.

"Maybe I was wrong about the whole leader thing." He sighs.

Beth has never been so embarrassed.

"I'm going for a walk," he stretches.

"Don't you want to sleep? You haven't eaten, slept, or even gone to the bathroom." Beth shouts, but he's already gone.

"Beth..." Adam won't look up and she can tell he is stricken with fear.

"What now?" she groans.

00:20 hours

"Stragglers." Adam points at the screen. *How?*

Beth notices on the CCTV odd stragglers of infected are making their way into the store. It is no longer safe to be on the shop floor... period.

"Grab everything."

They head up to the security rooms, scared for their lives. Matt and Damon carry Claire on a makeshift stretcher. Will slams the door shut on Tom, still taped up and injured in the bathroom. Amy and Adam have packed up supplies, and it forces them to see the rest of the night through cramped in with one another.

"We are leaving now."

"We have to figure out how the copper and Joel *and* the creepers got in here!" claims Will.

They prepare a supply and find a way out but with little means of escape, and a lack of reasoning.

"The same way I got in, but we take to the roof. There's a 20-foot drop." Beth folds her arms.

"I have a suggestion," a stifled voice calls from the bathroom. Tom feels everybody will want to hear it.

"SHUT the fuck up before I put the last two bullets in your arms and your legs," threatens Will.

"BAIT!" yells Tom.

"What did he just say?"

"Your pals. Feed them to the munchers. Bait them, it'll keep them at bay. It's what they want, isn't it?"

"The people you butchered in cold blood?" Beth yells over her shoulder.

"That... might not be the worst idea..." Damon suggests.

"Maybe if you used the rotting corpses of Val, Harry and Dylan, then throw in some of your copper and her minion, you could buy some more time. Since you put them on ice. AND YOU CALL ME SICK?"

Will flings the door open. "You don't get to say their names." He sees Tom's gag has fallen off.

"Come on, it's like a fucking depressing losers' convention. I get it, I've lost, you need an escape plan."

"Ignore him, he's just bitter and panicking cos he's fucked," says Matt.

Beth turns to Damon. "These were people. Ripped apart by him for no reason. Do you have any respect for the dead? Do you have any idea who you're talking to?"

"Yeah, I saw the tapes," Damon firmly remarks.

"Then you'll know this man will say and do anything to get on your side, in your head, and his hands on your insides," Will mutters.

You can smell the tensions between Damon and Will building.

Beth disturbs their standoff. "Regardless of how sick and crude the idea is, you can't feed those creatures. I doubt there is enough to go around and even if there was. That human meat is rotting. Even animals with basic primal instincts don't want rotting flesh."

"Well, what do you do after you've had a full banquet feast? You barely want to move, so I'm sure it's all the same to the people outside," Tom slyly says.

The group glare at him.

"Why don't you just hit the fucking road?"

"BECAUSE WE CAN'T LEAVE!"

"YOU HAVEN'T FUCKING TRIED!"

Will kicks him and Tom groans in pain.

"You really think they're going to stop? Mr Manager, those things would just vomit up what they ate and then eat the vomit, because they don't know any better," Matt responds.

"Like me on a Friday night," Adam playfully adds. The group then turns to him, and he apologises.

"We have the keys to a van," Will points out.

"It's wedged hallway between us and them. How are we going to get my sister on safely?"

"We gotta figure out what makes them tick," Will decides.

The others ask Will what he means. He explains to understand what they are up against and how to figure out their enemy's weakness, they will have to capture a zombie. There is murmuring among the group. Will walks to the CCTV and watches the dormant creatures stagger from pillar to post. He concludes if they work together, they could capture one.

"You can't seriously be considering trying to feed it?"

"You are sitting on slabs of fucking man meat. CHOP THEM UP!"

"Mate, I swear to God if you don't shut the fuck up…" Matt clenches his fist.

"Take it easy," Beth says.

"What you gonna do, fall on me? You brain damaged titted fuck." Tom mocks.

Matt leaps to life and storms into the bathroom to kick the shit out of Tom. It takes Damon, Will and Adam to restrain him.

"Matt, your nose," informs Beth.

He can feel it, the coldness of the drip; he thinks it is just a runny nose until he puts his finger up to his nostrils and sees blood. All that adrenaline and the rush to the head. Something is very wrong.

"Shit." He falls into the red sofa.

"I've got you, mate," Damon says.

"We are not chopping them up."

Tom grins. "I'll do it."

"Get fucked." Beth growls.

"Beth, you swore!" Will gasps.

"It's becoming a habit." She locks eyes with Tom.

"I DIDN'T SAY IT WAS GONNA BE A WALK IN THE

PARK NOW DID I, YOU BLONDE BARKING BINT? BUT. IT'S. WORTH. A. PISSING. TRY."

Tom screams as if he still has a say, only to be greeted by a sudden and very harsh left hook delivered from Damon. The others jump. One of Tom's teeth bounces away as he sniggers and lets the blood drool. That definitely had to hurt.

"Fine. How do we do it?" Amy speaks.

"I'll do it." Damon rubs his knuckles.

Who is this gun slinging, dark, killer punching boy? What's his game? Beth thinks, toying over other anxieties.

There is an outcry in the group, hands on heads, hands over mouths, trying to mull it over.

"You catch one, a slow one. I'll get bait."

"Well, there's one or two dawdlers on the lower ground, but a quick one could easily slip in and get us," reveals Adam.

Amy asks, "How did they slip in?"

"I don't know, this place is huge," Adam replies, "and Beth locked us in."

"Obviously it didn't work. How many are outside?" Damon says plainly.

Adam shrugs. "I don't know, like half and half."

"Get one of them." Beth has no choice but to concede.

"Beth! Are you really going to let him get away with what he's doing?"

She looks hesitant. "They have outvoted me, Adam, this is a democracy. He's right. We have to try."

"Some leader *you* are." Adam scorns her before storming off.

"Guess what? That's democracy!"

Damon follows Adam after laying Claire down. "There's 20-feet between us and them."

"So, we scoop one!" Matt claps his hands, ready.

"It's not fucking hook-a-duck," scoffs Will.

"Get me some rope, tape, bags, and wire. Meet me on the roof."

"Who *are* you?"

Rooftop

Matt throws down a long rope with a noose in front of Will and Beth while Adam monitors Claire and makes sure Tom doesn't slip away.

"What is this?" grunts Will.

"Noose lassoo!" Matt says without care.

"WHO ARE YOU?" begs Will.

"I grew up on a farm, okay? Lots of fixing of things, building from scratch. Engineer, remember?" He looks down at the squabbling and rowdy crowd of the undead reaching up for their dinner. So angry and full of hate. "You two are going to be weight. I'm gonna hook one of the slow ones and you're gonna pull as hard as you can. This might take a few attempts. Will, are you going to be okay with your leg?"

"I think the question is, are you going to be okay with your head?"

"Let's find out."

Damon

"I might as well be dragging 20 sacks of potatoes at once."

Damon heard somewhere human bodies get heavier after death, something to do with relaxing muscles. It sure feels like it. He does not know if that awful pungent smell is the rotting corpses or the rotting food. *Both, perhaps.*

No one else wants to do the knitty-gritty, dirty work. Maybe they've been through enough. Damon has always stomached it. He's always been the one to take on the arduous tasks no one else opts for, even if it makes him the sick bastard.

Matt

"HEAVE."

The trio pull with all their might. Simultaneously, Damon is dragging new bodies over to the deli aisle.

"HEAVE!"

And again, they pull. Out rises a corpse, confused as well as pissed off.

Damon

Damon slugs the last body in and gets to work.

Amy is trying not to watch from a far, head in her hands, as the slicing and sludging begins.

Damon mutters as he cuts through these bodies as if they were animal carcasses being trimmed down to sell. He slops piles and chunks of meat into bowls reluctantly. It's a bloody parlour game of a mess. Soon his watch, his clothes and his face are covered. It's almost like he is praying, carving what he can from their bones and their guts.

Matt

"Get it, get it, don't let wriggle free!"

They drag one onto the roof, slap bang into the paint that's still drying. It's a squabbling messy affair.

"The bags, get me the bags, hold his arms!" Matt is throwing orders around. "Good, good."

They have him held down. But Matt suddenly has a wave of light-headedness and a splitting headache. He lets go of the weight on the creature, and it jumps to life.

"MATT!"

"OH NO! GRAB IT!"

It lunges for Beth as Matt collapses in a heap, so it's up to Will. The creeper has Beth's forearm and leans in. She screams a split second before Will swoops in, tackling the beast by planting a shopping bag over its head. Will quickly uses the rope to wrap around its neck, throwing the other end around a mast.

"Stay, doggy!" He jumps over to Beth. "Are you okay? Did it get you?"

"No, I'm okay. Help Matt."

The creature is wondering, swinging its arms around, restricted on the rope as they come to their friend's aid.

"He's having a fit!"

"What do we do?"

"We don't!"

Beth ties her hair into a golden ponytail, loose hair falling all over her features that contort with effort. She takes hold of Matt, eyes rolling into the back of his head, jerking. She sings to him. Though helpless, she can at least make it bearable.

"Don't go, don't take him, please. This angel is not ready to go home yet." Tears are streaming. She rocks. Will can only watch in anguish. "It's my fault, it's my fault. I'm so sorry, it's my fault," she whispers. But Will doesn't understand why.

Damon places bags and bags of meat sealed in airtight pouches to the side. Adam tries not to feel nauseas, the anger and the disapproval helps.

"I'm sorry!" Damon sits in a bloody exhausted state.

"No, he's not." Tom grins.

"I thought we shut you up."

Will is navigating the beast they bagged. The undead individual kicks and screams.

"Wow, that is truly an awful sound!" Amy has made her way up, carrying water for them all.

Will slams the creature on the table as Damon stands,

pushes off most of the computers and tills, much to Tom's protests. Beth staggers in with Matt, who has seen better days.

"What happened?"

"He had a fit." She sits him down next to Claire, hunched over and calm. She wipes up the blood. "No more exercising for you," she urges.

"You just look more beautiful every time I see you!" He grins.

Nobody is looking, and Tom seizes a piece of metal that fell from the table. He moves his feet to drag it back and curls up to pass it to his hands. Will takes notice for a moment, before shaking it off, not realising his hands were in front of him and bound a second ago. Once the zombie is strapped down, they take off its bag.

"Straight from the supermarket to your door!" Will claps.

Adam and Amy recoil in disgust. It has a green-grey complexion, originally olive skin, black veins and bloodshot eyes, and its teeth are chattering and snatching. The decomposing process has begun. Will and Damon can't help but be fascinated by the creature and Beth looks on in despair as she tends to Matt. Before they begin, Will asks everybody in the group if they have any experience.

"Science? Medicine? Hell, even a weekend at a butcher's shop?"

Tom tries to raise his hand, which Will ignores. Damon pipes up and explains he's always had an interest in science; he doesn't know much about medicine, but he remembers reading a few books of Claire's she left lying around the house when she was studying.

"Look at its complexion." He comments on how most of the blood has left the body. "I'm not a scientist, but it's pooling in lower-lying portions, creating a pale appearance in some places and a darker appearance in others. Decomposing tissue is emitting a green substance, as well as gasses such as methane and hydrogen sulphide. Hence the dull complexion. The lungs and stomach are leaking fluid through the mouth and nose."

This is all Damon can come up with. Suddenly, the others fire questions at him.

"Why the killing and eating of human flesh?"

"Why the bile and blood?"

"Is it curable?"

Damon calms everybody and says all he has done is state the obvious. "These 'people' are certainly post mortem."

"So, once you get it there's no coming back?" Adam sits down from shock.

While they turn their backs, ogling their prize, Tom is chiselling away at his tape and chains, fixated on them.

"Now the million-dollar question," says Beth.

"Will the bait work?" Damon goes to one of his bags and picks out a nice chunk of man-chum, repulsing the others.

"Jesus Christ!" Amy turns, annoyed.

As Damon slowly teases the bloody human flesh, the creature goes from wriggling to spooked; it flexes its nostrils.

"It's like a sniffer dog!" claims Will.

"I will never get used to seeing all these entrails!" Adam shudders.

Damon has its attention. He brings it close, and it sniffs like a curious animal.

"Come on," he whispers.

"It's too rotten!" Adam protests. They shush him.

"Go for it!" Beth catches herself actually invested.

"WRAGUHHHHHHHH!"

CHOMP!

They savour the minor victory, bizarre and messed up, but still thankful. They study how long it takes to kill one, and from a few experiments, it appears to take only damage to the brain. Beth physically cannot be in the room while the dissecting is going on and Damon is the one to put it out of its misery by a sliding a knife through its ear.

"Its skin is so soft, like a knife in butter."

Once again, Will's theory is proven that the dead may walk and live off the flesh of the living.

"It's settled then, a clean blow to the head or brain will stop a creature for good," he says, triumphant.

Beth hugs Damon even though he is a bloody mess. She fits perfectly into him.

"I'm really glad you're here. Thank you!"

She rests her cheek on his chest, and he kisses her forehead. It's like a photograph. Those pictures where the background is blurred, where the only part in focus is the person pictured. That's how she feels. Not ideal, the image is blood-soaked and gory but it's a light in a dark tunnel. Every other detail of this room blurs as every part of Beth focuses on every aspect of Damon. Lovers are flames that breathe all the more deeply for being closer together; it is then they shine brighter. They become a source of light and love in the world, showering sparks of positive chaos into the dark. However, for some the burning isn't so passionate and flowing… instead, it hurts. Matt becomes increasingly jealous seeing Beth and Damon becoming closer while he sits weary and sick. Eventually, he sees them having a moment.

Tom uses his observation skills to put two and two together. He watches Matt's reaction and can almost feel the burning daggers toward Damon sweet talking Beth.

He grins. "Bingo."

Tom
00:00 hours

And the clock strikes 12, it's show time.

"Pssst… Pssst… PSSST! Fuck sake… OI, HELEN

KELLER!" Tom say's a little louder than a whisper to get Matt's attention.

Others are asleep or looting the shop floor. He looks over at Claire snoozing peacefully when Matt stirs from his slumber. His head feels heavy, like it's too big for his body. There's a ringing in his ears and a killer headache that he can't shake. Matt thinks his brain cells have been knocked out of his head.

"What the fuck do you want, pig?" He can barely see, but is irritated.

"Don't let them do this to me, eh?"

"You shouldn't have butchered your staff or their friends now, should you?" Matt goes to turn back over.

"Wait, wait!"

"Mate, if I had it my way, I'd feed you to the creeps… piece by piece. I saw what you did."

"They are going to kill me. Leave me here to starve. Or put me out of my misery!" Tom is quietly frantic and nervous, almost like he's genuinely concerned or showing some humanity.

Bullshit, Matt thinks.

"Let's hope it's quick."

"N-n-n-no. You're not like them! You're smart. You like mechanics and you build things, right? Yeah, yeah. That's it. They listen to you. You are useful and have the humanity."

"Mate, I used to raise cows, milk and breed them, then fucking shoot them for my barbeque. Don't talk to me like I'm gonna save you. You're nothing."

"I've seen this. I've heard them talking. I've heard them all talking! What they're gonna do with me, to me… but what they are gonna do with you after. Yeah!"

Now he has Matt's attention. "What the fuck do you mean?" He sits up slowly.

"Yeah… they think you're broken… retarded even… faulty products that's just going to weigh them down. Too much brain damage." Tom rapidly nods with a sweat on, probably from taking two shots—though they grazed him—to his legs. "I've seen it a thousand times as a manager! They will split you off from the team. Beth and Damon. Yeah, the lovers who bitch about you, laugh about you behind your back. You like her and she mocks you!" Tom hisses quietly.

"Mate, shut the fuck up or—"

"Ask yourself, go on, who is gonna be at the runt of the litter once they've done away with me? I will protect you! You're not broken, you have a beautiful mind. I've been watching you building."

He brainwashes Matt to try to use him as a pawn. Matthew isn't thinking clearly, it's got to be the head trauma.

Come on, you're better than this.

Tom realises it's going to take some work to win Matt over.

"I can sort that boy out, the one all over your girl. I promise. It can be our secret; she will be your queen and you can prove to her you ain't broken… all you have to do is let me go."

"Liar."

"I have nothing left to lose. And I am totally defenceless."

"I'm not a joke."

"Show them," Tom whispers.

Matt comes closer, sceptical of his promises. Tom deceitfully reveals his arms. He has hold of the sharp metal scrap and stabs Matt in the side. He breaks loose from his captivity, not before nearly losing balance. He hobbles away, leaving Matt to die.

CHAPTER 10:

WHERE'S THE MANAGER?

January 4ᵗʰ, 2012
00:07 hours
Matt

He doesn't see it coming. The loose shiv jabs his side; it
meets Matt's flesh, soft and pudgy, and makes a satisfying
squish as the tip of the blade sinks deep enough to make
Matt yelp but not loud enough to stir the others. It's too
much pain to do anything else. Tom twists the blade in his
hands, all the while plunging it deeper. Then, without
warning, he jerks it out. A cascade of Matt's life source
gushes in all directions. Copper hits Matt's nostrils.

Tom is back on the loose. He causes severe problems for
the group and tries to get them one by one. He plays them
against each other—the place is now heavily surrounded by
the infected, and time to deal with them is running out. He
slyly takes away food and belongings without making his
presence known to the others, and against everyone's orders,
Damon is busy feeding the infected the flesh of the corpses.
He hopes it will distract them to allow a safe passing, but
only makes them angrier and thirstier.

A feverish Claire wakes full of aches, pains, and is the
only one with medical experience under her belt. She
shivers. All she can do is wait for a pass of cool air from the
conditioner. Noise is distorted and her vision blurring—if
her temperatures spikes, her cells will die, and Claire's
biochemistry will slow. She knows she is dying but tries

with every fibre of her being to fight. In a moment of clarity, she comes to and sees Matthew's bloody and unconscious body.

She tries to call out to him, but Matt doesn't respond. The room is shifting, making it nauseating to see. She is too weak to yell to the others, so she tries to move from her bed and drags herself towards him. When she turns him over, she sees he has been stabbed, and the wound is still pouring.

She wipes the cold sweat on her forehead, glimpses herself in an obscure reflection in an appliance. She tries to drag herself to the medicines and fishes out a few needles, then injects him with something, but before she can register she's finished, she passes out on his chest.

It isn't safe here anymore. They have to go.

Everyone is too busy in the docking station downstairs where a few of the infected find their way in through vents, leading them to the store, which Beth and Damon struggle to contain. When they finally return to the office, Damon discovers his sister's condition as she rapidly spirals out of control. Claire and Matt are passed out on one another.

"What the hell?"

Damon drops the canned goods. He angrily tries to pull his sister back onto the bed when Will comes to see what the commotion is.

"What happened?" Damon's voice is soft and light.

"I don't know you that well, but she doesn't look good—she's suffering, man."

Something inside Damon unexpectedly erupts. Adrenaline hits his blood full pelt. He turns and, in a flash, he has Will by the scruff of his jumper against the office wall.

"And just what exactly is it you are suggesting, kid?"

"Fuck off me, man!" Will uses his fists to deflect Damon's hands and shoves him away. "I was only saying. She looks like she will not make it. I don't want to see her suffering, it's horrific to watch."

"You stay away from her!"

"I have been trying to look after her."

"You don't even know her. I heard you were the one who drove a truck through the entrance and probably got her into this mess."

"Fuck you!"

Damon suddenly gets the resurgence of adrenaline—an intravenous drip, so he attacks Will. Their heated words turn into an angry scrap because Will suggested she be put out of her pain and misery. Secretly, inside, he cannot bare to see her in agony. He is developing feelings for her.

They throw punches and thumps, falling into an office table, pushing each other's faces with their palms. Damon picks up a coffee mug, breaking it over Will's head.

"Oh, you want to play dirty?" Will immediately picks up a stapler and thrusts it into Damon's cheek.

In complete awe, Damon glares at Will, checking for blood. He picks up a letter opener. The atmosphere takes a drastic turn when Will sees the dagger clenched in Damon's palm. Sudden terror instils in time for Beth and Amy to barge in and break them up.

"Knock it off!" Beth sees the dagger and is appalled. "You can't be serious? Give me that thing, now!"

Beth looks down her nose at him, but Damon just ignores her, fixed on Will.

"Matt, sit up for me, honey," whispers Amy, helping him.

"HEY! If you dare threaten his life again, I will kill you," Beth says, as serious as a heart attack.

Will is ready, still wielding the stapler. Tensions are at their highest, secrets are out, and Matt tries to stay out of it, awkwardly trying to patch himself up. It's the only sound in the room.

"Hey, hey! Look at me. Do you understand me?" She cups Damon's cheek as a single drop trickles down his face.

Damon jerks her hand away. "He comes near me again... I kill him."

"You're a fucking psycho!" Will barks.

"You tried to suggest my sister be put down like some fucking dog," Damon snaps back.

Beth has taken the letter opener. "What?" She turns to Will.

"That's not at all what I said."

Beth has seen this dark streak in Damon before, the one that unsettles her to the core. Will tosses the stapler and storms to the bathroom.

"Where's the manager?"

"He..." Matt can't bring himself to speak. His face slumps as his nose bleeds again.

"BETH!" Amy groans, trying to lift his face.

"Tom is the one who stabbed him, but he has gone missing again."

"I can no longer play house while waiting around like sitting ducks, plus my sister is dying and the infected numbers are increasing every single hour." Damon has had enough.

"That's because you thought it would be clever to fucking feed them!" Will grunts in the distance.

Damon throws him a look that could kill if it took on a human form. Beth tries to calm things once again.

"I've not been here five minutes, yet I know that was a bit of a dick move!" Amy says to Will.

"I'm sorry, and you are?" Will sarcastically remarks. "Oh, that's right... an outsider."

Will storms off, leaving Amy hurt.

Shop Floor

Adam is packing bags full of water and food to drag up the stairs when he suddenly hears voices. He turns, a little nervous, thinking he is losing his mind, before spinning back, only to have a run in with Tom. A scream echoes, reaching to the security room. The rest of the survivors run to his aid and drag him up into the office, then barricade the door.

Things are at breaking point. Beth calls a group meeting to address matters once and for all.

Tom is loose in the store and picking them off like targets.

Matt and Damon dislike one another over their feelings for Beth.

Damon and Will dislike each other because of Will's feelings towards Claire.

Amy feels like a spare part as they all squabble like high school students.

And to make matters worse, the infected could break in at *any* moment.

"ALRIGHT, SHUT UP!" Beth silences the madness. "We yell any louder and those things will find their way in here. Do you want to be the special on the menu?"

When nobody responds, she leads them to the roof (the only safe spot she knows where Tom cannot sabotage or harm them).

"Hurry. I don't trust that Tom won't sneak into the offices and hurt Claire."

Damon runs his hand three times through his close-cropped hair in quick succession—Will fixes him a stare that could freeze the Pacific.

He growls. "It's locked, idiot."

"Enough."

Even though there is no heat in her voice, Beth's cold fury burns with dangerous intensity. It's these bitterly cold, slow burning rages that threaten to engulf them. It's clear there are some issues that need addressing if they are going to survive united as a group.

"We've spent only three days in here and we've let this

place go to shit."

Beth paces like her body has had too much caffeine.

"Not to mention, we let a murderer in." Will refers to Damon.

"You come for my blood; I spill yours. I know I'm not wanted or liked." He has had enough. His sister is dying, and rescue is not coming.

"We only did this because we were supposed to be waiting for rescue. If it was coming, it would be here by now."

"I'm taking Claire and leaving this instant."

"DAMON, STOP!" Beth yells with the wind, which is picking up.

"There's still time. Leeds is a big place," Amy speaks finally.

"And the army is bigger! We walked through that together, not a soul!" Damon says.

Will tries the peaceful road. "If you try to leave, you could put the others' lives at risk."

"LOOK AROUND! Their lives are already in jeopardy." He says, "Psychopaths and zombies running rampant."

"Isn't that ironic coming from you? Let him leave, let him kill his sister even slower and make her suffer."

"That's it."

Damon jolts to life and charges for Will, causing a frenzy among the others. It takes almost all of them to push him back and calm him down. Damon tries to leave when Will puts a hand on his shoulder, feeling bad for his comments; he tries to turn Damon, but is shoved back and falls through the door.

Matt calls, "Not again, please don't."

"OR WHAT? NOTHING IS GOING TO HAPPEN!" Damon yells until his voice croaks. The others watch awkwardly. "HELLO OUT THERE?" He turns to the wind and the distance of the empty city.

"Damon, stop it," Beth asks calmly.

"CAN ANYBODY HEAR ME? IS THAT HELP I SEE OVER THERE?" Damon shouts, ironically in a posh tyke.

"Fucking cunt!"

Will sees a mist red and goes to pick up a fire extinguisher. He attempts to launch it at Damon. Amy and Beth try to stop him, and Amy gets the full force of what was intended for Damon. She goes down hard. Will drops it by accident; it makes a dint in a weak part of the floor.

"Amy, I'm *so* sorry!"

Through Will's distraction, Damon comes bouncing back and punches him in the face. The two get into a fight that Matt and Adam must break up. Beth tends to Amy, holding her face to the floor.

"I'm a big girl, I'll be fine."

"That was a hard hit!"

Beth turns to the boys and is literally screaming at them. Matt and Adam look like rejected puppies, and Adam lowers his jaw, catching flies.

"What did I do?" He gasps.

"All of you are acting like imbecilic Neanderthals throwing your testosterone around."

A huge cracking sound silences them.

CRUNCH!

Damon breaks free of Will's grip, stepping back. Will and Amy look down at the floor, scanning their surroundings, as the cracking turns into creaking and suddenly the floor beneath them caves in, weakened by the commotion. They fall through the roof into the store below. Amy crash lands on the top of an aisle. Will hits the same aisle but rolls off and plummets to the floor. The infected are dotted around the store and slowly turn, drawn to the noise.

Beth and Matt peer through the hole.

"Are you okay?"

Beth spots a creeper slowly drawing in; already its

clothing is tatty where prey has clawed at the material, hoping to break free. It's covered in blood, suggesting they failed.

Damon has vanished; Matt calls for Amy not to move and Beth shouts at Will to get up and run, but Will isn't responding. It's apparent he is fading in and out of consciousness. A creeper is within reaching distance of his warm body when out of nowhere, Matt drops the hole and splits the creature's head open with his foot in a superhero-style landing. He then tries to get Will to his feet before noticing the red patch forming on his bandage.

Beth runs back into the store from the roof with Adam and finds Damon, ahold of his sister, about to leave.

Beth pleads for Damon to help his new friend, Amy, who is stranded on the top of an aisle while a sea of creatures, once from all walks of life, gnash their jaws and claw at her. Damon reluctantly puts Claire down and goes up to the roof with Beth. He gets on his belly at the edge of the hole. Damon holds his arm out, but only the tips of the fingers lock with Amy's.

"Shit!"

They have Damon's rifle, Jules's gun, limited bullets and an endless supply of gardening tools, but it isn't enough. Will comes to and the infected are surrounding them. He aids Matt as the two boys limp away, darting down the aisles. They see infected at the other end of the next aisle, so they turn back only to be greeted by more.

"We're trapped," Matt exhales.

Will shouts at Matt to start climbing.

"DON'T FAINT!" Will stresses.

They clamber up the shelves, hopping from one aisle to another—it's a struggle for Matt, still bleeding for Tom's attack.

Roof

"Screw it!"

Beth jumps down to land next to Amy, only to slip and land on her front. Creepers reach up, missing her nose by centimetres. Amy pulls her back to her feet.

"Follow!"

She helps Amy off the shelf at the end and onto the escalator. At the entrance, more of the dead slowly surround them. Beth doesn't understand how so many have filtered through the shop floor until she remembers Tom is still out there somewhere.

"He did this."

"Who?"

"The manager! He must have let them in somehow."

"Adam, take over," Damon says from the hole, but Adam has vanished.

He is in the store, aimlessly trying to help.

Store

Will and Matt reunite with Amy and Beth at the entrance, back-to-back weapons in their hands.

"There's no way out."

Will looks at Amy's face, bloodied from his fire extinguisher assault. With the guilt of his actions, Will's stupidity threatens more lives. They try to stop him from opening the barricade, so he can distract the zombies to ensure everyone leaves and meets later. Adam turns up; there's a cacophony of creepers between him and the group. This bunch of lunatics are docile and slower than some others, making it easier to push them around.

This is it, the undead are at every turn. They circle against each other. No way out, he's staring death in the face.

"Beth, what do we do?"

Will is out of options. He has no choice but to turn to her.

Think, Beth, think! Her brain goes into overdrive. She almost has an aneurism from the stress, and her eye twitches.

"We might just have to run," she says. "If we get separated, meet at the crash site, where the bus capsized on the edge of the dual carriageway."

Will turns back to the entrance and takes apart what he can for them to squeeze through. Despite death being imminent, Matt can't help but wonder how she knows about the bus pulverising the sea of cars.

"We never told you," he says.

Beth tearfully comes clean and says she was the one who drove and crashed the bus. "I did not know it was you boys in the car." She couldn't live with herself, or die, knowing she said nothing.

"MATT!" She weeps. "It's all my fault! Your brain injury. It's all my fault!"

Beth loses total control of her composure. It takes Matt back for a moment but he soon forgets with the incoming onslaught as they back up further.

Will is halfway through the barrier as undead hands from outside slip through, grabbing for him. He throws himself back.

"Leaving that way is not an option."

Beth screams. "WHY?"

"I think they really want the January sales!"

Damon catches up to them in time.

"Damon, mate, I'm sorry, I'm so, so sorry! Please!"

"Forget it. I'm sorry too."

"Beth… I think I love you! If we're going to die and we're doing confessions, I don't want to die not telling you! Even if you think I am broken, brain damaged or retarded," says Matt.

"WHAT?" she cries, sniffling.

He replies, "I think I'm dying, guys. My brain is bleeding."

"No! I don't think you're broken. Where did that come from?"

"Thomas said—"

"The man's a monster!"

"Oh, thank God!"

"Beth, I love you too!" Damon adds.

"Now is *really* not the time!"

"I know we don't really know each other, but it's true! I feel something I've never felt before. I promise if we get out of this, I'll watch more cartoons."

Beth struggles to make a choice with two men competing for her whilst also being approached by an army of the undead. This prompts Adam to confess his feelings to Will. It all comes out as the pressure mounts.

"Big surprise," Will sarcastically remarks.

"Oh, yeah, cheers!"

"Why's it always me?"

"Wow, big-headed till the end!" shouts Beth.

"Beth, I hate your cooking! Always have!" Will says like word vomit.

"WHAT? You're going to let me die with that reveal? Bastard."

"GOD, I WISH I NEVER CAME HERE! YOU PEOPLE ARE BEYOND PROBLEMATIC AND TOXIC," Amy says.

The impossible six have a rude awakening as it reminds them of an old problem. They are yet to deal with Tom! Beth spots him lurking on the other side of the creepers. The infected are within touching distance, so the survivors slice and dice for their lives to push back and regain control of their home.

A smack to the head here, a stab to the chest there. Limbs and guts fly. The group kick, push and shove as they grapple the undead and Beth sees a brief opening, but they have to take it now.

"EVERYBODY RUN" Beth screams.

She pushes over a docile infected. Damon helps Will break free from the grip of a monster and everybody scrambles to keep together as they run back to the security office. Damon says he needs to get Claire.

"We cleared them! We did it!" Beth laughs with genuine shock.

"Not for long," a voice says from behind.

"Tom!"

The game is on to escape his wrath and dodge the other infected loose in the store. They find Tom again in the butcher's section, causing them to have it out abruptly. Matt fires Jules's gun until it runs out. A lousy waste of two bullets, but it was worth it. The others throw glass and metal cans at the counter as he throws sharp cutlery back—both Matt and Beth get sliced by flying meat cleavers, but they are closer. Tom does something dastardly for ultimate revenge. He takes Adam hostage, working his way back to the front of the store with his butcher knife, which he holds to Adam's throat.

Beth and Damon slowly advance, pointing a cleaver and Damon's rifle as Tom continues to retreat closer to the front barricade. Things are noisy as hundreds of infected are bashing at the shutters and flocked around the aisles. Beth is shaky. She does not know how to control her arm but doesn't let it show.

"Don't do anything stupid now." Damon growls, eyes down the sight of his rifle.

"We can get out of this, Tom. I can forgive all if you just give us our friend back!"

Negotiations begin. Matt and Amy glance at what is happening, Matt knocks back into a zombie and taps Amy, and she gasps. Amy picks up a clay pot and throws it at a group of creatures coming from their right. They fall like bowling pins.

Amy grabs Matt, and they dart to the front of the store.

Without breaking eye contact with Tom, Damon pleadingly begs Will to get Claire. Matt and Amy continue to push and shove the infected away, slicing at their bodies to give the others room to negotiate on the move.

Oh no!

Drip… drip…

It's coming out of Matt's nose again. *Please, not now, not a fit.*

It's too late. He goes down and Amy roars.

Beth and Damon take it step by step. With each one Tom takes backward toward the shutters, Beth and Damon take one closer.

Adam gulps with the cleaver pressed against his neck because he can feel the pure sharp silver on his skin, prickling his chin hairs. They try to negotiate with him to not do anything stupid.

Hundreds of infected claw at the other side. The shutters flap and ache as the ferocious monsters bang and rabble against the metal wall. The only thing that separates them from the dead is Tom's finger teasing the button.

Anything could happen; the unpredictable trepidation throws everything up in the air. Beth can feel her heartbeat in her throat.

07:30 hours
Entrance

"GET UP!" Amy angrily seethes at Matt, jerking and tossing again.

Beth pleads. "Don't do this, Tom."

Amy has no choice but to drag him away but keeps dropping him to push back the creepers.

"FUCK OFF!" she cries tearfully.

"You've won, mate. You don't need to carry on doing this. We are leaving, the store is all yours." Damon surveys Tom's every move.

"You've desecrated my empire and now you must pay," Tom mutters.

CLICK. Brrrrrrvvvv!

In his truest moment of insanity, Tom presses the button to the shutters. He then pushes Adam at Damon and Beth, catching his throat in the slash.

"NO!" Beth screeches.

Tom destroys the entire entrance, and the store is shredded. The broken shutters struggle to rise as the power flickers on and off, and crumble against the lorry, still wedged in the middle. This causes the entire front structure of the store to collapse in a debris cloud. Falling metal rings out. In the mist's clearing and the fall of the barricade, a silhouette emerges through the dust.

"You have got to be fucking kidding me." Beth's heart drops.

A zombified Kieran, enraged and engulfed with fury, leads a pack of raging infected maniacs into the store, bombarding the survivors. Beside him are Darcy and Aiden, both plagued by Grime Flu. Kieran glares up at the cameras at Will from the CCTV.

"You have to be fucking kidding, of all people," Will echoes.

Will bursts to life and runs over to Claire, who isn't responding anymore. He picks her up.

Beth locks eyes with Kieran, then Darcy and Aiden Wolfe. She can't help but notice there is no Chris, but she remembers they tore him to shreds, so there is probably nothing left.

She mutters over and over. "They aren't people anymore." She tosses her knife into her other hand, ready for a fight. "He's not a real person. He's just a shell. A shell. He's dead. He's dead. That's not Darcy."

Kieran almost grins as he stomps into the room. He screeches like a barn owl. Then, suddenly, the rest of the undead storm in. They have a sloppy gait as they approach. Their jaws are dislocated, showing their torn tongues and blood-stained teeth. They moan and howl as they smell the blood in the air. Skin peels from their bones and organs, showing muscles. Although their hearts do not beat, the group can see how their organs were torn, how their blood has turned in to a thick, turbid goo of browns, blacks and greens, and how their stomachs slowly digests the flesh that is their own.

Game over, checkmate, the infected trample over one another to swarm the shop floor. Some of them shuffle aimlessly while the stronger creatures sprint and spit at the survivors.

Tom cackles with joy, but his joy is short-lived when a sensible part of his mind realises what he has done.

Endless undead flood the supermarket. Beth and Damon don't stick around. They flee. Tom trembles like the sensible part of his brain takes back over but he is struck down by the dead. He panics as he tries to break free but there are too many. He screams and swears.

"Come on then, pussies! I have plenty to go around."

They sink their teeth into his flesh. Blood draws to the surface like a tender medium rare steak, still juicy. They claw at his body, and suddenly his insides appear on the out. Disembowelled alive, he watches himself be ripped apart. They tear out his intestines, a pinkish grey. Then they take his organs. They steal and fight over his liver. His stomach is torn to shreds and split open, children trying to rip open candy bag, eaten before his eyes.

THLP! SLOP! KZWLLL! THLPTHLPTHLP!

Still, they take away his entire lower half, dragging his

legs away. He cackles, somehow still alive beyond belief. He looks at his ribcage, encouraging them to take his entrails.

"I HAVE BOWELS FULL OF SHIT. GO ON! EAT IT! FUCKING EAT IT!"

He squeals, still alive. They snap his bones and tear his nerves. Finally, they shut him up by tearing out his throat and they gouge out his eyes with their fingernails. Eventually, there is nothing left but a hollow torso. Kieran, one of the strongest creatures, rips his head off and drags his spinal cord out, still attached to his skull.

Beth looks over her shoulder as they run back to the security office. She can only see Damon and the lower half of Tom being thrown between the lions fighting over their meal. Despite the trauma, Beth can't say she isn't satisfied with his demise.

07:40 hours
Adam

Discarded like an old tissue, he limps away, clinging to his neck. Luckily, the strike from Tom wasn't fatal, and Adam gets to keep his life for a while longer. He applies pressure, then looks back at Tom, who is now a blended protein shake for the undead. His heart sinks and the fear of meeting the same fate overwhelms him.

He's lost. Adam loses sight of the others and now he has infected on his tail. He attempts to run downstairs, but he too is unsuccessful in fleeing.

He tumbles down the escalator, pursued relentlessly.

Beth & Damon

They bolt up the stairs to the security office.
"WAIT!"

Beth nearly falls over her own feet on the steps. She runs down and shuts the door a split second before a creature sticks its arm through. BANG! The monsters fly in and stick their arms out, pushing Beth.

Damon stops at the top of the stairs. Beth's screams echo at the bottom. He growls and aims his rifle at the waving limbs, trying to push through and marginally misses Beth; he screams at her to run. She waits for her moment and pulls herself up the stairs, letting the door fly open to the mountain of bodies trying to fight their way through.

She screams continuously as one of the undead misses her golden hair by the tips of its fingers. Damon holds out his hand and practically throws her through the security door. She finds Amy and Matt taking refuge and Will with Claire in his arms.

Damon darts through and bolts it shut.

Everybody tries to calm their breathing.

07:42 hours
Will

"What the fuck happened?" Will demands.

"He opened the shutters, and they swarmed. He got ripped apart. So did Adam. I don't know. I lost him." Beth pants, trying to catch her breath.

Damon takes his sister from Will. They all look at the security cameras.

Beth gasps. "They're everywhere."

End of the line. They surround both doors to the security office, sure to give way any second.

"There're hundreds of them now." Beth gulps.

"Where's that boy, Adam?" Amy asks.

Nobody knows.

"We're not backing down." Beth says. "We go out with a fight; slice our way out until they fall. Who's with me?"

349

The others look at her, shit scared, trying to process the fact they are going to die now. Eventually, they nod one by one and raise their weapons. Beth says her goodbyes and tells them all that the time she spent there was short but sweet.

Will picks up his weapon. "Hold your horses—" He believes he can give them a fighting chance.

"Will, no, you can't—"

"Don't even try, B!" Will insists it isn't up for discussion "Trust me, have I ever let you down?"

And before they know it, he's out the security door. Will attempts to slice his way to freedom but goes missing in the horde, now invading. Beth calls out for him, her heart breaks.

"NOOO!"

"STOP!" Damon tugs her from doing something stupid. "He's gone!"

Amy struggles to jam the door shut. Damon picks up Claire and races for the lift. She is too weak to do anything herself. Kieran targets the others and they run into the lift, barley escaping with their lives as the door shuts. He slams into the other side.

Matt, Beth, Damon and Amy try to shake off the shock and isolate themselves in the panic room as the store is rampaged and the zombies feast upon their human meals. A momentary panic sends the four into a further frenzy. Hope seems lost. The door to the office breaks in and they flood the room destroying any memory of them being there.

Kieran hounds the lift. BASH... BASH... BASH!

Even 20-feet above they can feel the room quake. It's a box.

"Why did he do that? Why did he just get himself killed like that?" Beth breaks down. "He just left us."

"Guys, I'm sorry!"

Matt falls into the wall again; it's bad this time, somehow

seemingly worse than the previous times, it's coming from his ears and his eyes as well has his mouth.

"Hold him!" Damon commands.

They gather round. He becomes weak and soft-spoken.

"It's okay." He puts his bloody palm on Beth's face as her teardrops hit his pale, loving face.

"I don't blame you, Beth. You're too much of an angel!" The others grimace, joined in their grief. "I could always be… God's engineer… I guess." Every breath he takes is shorter and shorter, harder to fathom. "I got… you all… a present…"

He unveils what looks like a home-made pipe bomb.

"What the fuck, Matt?" Beth cautions, laughing.

"So that's what you've been making with all those electricals and wires…" Adam says in awe.

"I figured for the first couple of collapses, something was wrong… in here…" He taps his noggin. "While you lot were playing happy families over the last day or two… I just figured… prepare for the worst… I'm not saying I knew this would happen, but it was just in case those things broke in… a last resort." Matt replies.

Damon gives his sister to Amy to hold while he investigates Matt's creation. "Just one problem. It's manually detonated. You have about three minutes to get the hell out, meaning one person stays to blow it up."

"No. Not a chance. Out of the question."

"Stop, don't make this hard." Matt suggests that because he made it, he should stay. "Look at me."

He matches Beth's eye line, staring into those ocean-strong sunlit currents and her back at his hazelnut rivers. Finally, the connection he yearned for. Her breathing becomes softer, the pensive look melting into a smile as soft as the morning light. Her body squirms just a little as her muscles relax. There is something about that gaze of his she'll never find in another man, as if in that moment their souls have made a bridge.

"I'm dying… it has to be me…"

"Where the fuck did you learn to make one of these?" Damon bounces it like a weight.

"The Dark Web," Matt jokes.

"Who are you?" He grins.

There is an argument, but there's no time. Suddenly, the horde reaches the security room and brays upon the doors.

"They must have climbed!" Amy darts around and finds a hatch. "Rooftop!"

It won't be long until they pulverise a way through. They look at the safety glass, already weakening, as these things (that were once people!) hurt themselves.

Damon shakes his head. "This is pure chaos."

"This is God pissed off with us," Amy adds.

Damon does his best to calm a hysterical Beth and settle a feverish Claire.

"Remember that I loved you. I loved life, I loved to create and the happiness that comes of simple pleasures. When you die, come sit with me in heaven as long as you wish… You are such wonderful company." Matt takes Damon's hand now, who tries to not get worked up. "We'd do it all again. It is a fine way to spend eternity, yes?"

"Yes!"

Beth takes hold of his cheeks. And their lips connect. In that kiss, it's the sweetness of passion, a million loving thoughts condensed into a moment.

Damon lets go of all the anger, the frustration, and the misery. He kisses Matt's hand before offering him a cigarette; they put their differences aside and Damon tries to be the bigger man. He apologises for their high school drama.

"Goodbye, Matt."

"Goodbye, angel."

Generation Dead

The safe room door begins to creek. Cracks appear around the edges as dust falls. Matt helps the others into the vents one by one, including a delirious Claire. He clings to his explosive creation.

Matt slumps down against a cupboard, putting the cigarette in his mouth. He tilts his head back, which opens the cupboard door.

"Hello," he says intrinsically.

Bottles upon bottles of white spirit and propane tanks from the DIY isles greet him.

"I wondered where you were!"

He exhales and smiles as he watches Damon, Beth and Amy escape through the vents above and crawl through the exit leading to the roof and a set of stairs. Beth remembers using the same one to enter the building, which seems like a lifetime ago.

They race down and see the horde now cover the entire car park. More and more are running from the trees to gather.

"What have we done?"

"Come on then peeps, I'm half price today!"

The zombies burst through the doors and savagely sink into Matt's body as he clings desperately to the bomb. They bite his shoulders, arms and face. Suddenly, the group is at a standstill as they take in the frigid January air. A swarm of zombies down below leave them stranded on the rooftop.

Beth looks around in streaming tears. "Well, goodbye everyone."

They hold hands; she shuts her eyes, and for a moment she prays for a miracle. Simultaneously, she hears a horn and perks one eye open. The group sees a superstore truck splatter through half the dead toward the four of them. They explode like watermelons being thrown on the ground as they collide.

No time for questions. Amy shoots between Beth and Damon, who follow with Claire in tow. Beth can't believe it.

Will is in the driver's seat, alive, yelling, "YOUR CHARIOT AWAITS, BITCHES!"

They soar through the air as Will pulls up in the delivery bay. They land on the roof and when everyone is on board, he drives off. He needs to pick up speed; the beasts are sprinting toward the truck.

07:45 hours
Adam

Downstairs in the wardrobe deportment a hysterical Adam climbs the shelves until he is on top on an aisle, out of the zombies' reach.

It's unclear whether he has been bitten—his wound to the neck appears savage but not life-threatening. He takes a moment to catch his breath and one to gather himself, before telling the venomous demons they will have to work for their food.

07:47 hours
Matt

CLICK!
    '10...9...'

07:47 hours
Will

The rest of the group hop in through the windows. Will tells them to cling on for dear life as he swerves and races away from the store.

07:47 hours
Matt

'7...6...5.'

07.47 hours
Damon

He tries to pat his sister awake.

Will swerves once more, running over straggling undead. Amy tells him to knock it off and concentrate.

07:47 hours
Matt

'3... 2... 1..."
  KABOOM!
The superstore is suddenly engulfed in a giant fireball; a tangled fist of orange and crimson punches through the main entrance, sending shopping baskets and carts flying. Windows shatter, smoke and shrapnel erupt, cascading into abandoned cars in the parking lot, triggering a piercing choir of alarms. Thousands of pieces of glass, brick and steel batter the undead. Those alarms—now shrill—smother the crackling flames. It's hard to believe a small DIY bomb can do so much damage, but it does. The explosion is seen for miles. Despite the chaos, it conveniently blasts half of the

attacking bloodthirsty creatures to smithereens, though the survivors—once strangers forced together—have created half-decent memories in that store. Now, however, those memories are consumed in flames. Everything from their film projector to the beds and the den is gone; their sense of home lost, their blanket of security quickly disintegrating. The blast wave ripples for miles, almost forcing their getaway truck into a lamppost.

Will spins the steering wheel to avoid a collision at the last second. It would've been game over—his new friends made lunch meat for the nearby battalion of undead man-eaters. Damon watches the supermarket explode and dives on his sister, Claire—praying he doesn't crush her tiny frame—to shield her. To their left, Amy and Beth are thrown to the back of the truck. Suddenly, Claire bursts to life from a bout of unconsciousness, still weak and in need of help. Damon cradles his trembling sister. He strokes her face, elated to see she's unharmed. Claire is equally bewildered to see him and passes out again in a hot sweat.

Now collapsed in Damon's arms, Beth glances back at the store—once their makeshift home. It is now a huge bonfire. Then she buries her face in Damon's sweater, emotionally drained. But at least they're safe... for now.

***

Kieran appears amidst the burning wreckage of the superstore, flames so high the Great Fire of London would have cowered in fear. He steps through the blaze like a machine, unphased by the bedlam, hell-bent on claiming a well-deserved prize after a long hunt on the scent of the fleeing teens in the delivery truck—a prize that will include his ex-boyfriend and the accompanying band of dishevelled teens. He screeches through the thick smog, foaming at the mouth. The remaining infected follow him like he was the leader as he charges for the truck. Kieran soon slows to a disgruntled stop, staring at the truck's arse end. Amy smugly offers him her middle finger as they speed off, disappearing over the horizon. She knows he'll be back, and nothing can prepare them for what is yet to come.

Author's Note

Good morning, afternoon, or evening.

Thank you for taking the time to read the scripture I have created. If you have made it this far, then I am both thankful and impressed already. I hope you are enjoying your time alone on the toilet, your flight (I recommend a double Jack), the bookstore, train, or your prison cell—wherever you have taken the time to embark on this adventure.

I hope you are reading this at the end of civilisation, perhaps—where humanity has rocketed off in 2125 (because we evil humans have finally sucked the life from Earth and have no choice but to terraform another planet). Hopefully, humans have saved the best literature to survive the apocalypse.

Where to begin? It has taken nearly ten years to perfect my *Generation Dead*. I was always a fan of writing stories and screenplays, ever since I was 11-years-old. *Generation Dead* originally stemmed from one short story—a series of 12 episodes (or chapters as you'll see them here), which after five years continued to 12 volumes. I hope people find them moderately interesting.

Ten years later the story is complete.

Teachers used to get me to write stories in order to concentrate because of my ADHD and Dyslexia. It didn't work, but I was a fascinating subject for the greatest minds in Geneva to experiment on.

A deep devotion to the sub-genre that is all things undead originally inspired *Generation Dead*. Like a moth to a flame, I was drawn to George A Romero's *Dawn of the Dead* and I haven't been the same since; my cool aunts and uncles would let me watch scary movies when my parents weren't looking. I thought, what if the movie didn't end, and it just kept going? I was always wanting to know what happened next, and never wanted the story to end.

So, I wrote my own.... that just kept going.

Then AMC's *The Walking Dead* came along, and slowly everything changed. Other influences from television shows, movies and games alike helped me create this never-ending world I can escape within to this day. It sounds strange, but it's true.

I often struggle to fit in with reality or conform to what I would consider the 'norm', so I make my own. I've always been quirky—the words follow me. I was reluctant to wear those badges, but now I feel they are an honour as they wouldn't have allowed me to create something I can call my legacy.

It occurred to me, aside from shows like *The Walking Dead, Z Nation*, etc., today, there aren't many shows around based specifically in a modern post-apocalyptic zombie world, especially that depict something from the start and the events leading up to a fateful outbreak. I wrote my own British twist on what I visualise, in my mind, as a TV show, taking inspiration from films, shows and games that influenced me growing up. But, I tried to be as original as possible to make it exciting until the end.

Every so often a movie, book or show would get released, currently existing as a subplot in *Generation Dead*, and I'd have to sulk and re-think and re-write, or I'd look like I had stolen the idea. Other influences include: *How to Get Away with Murder, The Strain, Black Summer, Children of Men, Utopia, Dead Set,* to name a few.

I've set the writing style in a series; read each chapter as an episode. In each episode, it explains what happens as the story unfolds. I broke the chapters into parts to give you a chance to reflect or take a break.

Sometimes, the story is detailed and picks apart specific points. In other sections, it is quite ambiguous. Each one is as detailed as the next, while only adding specific direct dialog. I did this because I feel we have not done it before— if it did get published, it would be easy to understand what happens. I want the reader to imagine what each character is saying below the surface, within the story, and interpret it as how they like.

It was supposed to stay short, but idea after idea flowed and I couldn't end it.

I fell in love with the story, the characters and the adventure. I remember it being an assignment for a two-page essay in my English class, which went a little far. I would make YouTube videos with my friends, creating these stories.

I don't think of myself as an author or writer, perhaps because of a lack of confidence, but this universe was inside my head... I had to bring it to life on paper. It was that or therapy. I have invested a lot of emotion and effort into this adventure and had literary friends read and review sections, giving me their intense critiques as readers and honest opinions. Each character and event in the past has been inspired and/or influenced by real-life events or people from my personal life.

I have tried to go over and over, leave some time between, and edit my book until I felt I was at a place I could give it my best shot, after being told it was worth something.

I decided upon the title, *Generation Dead* because I felt it was original; this is something that hasn't been done. I wanted to try to find a name that wasn't taken or too mainstream, that I came up with first in 2011... granted it may exist *somewhere*, but I thought I was being dead cool. The characters are the next generation of life, but the irony is... they may be the last.

At 25-years-old, I've achieved my dream, something many people can't say. To many, it may be a bag of shit. But it's *my* bag of shit—I hope you really enjoyed it.

K. J. McGuinness

About the Author

- www.kjmcguinness.com -

K. J. McGuinness likes to the think he's an award-winning, renowned, 25-time Academy Award nominee. At least that's the dream. In reality, he's a talented and creative health professional from Leeds, West Yorkshire.

He has qualifications in mental health, fashion marketing, psychology, paramedicine and many other award-winning achievements.

Kier is a trained paramedic and a trained one-to-one counsellor for overwhelmed young adults. He often works in the community running drag queen pageants, charity balls, and in his free time he continues his ongoing saga *Generation Dead*.

Lightning Source UK Ltd.
Milton Keynes UK
UKHW011012270921
391257UK00002B/360